DARKNESS FALLS

RACHEL WESSON

Copyright © Rachel Wesson, 2022, 2023

Previously published in 2022 by Londongate Publishing.

The moral right of the author has been asserted.

Ebook ISBN: 978-1-80508-128-9
Paperback ISBN: 978-1-80508-129-6

Cover design: Debbie Clement
Cover images: Arcangel, Shutterstock

Published by Storm Publishing.
For further information, visit:
www.stormpublishing.co

ALSO BY RACHEL WESSON

The Resistance Sisters

Darkness Falls

Light Rises

Hearts at War (WWII)

When's Mummy Coming?

A Mother's Promise

WWII Irish Standalone

Stolen from Her Mother

Orphans of Hope House

Home for Unloved Orphans (Orphans of Hope House 1)

Baby on the Doorstep (Orphans of Hope House 2)

Women and War

Gracie Under Fire

Penny's Secret Mission

Molly's Flight

Hearts on the Rails

Orphan Train Escape

Orphan Train Trials

Orphan Train Christmas

Orphan Train Tragedy

Genevieve, thank you for everything, not least of all your knowledge of all things French.

Note to readers: As the main characters are French, we have used the French rules re grammar i.e., no capital letters for nouns like Maman, Papa, mémé or resistance. Except of course where these words start a sentence.

ONE

MAY 1940, FONTAINEBLEAU, PARIS

The cool evening air circulated through the ballroom, the vaulted ceilings and large French windows, failing to dissipate the metallic smell of blood mixing with the scent of antiseptic. Sophie Bélanger, drops of sweat beading on her brow mixing with the blonde tendrils escaping from the clips she'd used to secure her long hair, struggled to restrain her patient. Nothing in the past three years of medical school had prepared her for this: not just the shelling, the horrific injuries, the sheer number of casualties, but the lack of properly qualified medics.

The patient continued to thrash from side to side as Sophie fought to keep her on the bed. "Give her more chloroform." Neither she nor the nurse should be administering anaesthesia but the textbook approach went out the window when they were swamped with casualties. The nurse didn't move.

Sophie turned to the nurse, her once-white uniform covered in bloodstains. "Did you not hear me?"

Noémie's lips trembled, her brown eyes widening as she looked around as if expecting someone to come to her aid. She stammered, "We're running out. Dr Murphy said to..."

"Give it to her. We must get her ready for surgery."

"I wish Elizabeth was here," Noémie muttered. "She'd know how to handle everything."

Sophie couldn't agree more. The head nurse at the American Hospital, and Dr Murphy's right-hand woman since the last war, was a formidable lady who could cope with anything thrown at her. But Elizabeth was needed at the main hospital in Paris. Someone had to look after the more serious casualties.

"Elizabeth would be very proud of the way her top nurse is coping." Sophie leaned closer and whispered, "Come on, show this third-year medical student how it's done."

Noémie managed a small smile before she poured the liquid onto the cloth and placed it over the patient's nose and mouth. "Please count to one hundred."

Sophie gasped with pain as the patient pushed the cloth away and dug her nails into Sophie's hand. "Monique ... my baby. Find her."

Noémie gently pushed the woman back, placing the cloth over her nose and mouth just as the woman muttered, "Mon Dieu, please find my child."

"We'll do our best. Lie still. You will make your injury worse," Sophie said, as fresh blood seeped into the sheets around the woman's injured arm. They had to get the bleeding stopped or she would die. "We will find Monique tomorrow. For now, please rest." She held the patient's hand and watched as she slowly stilled. Relief surged through Sophie as she spotted Dr Murphy – tall, bushy eyebrows above tired blue eyes – heading towards them, running a hand through his dark hair. She gently touched her patient's face. "Dr Murphy is here now. He'll help you."

The woman's eyelids flickered.

"Evening, madame. Dr Michael Murphy at your service." Despite his exhausted pallor, the doctor's American accent was upbeat and confident. Sophie wished she knew how he managed it. At fifty-six years old, he was more than twice her age, had worked through the last two days and nights as she had, yet he still radiated energy and reassurance. "Relax, madame. I will fix your arm while you sleep."

Sophie felt her patient give in to the anaesthetic. Only once she was certain the woman was out cold did she loosen her grip on her hand.

Dr Murphy examined the wound, muttering under his breath.

Sophie gently asked, "Sorry, what did you say?"

He looked up, catching her gaze. "I thought I saw the worst of battle at the Somme in 1917, but these new weapons ... they turn human beings into hamburgers."

At his words, the building swayed, showering everyone with tiny bits of plaster falling from the ornate scallop-edged ceiling medallions. How were they supposed to maintain hygiene in a deserted old casino?

Dr Murphy ignored the shelling sounds, concentrating on his patient. "I'll have to amputate the arm. Otherwise, she doesn't stand a chance. She's lost a lot of blood. She may not be strong enough for the operation. Does she have any family?"

Sophie shuddered, wondering where the woman's little girl was. So many were missing – not surprising given the number of refugees flooding in from Belgium and elsewhere. What was it like to be so terrified you had to abandon your home and take to the street? Were the Germans really that horrible?

Noémie spoke up. "She's lost her young daughter. I don't think there was anyone else; her husband's at the front. She said last month they were collecting funds to buy rosebushes for the Maginot Line."

Dr Murphy's eyebrows rose. "Rosebushes?"

"Yes, they were to make the view prettier." Noémie's voice trailed off at his incredulous look.

"Would have been better buying tanks and other weapons.

Rosebushes!" Dr Murphy rolled his eyes. "Sophie, can you take care of things outside? Noémie will help me, won't you?"

Sophie pushed down the wave of tiredness as she nodded. Noémie's brown eyes widened with terror, her lips pursed together, but she stood straighter. "Yes, Dr Murphy."

"Never thought I'd miss the smell of musty wards with a distinct undertone of disinfectant – did you?" Dr Murphy smiled at Noémie before turning his attention back to his patient.

He really was such a nice man, his care for his staff evident always. When Sophie qualified as a doctor, she wanted to be just like him. As she moved the blood-soaked linen to the correct bucket for the porter to take to the laundry, she wondered when that would be. Would the arrival of the Germans stop her studies? Would Jules return from being a frontline medic to complete his final year as a trainee doctor at the American Hospital? *If he is still alive.* He had to be. She closed her eyes briefly, seeing her lover, his brown eyes twinkling at her as he had on their last weekend together in April when they had talked and laughed non-stop. Since then, she'd had one letter and a hurried note and then silence. Unbearable, heartbreaking silence.

Sophie made her way past their other patients to the ambulance arrival point outside, some lying quietly waiting for death, others begging for water. All young men, some younger than her seventeen-year-old brother. They'd pretended to be older so they could fight. *La dole de guerre* was over; there was nothing phoney about these injuries. She had to focus on the next patient or the despair would envelop her.

The crunching of gears announced yet another ambulance. Had this one been targeted by the Germans, who seemed to take delight in strafing anything with red cross markings? Sophie restrained the urge to run. Doctors and nurses never ran. Even here, in a makeshift hospital in the grounds of an abandoned casino, they followed the rules. She pushed past the crowd at the door and out onto the area outside, once grass, now a sea of churned-up mud and goodness knows what else.

The middle-aged ambulance driver climbed down from his cab, swiping an arm across his face, displacing some flies.

"Sorry, Nurse, it took fifteen hours to reach you. Bomb craters or worse on the roads. Those poor boys, if they weren't badly off when I picked them off the battlefield, they are now."

Fifteen hours? They opened the back doors. Despite the warning, Sophie's stomach churned as the sickly-sweet smell assaulted her nostrils. Gangrene. Clenching her teeth, she worked in tandem with the ambulance driver and a couple of stretcher-bearers. They unloaded the ambulance, and she quickly checked each patient, sending them to the left or the right, a chance at life or certain death. It was a grim but necessary task. They didn't have the facilities or staff to help everyone. They had little more than the basics and even those were running out.

Hesitating for a second at the youthful, pale face lying on the stretcher, she glanced down and saw a large hole where his stomach should be. Darn it, this wasn't why she was training to be a doctor, to play God choosing who lived or died. Torn by doubt, she knew his chance of survival had been low at the time of impact, never mind fifteen hours later. They couldn't save him and, by trying, two or more other patients could lose their lives while they waited to be treated. She whispered something as she brushed his hair from his brow before indicating the orderlies take him to the right, to the tents where the priest waited to offer absolution to those who wanted it. Elderly nuns, those who weren't capable of nursing or assisting in the treatment of patients, helped the priest by writing letters for those soldiers still capable of giving their details. Their families, at least, would know what had happened to their sons.

Where was Jules? Was he safe or was someone making a

similar decision about him as she was now? She closed her eyes, saying a quick prayer to keep her beau safe. Then she felt the hairs rise on the back of her neck ... someone was watching her. She glanced up, meeting the eyes of the orderly holding the top end of the stretcher carrying the young soldier. She saw his shaking hands, almost causing the patient to fall off the stretcher.

"Please, Doctor. Try to help him. He's so young."

She wanted to scream at the orderly. Tell him it wasn't right that she, a twenty-three-year-old medical student, was making life-and-death decisions. She wanted to help them all, to heal them and return them to their loved ones just as she hoped Jules would return to her. She pushed her hands down the side of her coat and forced the instruction out of her mouth.

"To the right."

She turned her attention to the next patient, avoiding the orderly's stare. She couldn't afford sentimentality, not when so many lives were at stake.

The orderly's remark carried on the wind. "She may be a blonde beauty, but she's got ice for a heart."

Sophie pretended not to hear, although her hand stilled for a second before she continued to examine the next case. Noémie, having finished helping Dr Murphy, appeared at her side just in time to hear the comment.

"He doesn't mean it."

"He does, and he would be right." Sophie bit her lip, trying to keep her tears at bay. This wasn't doctoring. She indicated that this patient be taken to the operating theatre. He had a chance of life, albeit without his legs.

Noémie waited for the two orderlies to leave before rubbing Sophie's back, whispering, "They couldn't do what you're doing."

"I hate playing God, but we both know abdominal wounds like his are difficult to treat in a proper hospital. But out here?"

Noémie didn't answer. People were dying who should live. Noémie checked the ambulance was empty before directing two of the refugees to wash it out. They would work for food.

Then she turned back to Sophie, her trembling voice rising. "How can they expect us to save any of them? It takes too long to get them from the battlefields to us. Lice, flies, and filthy bandages don't help. What are the medics doing at the battle-field stations?"

"Quieten down. It won't do anyone any good if they see us getting upset. They are doi—"

The noise of an aeroplane cut her off. She glanced into the sky. *Please let it be one of ours.*

A staccato burst of gunfire had everyone diving for cover. Sophie threw herself over a group of wounded French soldiers sitting around the opening of the converted casino. The attack was over almost as soon as it started. She stood up, dusting down her filthy uniform, only to rub in dried blood and worse. Heart racing, she checked her patients. One tried to make a joke.

"Things are looking up, boys. Been a long time since such a looker threw herself at me."

She glanced at the soldier, but her rebuke died on her lips. She didn't wince as her gaze took in the degree of his facial burns. One side of his face was unmarked, the other unrecognis-able where the bandage had slipped.

"Where you from, soldier?"

"Lyon, at least originally. Just recently, the outskirts of Paris. They said we were going to the American Hospital." He tried to grin as he looked around. "I was told that it was in the wealthy part of Paris, with views of chestnut trees and the scent of lilacs and lilies. Wasn't expecting all this."

Sophie forced a smile to match his attempt at humour, taking a few seconds to find her voice. "I don't know. Who wouldn't prefer to operate in the countryside with the fresh smell of cow dung and mud in her nostrils?"

She shrugged, making more of them laugh. Then she kneeled beside him. "I'd better fix that bandage. It came loose when I threw myself at you. We can't risk it getting infected."

She hated touching him, his agony clear when he winced despite her gentle fingers, but he stayed quiet. His bravery brought the tears back to her eyes.

His mates watched in silence until she finished. Then one said, "Didn't know they'd let you nurses out of the wards."

Noémie answered on Sophie's behalf. "She's not a nurse, but a trainee doctor. Despite the lack of chestnut trees, lilacs, or any other flowers, you're in expert hands," Noémie confirmed. "Doctor, Dr Murphy said to use the alcohol."

One man tried to sit up, his once smart bottle-green uniform covered in dirt. "Great, just what we need. Pretty girls and a few drinks."

Noémie put the chatty soldier back in his place. "Not for that, silly. We need it to sterilise the wounds. We've run out of most things." Noémie caught Sophie's eye and then walked away, claiming she needed more supplies. Sophie knew she needed to hide her tears.

Sophie wanted to ask them whether they knew Jules, if he was one of the medics at the casualty station nearer the front. Knowing her beau, he'd be right there in the middle of it, all thoughts on the patients, none for his own safety. She didn't get a chance. Over the noise and commotion, she heard someone shouting for a doctor.

"Got to go. I'll be back to check on you."

"Look forward to it, Doc."

Blushing despite herself, Sophie hurried to a patient lying on one of the baccarat tables, stopping only to wash her hands in a basin of fresh, clean water an orderly supplied. She assessed the emergency. The nurse's blood-covered fingers were stuck inside a leg wound. Why wasn't she using more bandages?

"Get more bandages; you need to increase the pressure."

The frantic expression on the nurse's face should have warned her.

"We don't have any. We've run out."

"He's going to bleed out if we don't use something." Glancing around, Sophie couldn't see anything better than the sheet the patient was lying on.

"Hold him; keep the pressure on that bleed."

She ripped a length off the sheet and wound it tightly around the man's leg. The tourniquet worked. The blood stopped spurting. "That will hold for a few minutes. Might be enough time for Dr Murphy to see to him."

Sophie called two of the walking wounded soldiers capable of carrying a stretcher. "Privates, take this patient to the roulette table. Nurse, tell Dr Murphy the tourniquet won't hold for long; he needs to operate quickly."

The nurse stammered, "Yes, Doctor."

Sophie closed her eyes momentarily.

Her back ached, blisters covered her feet, yet she couldn't rest. Her stomach protested the lack of food and her throat was as rough as a sandy beach.

Noémie thrust a cup of hot liquid into her hand. "Sophie, drink this. Don't ask what it is, but it will warm you up."

"Merci." She didn't care for the taste, but the warm liquid helped offset the hunger pains.

Noémie leaned closer, whispering, "Is your family still in Paris? I heard that the Germans have already looted the city."

Sophie swallowed as her mouth went dry, her head feeling like it was in a vice, the tension making her eyes water. There'd been no signs of the Germans when she'd been home last week. Papa was adamant he was staying at their family home, but maybe he had changed his mind about leaving. She didn't want to think about her twin being at the mercy of the Germans. Jean-Pierre had joked once too often that his sisters were just the type of women the Germans loved: tall, blonde, slim but with curves in all the right places. She pulled her earlobe, the pain bringing her back to her senses.

"That's just gossip." She flashed her friend what she hoped was a reassuring smile. "Ambulances are commuting back and forth from Neuilly; the drivers would have told us. All they talk about are the refugees fleeing Belgium and other countries, or the Germans strafing them despite the red cross clearly visible on the vans." Sophie handed her friend the empty cup, knowing they needed to keep busy to distract themselves from the what-ifs. "Let's get back to work. Did the mother live?"

"For now. She woke up calling her daughter's name. She hasn't seen her since shortly after they left Paris. She thought it would be safer for her daughter to travel on a cart but the planes came and the cart overturned and..." Noémie's voice trailed off. As medics, they trained to remain stoic in the face of tragedy, but nobody had prepared them for this.

"We do our best. It's all we can do." Sophie echoed Dr Murphy's earlier words.

"Our best isn't good enough. People are dying and we are running out of all medicines. There's no food or shelter. Maria, from the village inn, says people are fighting over sleeping in the barn with the animals. When will it end?"

Sophie couldn't argue. She knew everything Noémie said was true, but it was better to allow the girl to let off steam.

Nothing could have prepared her for the vision in front of her eyes. There were hundreds of people, refugees and French soldiers, milling about. Some with obvious injuries, most showing signs of shock. She could only imagine what they had witnessed in the last forty-eight hours. Her throat closed over a lump, depriving her of the ability to speak to confirm she understood. She tried to smile but even that was difficult. Their eyes locked, the unshed tears reflecting on each other's face.

Looking embarrassed, Noémie took the empty cup from Sophie's hands. "We'd best get back to it. There's more coming."

As she headed for the incoming ambulance, a wounded patient lying nearby pulled himself up to a half-sitting position and grabbed Sophie's hand, his strength surprising her.

"Nurse, I've got to go back and help. Can't you just patch me up? I can still shoot. You've no idea how bad it is back there. My friends, they need me."

Sophie glanced at his name tag. "Private Reynard, you can go back just as soon as I tell you and not before. You're my patient now. We must see to those wounds. Infection has set in. You are running a temperature and if left untreated..." She didn't finish the sentence, hoping her message would convey itself.

The private lay back, his expression a mixture of relief and annoyance.

Sophie bent down. "Private, your request does you credit. But you will serve your friends and family better if you direct your energies into getting better. France will need all the help she can get."

"Vive la France," the private replied, half-saluting her, his weariness getting the better of him.

Time passed in a flurry of activity as more ambulances rolled in. The casino was full, all tables in use, yet still more patients arrived.

Despite being exhausted, Sophie put one foot in front of the other, again and again. It was the only way she could keep going. Dr Murphy said they were working longer hours than he ever had before, including the days of the worst battles of World War I.

Seeing Noémie sway on her feet, Sophie jumped to catch the nurse before she fell to the ground.

"Take a break."

Noémie shook her head. "Don't have time for breaks. Look at all these people. And there are more on the way. The

Germans dive-bombed refugees, men, women, and children. What will we do?"

The nurse's hysterical tirade ended with tears. Sophie took the woman by both arms and shook her gently. "We will do what we always do, the best we can for the patient we are dealing with. Forget everything else but this boy." Sophie gestured towards the child lying on the bed. "Then you need to take a break. I insist, as your doctor, not your friend." Sophie turned her attention back to the patient. "Who have we got here?"

Noémie's reply was less shaky this time. "Friendly fire hit the ambulance. He's lost a lot of blood, but I've stopped the bleeding for now."

Dr Murphy arrived just in time. "Who's next, Sophie?"

"This boy. Hit by friendly fire." Sophie quickly examined the patient. "Noémie did a great job on the bandaging. If the bullets hit a little higher, they would have got the artery. He was lucky."

Dr Murphy glanced at their surroundings before exchanging a sad smile with her. "Lucky?"

"Who can fault our facilities? The flies and the mud are a bonus. Isn't that what you stayed in France for?"

Dr Murphy seemed amused. "I stayed for my wife. We lived in the US back when we first got married, but my wife hated Maine. I think she might leave me if I threatened to go home." His eyes twinkled above his mask. Then their expression changed as he looked around. "How could I leave? Did you know Angela was a nurse in the last war? They gave her an award. That was supposed to be the war to end all wars!"

He fell silent for a few seconds as he examined the boy. He took out some shrapnel before cleaning the wound once more. "France needs our skills. Not just because of our medical knowledge, but because someone must stop the Germans. Angela insists on staying in our apartment even though they're likely to take up residence in Paris. I would prefer she and Philippe went to our country place, but my wife is a stubborn woman."

Sophie wondered if he realised Angela wasn't the only one who was stubborn; he was just as bad.

"You're right, Hitler can't win. The man is insane."

Dr Murphy wasn't listening to her; he was concentrating on closing the wound.

"He should live, if we can keep that wound clean," Dr Murphy said as he finished suturing the wound. Sophie pushed the sleeping child's hair back from his eyes. He was so young, he would recover quickly. But what of his family? He seemed to be alone.

Dr Murphy put his hand over hers and murmured, "At least he has a chance."

She squeezed her eyes shut to stop the tears falling at his unexpected gentleness. She loved and admired him as a doctor but at times his fierce temper and stern demeanour could inspire fear. In patients and staff alike. Yet watching him treating the boy brought a lump to her throat. Innocent children blown to bits. For what? Who had they hurt?

How many wouldn't survive? She wondered how the hospital in Neuilly was faring. It seemed like six months since she'd been home in Paris, not six days. How was her twin sister, Adèle, and the rest of her family coping; were they still in their apartment? Adèle was already a widow due to the war. And then Jules – her thoughts always returned to Jules. *Dear God, please keep him safe.* Reopening her eyes, she saw concern etched on Dr Murphy's face.

"Get some rest. When did you last sleep?" Dr Murphy asked her as they scrubbed their hands in the bowls of water provided by the porters.

Sophie shrugged. She had lost track of time completely.

"You look dead on your feet. Go to bed, that's an order."

Sophie hesitated; there were so many in need.

"I heard what you said to Noémie. The same applies to you. You can't help if you fall asleep or are so tired you make a mistake. Four hours won't make any difference to the tide of wounded. I fear things will only get worse. Now please, don't make me leave to escort you to your tent."

Worse? How could things deteriorate any further?

TWO

JUNE 1940

The wail of the air raid siren penetrated Adèle's deep slumber. She twisted and turned before half opening her eyes, settling her gaze on the familiar thick curtains covering the floor-to-ceiling windows. Why was she in her old bedroom? Where was Nicolas? What was that noise? It took a few seconds for reality to hit: Nicolas was dead, she was back home in her childhood bedroom and ... Paris was under attack.

Throwing the covers off, she jumped out of bed, hastily throwing on a dress and a cardigan. She wasn't going to the air raid shelter in her negligee. Her mother's screaming ratcheted up the noise level.

She picked up her hairbrush and pulled it through her long hair before twisting it into a knot, securing it at the base of her neck. Her hand had moved to her make-up out of habit when a knock on the oak bedroom door startled her.

Jean-Pierre put his head around her door. "Adèle, get down to the shelter now. I'll help papa with maman." She picked up her Jeanne Lanvin gas mask case and a bag containing her papers, jewellery and some francs, glancing around the room, wondering if her treasures would survive a raid, before heading out of the flat and downstairs. Sophie was at the hospital and Zeldah, their maid, had yet to arrive. She joined her neighbours making their way down the stairs.

A loud repeating noise rose up.

"What's that?" someone asked.

Adèle held her breath as the residents of their apartment block looked to the ceiling.

"It's just the ack-ack guns. They'll keep the Boche busy. Come on now." Madame Garnier, the concierge and also the shelter warden, directed them to the basement stairs. "Hurry now. That's right, everyone inside. It's the safest place for all of us."

Adèle picked a spot to sit at the far end of the basement, near to where her family and the other tenants stored their excess belongings. She waved to Jean-Pierre as he escorted their shaken mother into the shelter with papa following on behind, and they came over to sit beside her. The Litwaks' younger girl came in and lay down on some of the makeshift beds that had been prepared in advance. She was fast asleep almost as soon as her head hit the pillow. Adèle wished she could do the same. Instead, she stared at the supply of water and canned foods occupying one side of the shelter wall. Surely they wouldn't have to stay down here for long?

She closed her eyes, her thoughts going to her happy place: their finishing school in Switzerland, where she'd first met Nicolas. Even now after everything, her breath caught as she saw him perfectly in her mind's eye. She'd been overwhelmed that a sophisticated, older man was interested in her. She knew she was attractive, but in a finishing school, beautiful girls were two a penny. He'd wined and dined her – and then disappeared for over a year. She'd been crushed and Sophie had said he was just playing with her. What thirty-three-year-old man would be interested in a nineteen-year-old?

But then they'd met at Maxim's, on the night of her twenty-first birthday. He seemed fascinated with her. Despite being in his thirties, his debonair figure, ash-blonde hair and aquamarine-blue eyes turned heads. They'd made a very attractive couple and spent a year partying and touring Europe, her friends and their parents acting as chaperones. Her parents, while not liking his age, approved of his wealthy background and long-standing family connections. He'd charmed and conned everyone he met, including her.

They might never have got married but for her being careless. His dear mother had caught her coming out of his bedroom early one morning. Adèle sighed, remembering what a fuss that had caused. They'd been marched down the aisle *tout de suite*. And for what? Nicolas was dead three months after the wedding and she...

She winced as the building shuddered, the swaying releasing dust onto the inhabitants of the shelter. Her mother's nails dug into her arm but Adèle didn't complain. Was this how her life would end? Trapped under their apartment block.

"That's bombs exploding but they aren't near us." Jean-Pierre put his arm around her shoulders. "Don't worry."

"I'm not." She lied to her seventeen-year-old sibling. She didn't respond to her brother's raised eyebrows. He could think what he liked but she wasn't going to admit to being scared. "I hope Sophie is in a shelter somewhere."

Soon after, the all-clear sounded but they weren't allowed to leave. Madame Garnier, their concierge, went out to check that the block wasn't damaged before she called for them to make their way back to their own apartments.

Jean-Pierre stood up. "I'm going to go and check what's going on."

Her father stood, smoothing down his suit before lighting a cigarette. "Wait, I'll come with you. Adèle, take your mother back to the apartment." He glanced at his watch. "It's almost eight. Zeldah should be here shortly but if she's delayed, make some coffee."

Adèle opened her mouth to protest but it was pointless. Her father strode off without a backwards look. She took her mother's arm and half dragged her up the stairs back to their apartment.

"Ring the American Hospital and tell Sophie to come home." She clutched her hand. "I want us all together."

"Go back to bed." Adèle tried to hide her frustration. She'd thought she'd escaped her parents when she married, so being back here was even more annoying. Her mother only cared about her sainted twin. "Sophie will be fine. You know she'll have to stay to see to any wounded."

Adèle returned to her bedroom. She put away the emergency bag and gas mask before making her way to the bathroom. After rolling her hair in strips of rags, she returned to bed to catch up on some sleep. She had a date that evening and nothing, not even German bombs, was going to stop her from seeing Léo. She knew people would think it was too soon, but she didn't care – he was everything Nicolas wasn't. A proud working man with dark hair and deep, almost purple, eyes. He had a way of looking at her that made her wish they were alone. Of course her parents disapproved, her father saying he was only an engineer, but she didn't care what they thought. She wasn't getting married to him; it was just fun. He didn't claim to be someone he wasn't. Her lips curved into a smile as she anticipated the evening ahead. There were certain benefits to being a widow. If they were going to die, she wanted to live her last moments having fun.

* * *

Adèle swayed a little as she checked her chosen outfit. It would be better with her mother's solitaire diamond necklace.

Humming, she closed her bedroom door and walked down the hall into the sitting room where their mother was sitting on the edge of the armchair, staring at the empty hearth, her hands joined in prayer. Her mother was dressed as usual, her hair curled, wearing a day dress that accentuated her slim waist, her legs encased in stockings and high heels. Papa's wandering eye was well known but her mother would never let anyone say she'd let herself go.

"Maman, can I borrow..." Adèle stopped as her mother didn't acknowledge her; her lips moved as she prayed. Adèle tapped her foot. At last, her mother looked up.

"Yes?"

"Can I borrow your diamond necklace? I'm going to dinner this evening."

"Dinner? Our city has just been bombed."

Adèle fingered the brocade fabric of the couch, trying to keep her temper in check. Why did her mother insist on stating the obvious?

"You should stay home and wait."

"For what? I'm a young woman and I'm not going to wait around for the Germans to march into Paris. I want to have some fun while I still can."

Her mother stood and ambled over to the balcony. "What do you see when you look out there?"

Adèle peered over her mother's shoulder. There were people everywhere, some refugees travelling by foot, others with their belongings packed on top of their cars. A slight chill shivered down her spine. Surely those people were overreacting. They were safe in Paris. Weren't they? "They are foreigners on the run from the Germans, not Parisians. Papa would have made us leave if there was any danger." Adèle turned on her most winning smile. "Please. I want to make an impression."

"You don't need diamonds to do that. There will be gossip.

You should be in mourning for your husband, a hero for France."

Adèle couldn't stop the smirk.

"Why do you laugh? Nicolas must have meant something to you."

"I'm sorry he's dead, but he's hardly a hero. He was drunk and the car left the road."

Her mother frowned, pursing her lips. "He was buried with the honours due to an officer."

"Only because of who he was and the fact he wore a uniform."

Her mother paled, her hand going to her cheek. Honestly, she should be on the stage, she was so dramatic. Adèle took a deep breath and modulated her tone.

"Maman, please stop this. You didn't even like him. You only agreed to us getting married because you were worried I was pregnant."

"That's not true." But maman avoided looking at her.

"Yes it is!" She wasn't listening to any more lies. "We couldn't risk a scandal now, could we?"

Her mother sat down, her elbows on her knees, hands covering her face. When she lifted her head, she met Adèle's gaze. "I don't attempt to understand you. You are callous and self-centred. Whatever Nicolas was, he was your husband and he is dead."

Adèle's jaw tightened; her head started to pound. Nicolas was no saint; he'd never been faithful and considered her little more than a meal ticket. He'd made that clear. His family may have been descended from Napoleon but all their money was tied up in property, paintings, and other assets. Something they had hidden extremely well. He had seduced her on purpose, not that she'd ever admit that to anyone, not even Sophie, who'd never liked him. She closed her eyes, seeing the cold, calculating expression when he'd admitted not only the truth but the fact that he wasn't willing to change his behaviour. She could hear his taunting voice. *You get my name and connections, chérie, I get your money. It's a match made in heaven.*

"Look around you. There are plenty dead and more will die before this is all over. Even more reason I want to go out and live my life. While I still can."

She marched out of the living room back to her bedroom, but the ringing telephone stopped her. She waited for Zeldah to answer it.

"Oui, Madame Adèle is here. One moment please." She heard Zeldah hesitate before saying, "Bien sûr, I will pass on the message. Au revoir." Zeldah put the receiver back on the handle. "Monsieur Favreau sends his regrets."

Adèle waited for Zeldah to explain further but when the maid stayed silent, she snapped, "Why didn't he wait to speak to me?"

Zeldah shrugged. "He said it was chaotic and he would speak to you soon."

Adèle didn't look at the maid's face, not wanting to see her gloating. She turned on her heel and stomped off to her bedroom.

She paced the room in irritation. Why did Nicolas have to die? If he was still alive, she would be living in their home and enjoying complete freedom to see Léo whenever she wished. Nicolas would be off at war and she'd be enjoying the attention lavished on a new tragic bride whose husband was at the front. Now his brother and horrendous fat wife lived in the magnificent villa, and she was back at home being treated like a child. She took off her shoes and pitched one across the room before throwing herself across the bed. This stupid war had ruined everything.

* * *

Sunday morning, the church bells chimed, calling the faithful to Mass as always, but for once her mother stayed home.

She was sitting by her desk. "I can't breathe properly with those fumes and that smell."

"Why didn't you shut the window?" Coughing after inhaling a mouthful of dark smoke, Adèle closed the window with a bang. She was in a foul mood and her mother's whining wasn't helping. "First we're bombed and now we're being poisoned too. They set the large gas and oil tanks alight. They don't want the fuel landing in the Germans' hands." Adèle coughed again and sat close to her mother. "I've been listening to the radio. According to the news, children, old people, and those with chest problems are being admitted to hospital. Sophie will be busier than ever, although why she has to work in a converted casino rather than a real hospital is anyone's guess."

"She had to go where the casualties are. I hope she'll be careful. What is the latest news?"

Adèle stood up and walked across the wooden floor. She lifted the phone to listen to the news on the *informations parlées*. It was conflicting but depressing. She slammed down the receiver. It just couldn't be true. The Germans in Paris? What had happened to the unbreachable Maginot Line? The Allied armies had retreated via Dunkirk. Over dinner last night, her father had called them rats, leaving a sinking ship. Jean-Pierre had argued angrily that they were regrouping and would return. Father and son rarely agreed these days and Jean-Pierre increasingly spent time with his friends, avoiding mealtimes with their father whenever he could.

She moved towards the French doors leading to the small balcony.

"Look at the crowds leaving Paris. Maybe papa was wrong, we should leave." Adèle pointed down to the street beneath their third-floor window. "They must think the Boches will murder us in our beds."

Her mother stood up, her back straight, a look of defiance on her face. "I am half-German. Please do not use that vulgar word in this house. The Germans are a civilised people, not murderers."

Adèle wanted to scream at her and tell her to shut up. Had she not read the papers, seen the stream of refugees flooding through Paris from Belgium and other countries? Never mind the influx of immigrants from Eastern Europe. Adèle sniffed. They should have left Paris months ago and would have but for her mother. The last time her mother had dug her heels in had been to prevent Adèle from going to New York. A friend from school had invited her after Nicolas had been killed, but her mother refused permission in case Adèle became stranded in America. As if America was interested in joining the fight against Hitler.

Why, oh why, hadn't she gone? She wouldn't have to live under the restrictions already in place. She doubted any American would put up with no meat dishes being available in restaurants three days a week, or if you could get meat, you couldn't get pastries. And having a meal without wine – that was just unpatriotic.

"Where is Jean-Pierre?" her mother asked.

"Where do you think? He's packing old things into boxes up at the museum. Why does he spend all his spare time over there anyway?" Jean-Pierre had never willingly opened a book in his life, yet since war broke out he'd become an almost constant presence at the museum. There must be a pretty woman working there. "The Germans won't be interested in their treasures. Who needs old weapons or photographs of Morocco? They are after gold, diamonds, and anything valuable they can get their slimy paws on."

Her mother's frigid stare stopped her. "I wish he was here.

Sophie, she's needed at the hospital, but there is no reason for my son to desert me. Not at a time like this."

Adèle's stomach turned over, thinking of her twin, up to her elbows in blood and guts. Her stomach clenched as she fought the rising nausea; they may be identical in looks but that's where the similarities ended. She couldn't handle the sight of blood and didn't intend having to work for a living, whereas Sophie seemed to relish her chosen career.

When Adèle looked up, her mother had left the room. Adèle turned back to the window, watching the procession of people. She wiped the palms of her hands on her skirt.

A few air raids and the citizens of Paris had flooded the streets in their haste to depart, car roofs covered with their most valuable possessions. Those who didn't own a car went by horse and cart or walked. Some children were making a game of jumping over the sandbags protecting every building. Adèle inhaled. Just how far did they think they would get by walking?

Her father came into the apartment, slamming the door behind him. He strode into the sitting room, his suit creased – and was that a stain on his tie? Her normally dapper, unflappable father looked ten years older than he had done last night.

"Adèle, pack your things. We are leaving."

"But —"

"No buts. We are all leaving in an hour. The train stations have been closed, with gendarmes guarding the entrances. There is complete chaos out there. My contacts have advised us to leave, immediately."

Adèle stared at him, her mouth open. Her mother walked back into the room.

"Where are we going, papa?"

Her mother was gazing at her husband in disbelief. "Leave? We can't. What about our things?"

Adèle followed her mother's gaze, taking in the antique fireplace, the high ceilings, the silk wallpaper covered in paintings, each one more valuable than the last. Her mother walked over and picked up a Sèvres vase. "How am I supposed to leave all my precious things behind?"

Papa grunted. "They won't survive a bombardment, will they? What if Hitler levels Paris like he did Warsaw?"

"Papa, you can't compare Warsaw to our beloved Paris."

"Shut up. Just pack your jewels and your coats and off we go."

Shocked, she stared at her father. He rarely spoke to her like that.

Her mother protested, "What about Sophie and Jean-Pierre?"

Papa speared her mother with a look. "Your children have made their choices. We will drive to Lyon and leave word with the concierge of where we've gone. You can stay with your mother while I—"

Adèle frowned. "Lyon? Why do we have to go there?"

He ignored her question. "This is not a holiday. You have fifteen minutes to get ready."

Adèle ran to her bedroom, wondering what she should take. Not her prized possession. Her father would shoot her if she suggested she pack the Dresden china dressing table, a present from her mother's mother. Mémé hated the piece, said it reminded her of Germany. Adèle fingered the china. It was too fabulous for her to care where it had originated. She heard her father calling to say he was leaving. He wouldn't leave without her, would he? Was he serious about leaving Sophie and Jean-Pierre behind? How would they fare at the hands of the Germans? They wouldn't bomb a hospital, though, would they? Sophie would be safe, wouldn't she?

She jumped as her father roared at her mother. "I don't have time to wait."

"I'm coming. Don't leave without me." Adèle yelled from

her room as she swung her emergency bag over her shoulder and grabbed some clothes, stuffing them into a suitcase.

"Zeldah, where are you?"

Where was the maid? Had she left already? Perhaps she had gone to check on her invalid mother. Another one, like Sophie, who wouldn't save herself.

Throwing a few more things into the suitcase, Adèle slammed it shut and half-pulled, half-dragged it out to where her father was waiting. He attempted to lift the case.

"What's in there? Rocks?"

"Papa! You said to pack my most precious belongings. I had to leave half my wardrobe behind as it was. This is most inconvenient. Why couldn't our soldiers do a better job of protecting us?"

"Who knows? Help me get your mother downstairs and into the car. She is refusing to leave."

Adèle went to her parents' room to fetch her mother, who was sitting on her dressing table stool, staring ahead of her as if paralysed. "Papa won't wait. The roads are already busy. Come on."

Her mother gripped her hands in front of her chest, her eyes wild. "I can't leave without knowing Jean-Pierre and Sophie are safe."

"They made their choice. Papa made yours." Adèle picked up a bag on her mother's bed. "Have you put your jewellery inside? Money?"

Her mother just stared at the bed. Adèle wanted to shake her, but she knew that wouldn't help. "I'll take this to the car while you lock up."

Once outside, it quickly became obvious they had left it too late to make their escape. All around them, the other apartments and houses had shuttered windows and locked doors. Adèle climbed into the back seat of the black Citroën *traction avant*. People of all types, sizes, and, judging from the accents, nationalities jammed the roads. Where were they coming from?

"Belgium and other places." Papa answered her unspoken question. She looked out the window just in time to see Zeldah walk down the street.

"Monsieur Bélanger, you're leaving?"

Adèle saw her gaze running over the empty car seats. Did Zeldah want to come with them? Surely not. She was their maid.

"Yes. Please tell Jean-Pierre and Sophie we couldn't wait."

Zeldah's eyes flashed but she didn't say another word, simply turning on her heel and walking to the apartment entrance. Adèle watched as her mother came out of the building and greeted the maid. She appeared to be giving her a list of instructions.

Her father beeped the horn impatiently and finally, her mother came over and got into the front seat, and they were ready to leave. But they hadn't gone very far when her mother demanded they stop the car.

Fuming, Adèle drummed her fingers on the seat beside her. "Why?"

"Help these people. Look at them! That old couple, they look older than my mother. We must give them a lift."

Adèle leaned forward to put her hands on her mother's shoulders to calm her down – and make her see sense.

"You can't stop every time you see someone you think needs help. We will never make it to Lyon. Mémé will worry."

Her mother seemed to listen, and her father flashed Adèle a look of approval.

The endless tide of people kept coming, flowing out of Paris and away from the perceived danger. If only they had left when the news first broke! The hours passed as they made little progress, caught up in the melee. They would move faster if they got out and pushed the car. Everywhere you looked, there was evidence of desperation. Carts abandoned by street sellers, fresh flowers scattered over the roads. Vacant properties, some hastily deserted as evidenced by half-closed shutters. As they left the city, finally, the view began to change; farm animals grazed on small patches of grass.

Perspiring heavily, Adèle stared out the window, ignoring the people begging for a lift or for food. Her father had had the foresight to pack food and water in empty wine bottles. He was very well prepared, probably more so than the others in buses and other cars around them, never mind the poor unfortunates clinging to horse-drawn carts.

The time passed so slowly as their car inched forward. After four hours, they had travelled less than thirty miles, when in peacetime they'd have been near to Lyon.

"There's a town just over there. We can stop and get something to eat. A bath maybe?" Adèle used her sweetest tone, wary of her father's temper.

"Look at the number of travellers. We can't stop here. There's no room." Papa swore before driving on.

Adèle could see people sleeping on the floors of cafés and hotels as they passed. Some were even sleeping on the pavement. "There's a woman washing nappies in the fountain."

Her mother stretched, trying to see. "Should we turn back? Go home?"

Adèle didn't hear what her father said. She only heard the noise, which stopped and started, like a car backfiring. When people started screaming, she realised they were being fired upon.

"Papa, stop the car," Adèle screeched as she wrenched the car door open. "Get out! They are bombing us!" In her hurry to get out and away from the car, she knocked someone over but didn't stop to help them. She kept running, away from the obvious targets. Others followed, whole families splintering to find shelter. But there wasn't any.

Adèle threw herself to the ground and covered her head with her arms. Explosions shook the ground, pieces of rock and other debris raining down on her. She coughed as the scent of burning irritated her nostrils and then shrieked as the gunfire rang in her ears.

When would it stop? Adèle curled up as small as she could. Time ticked past as if in slow motion. She opened her eyes only to glimpse someone get hit, the splash of blood seeping from a wound where their mouth had been. Screaming, she clung closer to the ground. They were going to die.

* * *

At last, the planes seemed to go away. But just as Adèle was about to sit up, they came back, dropping more bombs and bullets as they went. Something landed with a thud beside her. Opening her eyes, she couldn't work out what it was, her brain refusing to believe what her eyes were telling her. An arm. She retched as the smell of blood filled her nostrils. She rocked back and forth, screeching, not caring who heard her.

"Adèle, where are you? I can hear you but can't see you."

"Papa, papa! I'm here. Come and get me please!" she begged as she waited for her father to come to her. She felt like a child again, unable to do anything but wait to be rescued. What if the planes came back? This was pure madness, lying in a field surrounded by strangers, being shot at by Germans.

"Are you hurt?" She saw her father coming towards her and he dropped down onto the ground beside her.

"No. Can we go home? Please, I want to go home."

He held her against his chest. She relished the unfamiliar comfort and support he offered. This was so unlike him, but she didn't question his behaviour. Nothing was normal any more.

They waited for a while but the Germans didn't come back, so they slowly made their way back to their wrecked car, the roof punctured by bullets, the wheels flattened. Her mother sat by the side of the road, a red-stained handkerchief at her fore-head. Adèle scrambled, falling over something as she went to her. She didn't stop to check what it was.

"Maman, you're injured!"

"It's just a graze. Are you all right?" Turning to her husband, she asked, "And you?" He nodded but didn't look at her, his gaze roaming over the carnage.

His hands shook, his face pale as his voice trembled. "How on earth are we going to get out of here now?"

Amazed, Adèle saw the attack had invigorated rather than defeated her mother. She stood up. "We'll walk, I guess. Just like everyone else."

Adèle stared at her mother, wondering if she had hit her head. Walk? In these shoes? Not likely.

But she did. They began walking back the way they had come, too tired, too hungry to care if the Germans were marching right through their apartment, never mind Paris. At first the bloated bodies of cows, horses, never mind humans, made Adèle ill, the eye-watering stench making her stomach heave, but in time she became immune to everything but the thought of putting one foot in front of the other.

THREE

The lights flickered. Sophie swayed on her feet from tiredness, and swallowed hard to fight nausea caused by the smell of unwashed bodies combined with blood and other bodily fluids.

"Pay attention, Mademoiselle Bélanger."

Sophie bit back a gasp at the harsh reprimand. Dr Thierry always behaved like a gentleman, showing courtesy to patients and colleagues alike. But in the last few weeks, the debonair dresser had changed, the intelligence lurking in his eyes dampened by a thousand painful memories, his aristocratic bearing replaced by an old man's shuffle, his short grey hair standing on end.

"Sorry, Dr Thierry." Sophie apologised rather than explain she was exhausted after a long, challenging ambulance trip escorting seriously ill passengers from the temporary hospital at Fontainebleau. Dr Murphy had ordered her back to the American Hospital with him, feeling it would be safer. An army medical unit had taken over the Fontainebleau field hospital. Nazi planes had strafed them as they drove through the working-class suburbs before reaching the leafy Neuilly streets.

"I'll show you again; observe closely." Dr Thierry lifted the scalpel and illustrated how the cut should be made. Sophie stifled a yawn, shuffling from one foot to the other, ignoring her hunger pangs. The young soldier in the operating theatre would only survive because of Dr Thierry's skills, so she could bear his temper. But she couldn't hide her relief when the operation finished and Dr Thierry retired, leaving Sophie to observe the patient.

Elizabeth, their head nurse, sidled closer.

"Forgive him." Elizabeth hesitated. "I worry about him. He has nobody to look after him, to stop him from working himself to death. Every night he was in the cellar operating while the Germans shelled the city. He says the condition of the wounded is worse than he saw during the previous war, the war that cost him his son."

"Dr Murphy said the same. Do you think they will flatten Paris like they did Warsaw? Or is it true Hitler wants to visit?"

Elizabeth ran a hand through her greying hair, her foot tapping continuously. "I wish he would. I'd like to get my bare hands on his scrawny neck." Elizabeth clenched and unclenched her hands several times before snapping the pencil she held in two. She threw it on the table beside her. "Look at us. Dealing with horrific wounds on soldiers and civilians alike. There are several ambulances missing; those young American drivers vanished. What did those girls ever do to anyone, will you tell me?" Elizabeth rubbed the side of her temple. Had she a headache too? She inhaled loudly, her eyes shimmering a little too brightly.

Sophie wanted to make her friend feel better but she couldn't. She wouldn't mind getting her hands on Hitler, either. She fingered the scalpel in her hands before putting it down again. What was she thinking? As a doctor, she had to vow to preserve life. But she hadn't qualified yet, had she?

Full ambulances continued to arrive at regular intervals at the hospital, carrying patients with a wide variety of injuries.

Sophie and Elizabeth accompanied Dr Murphy on his rounds.

"If the patient is too ill to be moved, remove their uniforms and burn them. They will be admitted as ordinary patients. We don't want the Germans putting these brave French soldiers in prisoner-of-war camps."

"You think the Germans are going to win?" Sophie wanted to put the words back in her mouth at the pitying look Dr Murphy gave her. He continued as if she hadn't spoken.

"They must receive the best care we can give them if they are to have a chance at recovery."

Elizabeth nodded. "How will you explain their injuries?"

"With the Germans targeting civilians, we don't have to worry about that, do we?" Dr Murphy looked up from the patient's notes. "We need to decide what to do about the ones that aren't severely injured."

Sophie wasn't sure what he was asking. What did he mean? Surely they would return to their units.

As if reading her thoughts, Dr Murphy continued. "The Germans will march into Paris any day now. If we patch these soldiers up and return them to their units, they will be taken prisoner. I don't feel right handing over more men that could live to fight another day."

Elizabeth glanced around before whispering, "They should die. At least some of them."

"Die?" Sophie sputtered. She wasn't at all sure she'd heard correctly. She caught the look of reproval Dr Murphy gave Elizabeth.

"What? Tell me what Elizabeth meant?" Sophie glared at the silent doctor.

"The ambulances leaving this hospital are not empty. Occasionally, we use them to deliver the walking wounded to friends further south. We can't save everyone, but a few is better than none. Those men must disappear so that they can escape

France, and join the Allies to fight back. The Germans may have won this battle but not the war."

"And what better way for them to go than to say they died?" Elizabeth explained as Sophie looked at Dr Murphy blankly.

Sophie couldn't stop herself. "But that's against the law. Several laws, in fact. You'll lose your licence."

She caught the irritation in Dr Murphy's eyes before he masked it.

"War is not a time of rules. You will learn that in due course. But I don't want you involved in this. Go, take your break now."

"But—"

"Now, Mademoiselle Bélanger."

Sophie hesitated. She'd upset him – but why? What he was suggesting was ludicrous. They would be caught and then what would happen? He turned his back towards her and she took the hint and walked away. If he lost his licence to practise medicine, how would this hospital survive? Why would such an intelligent man take such risks?

Later, she bumped into Elizabeth on another ward, but one glance at her friend's face warned her not to bring up their previous conversation. For a second, she thought she'd disappointed the senior nurse. Her stomach hardened with hurt, but she buried the feeling. She had other worries. Her shift was over. She needed to be with her family.

* * *

Despite feeling guilty at deserting the hospital, she was desperately worried about Adèle and the others. She walked past the taped-up hospital windows, the sandbags piled high around the entrance, forcing herself to ignore the patients waiting to be seen.

There were no buses – they had requisitioned most to move

troops to the front, and those that were left were hopelessly overcrowded. The same with the métro. It took ages to get back to their apartment, which was still standing and looked untouched. She walked in the front door, noting Madame Garnier's door was closed, which was unusual, but maybe the concierge was out shopping. Climbing the stairs to the second-floor apartment, she was about to put her key in the door when it opened and Zeldah threw her arms around her.

"Thank God you're safe. Jean-Pierre was so worried. He went to the hospital but you weren't there."

"I was at Fontainebleau; we set up a temporary hospital to deal with the wounded. I got back to the Neuilly Hospital yesterday but stayed to assist with some surgeries. We're so short of staff." Sophie glanced around; the apartment looked deserted. "Where're my parents? Adèle?"

"They left Paris two days ago. They went to Lyon to your grandmother."

Without me? Without saying goodbye.

"I was late for work that morning, delayed by the traffic, and by the time I got to your apartment, your father was already in the car, Adèle too. Your mother didn't want to go, but he wasn't in the mood to listen. I think they should have stayed here. I've been listening to horrible stories from neighbours and friends about the chaos on the roads, missing children, parents dead in ditches..."

Sophie shuddered, the images of the crumpled bodies she'd tended to over the last week coming to mind. Had her family got to safety? She didn't want to think of them being hurt or worse.

Zeldah was still speaking and she hastily interrupted. "How's your mother? Is the pain still bad? Will I check on her?"

Zeldah shook her head. "No, you should get to bed. You look almost as bad as some of those who've walked here from

Belgium. Have a bath first, although the water is not boiling, and go to sleep." Zeldah held the door open to the bathroom. "Mama is doing better thanks to your skill and medicine. You rest. When are you due back at the hospital?"

"Tomorrow morning."

Sophie gratefully took Zeldah's advice. She lingered in a tepid bath, the water turning black around her. Then she showered off and fell into her bed, not caring her hair was still wet. She fell asleep to the sounds of shells falling in the distance. Her last thought was the hope that Adèle was safe in Lyon.

* * *

The next day, back at the hospital, Sophie was startled by the sound of announcements outside and she moved over to the window, looking out as German vehicles fitted with loudspeakers invaded the streets, repeating the same announcement.

"... Paris inhabitants will stay indoors for the next forty-eight hours. Any resistance will be crushed by the most rigorous means... The Paris police remain on duty... Looting and sabotage will not be tolerated."

"Sophie, move away from the window," Elizabeth said, and turned to look at the sterile instruments to check whether Sophie had laid them out correctly. "I see you've mastered the art of surgery preparation. Everything has to be in the correct place, or the surgeons get upset."

Elizabeth indicated the trolley in front of her, but Sophie was too annoyed to concentrate.

"How dare they tell us to stay home. This is our city, Elizabeth."

"I know!"

The dry reply made Sophie smile just as it was supposed to. "Sorry, I'm still on edge because I haven't heard from Jules. I was sure he'd send word." Sophie couldn't push the feeling of impending doom away. Jules would have tried everything to contact her, not leave her to wonder if he was hurt or ... she closed her eyes. She had to stop thinking like that.

"Every time I think of Doctor Stein, it makes me smile. I miss him around the hospital, his kindness for the patients and of course, his handsome face. The female patients flirted with him constantly calling him the French Clark Gable." Elizabeth blinked, her eyes shining as her voice shook a little. "I don't miss his practical jokes. Do you remember when he left red berries on that trainee doctors chair, what was his name again? The real pompous young man who ordered us all around as if we were servants."

Sophie laughed despite her misery. "Doctor Vallin, an odious little man. He was such a bully, he had all the nurses in tears with his stupid demands. Well apart from you."

"Like most bullies, he knew who to pick on."

Sophie nodded. "His face was a picture when he sat down and jumped up again to find his trousers stained red. Even the patients downstairs heard him yelling. I thought Jules would be fired. Doctor Vallin was very well connected."

"His own father didn't have time for his attitude. Monsieur Vallin told me he was sorry he wasn't here to see for himself." Elizabeth laid her hand on Sophie's arm. "Dr Stein is a survivor. If he's been captured, he might not be able to write. They will let us have a list of prisoners soon, I think. Try not to lose hope."

Jules a prisoner? How would he cope? He didn't like taking orders and wouldn't stand by if anyone was ill-treated. Would the Germans treat the prisoners harshly? He was a medic. People respected those on both sides, didn't they?

"I'll try, it's just so hard not knowing. When Nicolas died, they sent word to Adèle straight away."

"That was different. They were married and he died in an accident, not at the front. You can't compare the two. How is

Adèle? You haven't said. She's so young and beautiful to be a widow. Were they together long?"

Sophie sighed. "She's fine." She hesitated. How could she explain her sister didn't appear to be broken-hearted without making her sound callous? "They first met at a party we both went to from that ridiculous finishing school our mother insisted we attend. The aim of that place was to find us a good husband; she succeeded, while I..." Sophie bit her lip as the pain of his loss hit her once more.

"Fell head over heels in love with a career in medicine and a rather charming, good-looking medical student." Elizabeth smiled. "I can still hear your father now, shouting at Dr Murphy for encouraging you to study."

Sophie's cheeks flushed at the memory. Her father had behaved so badly, making a show of them all at a charity dinner where Dr Murphy, Elizabeth, and some of the other senior staff had been in attendance.

"Papa was more in favour of Nicolas. Adèle wouldn't have to work, much less, God forbid, encounter any germs." Sophie finished setting up the tray, earning herself a nod of approval from the head nurse.

"You will make an excellent doctor. As for your twin, I assumed it was a match based on mutual benefit, his family name in return for her beauty, by looking at the society pages. He was a good bit older than her but his family are very wealthy. Does she still see his parents?"

Sophie shook her head. Even now, she couldn't understand how Adèle had married a man in his mid-thirties. Sophie and Adèle had been so close as children and at school, and she'd thought they'd remain that way forever. But when they'd toured Europe after the Swiss finishing school, their differences drove them apart. She loved to see the history of the European towns; her sister was only interested in what was happening socially.

She'd stay in bed all day after partying all night. Not that Sophie didn't enjoy a great party – she did. Elizabeth coughed.

Sophie looked at Elizabeth and realised she was still waiting for an answer. "Sorry, I was miles away. She moved home as soon as Nicolas died and his brother took over the villa."

Elizabeth didn't comment. She gave the theatre set-up a final inspection before leading their way to the hospital lobby. They were both due a break now.

"Looks like most people have ignored the warning." Elizabeth indicated the crowd outside. "Shall we join them?" Elizabeth winked. "I have some shopping to do and I won't be told by anyone how to behave in my own city."

"Let's go." Sophie was proud of her people. Parisians came out in their droves to see the Germans parade, to shop or just to prove they weren't defeated.

After a few days of such good behaviour, General von Studnitz rescinded the order in favour of a curfew.

FOUR

It took them five days to return home, their pace slow. Adèle lost her shoes along the way, but still they moved forward. None of them were fit, and the route proved hazardous, with abandoned vehicles, cases, clothes, and other items lying strewn about.

"When we reach Paris, we will stop at the first hotel we see."

Adèle nodded in response to her father, too tired to do anything else. But when they reached a hotel, they didn't stop. There were no rooms, refugees packed in every one. They kept walking through the outskirts of Paris until they reached their district.

Adèle couldn't believe her eyes; everything looked the same as it had when they'd left. It was like stepping back in time to see the neatly kept gardens full of exotic flowers, the riding paths clear of debris, their honey-coloured apartment building swathed in sunshine.

Papa greeted the concierge, who simply stared at them, for once rendered speechless. Madame Garnier stood there open-mouthed as Adèle, followed by her mother, trailed up the stairs to their apartment. Walking inside, Adèle burst into tears. She wanted to kill papa for making them leave.

Sophie and Jean-Pierre were sitting in the untouched sitting room surrounded by their mother's precious ornaments, looking as they always did. Adèle could hear Zeldah singing in the kitchen, the smell of something baking causing her stomach to rumble. Nothing would make her leave Paris again. She didn't care if every German national moved to France. This was her home.

"Adèle, maman, papa! You're home! We were so worried about you. Let me see your face. How did you get hurt?" Sophie jumped up and rushed towards them, examining each individually. Adèle pushed her twin away.

Her mother hugged Sophie close. "It is nothing. How are you? And Jean-Pierre? You are not injured?"

"Do they look hurt?" Adèle snapped as her mother fussed over her children. "Were they bombed, shot at, or forced to walk until their blisters had blisters?"

"I missed you so much." Sophie gathered her into her arms. "Come with me. I'll run you a bath. I have some salve for your feet. You poor thing! Zeldah will make you something to eat. We're so glad to have you home."

Adèle got into the bath and let her sister wash away the blood, hay, and whatever else covered her body. She could hear the thud of the bullets ricocheting off the ground around her, the screams of the people hit, the stench of the dead and dying... She squeezed her eyes shut to stop the tears, wishing the memories would stop tormenting her.

"Are you all right?"

Adèle opened her eyes in response to her sister's question. "I'm fine. I can wash myself."

But Sophie shook her head. "I'll wash your hair."

Reluctantly, she settled back as Sophie's fingers massaged her scalp. Why had she left with her father? She should have stayed at home in safety. She stared at the water covering her body. When she was finally clean, she wanted to lie still in the water and close her eyes and forget the last few days had ever happened. But Sophie wouldn't let her wallow in peace.

"Did you see those horrible flags? They fly from every building. Gaudy blood-red things with that black swastika in the middle."

"Oui." Adèle added more hot water to the bath.

Sophie smiled as she handed Adèle a towel. "You'd best get out before your skin melts off."

Why couldn't Sophie disappear and leave her alone? Her sister's chattering was making Adèle's head hurt even more.

"Those Nazis had to climb the Eiffel Tower by foot. Our soldiers sabotaged the lifts. Imagine climbing three hundred metres just to hang a flag."

Why was Sophie so concerned about the flag? She thrust her twin away and glared at her. "Imagine if our soldiers had put more effort into defending our country than sabotaging lifts. I wouldn't look like this. I would never have had to leave."

Sophie turned on her, her eyes flashing. "Adèle Bélanger, never do I want to hear you criticising our brave men again. Do you know how many of them are lying dead on the fields? Not even a decent burial for them. If you saw the state of the men who arrive at our hospital ... I haven't heard from Jules. He could be anywhere."

Adèle felt guilty for about a second. She thought of what she had seen – the destruction of war mangling innocent people who were only trying to escape to safety. She wondered if she could ever confide in Sophie, tell her how horrific it had been. She turned to her twin, but Sophie walked away. *Suit yourself.* Adèle walked to her bedroom and took a long nap.

When she woke, it was almost evening. She walked into the sitting room where her family had congregated. Papa was giving instructions as usual.

"I want you to give up working at the American Hospital. The Germans are here now. It's best for everyone if we stay together until we see what happens over the next few weeks."

Sophie jumped to her feet. "Glad to see you up and looking better, Adèle. Sorry, papa, but I have to go to the hospital. I can't expect someone else to cover my shift. We're short-staffed as it is and it's going to get worse."

"Sophie, you must stay here. You've no idea what they did to us out there." Her mother's tendons stood out in her neck, her hands jammed into her armpits, a look of terror on her face. "You tell her, Adèle. Tell her how awful it was."

Adèle caught Sophie rolling her eyes. "Let her go. Maybe she thinks just because she's a medic she's untouchable."

Her mother made a disapproving noise. Adèle knew Sophie's feelings would be hurt, but she didn't care. She turned on her heel and went back to her room. Her mother's reminder of what they'd been through had brought horrible visions to her mind. She threw off her shoes and lay on the bed fully clothed. She heard the apartment front door bang as Sophie left. It used to be her who was the adventurous one, the rebel who went against their parents at every opportunity. Sophie was the one who always obeyed the rules, no matter what they were. She didn't speak out in class, never cheeked a teacher or wore her top blouse button undone. She'd never jumped a subway without a ticket nor dropped a sweet wrapper on the ground. In the last couple of years, she'd challenged everyone, from the decision to go to medical school to becoming unofficially engaged to a trainee doctor beau, and now she was disobeying papa over the Germans. What next?

FIVE

15 JUNE 1940

Nobody stopped Sophie on her way to the hospital. It was a relief to be out of the apartment, where the atmosphere was strained: Adèle seeming withdrawn and angry with her, Jean-Pierre often out with his museum friends, and their parents' tension.

If Jules were here, he'd find a way to make her smile. Only he knew how frustrating she found her twin and how angry her father's attitude made her. Jules had his own family issues. His parents had selected a suitable wife and had his future planned out. If Madame Stein had her way, Jules would become the best known surgeon in Paris, no make that France. His wife wouldn't work but would provide him with a large family of sons.

Would he come back and marry her or would the war and the Nazi propaganda from Germany make him bow to his parents' wishes? Did he love her enough to go against his mother? The old woman had threatened to sit Shiva for him if he did. She forced those thoughts out of her head. If Jules was here, he'd kiss her worries away, reassure her of his love.

The métro was quieter than usual, those who'd ventured

out looking rather glum. And so they should. The Germans had taken over Paris without a single shot being fired.

She got to the hospital and climbed the stairs to Dr Murphy's office. He wasn't there, but she stood looking out of his window, wondering what the people scurrying around on the streets below really thought of the occupation.

Sophie looked up as Dr Murphy walked into the room, his face grey. A few medical staff, including Elizabeth and Noémie, followed him in.

His voice trembled with shock as he said, "I regret to inform you our esteemed colleague, my friend, Dr Thierry, has taken his own life."

Sophie couldn't believe her ears, although the devastated looks on her colleagues' faces echoed what she had just heard Dr Murphy say.

"It was clear he was struggling, had been for some time, yet I didn't believe he would do something like this." Dr Murphy shook his head, his eyes darting from one person to another as if hoping someone could explain. "I blame myself. I should have done something, said something."

"Dr Murphy, there was nothing you could have done. Dr Thierry had an iron will," Noémie said. "He knew what he was doing, and it was his choice."

Dr Murphy rounded on her, barking, "His choice? He couldn't bear to see the Germans in our beloved city. He paid a heavy price last time, losing his only son to the Boches."

Elizabeth cut him short by putting her hand on his arm. "Noémie isn't to blame. Don't go shouting at her; she has more reason to hate the Boches than most of us."

Sophie glanced at Noémie's pale face. The nurse had confided her worries for her family after receiving correspondence from relatives in Germany over the last few years. Life for Jews had worsened year by year since Hitler had taken power in 1933. Horrified at what Noémie had told her, Sophie had quickly reassured her friend nothing like that would happen here. Not in Paris or anywhere in France.

But with the news of Dr Thierry's suicide, Sophie wasn't sure of anything any more. The Germans had overwhelmed the French army in an embarrassingly quick time and now they were marching down the avenue des Champs-Élysées. Dr Thierry, a highly intelligent pioneering surgeon, had decided death was better than living under Hitler's boot. Who was she, not even qualified yet, to argue with that?

"Who will take over now?" someone asked.

Everyone looked at Dr Murphy, who sat slumped in his chair, staring at the floor. Sophie wanted to comfort him. Paris would mourn for the aristocrat and eminent brain surgeon, but Dr Murphy had lost something more precious. His mentor and his friend.

She watched as determination replaced devastation in the man she admired. Dr Murphy stood up and, turning to the surrounding group, announced, "They have offered me the role of director. I aim to run this hospital just the way Dr Thierry would have wanted. For as long as I am alive..." He fell silent for two seconds, glancing at Elizabeth. "This hospital will continue to serve the citizens of Paris. Those who belong here!"

Stunned, Sophie stared at her mentor. What did that mean?

"Parisians will fill every bed. I refuse to have the Boches billeted in this building. Anyone who disagrees with my decision is free to leave. Today."

Sophie glanced around at her colleagues. To a person, they moved closer to Dr Murphy, admiration lighting up their faces.

"Vive la France," someone shouted. Sophie couldn't breathe. She was exhilarated and terrified, not for herself but for this brave man in front of her. The occupiers were unlikely to approve of his terms.

* * *

After a long and frustrating double shift at the hospital, Sophie waited until she could leave under the German curfew and made her way home. She sat in the back of the métro on purpose, not wanting to see a German officer, never mind speak to one.

Pushing open the door of their home, she hoped her parents had gone out for the evening now that people could venture outdoors once more. She didn't want to do anything other than soak in a hot bath.

Her mother called to her almost before she had the door closed.

"Sophie, is it true? Did Thierry commit suicide by injecting poison?"

Sophie took off her coat, hanging it on the coat rack near the door, weariness seeping through her bones. Glancing in the mirror, she saw her mother sitting on a chair near the fireplace in the drawing room. The last thing she wanted to deal with was her mother's preoccupation with gossip.

"Yes, maman. He is dead." She didn't enter the drawing room but stood at the door, not wanting to engage in a conversation. She wanted to grieve not just for the loss of a brilliant doctor and role model, but for the whole situation.

"But why would someone like him do that? He is an aristocrat, an eminent physician, a brain surgeon. What could he fear from the Germans?"

Sophie walked into the room where her mother sat, the newspaper spread over her knees.

Her mother looked genuinely bewildered, yet Sophie couldn't stop the irritation rushing through her.

"Why? You know why, maman, he couldn't bear to see our country overrun by the Boches again. He fought in the last war; he lost his son. He couldn't do it again. So, he took, for him at least, the only way out."

Her mother sniffed, although whether at Sophie's less than

respectful tone or the bare facts she had just been faced with was anyone's guess.

"I never expected a man like him to be a coward."

Sophie didn't argue. There was little point in trying to convince her mother that suicide wasn't the coward's way out on any occasion. She turned on her heel and left the room, wondering just how many others would die, either by their own hand or that of the enemy, before France was free once more.

SIX

22 JUNE 1940

Sophie took her sandwiches to eat in the canteen. The small room was fairly busy with porters and male orderlies sitting smoking at one table, discussing the war. She headed for the table of nurses, Noémie moving up to let her sit down.

Victor, one of the young male orderlies, threw his newspaper down on the table, grinding his cigarette out on a plate. "I can't believe that little runt made our government sign the armistice in the same train car as they used in 1918. He is a..." Victor turned red as if he realised he was in the company of ladies. His uncle Oliver, a seasoned member of staff, gave him a look that had Victor reclaiming his seat in seconds.

"Master manipulator," Dr Murphy supplied as he stopped by the table and picked up the newspaper. "Hitler wants France to experience the humiliation he feels his country received after the last war. Many agree with him."

Victor gawped at him. Sophie didn't blame him; she couldn't believe what Dr Murphy was saying. He sounded as if he agreed with Hitler. He couldn't. He wouldn't. He was American, though, so perhaps he didn't understand the French viewpoint. But even as that thought skipped into her mind, she dismissed it. This was Dr Murphy.

"You can all stop glaring at me," Dr Murphy said. "I didn't say I agree. But there are those who believe the Allies were too keen on humiliating Germany and bringing that country to their knees. This is payback. At least that's how they see it. I believe this photograph has to be one of the saddest things I have seen for a long time."

Sophie glanced at the newspaper on her own table, seeing the photo of the railcar with the Germans standing tall and the French men looking like they wanted to disappear. Compiègne would go down in history for all the wrong reasons.

Her stomach churned as she found it difficult to breathe. She needed some space, away from her colleagues, her friends, France. She stood but couldn't bring herself to leave the sandwich behind. Zeldah had gone to so much trouble. She glanced around, catching Noémie eyeing Sophie's lunch. She pushed it towards her friend. Mumbling an apology and placing her hand on her stomach, she left quickly, deciding to get some fresh air.

But there was no escape. Outside the hospital, there was more visible evidence of the occupation with the flags and the soldiers. She turned back towards the wards.

She needed to keep busy. It seemed increasingly likely Jules must have been captured since there was no official confirmation and no word from him for so long. She read the papers, but who knew whether you could believe them. Rumours abounded all news had to be checked by German officials, and would they print the truth?

* * *

Later that afternoon, she climbed the stairs and knocked on Dr Murphy's door, opening it to find him and Elizabeth in deep conversation. The smell of roasted coffee beans hit her, her mouth watering.

"Sorry, it's not important. I will come back later." She turned to leave, but Dr Murphy told her to stay.

"You'd best listen to what Elizabeth has to say. Take a seat. Have a proper cup of coffee."

At Sophie's glance, he continued. "Gift from our occupiers. As a sign of good faith, he said."

Sophie saw the tension lines around her boss's mouth. He was exhausted and, away from the wards, looked older and more forlorn. His sadness frightened her. Despite wanting coffee, she had to leave.

"I'll come back later."

"Sophie, sit down. Please. I have some news I think you should hear." Elizabeth's grave expression turned Sophie's stomach rock-hard. She fought the instinct to turn on her heel and leave.

Taking a deep breath, she took a seat. Elizabeth poured a cup of coffee and handed it to her. "I was just telling Mike about something Langeron told me. We've been friends for years."

"The police chief?" Sophie picked up the coffee, revelling in its smell.

"Yes. He called to my home yesterday. He wanted to pass on a warning. You can't repeat what I say, Sophie. Not to anyone, not even Adèle."

Sophie nodded. Her sister wouldn't be interested unless it related to clothes, make-up, or going out. Sophie doubted the chief of police would waste his time over such trivialities.

Elizabeth took a sip of coffee before saying, "Langeron suspects the Germans have had spies here for a long time."

"Like the rest of Paris." Sophie saw her joke fell flat as Elizabeth didn't attempt a smile. "Sorry, I didn't mean to make light of things."

Elizabeth shrugged. "It's true. It makes sense when you think of how they seem to know exactly where the best places are for their officers, the apartments they have commandeered, etc. But Langeron says it is worse than that. It isn't just the German army who've arrived in Paris. He had a visit from the Sicherheitsdienst, or SD as they are more commonly known."

"Who?"

"You might never have heard of them. The SD are the security, intelligence, and policing arm of the organisation known to many as Schutzstaffel or SS. Some just call the whole lot the Gestapo."

A chill went down Sophie's spine. She'd heard stories about the SS from the refugees who had flooded in from Poland and other countries over the last five years. They put people in jail without explanation, if they didn't murder them first. What did the secret service want with Langeron? She stood up and walked over to the window, looking out at the terrace from which you could see the courtyard below where the ambulances pulled in. How long would it last? She didn't want to hear what Elizabeth had been told about the German secret police, but then she couldn't not know either. She turned her back on her city to listen.

"The police hold files on everyone from those involved in petty thieving to communists and other gang members."

Dr Murphy inhaled sharply. "More than a few of those same people have been very helpful to us over the last few months, providing medicine, trucks, petrol, bribes, and goodness knows what else."

"My thoughts exactly." Elizabeth nodded. "In anticipation of the SD using the records for their own nefarious purposes, Langeron ordered the files to be sent by barge down the river. He only used his trusted men, who then loaded the barges with explosives."

Sophie put her hand over her mouth. It was an offence to

destroy records. Langeron was the chief of police. Before she could say anything, Dr Murphy spoke. "So, if ordered to comply with the occupiers, they can't hand over what isn't there?"

"Exactly." Elizabeth allowed herself a small smile. "But it was a risk. Langeron said four of the police superintendents were taken away for questioning. Nobody knows where they are."

Sophie moved back to take her seat, leaning forward, putting her coffee cup on the table. She shivered, although the office wasn't cold. "They can't do that. Police officers don't just disappear."

"Langeron said to be careful. He knew we had sent some men down south instead of sending them back to the prisoner-of-war camps."

Sophie's mouth fell open.

"Don't worry, Sophie. He's not going to tell anyone. But he warned us to be more careful. He figures spies have been lurking and watching those of interest for some time. We think they may have been gathering information about the hospital – about those of us working here."

Sophie slumped in her chair. "But that means their spies could have told them about Dr Murphy." She glanced at Dr Murphy. "I mean the fact you said you wouldn't treat Germans."

Dr Murphy nodded. "That isn't a secret. The Germans have their own doctors."

Elizabeth glanced at the wall behind Dr Murphy. "We all must be more careful. We must pretend as if we agree with this regime so that we can continue to help all our patients. Do nothing to stand out or make yourself noticeable."

Dr Murphy shook his head. "We can't let them win."

The three sat in silence for a few minutes while they absorbed the changes in their world. Then Elizabeth smiled.

"What's so funny?" Dr Murphy asked.

"Langeron told me that the Germans have picked out certain bordellos, which they insist will be used for the sole pleasures of the German armies. I know one madam of a chosen house. She told me she had suggested to her girls they smear mustard on certain parts to add spice to the evening."

Sophie grimaced as she thought of the discomfort the girls would be in. Looking up, she spurted her coffee at the expression on Dr Murphy's face. Despite being a married man and a doctor, his cheeks turned crimson as he shifted in his seat. Sophie, concerned for the poor sex workers, asked, "The girls won't take her advice, will they? I can't imagine the soldiers taking that lying down."

At her unintentional pun, Elizabeth laughed and then all three of them were laughing with tears rolling down their faces.

Their laughter subsided, and they agreed not to divulge the content of their conversation with anyone.

Dr Murphy said, "There are some in the hospital who are friends of our occupiers. Be on your guard, ladies. I couldn't run this hospital without the two of you."

"You too, Mike," Elizabeth countered. "You are far too vocal in your views on Hitler and his friends."

"I'm an American. We aren't in this fight, and everyone expects us to be brash and loud. Worse than the Germans."

Sophie knew he was joking, but she didn't smile. She hoped this wonderful man would live to see the Paris they all loved revert to normal. But when that would be was anyone's guess.

* * *

Sophie walked through the main hospital door, looking forward to a bath to soothe her aching feet.

"Miss..."

Sophie glanced behind her at the whispered greeting. A man, his face covered in stubble, his tattered clothes a testament to his having travelled some way, took a last drag of his cigarette before stubbing it out.

"Can I help you?"

"Are you Sophie Bélanger?" The man appeared edgy, his eyes glancing at the visitors coming and going from the hospital.

Sophie put her hand on her bag, edging closer to the hospital door. "Yes. Do I know you?"

"No. But I have a message for you. Dr Jules sent me. He saved my life. He said if I got back to Paris to find you and tell you."

Sophie wanted to hug the man but caught herself in time. "When?"

The man paled, reaching out his hand to lean on the wall. She offered him her arm and led him to a bench.

"Sorry, I haven't fully recovered, but it was important I got this message to you. I owe him everything." The man's eyes filled up. She looked away, pretending not to notice as he wiped his hand across his face. "You've no idea how bad it was. They just kept coming, wave after wave. We couldn't stop them. But we tried, I swear we tried."

"Shh. I was at Fontainebleau. I saw enough. Please tell me when you saw Jules. Was he all right? He wasn't injured or anything? Just I haven't had any word from him and ... I ... worry."

The man took her hand and squeezed it before he sat down on the bench with a sigh. "He was alive and well on 22 June when the armistice was signed. He patched me up and then I got sent back down the line to a hospital. I've been there since. I should be in a prisoner-of-war camp but I had to find you. I promised I would."

"Thank you." Sophie could barely speak past the lump in her throat. Jules was alive. The man leaned back against the bench, his eyes closing. Guilt flooded her. "Please come inside with me, let me get you something to eat. And you should be examined too."

He let her guide him into the hospital. She spotted Noémie and quickly filled her in and passed the man over to her care. "Noémie will look after you. She's one of our best nurses. I have to tell a few people about Jules. They will be so relieved. Thank you." Sophie kissed the man on the cheek before heading off to find Elizabeth and Dr Murphy.

They were still in Dr Murphy's office. She burst through the door, causing them to both jump to their feet.

"What's wrong?" Elizabeth asked.

"Nothing. Jules is alive. He's alive. There's a man downstairs. He saw Jules on 22 June; he looked after this man's injuries. Oh, Elizabeth, he's alive." She could hear herself repeating the word "alive". But her friends didn't appear to hear her; they were avoiding her eyes. Her mouth dried as her pulse quickened at the look that passed between Elizabeth and Dr Murphy. "What?"

"Nothing," Elizabeth quickly reassured her.

"Don't do that. I saw the look you two exchanged. Do you know something I don't?"

Dr Murphy took her hand and led her to a seat. "Sophie, we only heard rumours. Nobody knows anything for certain at the moment."

"But?" she prompted, even though she didn't want to hear what he was trying to say.

He glanced at Elizabeth, who came to sit beside her. "Dear Sophie, we must remember Jules is Jewish."

"What does that have to do with anything?" Genuinely confused, Sophie waited for an explanation.

"He's Jewish. That's all the Germans care about. They don't believe Jules or anyone else of his race are human beings, let alone excellent doctors." Elizabeth inched closer to Sophie.

"There are many rumours spreading about how the Germans are treating Jews."

"Yes, I know about people being put in ghettos in Poland. But this is France. Jules is a medic." She waited but they just stared at her. "They are just rumours, surely. I mean the ones about people being shot in the streets just for being Jewish. That's barbaric." Sophie looked at Dr Murphy, but he stared at the table. Elizabeth fidgeted. Sophie kept talking, although who she was trying to convince, she wasn't sure.

"I can understand why some foreign Jews might get nervous. Those that are here without papers and such things. But not the French. Jules sees himself as French first and ... well, he doesn't even attend the synagogue. Only when his mother insists."

Elizabeth put her hand on Sophie's. "You know how much I like Jules. He is a wonderful doctor and his sense of humour makes me laugh. I want to see him come back here. But ... oh, Sophie, the reality is the best we can hope for is he will be kept as a prisoner of war and sent to Germany."

Sophie jumped up, putting as much distance as she could between them and her. "What are you talking about, the best we can hope for? The man I just spoke to said that Jules is alive and treating the injured. Jules is coming home. I just know it."

She turned on her heel and left the office, not caring what they thought. She was right. She had to be.

SEVEN

JULY 1940

Adèle paced the apartment, fed up with being stuck inside. Sophie had the hospital and Jean-Pierre was never home. He was always heading off on his bicycle, disappearing for days, or else he went to the museum. Of course, being a boy, he could come and go as he wished. Her father didn't say a word and her mother just said he was young and might as well enjoy himself until the schools and universities reopened. Even Zeldah got out to do the shopping.

But she stayed indoors. Well, no longer. She was young and, despite her mother's beliefs, Adèle wasn't about to start wearing black clothes and lock herself away. Today she'd taken her father up on the offer to go out to dinner. Opening her closet, she chose a new dress, some silk stockings and her best shoes.

She had just finished her make-up when Sophie walked into the bathroom they shared. Sophie stared at her.

"Where are you going? Why are you wearing my new dress?"

Adèle glanced down at the evening dress, brushing a stray blonde hair from the bodice. "You never go anywhere to justify this dress, unless you want to join us. Papa is taking me to Maxim's."

"I'm having an early night." Sophie hesitated.

Adèle looked at her sister. Was she having second thoughts? She tried to convince her. "You can sleep when you're dead. Come out with us."

Sophie shook her head, her eyes shining with anticipation. "I met someone at the hospital. He said Jules was alive when the armistice was signed."

"Really?"

Adèle felt a twinge of guilt at the look of hurt in her twin's eyes at her lack of interest, but she wasn't about to pretend any fondness for Jules Stein. Their parents disapproved of the match for good reason and so did she. He was a trainee doctor; even when fully qualified he wouldn't earn enough to keep Sophie in the style she was used to. Sophie could make a much better match, one where she wouldn't have to work after she married, especially as a doctor. Adèle shuddered as images of injuries and germs crossed her mind. She forced them away as she continued to apply her make-up.

Sophie studied her intently, as if she wanted to say something but couldn't. Adèle didn't encourage her either way. She turned to the mirror to fix her hair, although it was perfect.

"Adèle, do you think you should? The Germans go there."

Adèle pivoted. "So what? They have nice food, and I deserve to enjoy myself after what I've been through. I don't have to talk to the Germans, do I?" Adèle didn't know why she protested so much. Really, what was the harm in talking? The Germans were here now.

"Adèle! Have respect for your country."

"Sophie, you have enough for both of us. I'm hungry and I need some fun. You don't know how we suffered out there. Maxim's will take my mind off things. Best go, papa is waiting."

Adèle could feel her sister's eyes drilling a hole in her head, but she didn't care. She needed some fun.

Papa's look of approval when she met him in the hallway made her feel good.

"You look beautiful tonight. I'm glad you're coming out with me. Your mother took to her bed. I shall be the envy of many gentlemen when I walk into dinner with a young girl on my arm."

"Not so young now. We will soon be twenty-three."

Papa's mouth thinned. "No need to talk about age."

She didn't take any notice of his rebuke. He hated getting old, but that was his issue, not hers.

Papa offered her his arm as they walked down the stairs past the *loge* with a nod to the concierge. Adèle walked faster so her father wouldn't engage with Madame Garnier; the woman was too nosy for her own good, but you had to be careful not to offend her. They moved outside onto avenue Kléber. After they walked a few steps, she heard the clip-clop of a horse as a fiacre appeared. The driver stopped in response to her father lifting his arm. Adèle climbed into the four-wheeled carriage with her father's assistance. Then he climbed up, closed the door and they were off.

As they neared the restaurant, the carriage had to wait in line as the German cars ahead of them dropped their guests at the restaurant. Maxim's red awning stood out as a beacon of light after the last dreary few days. Butterflies danced in her stomach as they got nearer. Papa paid the fare before helping her gracefully exit the carriage. She smoothed down her dress, and, shoulders back, walked into the restaurant ready to conquer the world.

As they entered, she looked around her with interest, thrilled to see nothing had really changed. Well, if you ignored the fact that the men were mostly Germans, the women unmistakably French. The tables to the front were busy, with waiters ducking back and forth attending to their guests. She recognised several staff from previous visits but of course she didn't acknowledge them. Only Octave was absent. She'd liked him; he always knew the exact compliment a woman wanted to hear.

"What did they do with Octave, papa?"

Her father put his finger up to his mouth in a shushing motion. Whispering and using his eyes, he highlighted another man in conversation with a German officer. "That is the man in charge now, Monsieur Otto Horcher."

"Poor Octave, it must devastate him to lose Maxim's."

"Keep your voice down, Adèle. Octave and Monsieur Horcher are old friends and business colleagues. I'm sure the Vaudables will be fine. Now please drop this subject."

A man dressed in a splendid dark bespoke suit approached them, his smile broad, his eyes assessing their suitability for his establishment before widening with recognition. He acknowledged her father before addressing her.

"Bonsoir, mademoiselle. May I say how wonderful it is to have such a beauty in our presence." He bowed over her hand.

Adèle smiled at the man.

"Adèle, this is Monsieur Otto Horcher. You will have heard of the famous restaurant in Berlin." Papa bowed to Monsieur Horcher. "My daughter, Adèle."

"Enchanté, mademoiselle." His manners were impeccable, if a little formal, the clicking of his heels slightly too much. He was far too old to hold her interest so her gaze wandered. She hoped her father wouldn't sit beside the larger tables. The maître d'hôtel arrived with a smile that seemed to connect his ears. Papa requested a quiet table for two.

Relieved they didn't have to wait, she would die rather than admit to being intimidated. The room was full of uniforms. These men were on the same side as those who had terrorised innocent civilians, refugees fleeing Paris. Closing her eyes, she could smell the scent of death mixed with mud. She squeezed the memories of the field from her mind. For a second, she wished Léo was with her but quickly dismissed the thought. Her beau wouldn't be caught dead in Maxim's.

A bottle of Veuve Clicquot Champagne arrived at their table courtesy of a group of officers dining near them. She inclined her head in thanks and, never one to decline, accepted a glass. It was vintage, the bubbles crisp as they melted in her mouth. She surveyed her surroundings over the edge of the glass. The women were dressed in spectacular dresses, diamonds and other gemstones sparkling at their necks, wrists, and ears in the soft candlelight. There was no thought of war as she saw them laughing with men decked out in dress uniforms, their black boots polished to a high shine. Silverware clinked against plates as champagne corks popped. Waiters in black and white livery carried trays of food and drinks to the tables. Occasionally, a raised voice interrupted the ambiance, but it was only someone addressing an old friend.

Thinking of friends, where was everyone? She spotted a few familiar faces among all the strangers. Had they all left Paris? A waiter appeared to take their order. Adèle bowed to her father's choice.

The waiter offered some suggestions and then, with a recommendation for a bottle of white wine, departed.

"No shortages here," she said.

Her father topped up her champagne. "What did you expect? This is Maxim's. Nothing good about Paris has to change. In fact, I think you'll find things in many areas improve. The Germans have some good ideas."

Adèle opened her mouth to argue. The French had the best cuisine, fashion, and perfumes. What could the Germans offer? Bombs and... She stared around; it was difficult to see so many uniformed men in one place and not a French uniform at that. But before she could speak, a friend of her father stopped to speak to him. Recognising him as one of those men who liked to stare at her chest, she excused herself.

Adèle took her purse and walked to the ladies to powder her nose. It also gave her ample opportunity to check out the more distant tables. The men with blonde hair and blue eyes looked rather dashing in their uniforms. She noticed they felt a similar attraction, judging by the way their eyes surveyed her dress. She smiled with satisfaction; she may not be interested in dating these men, but it was nice to feel wanted.

On entering the ladies, she nodded at two women who were reapplying their lipstick – more than a little intoxicated, if their laughter and rather racy conversation were anything to go by. Despite their lovely designer dresses and fabulous jewels, they weren't the usual class of Maxim's customers. She walked into the cubicle, listening intently as they swapped small talk about their dates and what their favours may provide them. Real coffee seemed to be the catalyst for much laughter. Despite having been a married woman and thus experienced, she blushed on their behalf.

She waited for them to leave before she flushed the toilet and came out to wash her hands and reapply her own lipstick. She checked her hair, replacing a couple of pins that had escaped. Her powder wasn't quite sufficient to cover the dark circles under her eyes, evidence of the sleepless nights since the attack from the planes. The aircraft piloted by men acting under orders from officers eating in here. Sophie had been right. It wasn't a good idea to come to Maxim's.

On her way back, she spotted an old friend of the family, Auguste Citerne.

"Auguste, how lovely to see you." He looked thinner than she remembered, his glasses making him look older than his thirty years. It was his sight that prevented him from joining up, hence his presence. Every other young man of his age was wallowing in the prisoner-of-war camps, awaiting release.

"Adèle, how delightful you look. A sight for sore eyes in this dismal place. How is young Jean-Pierre?"

"He'd be upset to hear you call him that; he's not a child but turns eighteen shortly."

The woman with Auguste looked at Adèle, a bemused expression on her face as her eyes looked her up and down. It was almost as if she was trying to place her, but Adèle didn't recognise her and wasn't at all sure she liked the inspection.

"Have we met?" Adèle prompted when it appeared Auguste would not introduce them.

"No, I don't believe so," the woman replied, her American-accented tone as frosty as possible. She turned away in dismissal.

Adèle froze. How dare this frumpy old American treat her so rudely? She was at least mid-thirties, and still single, judging by the lack of a wedding ring. Not only was Adèle younger, wealthier, widowed and much more attractive, but France was her home. Fuming, she wasn't sure what to do: whether to walk back to her papa's table or to ask this woman what her problem was. She glanced towards papa but he was deep in conversation with two men, one of whom was in a German uniform. Admiring the occupiers' looks at a distance didn't mean she wanted to talk to one in person.

She turned her attention back to Auguste, catching the amusement dancing in his eyes. She gritted her teeth, her forced smile hurting her cheeks. She waited for an invitation to join them; when it failed to come, she invited herself.

"I shall join you, Auguste, thank you. Please don't speak about the war. It consumes papa. So boring."

Auguste coughed as if trying not to laugh. Adèle glared at him, but it was his companion who surprised her.

"Why would you believe you were welcome to sit with us? I may not be French but if I were, this is the last place I would come."

That was enough. How dare she? "Pardon me? What brings an American to Paris, especially to Maxim's? You don't look like their regular customers."

Auguste snorted but, at a look from his companion, twisted it into a cough before protesting, "Adèle Bélanger. Don't be rude."

Adèle smiled, her hand dabbing his arm. "Stand up for me. I seem to have caused your friend some discomfort." Adèle leaned in, nearer to his ear, to whisper, "Or does she usually look like she sucked a lemon?"

Auguste flushed, but Adèle ignored him. Satisfied, she saw her remark had hit home with the American now gawking at her, her lips thinned in disapproval. A chill made its way down Adèle's spine, despite her strapless gown feeling too warm, her shoes too tight.

Adèle turned her attention to the American. "What?"

Auguste spoke to the woman. "Dolores, I assure you, Adèle is usually charming company. She's obviously finding it difficult this evening. Perhaps it's the number of Fritz in the room." He gave Adèle a look that told her he found her behaviour petty, before saying, "Dolores is a journalist and a good friend of mine. She writes stories about life in Paris and sends them back to the newspapers in the States. Now, if you will excuse us, we were just leaving. Give my regards to your papa."

Auguste stood up and held Dolores's chair for her. Adèle stood as the other two left. Nobody could say she didn't have manners. Realising she was standing alone at an unoccupied table, staring at the departing guests like a fish out of water, she smiled her most dazzling smile at the nearest table before making her way to where her father was sitting.

Papa was talking to someone different now. Adèle barely registered the strange man, who didn't look up when she approached. His lack of appreciation for her charm made Auguste's behaviour cut deeper. Why would Auguste behave like he had? He could have offered to have a drink with her, at the very least. Shifting in her seat, she wished her father would dismiss his friend.

Her meal had arrived while she was at the ladies but she pushed it aside, all appetite disappearing. The men continued to talk, ignoring her completely. She looked up to find a man in uniform staring at her as if she was a large steak and he'd been on a forced vegetarian diet. She moved closer to the table and, picking up her glass, held it out, waiting for her father to refill it. Thankfully, she got her father's attention.

"Adèle. Forgive us. This is Roger Desrosiers, a business associate. Roger, my daughter. I will see you tomorrow, Roger."

Roger took the hint, stood and clicked his heels as he bid them goodnight. She waited until he had walked away before saying, "Can we go home, please? I'm not feeling too well."

Her father glanced at his full plate, opened his mouth to say something, but she put her hand on his.

"I keep hearing machine..."

He stood up just as she thought he might. Anything to avoid a scene and upsetting the occupiers.

"Of course."

She let him help her into her coat, chatting as he did so. He said something about the war having the potential to be very profitable, but she wasn't listening. She couldn't get the American's disdainful expression out of her head.

EIGHT

After a sleepless night, Sophie took the métro to Gare de Lyon and from there, the electric train to Moret-sur-Loing. Her heart beat faster as the minutes ticked by until, less than an hour later, she arrived.

Rushing through the beautiful village, she paid scant attention to the medieval buildings, or the church consecrated by Thomas Becket. She'd talk Jules into giving her a proper tour when he came back, as they shared a love of history. She walked down the Canal du Loing, leaving the town behind her, and soon arrived at Jules's. The house looked like something from a painting with beautiful trailing roses decorating the brickwork. Madame Stein had kept up the flowerbeds at the front of the house and she could see a vegetable garden to the side.

The Steins had moved to the pretty little farmhouse in Moret-sur-Loing before the invasion. Jules's father, believing the Germans would level Paris in the event of war, had decided his family would be safer on the outskirts. He said even Hitler wouldn't bomb such a beautiful place.

The chickens squawked as if in greeting as she opened the

gate then closed it carefully behind her. She glanced around at the fields full of wheat rocking gently in the breeze, the cows grazing on the grass. She could see what had attracted Monsieur Stein. It was a pity he hadn't lived long enough to enjoy it much. No one had known he had heart trouble, not even his son, the medical student. It had devastated Jules when his father had died last August, but he didn't have long to grieve before the war came and he joined up.

She hesitated before knocking. Was she wise getting Yvette's hopes up? She could hear Elizabeth's warning in her head, see the look on Dr Murphy's face when she'd told them Jules was alive. Oh for heaven's sake. She was here now and Jules's family deserved to know what little she did.

Yvette opened the door, her eyes widening in surprise.

"Sophie, what are you doing here? Oh, you look so tired."

"That's a lovely welcome." Sophie hugged her friend close before surveying the room behind Yvette. "Where's your mother?"

"In bed. She takes a nap every afternoon now. Come into the kitchen." She walked fast, Sophie trailing after her. Yvette closed the door before asking, "What is it? Tell me. Is it Jules?" Yvette rubbed her hands together, her eyes glued to Sophie's face.

"A man came to the hospital to see me. He had a message from Jules."

Yvette sank into a chair. "He's alive."

"He was when the armistice was signed. He tended to this man before sending him off in an ambulance. The man didn't have any more information. He may have been taken prisoner since then, but we won't know for sure until the Germans release the names." Sophie watched her friend closely, her muscles tightening as she watched Yvette's emotions flit across her face, hope battling with dread. "Yvette, he was alive. We have to focus on that."

Yvette inhaled before standing up, her hands patting down her skirt. "Yes. It's good news. I'll let Mother sleep as she needs the rest but she's going to be so pleased. Thank you for coming to see us."

"I missed you."

"Same." Yvette picked up two cups and opened the cupboard to retrieve some plates.

Sophie watched her warily. What was wrong? Yvette wasn't as happy as she'd anticipated.

"Yvette?"

"Do you know when they will confirm the names of the prisoners? Have they said anything in Paris? It's so horrible not knowing. My mind keeps imagining all sorts." Yvette's words tumbled from her mouth, expressing Sophie's thoughts. She couldn't stop a tear escaping, quickly followed by another one.

Yvette pulled her into a hug. "Cry. Let them out. I've done it until I'm not sure I have any tears left."

Sophie sobbed and then pulled herself together. This wasn't helping and with the noise she made, she may wake Madame Stein, something to be avoided at all costs.

"No, we haven't heard a word. It can't be long surely?" Sophie asked, even though Yvette wouldn't know any more than she did. "I mean they say the Germans are efficient."

Yvette gave her a dark look. "That's not all they say about the Germans."

"You're supposed to be making me feel better," Sophie reminded her friend, playfully patting her arm. Yvette gave her another hug before she held out a chair.

"Sit down. Tell me how things are in Paris." Yvette set the water on to boil.

"There's no fighting if that's what you mean. There's the time difference, the red flags hanging from every building and the fact that they've changed the road signs; they're all in German now." Sophie frowned. "People keep getting lost, including the German soldiers." She smiled at the memory of sending the last German soldier who'd asked for directions in a loop around Paris.

"What?" Yvette asked. "You always screw up your nose when you are thinking, do you know that?" Yvette poured the boiling water into the coffee pot and set it on the table.

Sophie smiled at her friend's teasing. She had missed Yvette.

"I didn't know what to expect, especially after all the rumours coming from Poland. But the individual soldiers are nice, if that's the right way to describe them. They're polite and try to be friendly." Sophie found it hard to put her description of the enemy into words. After all the rumours, she had been pleasantly surprised by how well the soldiers had behaved. But then she thought of what Elizabeth and Dr Murphy had said. She screwed her eyes shut to clear the memory. She wasn't sharing their comments with Yvette. But her friend hadn't noticed. She was too busy chatting.

"Much good that will do them. We hate them. The letters my mother had from her friends and family in Germany and elsewhere before war broke out would make you lose sleep. I tell you, Sophie, if only half of what they say is true, we're in trouble." Yvette gave her coffee a vicious stir.

Sophie could imagine what Yvette would do if she came face to face with a German. Jules used to say Yvette should have been born a boy. She was always getting into arguments. It was probably best that her friend had left Paris.

"Not everyone feels the same way we do, Yvette. You should see the clubs and bars every night. They're full to over-flowing. The girls who go there have the latest dresses and the make-up! The Germans throw money around like it's water. A shopkeeper told me they're buying up souvenirs, to send back home to their sweethearts."

Yvette rolled her eyes. She took a sip of the coffee, her nose twitching with distaste. "It's awful. No matter what I add to it, I can't make it taste like real coffee. Would you prefer water?"

Sophie shook her head. "I'm used to drinking this now."

"I bet Adèle is having a great time. She was always at the centre of every party."

The remark did not surprise Sophie, knowing her friend hated Adèle with a passion, and with good cause. Adèle had behaved badly when she'd met Yvette, not to mention her reaction to Jules. She found herself torn; she loved her sister so much but she didn't like her attitude most of the time. If only they could have remained close like they'd been when they were younger.

Sophie sipped her coffee.

Yvette was waiting for an answer. "She seems to cope," Sophie replied carefully. "Although she seemed a bit subdued after an evening out at Maxim's last night. Papa asked her to go for dinner as maman refused. Maman believes she should stay at home and mourn for her dead husband. She's a grown woman so she'll do what she wants." *Regardless of how it looks or the impact it has on our family.*

Yvette, perhaps seeing how uncomfortable she was, changed the subject. "How is the hospital?"

"Busy. Dr Murphy has ordered us to keep every bed occupied. He insists we won't treat any Germans."

"Good for him! But won't that get difficult with them setting up offices around the hospital?"

"Oh, you heard? News travels fast."

"Bad news does. Maman is still in contact with many of our previous neighbours in Neuilly. We were lucky to sell our house when we did. An SS officer threw out the people who bought it from us, and moved in. They couldn't protest either, for fear of what he would do. Can you imagine that? At least we had already left so maman didn't have to deal with the humiliation. Nobody is talking about the fact the SS have taken a liking to Jewish houses. In fact, there's no announcement in the papers about them even being in Paris." Yvette slapped her hand against her leg. Sophie could understand her frustration. It wasn't fair for people to be stripped of their possessions. But how did Yvette know so much?

Yvette seemed to read her mind. "I have many visitors. They come to see maman and also to trade with other villagers. A few of our friends have disposed of gold and jewellery to try to turn assets into cash. Just in case."

A chill travelled down Sophie's spine.

Yvette looked at her. "I'm surprised they've left the hospital alone."

"Dr Murphy lives on avenue Foch. The Germans have taken over most of that, but they won't touch the hospital. Countess de Chambrun has made sure of that."

"How so?"

"She's American, and she was rich before she married General de Chambrun. Her name was Clara Longworth. You know how the Germans like money." Sophie couldn't help but be cynical. Money talked in all societies. "They won't touch a high-profile American woman."

"Especially not one who is married to a general and friend of Pétain. De Chambrun's son is married to Laval's daughter, isn't he?"

Nothing seemed to escape Yvette. Sophie nodded in amused confirmation.

Yvette stood. "Let's not talk about them any more. Can you stay the night?"

"No, I have to get back." Sophie wanted to make up with her sister. She'd pretended to be sleeping when Adèle got back early last night. Now she wanted to find out what had upset her twin. Plus being here with Yvette, while lovely, made her miss Jules all the more.

Yvette wasn't quick enough to hide her disappointment.

"I will come again and stay. In the meantime, are you going to invite me to eat?"

Yvette put some potatoes and a knife on the table. "Make yourself useful and peel them. I have some carrots and garden peas. Would you like cheese or dessert?"

"Depends on what dessert? Has your mother been baking?" Sophie could almost taste Madame Stein's pastry on her tongue.

"Yes, she has. So, dessert it is. I don't have any meat but some fresh eggs to make a nice omelette."

"Perfect." Sophie picked up the knife and prepared the potatoes while Yvette bustled about the kitchen. She didn't feel the need to fill the comfortable silence.

"I have to come down here again soon. It is so calm and peaceful. The food is divine and the company isn't bad either."

Yvette glanced at the table. "It is simple." She shrugged. "You would think you had arrived on the Sabbath."

Sophie didn't think Madame Stein would be too welcoming, but she didn't say that. Jules's mother had never fully accepted her relationship with her son. "Is your mother not joining us?"

Yvette shook her head. "I will take a tray up to her later. She isn't eating much in this weather." She covered the table with the cloth Yvette had given her and then set it for the two of them. Yvette placed the breadbasket in the centre. Sophie nearly inhaled the contents. The smell was so tantalising.

"Sit, please. Don't stand on ceremony. My mother can't see us."

Sophie smiled. Madame Stein was a stickler for tradition. Sophie had been going out with Jules for over a year before his parents invited her to dinner. They had taken them to a restaurant. It had been another three months before Madame Stein had invited Sophie to eat at her home.

Sophie's stomach rumbled, causing them both to giggle. Taking a piece of bread, she broke it in two, leaving part of it on the table. The bread melted in her mouth, it was so tasty.

Yvette poured two glasses of wine and two of water. Holding her wine glass high, she said, "Cheers. To the end of the war. And Jules's safe return."

Her mouth full, Sophie finished her bread quickly before clicking her glass with Yvette's. She didn't want to talk about Jules; it was too painful. She changed the conversation.

"How do you enjoy living back with your mother?"

Yvette threw her eyes to heaven. "She's delighted to have me home so she can harass me. She wants me to get married. She thinks having an older husband would protect me."

Fear made Sophie's stomach feel like she had swallowed lead. "Protect you from what? You aren't having trouble, are you? Yvette, don't push me away. Tell me, please."

Yvette stood up. "I have to check on a cow. She is about to calve and I am not too keen on how she looks. Maybe you could check her."

"Yvette! I am almost a doctor, not a vet."

"Jules would do it," Yvette replied. She covered her mouth with her hands as tears filled her eyes.

Sophie moved to take her friend in her arms. They shed tears before Sophie pulled away. "We have to believe he will be fine." She changed the subject. "Where is my patient, then?"

"Put this on; you don't want to get your shoes dirty." Yvette gave her an old pair of farm boots and a coat. Together they walked out to check on the mother-to-be.

"How will you manage on the farm?" Sophie asked as they walked. "Will your cousins help again, like they did when you volunteered?"

Yvette shook her head. "They left. All of them. They are hoping to get a ship to America or somewhere safe. They were planning it for months but didn't think to ask my mother and I."

Sophie put her hand on Yvette's, hating the bitterness in her voice. When Yvette said nothing, Sophie asked, "I don't know a lot about farming, but don't you have to bring in the harvest?"

Yvette's eyes darkened, as did the look on her face.

"What did I say?"

"Nothing, Sophie. It isn't you. A German officer called last week. He said I had to have the wheat harvested and ready for collection by this weekend. He can't spare the men to help me, but he will arrange for it to be collected." Yvette's sarcasm didn't quite mask her feelings of hurt.

"Yvette, they can't do that!"

"They can and they will. No matter how well they appear to behave, Sophie, they're in charge now. They said people in Germany are starving. I asked what we were supposed to use for food and fuel. One of them offered to warm my bed if I got cold. I'm glad my mother was upstairs and didn't hear him."

"Oh, Yvette. What a beast! I can't believe they're doing that. How are you going to get the harvest completed on time? Can you not speak to the prefect?"

"I did. He can't do anything, or he won't. I'm not sure which it is, but his son's farm seems to have been left alone. Maybe they'll change their minds. But to answer your question, my neighbours will help me, just like I helped them with their harvests. I like it here, Sophie. This is a friendly community."

* * *

Thankfully, the cow co-operated. "The baby, I mean the calf, hasn't turned yet. Nature should take its course, but if you are still worried, call the vet. I don't know enough to attempt moving it." Sophie wasn't even going to try. The look the cow had given her, combined with the smell in the small barn, was enough to turn her stomach. She made to leave the barn. "Look, I'd best get back. I have a shift this evening."

Yvette slapped her on the back. "I never thought I would see the day where Sophie Bélanger was afraid of a dumb cow. You didn't show such fear with my parents."

"Don't remind me." Sophie didn't want to think about how hard she and Jules had fought to be together. Her mother liked him, but wouldn't agree to Sophie marrying a Jew. It upset Sophie to find Jules's parents agreed. Sophie was not the wife they wanted for their son.

Yvette said gently, "Flora Adler, the girl maman wanted Jules to marry... She's in Palestine now. Her father sent her and her sister with some group. From all accounts, she didn't put up much of a fight."

Sophie couldn't stop her heart from skipping a beat. Although she and Jules had promised to get married, their engagement wasn't official, as his parents wouldn't give their blessing. But with this girl gone, perhaps Madame Stein might be persuaded. That was assuming Jules turned up safe and sound.

"Yvette! You never used to be so judgemental."

"Who would leave their elderly parents behind at a time like this? Families should stick together."

Sophie hugged her. "We are family. You know where to find me if you need me."

Yvette nodded. "Be careful, and please come back and visit soon."

Sophie kissed her friend goodbye, promising to return. Madame hadn't appeared, for which she was thankful, although she felt sorry for the woman. Not knowing where her son was must cause her heartache.

Sophie wanted to get back to the hospital and drown herself

in work. Spending time with Yvette, while wonderful, high-lighted how lonely she was without Jules. Of all the things they'd thought would separate them, the war hadn't even come in the top five. But now they were apart and for how long? At least until the war ended. But what of the rumours she had heard? That was all they were, rumours, she told herself firmly.

NINE

16 JULY 1940

Heading out the front door of their apartment building, Sophie almost groaned as she heard the concierge call her name. What did she want? Papa had confirmed their details for Madame Garnier for the census ordered by the Germans. Sophie shifted her doctor's bag to her other hand.

"Good morning, Madame Garnier."

"Please come inside. Please."

The last thing she wanted to do was go into the woman's lair, as she and Zeldah called the *loge*. Madame's ability to gossip would have won her the top award if one existed. But today, she looked different. Less pompous, frightened. Sophie couldn't help herself. "What's wrong?"

Madame Garnier closed the door behind Sophie, standing against it as if thinking Sophie would make a run for it.

"Madame?"

"Sophie, I need your help and your discretion. You can't tell anyone. You must help me; there is nobody else." The woman was getting more worked up as she spoke, her voice shaking as the words came faster and faster. "I can't lose him too. It would kill me. I can't."

"Madame Garnier, take a seat. Have some water. Are you feeling ill?"

"Non, not me. My son."

"Matthieu? He's been released by the Germans?"

Madame looked at the floor. "He came back during the exode."

The *exode*? It had been almost a month since the armistice had been signed; had his mother cared for him all this time?

"He's afraid for his life. The French police ... they already came looking for him."

"Why? The French police don't..." Sophie trailed off. "You mean he deserted and is wanted for treason?"

"Shush." Madame glanced around, a terrified look on her face, as if she expected the gendarmes to arrive any second.

"He's wounded. He wouldn't have deserted otherwise. My son is a brave man."

Your son is a traitor. It took every ounce of self-restraint for Sophie not to put the thought into words.

"I've been tending to him, but..." Madame twisted the hand-kerchief in her hand. "He isn't getting better."

"Where is he?"

Madame didn't answer, her eyes darting around the room.

"Madame? Does he need to go to the hospital?"

"Non!" Madame snapped. "I'm sorry. It's my shattered nerves. He is all I have, you understand?"

"Yes, but I can't help you if you don't tell me where he is."

"Do you think you could have a look at him?"

Tempted to remind the concierge that not that long ago, the concierge had told everyone who'd listen that decent French girls got married and had children, not became doctors, Sophie sighed. She didn't like Matthieu. He was a bully, a mother's boy who'd teased Jean-Pierre about not being old enough to go to war. But the man was a French soldier. *Who deserted*. She shut off that voice.

"Take me to him. I'll see what I can do."

Madame gave her a hug before opening the *loge* door, looking out both ways before leading Sophie up the stairs. "He's in the attic apartment above the Litwaks."

"Aren't you worried they will hear him?"

Madame Garnier rolled her eyes. "Who would they tell if they did? They're Jewish. They wouldn't be running to the authorities. They want to keep a low profile now that the Germans are in charge."

Sophie stopped walking, wanting to take the woman to task for her horrible remark. *She's just worried about her son. She didn't mean it.*

She followed the concierge to the top floor, watching as the woman unlocked the door. "How are you feeding him? He won't have ration cards."

Madame shrugged her shoulders, which didn't help Sophie's sense of unease. She followed the woman's example and slipped off her shoes.

Matthieu was lying on the bed but, despite the copious amounts of bandages, didn't appear that badly injured. Not if the light of lust in his eyes was anything to go by. Sophie shivered, wishing she hadn't agreed to examine him.

"Is that Sophie or Adèle? No – Sophie. Adèle wouldn't get her hands dirty coming up here. As you can see, my mother has been doing her best."

"Your mother has put herself and all of us at risk protecting you." Sophie unwrapped the bandage covering his head. The wound was not deep and healing had already started. Opening her bag, she took out some iodine and put some on the cut, taking pleasure from the gasp he gave at the sting. Using a much smaller bandage, she covered it again.

"Where else are you injured?"

He lay back on the bed. "Why don't you examine me and

find out?" His meaning was unmistakable. Madame flushed with embarrassment, Sophie with anger.

She grabbed his bandaged arm. He winced but she didn't release the pressure.

"Ow, go gently. You'll do more damage."

"Behave yourself or I'll do worse." She unwrapped the bandage on his arm. The deep gash had been neatly stitched and showed no signs of infection. "Madame, you've done an excellent job. You kept the wound clean. You've done this before?"

"Oui – in the previous war. I didn't think I would have to use those skills again." The woman shuddered. "You don't think he will die?"

Why had the woman got her involved? Her precious son was well on his way to normal health.

"Matthieu is fine. He's a little underweight but those wounds are healing well. I will leave you the iodine; feel free to use it generously on the wounds. He should recover completely in a couple of weeks."

Madame nodded, but her hands worked feverishly on the handkerchief. "I don't know how I am going to find the money to buy good food for him. He needs the extra nourishment."

Ah, that was why Madame had engaged her services. Now she was complicit in Matthieu's escape and if she didn't contact the police, she was just as guilty as Madame. But how could she hand over another Frenchman? So many had died fighting the invasion and the ones that survived were prisoners of war. The armistice had been signed, what was the point in reporting him?

Matthieu grinned. "I told you. Get it from the Jews downstairs. They've got plenty."

"You leave that family alone! I can get you extra rations for now. To help you recover – but you'll have to make plans to get away. Or get papers to allow you to stay in Paris, legitimately." Sophie stood up. "I have to get to the hospital."

He grabbed her hand. "But you will come back to check on me again, won't you, *Doctor*?"

"Of course, if only to conduct your autopsy."

Sophie snapped her bag shut and walked out, straight down the stairs. Madame called after her, but she pretended not to hear. She was late for the hospital and the lovely patients she enjoyed dealing with.

* * *

She found Dr Murphy observing a new surgical patient. He looked up as she entered, surprise fighting with anxiety clouding his eyes. "Oh, I thought you were Elizabeth."

"She's not on until later. Will I do?"

Dr Murphy looked troubled, not at all pleased to see her.

"Please let me help. You're tired and I can look after the patient."

He walked behind her, closing the door before whispering, "Sophie, this is a challenging situation. If you are not comfortable, please leave and I will find someone else to help me."

Sophie would have rolled her eyes but for him being so serious. "I will help. Who is the patient? An escaped convict?"

Her joke fell flat as Dr Murphy didn't respond and her sense of unease escalated. Finally, Dr Murphy broke the silence.

"His real name is Captain Marchant. The Germans must not find him, so I have not registered him like we would normally when the wounded come in from the prisoner-of-war camps."

Curious, Sophie remained silent.

"Sophie, I am asking too much of you. This man is wanted by the Germans. You're putting yourself in danger by helping me."

"I can always pretend I didn't know who the patient was.

He's not wearing a uniform and he doesn't look like a French officer. He looks like a corpse."

Dr Murphy gripped her hands in thanks. "He needs to be monitored closely. I removed his appendix, but the idiots at the camp left it too late to call us. If he pulls through, it will be a miracle."

"We won't let him die. Too many already have. Now go on. I will stay with him."

"Thank you. I will send Elizabeth to take over when she arrives. Please don't let anyone else know."

"I promise." She waited until he left before approaching the bed. The poor man hadn't stirred. She took his vital signs and noted them on his record before taking a seat at his side.

"So what shall we call you, then? Percy, I think. After my favourite hero, the Scarlet Pimpernel. He escaped his enemies and so shall you." Sophie continued to whisper to the patient as she observed him. "It's a well-known fact I could talk someone to death but in this instance, I'm hoping you can hear me and come back to us."

TEN

Adèle fingered the light blue silk wrap her mother had lent her as the driver pulled up outside the German embassy on rue de Lille. She saw the reaction on some of the faces they passed. Some people simply stared at the car with the Nazi flags flying at the front but one man spat at the floor, his contempt for the vehicle and its occupants apparent. She didn't know why the embassy had sent a car to collect them.

Her father smiled at her, whether in encouragement or because he was happy to be here, she wasn't sure. The uniformed driver got out of the car and walked around to her side, holding the door open for her to exit. He then did the same for her father, not muttering a word to either of them. He didn't have to voice his disapproval; it radiated in waves. He got back in the car and drove off with not even a glance in their direction.

Her father offered her his arm to escort her inside. "I believe he thinks us French shouldn't be invited to his embassy."

"He should remember we are in France." Despite her words, Adèle couldn't ignore the disdainful glances coming from her French compatriots on the street. She stood straighter. "Shall we go inside?"

Despite her bravado, she couldn't shake the feeling it was wrong to be here. Léo hadn't been happy when she told him she was going but she wanted to see Suzanne Abetz in her full glory. The French woman had gone from being a secretary to one of the most influential women in Paris, a true Cinderella tale. Aside from the fact that Otto Abetz was hardly Prince Charming. An art teacher, he'd risen to the ranks of ambassador before he was expelled from France in 1939, something to do with some articles that had been published in the press. She hadn't paid any attention to the news at the time. But talk about a triumphant return. Now he was holding court to the crème de la crème of Paris, or so it was said.

She walked through the door, allowing the black-and-white-liveried servant to take her wrap. A woman, dressed in what looked like a Chanel jacket and fitted skirt, walked over to greet them. Enveloped in perfume as the woman leaned in to kiss her on each cheek, she watched as her father greeted Madame Abetz as an old friend.

"Suzanne, you get younger and more beautiful every time I see you. Life is treating you well?"

The woman smiled flirtatiously, letting her hand linger on his arm longer than necessary. "It is, Noël, thank you. Of course, Otto works far too hard and leaves me alone for hours at a time, but I manage."

"She shops and then she shops some more, don't you, darling?" The thin man with no chin held out his hand to Adèle. "Enchanted to meet you, at last, Mademoiselle Bélanger. Your father has spoken about you a lot although he didn't do justice to your beauty. No wonder men believe Frenchwomen to be the most beautiful in the world." He flashed a smile at his wife as he spoke.

"My Otto is such a charmer. Please go ahead and mingle. We have a buffet laid out in the next room. We thought it would be fun to pretend we were at a picnic." Suzanne tittered as she ignored Adèle completely.

Her father took her arm and led Adèle into the salon, where her eyes were immediately drawn to the giant swastika fashioned with red and white roses sitting on the polished marble countertop where glasses of champagne were laid out. A framed picture of Hitler adorned the walls, which were covered in silk wallpaper. Despite herself, she thought it was tastefully decorated or at least it would have been if there wasn't a large Nazi flag hanging from the ceiling. Did these people think everyone would forget what the horrible red and black spider represented if they failed to shove it in everyone's faces? She turned to speak to her father but he'd disappeared into the crowd. If only she'd listened to Léo – he'd laughed when she said she wanted to meet Chanel, Arletty and maybe even Serge Lifar, dancer and director of the Paris Opera. She loved opera and was thankful the Germans had kept it open.

Everyone seemed to know one another so, rather than standing alone, she wandered around admiring the furnishings and paintings that decorated every room. Her mouth watered at the scents coming from the buffet table. Mounds of croissants, pastries and other delicacies that hadn't been seen in months decorated one table. The next held an array of cold cuts such as ham and beef. The scent of salami tickled her nose.

"Hideous, isn't it? So much food yet the real people of Paris couldn't buy any of this even if they had the money."

Adèle turned at the woman's voice coming from behind her. She recognised her face but couldn't remember her name.

"He makes a good effort, to be fair." The woman took a sip of her champagne, her gaze focused on Otto.

Adèle moved to take a glass of champagne from a tray presented by a waiter. "Thank you." She turned back to the woman. "I'm Adèle Bélanger. I don't believe we've met."

But the woman didn't give her name. "He pretends to be a

good German, civilised and all, throwing these parties, talking about wanting France and Germany to lead the new Europe. But underneath it, he's just the same as the rest of them. Racist, anti-Semitic buffoons."

Was the woman insane? They were surrounded by German uniforms of various shades of blue, grey and green, never mind the secret service spies dressed in civilian clothes. Adèle coughed, her champagne having gone down the wrong way. A man clapped her gently on the back. She turned to find herself looking into the face of an Adonis. Tall, blonde, green-eyed with the most beautiful smile. Butterflies exploded in her stomach; he was too perfect and for some reason that scared her. She wanted to leave now. She looked around the room but couldn't see her father. She coughed again.

"Please have a drink of water. It will help." The man, dressed in civilian clothes, held out the glass, his accent a mixture of American with a faint trace of German.

"Sorry, the champagne," Adèle murmured, all the while hoping he hadn't heard the remarks made by her female companion, who had now lit up a cigarette. Adèle wished she'd never come. She should have listened to Léo.

"Has Ceci been talking too much again? Honestly, darling, you will have your head cut off if you continue. Look at what happened to Marie-Antoinette." The man smiled but the warning in his eyes was clear. "And put that cigarette out. You know their views on smoking."

"Yes, they have a view on everything, don't they? But why should we just do what they say?" Despite her brave words, she ground out the cigarette on a plate.

"Because they are in charge now and you need to earn a living." The man's retort caused the woman to flush, her eyes to glisten as if she was about to cry.

She was an actress. Adèle couldn't remember her name or

any of the roles she'd played but now was not the time to mention that.

"Excuse me. I must powder my nose." Ceci left, taking her purse with her.

Adèle was about to make her excuses and leave but he moved closer to her side, his voice low and intimate.

"Poor thing. I have some sympathy for her, but she needs to accept reality. The Germans are here now, and they aren't going anywhere. But enough about her. So tell me, what do you do? Are you an actress too?"

Adèle didn't know whether to be flattered or insulted. In some eyes, actresses weren't too different from courtesans. She stayed silent, her eyes searching the crowd to find someone she recognised.

"Forgive me for being rude. My name is Karl Follen."

"You're an American?" Adèle avoided giving him her name.

He bowed. "Guilty as charged. Well, at least partially. I was born in America but my parents are German; they emigrated in the 1920s. And you, madame, you are a Parisian through and through?"

Adèle's eyes locked with his. She couldn't help staring at him; it was as if he had some magical ability to command all her attention.

"You are not only beautiful, but your style screams chic. Your hairstyle, perfectly shaped and sized diamond earrings, and that dress ... cut to..."

She gaped at him.

"Karl, can we go home now please?" Ceci demanded as she walked up to them. Adèle jumped, not having seen the woman.

"Don't be ridiculous, Ceci. You know we are here to work. Herr Goebbels may arrive at any minute." He spoke as if to a friend but there was an underlying note Adèle didn't understand.

"All the more reason to leave. That man can't keep his

hands to himself." Ceci turned to Adèle. "He puts a whole new meaning on the word 'casting couch', and the movies he wants to make … the things he wants to portray on film, all lies but he believes the public will buy it. And they will." She shuddered but it wasn't her words that horrified Adèle but Karl's reaction.

His lips twisted as he muttered under his breath, "Shut up, you stupid girl. I haven't worked this hard to have you ruin it. Herr Goebbels has promised us a glittering future. If you don't make this film, you might as well earn your living on the streets. You won't act again. You're not good enough for Hollywood; you proved that."

Ceci's face crumpled, but Karl's didn't show an ounce of pity.

Adèle spotted her father across the room. "Please excuse me. I see someone I know." She didn't wait for Karl's reaction but fled.

ELEVEN

26 JULY 1940

Sophie looked up as Elizabeth, her face as white as her uniform, entered the ward and beckoned Sophie to come with her.

"Excuse me, Captain, I need to go now, but I will check back on you in a little while." Sophie squeezed the patient's hand but there was no response. She hurried after Elizabeth, who was holding the door open. "Jules?"

In the corridor outside the ward, Elizabeth put her hands on either side of Sophie's shoulders. "The list of prisoners has been published. Jules's name isn't on it."

"What? But it must be. He hasn't come home, and he was alive at the end of the fighting, so where is he?"

Elizabeth didn't speak. Her eyes, full of sadness and pity, held Sophie's gaze.

Sophie shrugged off Elizabeth's embrace. "No, I refuse to believe it. Jules can't be ... gone. I'd know. In here." She patted her heart. "There has to be a mistake."

Elizabeth put her hand out as if to pull her into a hug but she took a step back. Elizabeth opened her mouth to speak, paused for a moment and then said, "You've had a shock. But denying the truth isn't going to help, Sophie. The Germans keep meticulous records. Enough time has elapsed between the armistice and now. If he was..." Elizabeth's eyes filled with tears as she swallowed hard. "... alive, he would be here. With you – or at least have sent you word."

Sophie covered her face in her hands, bending from the waist. "No, don't say it. He can't be... I love him so much."

Elizabeth pulled her into a hug, ignoring Sophie's resistance. The older woman held her as the tears flowed. All these weeks of longing for news, hoping despite the silence that he would come back. To feel his lips on hers, see him laugh, and hold him.

"Elizabeth, how am I going to go on?" Sophie shuddered as she tried but failed to stop the tears. "Oh my goodness, I need to tell Yvette. They won't write to the family of those not on the lists, will they? How would they know who was missing – or would their *excellent* records hold that information too?"

Elizabeth didn't answer, just held her, handing her a handkerchief to dry her eyes. Her voice trembling, the older woman pushed the hair back from Sophie's face, placed a finger gently under her chin, forcing her to meet her gaze. "You are strong enough to handle this, Sophie. You will continue the fight and then when peace comes, you will become the best doctor Paris has ever seen. For you and Jules. He wouldn't expect you to fall apart. You're strong. Time is a great healer." The woman's eyes clouded over. "Many of us learned that lesson in the last war."

Sophie dried her eyes, pulling her strength from her toes. She had to finish her shift as they were short-staffed as it was. She'd grieve in her room later, but for now, her patients needed her.

"Thank you, Elizabeth, for coming to tell me and for being my friend."

Elizabeth leaned in and kissed her on the cheek. "I loved Jules; everyone in the hospital did. He loved you with every ounce of his being. Remember that in the dark days ahead."

Elizabeth blew her nose noisily before turning on her heel, exiting the small ward office, leaving Sophie alone. She sagged against the wall, closing her eyes so she could picture him, but her mind refused to co-operate. An alarm bell rang in the distance; someone needed a doctor. Taking a deep breath, she forced herself to stand tall. Jules would want her to carry on. To avenge his death in whatever way she could.

TWELVE

Later that evening, Sophie pushed the door of the apartment open. Madame Garnier, in deep whispered conversation with a neighbour, barely glanced at her. For that, she was grateful as she couldn't deal with Matthieu or his mother today. She forced herself to climb the stairs. Before she entered the apartment, the most delicious fragrance tantalised her taste buds, making her mouth water. Opening the door, she walked down the hallway to the kitchen, from where she heard voices.

Her eyes widened at the sight of the basket of croissants and pastries – she hadn't seen such treats since before the war. Her twin was standing on the opposite side of the table, arranging a bouquet of roses in a vase.

"Where did this come from?" Sophie asked pointedly.

Adèle jumped at Sophie's snarl. "Sophie, I didn't hear you come in. What's with the bad mood? It's only flowers and some pastries from an admirer. Fresh, too. Want one?" She put down the flowers and held out the plate towards Sophie, who angrily shoved it away. The plate smashed to the ground, sending pastries everywhere.

"What did you do that for? Do you know how difficult they are to find?"

"Not hard enough. How dare you? If you want to tramp about with Germans, go to their restaurants and coffee shops, that's your choice. But do not bring their bribes into this house."

Jean-Pierre came in at that moment, clapping his hands. "You tell her, Sophie; she might listen to you."

"Oh shut up, both of you; it's only a few flowers. I haven't committed treason."

Sophie gripped her hands tight together for fear she would slap her twin. "In the eyes of some people you've done worse. They'll deal with you, papa, and the others who think they can mingle with the Boches and not face consequences. If this was my house, you would be out on the street." With that she burst into tears and ran for her bedroom.

Startled, Jean-Pierre jumped out of her way before following her.

"Sophie, what's wrong? Tell me." He walked over to the bed where she sobbed into her pillow.

"Jules. He's dead."

Jean-Pierre patted her awkwardly on the back. "I'm sorry. I liked him a lot."

Zeldah must have heard the commotion as she came into the room and sat near the top of the bed, massaging Sophie's shoulders. "Cry, let the tears out. There now, that's better." Zeldah stroked her hair as Sophie gave up any attempt to hold back her emotions.

After a few minutes, she composed herself a little. "I have to get a train and tell Yvette and her mother tomorrow. I must do it in person."

"You need to rest. You look like you would fall over in a strong wind." Jean-Pierre reached out to touch her but withdrew as if afraid she would break. "I'll go and tell them."

"But..."

"No, let me. Please. I liked Jules a lot. I like Yvette. I can do this; as your brother it's my job to protect you."

"My little brother."

He stood up, stretching his height. "Not so little any more."

She appreciated his attempt to make her laugh, although it failed. "We'll talk about Yvette in the morning." The heaviness in her chest threatened to overwhelm her. She took refuge in anger. "I can't believe Adèle is consorting with them. They killed Jules and goodness knows how many others. What is she thinking?"

Jean-Pierre's voice was gruff. "She isn't. You know what she's like. Out for a good time. I feel sorry for her; someone is going to take her to task. And that won't be pretty."

Sophie sat up at his knowing tone. "What have you heard? Are people already speaking about Adèle?"

Jean-Pierre fingered the bedcover, his gaze moving to Zeldah before he walked over to the window. "Things are becoming more difficult. People have long memories. I... Oh, forget about Adèle. She can look after herself. Tell us how you heard about Jules, if it isn't too distressing."

Sophie explained how his name wasn't on the list of prisoners. "Yvette hadn't heard from him last week when I was there. The patient who came to the hospital confirmed he was alive, so he didn't die during the war. He just ... disappeared."

"But that doesn't..." Jean-Pierre started to protest, but Sophie saw Zeldah silence him with a look. He shrugged, mumbling, "I was only trying to make her feel better." He turned back to Sophie.

Sophie looked at Jean-Pierre as if seeing him for the first time. Her younger brother was growing up. Not just physically, although when had he got so tall? His face was leaner, he'd lost the baby look and grown into a man. He still had the same soft heart, though. A surge of love for him flowed through her; he would treat Yvette and her mother with kindness. Still, she should go with him, be there when they found out...

Adèle knocked at the door, walking into the room.

"I threw out the flowers and the pastries. I'm sorry." Her eyes held Sophie's and she could see Adèle genuinely meant it. Then her twin added, "I hate roses. So unoriginal."

Sophie almost screamed but then saw how Adèle hovered at the door, clearly uncomfortable as silence filled the room.

It was Zeldah who broke it. "I must get back to making dinner." She kissed Sophie on the cheek. "Jules loved you, remember that." Jean-Pierre stood up and followed Zeldah out of the bedroom, closing the door behind him.

Adèle took a seat at the bottom of the bed. "I'm sorry, Sophie."

"You didn't even like him."

Adèle didn't deny it. "That doesn't matter. You loved him and now you're hurting. I love you. Can I do anything?"

Sophie closed her eyes, shook her head before she curled into a ball, the pain threatening to overwhelm her. Adèle lay on the bed, curling up beside her and hugging her. "You knew real love, Sophie. That's a gift."

Adèle held her, ignoring the call for dinner, as Sophie finally gave in to the exhaustion. When she woke some time later, Adèle was still cuddling her.

* * *

The next day, when Sophie woke up, dressed in her nightgown, Adèle was gone. Zeldah brought her breakfast in bed.

"Thank you, Zeldah, and for last night too. Where's Adèle?"

"She's still asleep. Jean-Pierre already left. He went to see Yvette and her mother. He said you were not to get out of bed. You were already working too-long hours before all this."

Zeldah plumped up the pillows before straightening out the bedcovers.

Tears pricked Sophie's eyes again.

"I should have been the one to tell them. I feel guilty not going with Jean-Pierre."

"Why? Your heart is broken. Now, you can't handle their pain. A few days' rest and you will be stronger. Then you can see Yvette; she will understand." Zeldah passed the cup from the tray into Sophie's hand. "Drink and eat. Then sleep."

She took a gulp of coffee, but it threatened to reappear, so she pushed the bread away. Zeldah pursed her lips but didn't say a word as she left the bedroom with the unfinished breakfast.

Opening her wardrobe, Sophie stood on her toes to reach the box at the back of the shelf. This was where she'd kept every note or letter Jules had sent her. From the notes, he slipped her in the hospital when they first met to the letters written from the front. She sat on the bed picking out several items, a small ornament, a brooch belonging to his grandmother, the pressed petals from the first rose he'd given her. She closed the box as the memories assailed her, the tears flowing unchecked. They'd had a wonderful life planned and now it was gone.

Sophie closed her eyes. Yvette would understand, but even if she didn't, Zeldah was right. At this moment, she couldn't deal with anyone else. Not now when the pain was so raw.

THIRTEEN

A few days later when Zeldah came into Sophie's bedroom, she handed her a note and her clean uniform.

"Jean-Pierre asked me to give you this. He had to leave. He also said he didn't think it was wise you go back to the hospital today, but I've pressed this ready just in case."

Sophie took the note, recognising Yvette's scrawl. Jules had teased his sister about her lack of penmanship. Her stomach churned.

"Sophie, can I get you something?"

"No, thank you, Zeldah. I'm fine, thank you." She reached out and squeezed the girl's hand, too choked up to say anything. Zeldah nodded, hung the uniform in the wardrobe and left, closing the bedroom door behind her.

Sophie fingered the note for a few minutes before opening it.

Darling Sophie, my heart is breaking as yours must be. Jean-Pierre was so kind and considerate, and I completely understand his reasons for coming in your place. You always work too hard and now with ... this shock...

Sophie struggled to read the next words as the ink was all

blotchy. She could picture Yvette crying as she wrote it. Tears flowed down her own face.

I cry not just for the loss of my brother but for what that means. I won't have you as my sister-in-law, I won't get to spoil my nieces and nephews...

Sophie choked back a sob; all their plans had been destroyed.

She struggled to read to the end.

I love you and as far as I'm concerned you are my sister. Please come and see us soon. Yvette, x

Sophie folded the letter and put it in her drawer. Picking up the picture frame on her bedside table, she looked at the photograph of herself and Jules on the steps of the Louvre. She fingered his face, his smile. "I'll love you forever, Jules."

* * *

The return to the hospital was difficult with so many people stopping her to express their condolences. Even Victor, Oliver's passionate, hot-headed nephew, blushingly mumbled how sorry he was. She smiled, thanking everyone all the while wishing they would stop. She was trying to forget Jules was gone, but that was like wishing dawn didn't come every day.

She was glad of the distraction work provided. Sophie and Elizabeth took turns nursing the captain, who remained unconscious. One morning, as Sophie washed his face, he opened his eyes.

"Bonjour."

"Good morning to you, too. How are you feeling?"

"Like I fought with a tank and it won." The captain tried to sit up but fell weakly back on the pillow. Sophie put her arm around his back and helped him to sit up.

"I feel like a newborn. What happened to me?"

"Your appendix burst, causing peritonitis. You would have died but for Dr Murphy."

"Ah, the American. I prayed they would send me here, although not to die. I must get out of France. Go to de Gaulle."

"That's what everyone wants."

He grabbed her hands, his strength surprising her. "I must get out. The Germans they told me they won't treat me as an officer but as a Jew. You must help me."

Sophie's legs gave way as she grabbed the bedside, his words echoing Elizabeth's warning. "What do you mean, as a Jew?"

The man mimed the action of a gun to the back of the head and muttered something like "pft".

She thought of Jules. Oh dear God, was that what had happened to Jules? Had he known he was going to be murdered? What had his last thoughts been? She gripped the bed rail.

"Mademoiselle? You're very pale. What did I say?" His eyes examined her features.

"My fiancé beau, Jules Stein, he's a ... was a doctor. He was alive at the end of June but his name wasn't on the list of prisoners of war they published on 25 July." Her voice quivered with unshed tears.

"I apologise. I'm sorry for your loss. I should not have said what I did." He closed his eyes but whispered, "Now is not a good time to be a Jew."

She couldn't agree more. He had fallen back asleep. She went to find Elizabeth to update her on his condition.

* * *

When Sophie got home that evening, she walked straight into the kitchen, where Jean-Pierre was waiting for her.

"I was watching for you to come home. How are you?"

She choked back her emotions. Jean-Pierre was her younger

brother; she didn't want to burden him with her heartbreak. "I'm all right. Thank you for the letter from Yvette. She said you were very kind."

Jean-Pierre glanced away, his cheeks flushing. "I just thought of you and what you were going through. She was so strong but her mother ... she started screaming, Sophie. Ranting and raving about murderers and God turning his back on them and all sorts of things. To be honest, I was glad to leave."

Sophie brushed her hand across her eyes. Of course, Jules's mother was devastated, but a selfish part of her was glad she hadn't been there.

"Where did you go after you brought back the letter? Zeldah said you went away."

Her brother shifted from one foot to the other, staring at a spot over the top of her head. "Just a job for the museum, nothing serious."

Was it her imagination or was he trying to hide something? He was lying, she would almost bet on it. What was he up to? But then he smiled, a look of devilment in his eyes.

"Sophie, stay here for a few minutes and then come outside. I want to show you something."

She didn't want to wait around; she wanted to go to her room and cry her eyes out for Jules. But she also wanted to tackle him for lying.

"It seems like I haven't seen you in ages with my schedule at the hospital and you working at the museum. Why can't you stay and chat with me?"

"You talk too much, big sister. Now stay here and I will call you in a few minutes."

Sophie waited at the kitchen table. Where did he go when he went away to see friends? He seemed to have developed a wider circle of acquaintances than before the war. Always visiting this person or that. It seemed to take forever, but about five minutes later, Jean-Pierre came back with a big smile on his face.

"Come, close your eyes, I've a surprise for you."

She did as he said, following him into the sitting room, smiling at his antics. How glad she was the occupation hadn't changed her cheerful younger brother.

"Now you can open them."

Sophie opened her eyes to see Jean-Pierre balancing on her bicycle, pretending to be German using a horrible French accent. "You must ride ze bicycle just so. You must put both feet on ze pedals and both hands on ze handlebars. Do not cycle with a friend. You could be ze terrorist."

She giggled until her sides hurt. "Stop it, please. You will make me sick laughing."

"I am being serious. You must obey ze rules and you must have ze yellow marker on your vehicle. Like so!" Jean-Pierre pointed at the yellow tag he had fixed on her bike.

"What is that for?"

"All joking aside, sis, there are now rules about riding a bicycle. Seems the Germans are afraid the French will attack them on bicycles. I don't know whether we should be insulted or laugh. The yellow tag is mandatory. Warn your friends. They have already taken the cars. Let's not give them an excuse to take our bikes."

"I haven't seen papa since they took the cars. He loves his car more than anything, maybe even us. How is he taking it?" Sophie stopped joking at the look in her brother's eyes. "What?"

"Papa isn't obliged to obey the new law."

Sophie saw he wasn't meeting her gaze. She put a hand on his arm.

"But why? He isn't a doctor."

"Don't ask questions to which you don't want the answers," Jean-Pierre snapped.

Sophie pulled her hand back, surprised at her brother's

change of mood. But she was to blame, asking when she suspected the answer.

She knew her father had connections with the Germans and he'd surprised them often with food packages the likes of which hadn't been seen since before the war. Fresh meat, real coffee, sugar, flour, and chocolate. There was plenty of everything.

Her father hadn't hidden his admiration for the Germans or Pétain but, secretly, she suspected it was worse than that. Could he be a collaborator? He boasted about how good he was to buy businesses from the Jews even though she gathered he paid rock-bottom prices. Still, it was one thing for her to think these thoughts, different when Jean-Pierre pointed it out.

She forced herself to be jovial.

"Thank you, little brother, for making sure I obey the new rules. Better be careful or they will put you in a uniform. I think the grey-green will suit you. You will look like a good beetle."

Laughing, Jean-Pierre saluted before lighting a cigarette and heading off in search of his friends. Sophie watched him go, her heart filled with love, pride, and a little fear. How would her brother survive this horrible period? He might joke with her but she'd seen his serious side. She knew he was sensitive to how the occupation was affecting the people of Paris.

FOURTEEN

MID AUGUST

Sophie woke to her sister shaking her.

"You were screaming so loud, you woke me up. I thought the Germans had invaded the house." Adèle didn't hide her irritation.

"I was dreaming about Jules." Sophie sat up in the bed. "I keep dreaming about him – not knowing how he died and where his body is, it's killing me."

"That's pointless; how would having a grave change anything?"

"Adèle! Honestly, you can be so annoying."

"I don't mean to be. I never go to see Nicolas's grave." Her sister shuddered. "Don't want to think about that." Adèle moved to Sophie's wardrobe. "Can I borrow your blue dress tomorrow? Léo is taking me out to dinner. Only don't tell maman, will you, as she'll only give me a lecture. I've been widowed for almost a year. I'm entitled to have some fun, surely?"

How could someone be her mirror image in looks and not understand her?

"Get out." Sophie flung her pillow at her sister. "Go on. Out. I hate you."

Adèle took the blue dress and slammed the door behind her. Sophie dissolved into floods of tears. She didn't realise her mother had come into the room until she felt her hand on her shoulder. "Darling, what's the matter?"

"Oh, maman. Why did this war have to start?"

"Oh, my baby. You're grieving, but you are young. Give yourself time to grieve. You won't forget Jules but you will learn to live with the pain."

A surge of love for her mother inspired her to give her a hug.

"That's better, darling. Now, why don't you get up and have a bath? You'll feel better after you have something to eat. Keep busy. That's the best thing to do in these circumstances."

Her mother left but Sophie stayed in bed. Keep busy? She could work more hours in the hospital, but what she wanted most of all was to get rid of the Germans and for this war to be over.

* * *

Sophie pushed open the door to the ward where Captain M was recovering, concerned to find a six-foot-tall nun standing over his bed. Dr Murphy had said no visitors. The woman turned to smile at her.

"Bonjour, Dr Bélanger."

Sophie couldn't hide her surprise. They had never met, yet the woman knew her.

"I'm Sister Marie-Laurence from the hospital in Béthune. I'm here to take the captain out of Paris. I assume you agree we can move him?"

Sophie could have listened to her speak forever, the soft Irish lilt clear despite the perfect French.

"You're far from home, Sister."

"You mean Cork? I haven't been back to Ireland in years, but you never lose the accent. It comes in quite handy. Some of the Fritz still have respect for nationals from neutral countries, if not the uniform I wear."

Sophie could imagine the woman charming everyone she met; she spoke to you as if you were the most important person in the room.

"Captain M has recovered nicely but his health is still frail and, being a stubborn Frenchman, he refuses to rest as much as he should."

"Sure, Irish men are the same. Still, he'll do as I tell him, won't you, Captain?"

"Yes, Sister."

Sophie's mouth fell open at the meek agreement.

"I don't have any secret powers, Doctor. I simply explained to the captain that if he didn't agree to my rules, I would leave Paris alone. I have others who depend on me."

Sophie could only imagine. Between Allied prisoners of war on the run and Jewish refugees, all the escape lines were flooded.

"What can I do to help, Sister?"

"Bless you, child, you have done all you can with our captain. But I would like to speak to Elizabeth. I've been looking for her but she seems to have disappeared."

Sophie chewed her lip. "She's away at the moment, due back next week."

The nun didn't hide the concern in her eyes fast enough. Should she tell the nun Elizabeth was in the free zone having escorted some orphaned children? No, Elizabeth had said to keep the details secret.

"I can pass on a message if you wish."

The nun took a few seconds to think before walking to the far end of the ward. Sophie followed her. Once out of earshot of the captain, the sister whispered, "Warn Elizabeth to be careful."

Sophie's heart thumped faster as she wiped her clammy hands on her apron.

"I've heard rumours about this hospital. It's gaining a reputation as a place to seek refuge from the occupiers. A few names have been mentioned. Mainly Dr Murphy and Elizabeth's." The nun put her hand on Sophie's shoulder. "Dr Murphy gave me your name, no one else."

"I worry about Elizabeth. She says she has nobody, but we'd all be devastated if anything happened to her. She's the linchpin of the hospital."

"She's a lot more than that. I will pray for her. But it wouldn't hurt if you gave her a lecture too. Now I'd best get on my way."

"How are you going to get back to Béthune?"

The nun tapped her finger against her nose. "The less you know about my activities, the better. I hope we meet again but under nicer circumstances. You come from a brave family." The nun kissed her on both cheeks. "Au revoir."

The next morning, when Sophie arrived at the hospital, the captain and nun had left. She thought of what Sister Marie-Laurence had said. What did she know of Sophie's family? Or did she mean the American Hospital family?

FIFTEEN

OCTOBER 1940

Over a year since the war had started and yet it seemed so much longer to Sophie, especially when she thought about Jules. How she missed him. She shivered, pulling her coat around her. Now there was another census despite the last one being in July. But this time, they were only counting the Jews. Jean-Pierre said it had something to do with the Vichy government, but she wasn't sure what he'd meant. They hadn't had a chance to discuss it as papa announced Pétain knew what he was doing and that was the end of the conversation.

She went into the kitchen and gathered up some supplies from their well-stocked cupboards. Zeldah helped her without being asked.

"People are complaining they can't find rutabaga to eat and your papa finds all this?" Zeldah's arm swung towards the cupboards full of sugar, real coffee and everything else they had enjoyed before the war.

"Don't ask questions and you'll hear no lies," Sophie said. She packed a couple of bags but was careful not to take too much. It wouldn't do to upset her father, but worse, she didn't want to be stopped by the Germans. They may think she was a black marketeer.

"Make sure you take some food for your mother. She needs to eat better to fight off her illness." Sophie crossed her fingers at the white lie. No amount of food would cure cancer, but she didn't think Zeldah was ready to admit her mother was dying.

"My mother refuses to eat anything other than what I can buy in the shop." Zeldah's cheeks pinked up. "She won't allow me to bring home anything from my job."

"What?"

Zeldah hesitated before saying, "She says it's tainted."

Sophie glanced at the coffee in her hand. "She could be right, but at least we can use it for a good cause at the hospital. We can trade it for food for our older patients. Their rations are ridiculously low."

"Not just for the old." Zeldah turned away with tears in her eyes. Sophie put a hand on her back, but really, how could she make the girl feel better?

* * *

Elizabeth didn't seem too surprised to see her. "You lost?" she teased, but her eyes looked troubled. "What's wrong?"

Sophie placed the goods she had liberated from her home on the table. "Nothing. Everything." Sophie sighed. "I went for a walk but everywhere you look there are ugly flags, uglier soldiers, or guns."

"So you don't find the Aryan race attractive? Hitler will be disappointed." Although Elizabeth was joking, the concern on her face showed she was worried for her.

"I'm serious. I just want Paris to go back to the way it was, when we had full shops, when people were content to say hello or stop and chat. When we had food and ... oh darn it, anyway." Sophie wiped away a tear. "I'm not crying because I'm sad about Jules. I miss him so much, but it's not just that. How long will this war go on? I'm just so frustrated."

"It could be worse – you could be over in Britain. Wouldn't want to live in any of their big cities right about now. They are being bombed to pieces."

Guilt turned her stomach. Elizabeth was right: things were much worse elsewhere. British families were being blown apart, children and babies killed in their hundreds at home while their fathers were fighting the war. The British were fighting back, not feeling sorry for themselves.

"Can I help you with anything, Elizabeth? I need to keep busy rather than have time to think."

"You must be desperate to volunteer to do the stocktaking with me."

Sophie gave the older lady a half-smile. Elizabeth always cut straight to the point. She took the list from her colleague's hands. It was rather depressing. They had so little in stock, it would not take long to check things off.

"I want to do more. To help."

Elizabeth busied herself with some bottles, avoiding the conversation.

"Elizabeth, I'm serious. I know you and Dr Murphy are up to something more than just sheltering the odd French officer. Dr Murphy spelled out the risks before I started looking after Percy, I mean Captain Marchant. I'm not blind. The nun that came to see you told me to warn you that you and Dr Murphy had been mentioned, and you should be careful. I know she wasn't talking about a few extra food parcels. Credit me with some sense. We have Captain M here and suddenly she arrives to take him away. Not to mention the fact that when she came, you were crossing to the free zone with the 'French' orphans."

"What's that supposed to mean?" Despite her question, Elizabeth didn't look up.

"Those children didn't speak a word of French and we both

know it. I see the whispered conversations, the comings and goings. You and Dr Murphy are involved, fighting back in some way. I want to help. Surely there is something I could do?"

Elizabeth closed the door behind them and drew Sophie further into the storage room.

"You can stop shouting. These walls have ears, you know."

Sophie clasped her hands in front of her before apologising.

Elizabeth spoke at such a low volume, Sophie had to strain to hear her. "You have a wonderful future ahead of you. When this war is over, you will qualify as a doctor. You were born to be one. You have empathy with the patients and that means more than any textbook knowledge or qualifications."

"When will the war be over, though? Every newspaper headline commends Hitler on his latest victories. Soon the whole of Europe will march along the streets, giving themselves dislocated shoulders with that ridiculous hand signal. I want to do something. I need to be useful."

Elizabeth gave her a long, hard look. "It's not about what you need."

"Please think about it. I want to help those in need. I want revenge for what happened to Jules. I won't take a life, but I won't let the Germans just walk over us. I mean it."

* * *

Sophie got her wish to help much sooner than expected. Two days later, she'd just parked her bicycle in a space the porter had promised would be secure, bicycle parts becoming as valuable as gold, when Elizabeth found her.

"We have some special patients who need help. Dr Murphy is busy, so I thought you might handle it."

Sophie swallowed, butterflies flying loose in her stomach. She knew what Elizabeth was asking. She was being invited to join in the résistance. In the past, she'd obeyed all the rules, but the war had thrown the rule book out the window. She nodded, unable to speak because of a combination of pride and, if she was honest, a little fear. There was no turning back now.

Elizabeth spoke softly as they walked through the hospital, greeting those they knew with a smile.

"Unfortunately, they had to hide for a couple of days before we could bring them here. One has a nasty leg injury. It's infected."

"Thank you for your faith." Sophie followed Elizabeth through the various wards until they came to one labelled 'Highly Infectious'. Following Elizabeth's example, she donned a gown and mask, even though both knew there was nothing to fear from this ward.

"The Germans never come in here, too terrified of their own shadows, the little pipsicles."

Sophie grinned. To look at Elizabeth, she seemed like such a lady. Nobody expected her to curse. But she did, even if it was just made-up words like 'pipsicles' as she made her feelings clear.

The heavy smell of disinfectant greeting them helped to prove their cover story. Sophie spotted the first patient, wondering how on earth he'd got through Paris as he looked exactly like what you would expect a dashing young Englishman to look like. His hair was cut short at the back, but he'd left his blonde fringe long on his finely chiselled face, his lack of beard stressing his youth.

"This is Pilot Officer Ian Stewart." Elizabeth introduced the Englishman. "He was lucky to escape, having landed in the grounds of the chateau at Sceaux."

Sophie gasped. Sceaux was almost an hour away by ambulance. He'd been even luckier than she imagined, having got here safely.

Elizabeth ignored Sophie's reaction and continued talking in a calm, confident tone. "His parachute caught on a tree, and locals cut him loose. A farmer bandaged his leg, but it's still bleeding. There might be some fragments of the shell that hit the plane still in there."

Stewart, grimacing from pain, spoke in English. "I chased a Jerry too far and then found myself out of fuel, trying to avoid the chateau. Didn't see the tree. It could have moved out of my way, in all fairness." The man sounded like a BBC broadcaster. Sophie admired his spirit. He was white with pain, sweating visibly, yet still trying to be cheerful.

"Do you speak French as well as you understand it, Ian?"

Ian shook his head. "Never mastered the accent."

"I speak a little English, so between us, we'll manage. Now I will examine your leg. Lie back and try to relax."

She quickly examined his leg and found that Elizabeth was right. The area around the wound was a nasty shade of red, lines moving up his leg away from the wound site, a worrying sign of infection. She probed gently, but the man's sharp intake of breath told her he would need to be out cold if she was to examine him properly.

Sophie searched for the correct phrase. "We will have to knock you out, Ian." She didn't want to alarm him more than necessary.

His eyes widened as he looked around. "No. Can't do that. I have to keep my wits about me."

Sophie took his hand, looking straight at his face. "You are safe here. The Germans believe this is where we keep the most contagious patients and won't come in." She sensed he didn't believe her. She didn't have time to waste trying to convince him. "I must get started at once. That leg wound needs fixing, and fast."

The man looked around again in response to Sophie's firm tone. "But you're only a girl. Where's the doctor?"

"I am the doctor." Sophie crossed her fingers at the small white lie. She would be one in a few years' time, assuming the

Germans didn't get in her way. Given the situation, she couldn't call the doctor on duty or the surgeon. "Now, Nurse, can you put him out, please?"

Ian protested even as Elizabeth produced the chloroform. Sophie quickly sterilised her hands. She would have preferred to do this in an operating theatre, but that was impossible. The Germans would look for this man and the other patients like Captain Marchant hidden around the wards. The less attention they brought to themselves, the better.

"He's out but I can't say for how long," Elizabeth confirmed.

Sophie concentrated on the man's leg, using a small scalpel to help her probe the wound. "I see it. A bullet fragment, I think. Or maybe some flak. Hard to tell."

She extracted a piece of metal the size of her thumbnail, as Ian winced, adjusting his position. Elizabeth gave him a little more chloroform, allowing Sophie to make sure she cleaned the wound thoroughly before she stitched it back up.

"He'll have to stay here for a few days to check on that infection, but hopefully now the shrapnel is out, he'll recover quickly. With his looks and accent, he'll have to stay out of sight."

Elizabeth raised an eyebrow. "We've done this once or twice before, you know."

Sophie grinned back. "Sorry, I'm teaching you how to suck eggs. Forgive me."

"I'll think about it. We have another patient to see."

* * *

Another injured pilot sat on the next bed, an American from Texas. He called Sophie 'honey' and 'doll', but didn't mention her age or the fact that she wasn't a doctor. His injury was much easier to treat. A dislocated shoulder, which she quickly popped back into place, with Elizabeth's help. Tex, as he insisted she call him, didn't complain; his only reaction was the hiss of breath coming through his clenched teeth.

To distract him, Sophie asked, "What are you doing over here? America hasn't joined the war."

"I couldn't wait at home. Mom was from England, so I left and signed up for the RAF. There's a bunch of us flying for them. They need us."

Sophie knew they did. Dr Murphy had told her about the serious lack of qualified British pilots, especially now after so many died or were wounded during the Battle of Britain. It made the resistance role of rescuing downed pilots more urgent. They needed every flyer they could get back to Great Britain.

"How soon can we leave this joint?" Tex looked around him. "All the grey uniforms hanging around aren't helping my appetite. Someone said they had a command centre across the road from the main gate to this hospital."

Sophie answered as she bandaged his arm. "That's right. The Kommandantur is directly opposite the hospital, but the Germans don't pay us much attention. You can relax."

"Relax? Are you joking?"

"Shut up, Tex. You're always complaining. You heard the doctor. We've got to wait and do what we're told. It's not just our lives in danger, but these good people too."

Sophie hadn't noticed the other man until he spoke up. She blushed at his scrutiny, the look in his eyes reminding her of the way Jules looked at her sometimes.

Tex turned a rather becoming shade of red. "Sorry, Nurse, Doctor. I let my mouth run on."

Before the ladies could reply, Tex's companion spoke again.

"Don't worry, Tex. You'll be home soon, buddy. Soon enough you'll be complaining about warm British beer and damp weather."

Sophie followed Elizabeth into the storeroom, closing the

door behind her. This seemed to be the safest place in the hospital to have these conversations.

Whispering, she stepped closer to her friend. "Thank you for letting me help, but I want to get more involved than just seeing to some patients."

Elizabeth rolled her eyes. "You're never happy."

Sophie ignored her. "I know you are more involved than anyone else. Don't bother arguing. Someone gets these airmen to the hospital. And somebody, maybe the same person, gets them back out when they have recovered or been patched up. I think you're that person."

Elizabeth concentrated on a bottle label. "You give me too much credit." Sophie noticed the red tinge to her friend's neck and the way her hand shook slightly. Was she scared? Surely she knew Sophie wouldn't betray her.

"Elizabeth, please. We are friends. Don't insult my intelligence. Who else could it be? That nun from Béthune, she knew your name and said I was to tell you to be careful. Dr Murphy is too busy at the hospital but you, you go missing on a fairly regular basis. I know you have time off but even when you are supposed to be on shift, someone covers for you. Noémie a lot of the time. Every path leads to you."

Looking troubled, Elizabeth put the bottle back on the shelf and sat down on a dusty-looking chair.

"I have no one. My husband left years ago, and my sons ... I can afford to take risks. You have a family, a future."

"Jules is dead; they killed him. I don't have a future until France is free. And you're wrong. Many people care about you."

"I wasn't looking for pity. I mean, the Germans can't use anyone to hurt me. What would you do if they arrested Adèle and used her to get to you? Don't look so horrified. You do not understand what those monsters can and will do. I don't want to involve any more people I love. So please, be content with what you are doing. Now, where are we going to get fresh supplies? We can't treat patients without medicines."

"We can use herbs and make natural remedies for some things, but that's not what I want to talk about." Sophie pulled her friend around to face her. "I respect you not just as a nurse, but as my friend. You know that. But it is my choice, not yours. I am not a child."

With no response from Elizabeth, Sophie moved to the door. "If you won't help me be of more help, I will find someone who will."

Elizabeth's eyes widened, her temper flaring. "You are a stubborn brat. Don't you threaten me. I knew you when you first arrived here, blonde hair flying about your shoulders, wide blue eyes staring at Dr Murphy and the rest of the doctors like they were gods. You've changed."

Blushing, Sophie turned back to her friend. "Who helped change me? You did. You told me women could and should be anything they wanted to be. So, stop trying to protect me now. I can help. I know I can. So, let me try."

Elizabeth sighed. "He'll kill me for this."

Sophie assumed she meant Dr Murphy, but she didn't really care. She'd decided she wanted to fight back.

"We need supplies. Not just food and medicines, but other things. Our guests cannot register with the authorities for obvious reasons, but we can get them false papers. But that is only the first hurdle. The queues for bread, sugar, milk, and everything else that is rationed are bad enough. Queues are full of collaborators. Those who would sell their soul for a couple of francs. We have to be very careful who stands in line on behalf of our guests."

Sophie didn't say a word, but listened. She had given no thought to these difficulties.

Elizabeth continued. "Paperwork, or rather the lack of it, is an issue. These additional measures they have introduced are hurting us. The rationing is a way of controlling the population. How can our airmen or other refugees sign up with their local *boulangerie* or *boucherie*? Getting the tickets from the *mairie* is easier, not easy but not as difficult as finding willing bakers and butchers who will add our clients to their lists."

Sophie hadn't thought about that. When the rules came in to register with your local baker, butcher, etc. she had just obeyed them. She hadn't thought of the people in hiding who couldn't do that. How did they get their food?

"Can we use the black market? I know it's not patriotic, but who cares about that if we can help people, right?"

Elizabeth rolled her eyes, making Sophie feel foolish. "That costs money. There are people out there making a fortune from the black market. They go to visit their relatives in the country and bring back as much as they can carry. The police recently arrested two couples. Those four had made half a million francs already. The hospital doesn't have those resources. With winter coming, things will get worse."

Sophie thought for a few moments.

"Papa does. I'll get Adèle to help me. She is papa's favourite. She can talk him into anything."

Elizabeth pursed her lips, her eyes narrowing. "Your sister isn't likely to want to help us, is she? Adèle seems to enjoy the occupation."

The hairs on the back of her neck standing up, Sophie stared at Elizabeth. She'd never heard her be so disparaging about anyone before. Adèle wasn't doing anything wrong. But, even if she was, how did Elizabeth know what Adèle was up to? They hardly moved in the same social circles.

"She's just enjoying herself." Sophie hoped her cold, confident tone convinced her friend.

Elizabeth looked at her, her expression a mixture of pity and anger.

"You and I both know that's not how it looks. She travels

with them, she eats with them, dances with them. Who knows what else she does?"

Sophie's cheeks heated at Elizabeth's implied meaning. "Adèle wouldn't sleep with them. True, she goes to their restaurants. She has always travelled first class. But it means nothing. Adèle isn't political. All she cares about is having a good time, so when Léo is working, she goes out with Papa or her other friends. You know that. You know our family."

"I know it, but not everyone does. Your sister can't just flutter around like a butterfly, landing where she likes without thought of the consequences. When this war is over, we will deal with those who sided with the Germans."

Sophie laughed nervously, although Elizabeth's words echoed those of Yvette. "Now you are being ridiculous. Adèle isn't on the side of the Germans. She doesn't like them being here any more than you or I do. She wants everything to go back to what it was like before. Only the other night she was complaining about the curfew and Paris turning into the city of darkness, not light."

Elizabeth put her hand on Sophie's arm. "Your sister hasn't only been seen with Germans – she speaks their language."

Sophie moved slightly. Elizabeth's hand fell back to her side.

"We all speak German. My mother is half-German. Since when is that a crime?" Sophie put her hands on her hips, her nostrils flaring. "You know my family. Do you suspect me of being a spy too?"

"No, of course not. But you can't assume Adèle will want to help us, or that she won't mention what we are up to to her German friends."

Sophie couldn't find the words.

Elizabeth's belt was pulled tighter around her waist, emphasising her weight loss. There were new lines around her eyes and her hair was almost completely grey now.

"Sophie, it's not just the fact I, we, find it difficult to trust someone that acts like your sister does. It's a fact that most people in Paris don't want to get involved, they want to wait out the war as safe as they can. All they can think about is their own needs and those of their families – and given what our country went through in the last war, there're many that don't blame them for feeling like that."

"Adèle won't betray me – I mean us."

"You need to speak to her. Tell her people are watching."

"I will, but back to more important matters." Sophie stared at the other woman, holding her gaze. "What do you need most? To help?"

"Couriers."

"What?"

"Couriers, the people who bring the aircrew and others to safety in the free zone. Well, relative safety, as there are arrests happening there too. But you can't do that. You are needed here. Your absence would be noted and commented on."

Sophie didn't know what to say. Was Elizabeth expecting her to volunteer people to become couriers? Did she know anyone? Could she ask someone to take the risk? It was one thing to treat injured people in the hospital. She had some chance of protesting innocence on the basis she had to treat a patient. But those escorting the British and American fly boys were taking tremendous risks. There was no excuse for them if caught.

Elizabeth continued talking. "Next to couriers, we need money and paper. For ration cards and tickets and identity papers. We have some people willing to supply us, but they need things in return."

"Coffee, tobacco, luxuries like that."

Sophie beamed. "I can get paper. Papa has loads of it. I may be able to get some money too."

Elizabeth made a "tsk" sound, her head slightly tilted to one side. "I wish I still had some of your innocence. You can't just walk into your papa's business and take reams of paper."

Sophie bristled at her friend's pity but Elizabeth put her arm around her shoulders.

"Don't take any risks at home. If you can liberate tobacco, coffee, paper and anything else, then do. But don't get caught."

"My father wouldn't betray me." Sophie heard herself echoing what she had said about Adèle. She'd stand behind Adèle a hundred per cent, but her father...

Elizabeth looked at her sadly. "I hope that's true."

Sophie swallowed hard. "I know. He has no love for this hospital or Dr Murphy. He blames you for letting me follow my dreams. And for encouraging my relationship with Jules."

"You just need to be very careful."

Sophie didn't reply. What could she say to the truth?

SIXTEEN

LATE OCTOBER 1940

Adèle waltzed out of the *salon de couture*. Jeanne Lanvin always had the latest styles. The emerald satin would look...

"Ugh!" She withdrew in shock as a woman spat at the ground beside her.

"Whore!"

The woman had gone before Adèle said anything. Blushing, she realised many people were glaring at her, but why? She had done nothing but buy a dress. She tried hailing a vélo-taxi, but it sped past her despite being empty. When it happened a second time, she wondered if there was a neon light above her head. She bit back tears of frustration as it began to rain. There was nothing for it but to walk to the métro and catch a train home.

When she finally reached their apartment, soaked to the skin, she almost collided with Jean-Pierre on his way out. His eyes widened when he saw the bag.

"You've been shopping."

"Yes, I bought a dress. When did that become a crime?" Adèle snapped.

Her brother shook his head in disbelief. "People are struggling to meet the cost of food and you flaunt a couture dress. It's a wonder you got home alive."

"I'm not in the mood for this. One woman spat at me and called me a horrid name, a vélo-taxi refused to stop, so I had to get the métro. Look at the state of me." She glanced in the mirror above the hall table. "I look like they dragged me through a bush backwards."

Her brother laughed, but it wasn't nice. Glaring at him, she waited for an explanation.

"You just don't get it, do you? The only people with money to spend at..." He peered over her shoulder at the bag. "... Jeanne Lanvin are collaborators and their wh... mistresses. You might as well have taken out an advertisement on the wireless."

Adèle gritted her teeth, but her brother hadn't finished. "Papa is taking you to some event, isn't he? That's why you went shopping."

"I needed a new dress. Everything in my wardrobe is ancient." She pushed past him. "Excuse me, I need a bath."

He put a hand out to stop her. "Be careful, Adèle. You know what they say. If you sleep with dogs, you'll catch fleas."

Adèle shook his arm off. All this fuss because she'd bought a dress. She'd love to be able to give him a smart answer but he had the brains of the family. Well, him and Sophie – perhaps that's why they got on so well. Her chest burned, although she'd never admit to being jealous of the bond between her siblings.

Jean-Pierre picked up a satchel.

"Are you off out again? Where do you go that has you so enthralled?" she asked, curiosity getting the better of her. He was out more than she was in, these days. When he was home, he was closeted in the kitchen, whispering to Zeldah. He hesitated at the door, giving her a pained look full of disappointment and – was it anger? He couldn't be that annoyed that she'd bought a dress, could he?

"Jean-Pierre, I..." The bang of the door closing after him cut off her words. Her ears pounded and her stomach tightened. Why did his opinion of her matter?

She spun on her heel and stomped down the hall to her room. Once in her room, she allowed the tears of frustration to fall as she took the dress out of the bag. She wasn't even sure she liked it any more. Maybe she'd give it to Sophie.

* * *

Adèle's mouth was sore from forcing the smile on her face as she listened to her father entertain his guests. She'd thought papa was treating her to dinner à deux; if she'd known he had invited these people, she'd have stayed at home.

"You are very quiet."

Adèle picked up her glass, her fingers tightening around the stem. "I don't know that I could add to your conversation, monsieur." She didn't add that it seemed everyone agreed with her father that the Germans being in France had opened up more revenue streams. If she had to guess, they were almost pleased to have been invaded. She squirmed a little, wishing she could go home. Her brother had been right: these were the people Jean-Pierre had tried to warn her about.

"Desrosiers, Roger Desrosiers." He inched closer, the smell of his breath making her want to gag. "I don't believe that for a second. A well-educated young lady with your beauty and charm, the toast of French society, will hear all sorts of things. You could be very useful to us."

Adèle took a sip of champagne, playing for time. "I've no idea what you are talking about, Monsieur Desrosiers. I don't have any interest in politics."

His eyes glittered. "You like being rich, don't you? Having money to spend on couture gowns and baubles like that diamond necklace."

Her hands fingered the jewels her father had given her a week or so before.

"I was there when your father purchased that pretty piece. For a song, too. The people who sold it were in a hurry."

His tone suggested he relished bullying those who needed to sell. She'd heard enough of the conversation to know that her father and his cronies were taking advantage of those who were leaving Paris for America or other places. Those whose names appeared on certain lists. Such as the social democrats who had already fled Germany when Hitler had first come to power, the artists, musicians, and other talented people who had spoken out against the Nazis.

Ignoring the man by her side, she stared at her father across the table. How could he look so relaxed, as if he was discussing ordinary business deals, not taking advantage of those in need?

* * *

On the way home, she asked him how he could get involved with such people.

"It's purely business, my darling," he said with a brusque smile. "My friends introduce me to those who are in a hurry to liquidate their assets. I provide them with the money they need in return for their businesses or property or..."

"Diamond necklaces." She fingered the piece around her neck. It had been a little tight, but now it felt like it was strangling her.

"Yes, darling. I buy whatever I see has value."

"At rock-bottom prices, papa, from those who are running for their lives."

He gave her a disparaging look. "Hardly, sweetheart. You haven't seen anyone being shot down in the street, have you? Our German friends are well-behaved and courteous."

She wasn't about to be sidetracked. "You're taking advantage of people's misfortune."

"Don't be ridiculous. Those people who need to leave should have kept their mouths shut. Who are they to criticise such a wonderful regime? You've seen the results for yourself. Germany is prospering, with full employment." He gestured at her outfit with his finger. "I'd expect such a remark from your twin. But you, my darling, you and I are made from the same cloth. We both love the fine life, and this is a way to increase our holdings. Our name is recognised. We are moving in the best circles and I'm making more money than ever before." He leaned back in the car, a self-satisfied expression on his face.

But at what cost, papa? Adèle undid the necklace and shoved it in her handbag, feeling queasy at the idea of being made from the same stuff as her father.

SEVENTEEN

1 NOVEMBER 1940

La Toussaint, the Feast of All Saints, was one of their mother's favourite days and she insisted the whole family attend the meal.

Sophie took her seat at the table, plastering a smile on her face. She'd been avoiding home but had come to support her mother. At least she'd tried to comfort her over Jules. There was a funny atmosphere in the room. As if they were all walking on eggshells. Her mother looked white and much older than in the summer. Papa was sullen. Jean-Pierre hadn't arrived yet. Only Adèle was in her usual gay mood, dressed to the nines, wearing make-up. Her twin's physical appearance made Sophie wish she had taken more time getting ready.

The array of food on the kitchen table was mouth-watering, but she couldn't help feeling guilty. Where had it all come from? Despite the war, all the signature dishes were here. They had *coquilles Saint-Jacques*, the scallops looking perfect in the delicious-smelling sauce. Several cheeses took pride of place on a cheese tray: Saint-Marcellin, Sainte-Maure, Saint-Gilda and her personal favourite, Saint-Albray. There was even a Saint-Honoré cake, at a time when most people couldn't find sugar.

Even if Zeldah had been queuing for hours, she couldn't have sourced all of this. Not when the Germans were using France as their own Garden of Eden, transporting food, grains, animal feedstuffs, and leather back to Germany. People were eating rutabaga and dandelions, with boiled acorns as a coffee substitute. It was easier to find a bottle of wine than a loaf of fresh bread. Before she could comment, Jean-Pierre came in, kissing their mother on the cheek.

"Maman, you have outdone yourself. You and Zeldah must have queued for hours." With a wink at Sophie, Jean-Pierre passed through the kitchen to the dining room where his father and sister waited. He held out the chair for his mother to sit and then did the same for Sophie before taking his own seat. Taking the napkin and unfolding it, he asked, "Did you do your bit, Adèle?"

Adèle turned on him. "Me? Queuing. Are you joking? Why should I join the lines like peasant women?" Adèle took a sip of her wine, savouring the taste before explaining, "Papa brought home most of this. Zeldah queued for a few items. Maman and I went shopping. Although why we bothered is beyond me. Those Germans have the exchange rate benefiting them and dress designers have adjusted their prices accordingly. Not that they will let us have any of the decent material. They are too busy dressing those hausfraus, the wives and mistresses of our occupiers."

Sophie marvelled at her sister's nerve. She didn't mention the dress she'd bought at Jeanne Lanvin not that long ago. Although, to her knowledge, Adèle had never worn it. She wouldn't even know about it had Jean-Pierre not given Adèle a hard time about it.

Elizabeth's words about Adèle repeated through Sophie's brain. Her twin was totally self-serving.

"Hardly worth complaining about, is it? People are going hungry. Who cares about dresses?"

Adèle gave her a look more fitting for a badly behaved child before asking in a scathing tone, "Who is going hungry? That is just rumour. Have you seen people fading away?"

"Not in the circles you move in. If you came to the hospital you would see plenty of evidence." Sophie swallowed to regain a level tone, and glanced at her father, wondering if he would react to her words. He remained silent so she continued. "The temperatures are plummeting. The elderly patients have been hardest hit aside from the ridiculously low levels of rations assigned to them. Not everyone has someone to join the queues, and it's difficult for them to find coal, so they are freezing. If you bothered to look in the shops, the shelves are all empty. Someone should do something."

Jean-Pierre passed the breadbasket before joking, "Ask Pétain. There are pictures of him everywhere. He is the all-powerful one; he can do everything."

Sophie's knife fell out of her hand as she jumped in response to her father shouting at her brother. "Jean-Pierre, mind your manners. Pétain is our hero. Without him, where would France be?"

"Not under the yoke of the Germans." Jean-Pierre hadn't raised his voice. He didn't need to.

"Enough. I will not tolerate those comments under my roof. Show some respect, boy. Pétain is a war hero, the hero of Verdun. He is right: the Germans will help make France powerful again. Show us a better way to live."

Sophie looked pointedly around the room, her eyes focusing on the huge fire before moving to the silver cutlery, cut glasses complete with an expensive red wine. The dishes ready to be served from the kitchen could feed one family for a week in the current climate. "You're hardly living in poverty."

Her father's face flushed as her mother reprimanded her. "Sophie, hush. Don't talk to your papa like that. Apologise. Since when did we speak while we ate? Manners, darling."

"Sorry, maman, but I don't agree with papa. I'm a grown woman, a trainee doctor. If Pétain had his way, women would have no rights at all. I couldn't be a doctor."

Her father slammed a fist on the table, making the dishes and glasses ring. "Good. A woman's duty is to marry and have children." Her father chewed some cold meat. "Pétain has done away with the old motto of *Liberté, Égalité, Fraternité*. About time too. The new values are much better. *Travail, Famille, Patrie*, work, family, fatherland. You children should respect your parents."

Sophie opened her mouth to argue, but Jean-Pierre got there first. Her brother's eyes were shining, his fists balled. His voice quivered, she suspected, from trying to keep it civil.

"How can they want to make us powerful when they're setting up so many prison camps? Who are to fill these camps?" Jean-Pierre asked. But he didn't give his father a chance to reply. "What about the surrender on demand clause?"

Sophie risked a glance at her father. His face was thunderous with rage. Her mother paled, but Adèle kept eating and drinking as if life was perfect.

"What's that?" her mother asked.

Jean-Pierre glanced at her. "It means Pétain and the rest of his minions must assist the Germans in tracking down so-called 'undesirables' and deporting them."

Papa's fist hitting the table made the dishes jump this time. Everyone stared at him.

"It's about time. There are too many foreigners in France; they took over the banking and the money, and everything else. They need to go back to where they came from."

"Papa!" Sophie stared at her father. "Some of them are French."

Her father held her gaze. "Not any more. They revoked their citizenships."

"Noël, darling, please stop shouting. The neighbours might

hear us. You know how every sound echoes through these apartments."

Sophie didn't think her father cared about the neighbours or anyone else. He believed every word of what he said. She hoped the Litwak family upstairs couldn't hear him. Her face burned with anger, but her stomach turned over with fear. If her father, an educated man by anyone's standards, could hold such horrible opinions, what hope was there?

She sent Jean-Pierre a look, begging him to calm down. She didn't want the day ruined. Her mother looked fit to cry. Zeldah stood stone-faced. Only Adèle seemed unaffected by the argument.

Jean-Pierre spoke again. "I do not wish to be disrespectful, but I can't agree with you. Pétain is taking away all our civil liberties. He even repealed the Marchandeau Decree."

Papa's face grew redder, if that was even possible. Sophie didn't think now was a good time to remind him of his blood pressure. He roared at Jean-Pierre. "How is that removing your liberty? Papers can now print the truth without risk of falling foul of ridiculous racial libel laws."

Sophie had heard enough. Papa had forgotten Zeldah was Jewish. "The papers you read blame the Jews for everything." Sophie gave up any pretence of eating. "What about Jules and his friends? They fought for France and are now dead."

Papa banged on the table again. "France was, and never will be, a country of Jews or Bolsheviks. You complain you cannot feed your patients. The people are starving. Why? Why are they starving? Because the Jews took everything. They stockpile goods and keep the food from the good French people."

Horrified, Sophie didn't know what to say. Zeldah left the room on some pretext.

Her mother put her napkin down. "Noël, please. Zeldah is Jewish."

Her father misinterpreted her mother's reprimand. "Yes, we must replace her. Look into that."

Sophie was glad papa's remark caused Adèle to stare at him in shock. So, her twin felt something. Sophie was about to make her excuses and leave, but papa spoke again.

"Now Zeldah isn't here. I can speak more freely."

Good grief, how much more hatred could he spread? Sophie wanted to put her hands over her ears and pretend she wasn't there. She caught the furious glint in Jean-Pierre's eyes.

"I do not want any of you children bringing shame to this house. Do you hear me? The name of Bélanger means something, and by the time we finish this war, it will mean even more. I want you to cut off all contact with any communists or other undesirables. If you intend living under my roof, you will abide by my rules."

Sophie and Jean-Pierre exchanged glances, but it was Adèle who spoke first.

"I don't know any communists, do I?" Adèle asked, her eyes wide. "I wouldn't associate with them. Not on purpose. They have some funny ideas. It's not possible for everyone to be equal."

"No, Adèle, I don't imagine you do." Papa smiled at her before glaring at his son. "Jean-Pierre does. Georges Monier and that awful mother of his. That man, Boris Vildé, you work with. You must consider your position, your reputation."

Jean-Pierre pushed back his chair, his eyes wild. He looked as if he wanted to throttle their father.

"Boris Vildé isn't a Frenchman, but he is my colleague and I am honoured if he sees me as his friend." Papa opened his mouth, but at a look from Jean-Pierre pursed his lips. "Georges is a close friend since we were boys and that won't change, despite his politics. France – the France I want to be a part of – celebrates our differences as people. It is a democracy where people are entitled to their opinions, to develop their beliefs, not fall in line with some idiotic brainwashed teachings based on nonsense."

"Jean-Pierre, this is my home."

Sophie guessed her brother didn't even hear their father's comment.

"Georges and I don't agree on everything, but I know he would be as shocked as I am to hear a Frenchman talk the way you have. Unlike you, he wouldn't be found dead eating in Lapérouse, surrounded by our enemies spouting rubbish."

Papa's eyes bulged but, stung by the criticism, Adèle retorted, "I like it. Nicolas used to take me there; it was so romantic."

"Nicolas, a French officer, would turn in his grave."

"Jean-Pierre, don't be coarse. Nicolas would expect me to live life for the both of us. His friends go to Lapérouse. The chef is wonderful, the food superb, and the piano player talented. Why shouldn't we eat there?" It was a rhetorical question, as she continued. "Georges Monier is an ignorant peasant. I haven't met his mother, but she is probably the same. How mémé tolerates her company is beyond me. You shouldn't see him, Jean-Pierre. Papa is right."

Jean-Pierre didn't look at Adèle. "I'm hardly likely to see Georges. He is in the unoccupied zone."

"Good!" Maman picked up her napkin, glancing from her husband to her son. "You should be careful about some of your other friends. You need to accept how it is now. I'm not saying I like the Germans here; I don't. But they are here now and there is nothing we can do about it. Now can we all please stop arguing and eat our dinner. It is getting cold."

Sophie's appetite had disappeared. She wanted to – no, needed to – get away from her family before she said things she'd regret. They had all forgotten Jules, even Jean-Pierre. She didn't have a grave to visit. She wasn't a widow. It was as if her beloved had never existed.

"I have to go back to the hospital. My apologies, maman."
She ignored the disappointment on her mother's face. Turning
to her father, she said, "I'm sorry, papa, but I agree with Jean-
Pierre. We can't just sit here and do nothing. Not while
Germany strips France of everything, including our national
pride. It is my duty as a doctor to treat people regardless of religion or background, or politics. I will not refuse to treat anyone
because people like Pétain, Laval, and his other minions believe
they are not deserving."

"You wouldn't treat a German, though, would you?" Adèle
taunted.

Sophie preferred not to answer that question. It was one she
had asked herself many times. But if she wanted to be a doctor,
she couldn't distinguish. "If his life was in danger and there was
nobody else, I would, but not out of choice."

Papa pushed back his chair so violently that it fell over. "I
was wrong to let you go to the American Hospital. Those
people have ruined you. Putting silly ideas in your head about
everyone being equal. You mark my words, girl. That doctor you
think so highly of will land you in trouble."

"That hospital received the Croix de Guerre with Palm,
papa! The French government thought highly of Dr Murphy
and the rest of the staff just weeks ago." Sophie pushed her plate
away. "Maman, I'm sorry, but I need to leave now before I say
something I'd regret."

Jean-Pierre stood up and followed her. "I will walk you
down to the end of the street. I need some air."

Together, they left their apartment. Sophie was tempted to
find Zeldah, but she was too afraid of dragging the girl into the
argument. The last thing she wanted was to push her father into
taking revenge. Zeldah needed a job.

"You are so brave, Sophie. If you were a man, you would be
a general."

Sophie linked arms with her brother. "I'm terrified. I can't believe papa believes all the horrible things he says. When will this nightmare end? Poor Zeldah. She must think we are all animals."

"I'll check on her when I get back, make sure she is all right. Zeldah knows you are her friend and always will be. Look after her. She isn't as brave as she makes out. I wish she would move to the unoccupied zone. I think it might be safer for Jews down there, but she won't leave her mother. The old lady wants her to go. They argue about it almost daily."

Surprised by his knowledge of the family life of their servant, Sophie was about to question him but they'd arrived at the station entrance.

"You'd best go back home. Thank you for walking with me. Try to avoid papa. When he is in a mood like this, he wouldn't listen to anyone. Not even the great Pétain himself."

Jean-Pierre grinned at her comment, gave her a quick hug, and turned back the way they had come.

She scurried down the steps into the métro. Someday, things would go back to normal. Whatever that was.

EIGHTEEN

DECEMBER 1940

The band played another waltz. Adèle smiled as Léo stood in front of her.

"Would you like to dance?"

"Léo, finally! I am very upset." Adèle brushed her fingertips along his shoulder as her eyes held his gaze.

"Sorry," he stammered, his eyes widening. "I asked Sophie to dance thinking it was you. The least you could do is warn me in advance what colour dress you'll be wearing."

She half turned away from him, her gaze scanning the rest of the room. "Don't pout, Léo. It's not attractive. I always wear bright colours. Pink and pastels are Sophie's colours. She likes the insipid look."

"Adèle, be nice. Your sister doesn't deserve that. She is gorgeous, as are you."

Adèle didn't respond, eager to avoid further discussion about her angelic sister. She twisted as her brother approached.

"We'd better head home soon. Don't want to get caught outside after curfew," Jean-Pierre reminded them. "Adèle, go and say your goodbyes."

"Jean-Pierre, I am not a child. Léo will walk me home. We

aren't ready to leave yet, are we, darling?" Adèle asked, caressing Léo's arm with her fingertips.

Léo didn't answer, and Jean-Pierre's expression darkened.

"Adèle, do not defy me. You are leaving now. Maman and papa left hours ago."

"Stop being such a girl, Jean-Pierre." Adèle's dismissive tone made her brother turn crimson.

"Adèle Bélanger, we are going home now. Do not make a scene. Collect your coat." Jean-Pierre's sharp retort stung. Though he was younger than the twins, when their father wasn't present, Jean-Pierre took his role as the man of the family seriously.

Before Adèle could reply, Léo answered for her.

"We are leaving now. I will walk Adèle home, Jean-Pierre."

"We will all walk together. We are safer in a group."

Safer! Her brother was such an old woman. France was their country. They should be able to walk where they liked, when they liked. She opened her mouth, but shut it again at the murderous expression on Jean-Pierre's face. If he told their father she had disgraced their family name by causing a scene, he might make her stay home like her mother wanted. To live out her widowhood dressed in black, knitting or something equally as boring. She needed to stay on her father's good side.

Léo came back with her coat and helped her into it, the touch of his hands on her bare arms sending delicious chills through her. Pity Jean-Pierre was walking with them. He wouldn't stand for any kissing or cuddling. Honestly, with the efforts her brother took to protect her honour, you would think they'd promised her to a convent. She'd been married after all!

"Where is Sophie?" she asked.

"She left ages ago with Bruno." Jean-Pierre's short tone irritated her.

"You let our sister walk home with Bruno, yet you have to escort me?"

"Like Léo, Bruno is a man of honour. But unlike you, Sophie is trustworthy. Let's go."

She resisted the temptation to stick her tongue out at him.

Adèle and Léo joined Jean-Pierre, Louis, Adam, and a few other friends as they walked home. Her feet hurt as she tried to keep up with the pace set by Jean-Pierre and the others. They wouldn't be walking so fast if they were wearing heels. Why couldn't they have taken the car? Jean-Pierre kept a closer eye on their limited ration of petrol than the Germans did. He would make a good German officer with his rules and regulations.

They were practically at the train station, less than twenty minutes' walk from her home, when Léo came to a sudden stop.

"*Merde!*"

She glanced up at Léo's curse. She hadn't spotted the Wehrmacht soldiers moving towards them. Judging by their raucous sounds and lumbering gait, they were drunk.

"Adèle, go with Jean-Pierre now. He will take you home safely. I will see you on Wednesday." Léo kissed the side of her head before pushing her gently towards Jean-Pierre.

"I want you to walk me home."

"I want that too, chérie, but another time. Tonight is—" But the soldiers shouting cut off what he was about to say. One soldier reached out towards Adèle, saying something in German. She couldn't hear what he was saying, so didn't understand his slurred words, but Jean-Pierre did, and he replied in perfect German. The look of surprise on the soldier's face was classic. One of the soldier's colleagues stumbled into Louis, who pushed him away. A different soldier retaliated by punching Adam, who reacted instinctively and hit him back. Whistles blew.

"Adèle, go now. Jean-Pierre, take her. Go."

Léo got dragged into the fight.

Adèle didn't have time to say goodbye as her brother half-shoved, half-pulled her away. The heel of her shoe gave way, but Jean-Pierre didn't listen to her protests. They could hear whistles as more soldiers arrived on the scene. Jean-Pierre pushed her through the door of the closest hotel, announcing himself to the concierge d'hôtel as they entered.

"Monsieur, it is almost curfew, we are closed," the man said. He looked apologetic but remained firm, holding the door to encourage them to leave.

"We need a room for the night. They hurt my sister." Jean-Pierre pulled a bundle of francs from his pocket. Adèle saw the glint of greed in the concierge's eyes. He ushered them inside, closing the door behind them, his expression warm.

"Bien sûr." The concierge had only one room left, but he took their names and gave Jean-Pierre the key.

"I need to telephone our home."

"This is not possible. I am sorry, but the Germans..." The concierge was so servile, Adèle half-expected to see him lick Jean-Pierre's boots.

Frustration made Adèle turn away, and she looked out the window. The moon hid behind some clouds. She couldn't see or hear any soldiers or gendarmes in the street outside. They could have kept going until they reached home. There she would have had a warm bath and her own bed, but Jean-Pierre had to ruin everything, as usual.

Crumpled and furious with Jean-Pierre, Adèle didn't sleep all night. He insisted on sleeping on the sofa in their room, in case anything else were to happen. Her honour, her reputation, was at stake.

* * *

They arrived home early the next morning, creeping past the *loge*, hoping Madame Garnier wouldn't come out. Jean-Pierre put his key in the apartment door. "If we're lucky, maman will have slept through the night and we can pretend we did too."

But luck was against them. Their mother was at the door of the sitting room, she must have heard the door.

"Adèle, Jean-Pierre! My children! I was so worried." Her mother's whiny tone infuriated her; she was constantly fussing over them.

"We are fine, maman. We stayed in a hotel because of the curfew." Adèle walked into the sitting room, warming her hands at the remains of the fire. Her parents must have stayed up all night.

Her mother followed. "Why did you leave the party so late? Sophie was home on time. Papa told you not to stay too long."

Adèle didn't answer her mother, assuming this was another one of her rhetorical questions. Next would come the lecture about her behaviour and the family name. She adopted her usual mask of indifference as her mother twittered on and on. Papa walked into the room, but rather than the stern expression she was expecting, his face flushed with impatience.

"Jean-Pierre, thank God you are home. Léo's father has called several times. He is taking our old acquaintance for granted. Léo is a grown man, an engineer. What was he doing at the party, anyway? I wouldn't have thought he was of the same social standing."

"Léo has been a friend of ours for years." Adèle caught herself. Why was she standing up for Léo when he'd told her off last night?

"Léo never made it home; was he not with you?" papa asked Jean-Pierre, a hard look in his eyes. His hand rubbed his moustache before he lit up another cigarette. He ignored Adèle, leaving her in no doubt that she was in his bad books. That didn't sit well with her. She'd always been able to wind her father around her little finger.

"He was, papa, but we ran into some trouble," Jean-Pierre replied.

"What sort of trouble?" Her father's haughty tone told Adèle he was more than angry with them. Was there a hint of fear in his voice? What could he be afraid of?

"Some drunk off-duty soldiers. They made some disgusting remarks. Léo stayed with the others while I got Adèle away."

Her father gave her a look before turning to stare into the fire. "Disgusting behaviour. I shall complain to the officer. He said his men would behave in our streets."

"He's German. Since when have they ever told the truth?" Jean-Pierre asked.

"Jean-Pierre! Have some respect!" Their mother's voice shook with emotion as she visibly swayed before taking a seat. "Your grandmother and I are German, as are some of our closest friends. Please do not dismiss the entire German population because of the antics of a few bad eggs."

"Sorry, maman."

Adèle could see her brother was far from sorry, but he wasn't willing to upset their mother. Their grandmother had been born in Berlin, but had moved to France as a young girl where she had met Adèle's grandfather.

Her father ground out the cigarette into the ashtray. "Adèle, go to your room. We will discuss your behaviour this evening. Jean-Pierre, take a bath and change. Then we will find out more about what has happened to Léo."

"Yes, papa," Jean-Pierre answered. He glared at Adèle, pulling her towards the door. She read his warning not to push their parents further, but she ignored it.

She turned to her father. "I am sorry. I was having so much fun I lost track of time. I know I was silly, but it's just ... with the war and everything, we never get to get dressed up and have a good time any more. I promise to be good next time."

Her father glowered at her, but she kept the innocent look

on her face. After a few moments, her tactic worked. The glare dropped away as he smiled benevolently at her, opening his arms to envelop her in a hug.

"Darling, trouble always finds you." She ignored the stink of tobacco as he kissed the top of her head. "We were worried when you didn't return from the wedding. Go to bed and have a couple of hours' sleep, sweetheart, you look drained."

Somehow, his change of heart irritated her rather than placated her. She wasn't a baby.

She didn't want to go to bed. Hungry and curious about what had happened to Léo, she wanted to stay awake. If he had gone on to a forbidden party without her, she would be cross.

"Can I please have breakfast first?"

Papa smiled. "Zeldah will have something for you. Go and ask her."

Her mother glared at her before turning to her father.

"Noël, please. The girl put herself and Jean-Pierre in danger. You should reprimand her."

Adèle stood waiting for her father to reply. She didn't trust herself to be civil to her mother, who was always interfering and trying to make her life more miserable.

"Adèle, go and get something to eat." Papa's tone was final.

Adèle couldn't resist giving her mother a triumphant look as her father ignored his wife. Glancing at Jean-Pierre to make sure he caught her smug expression, she headed to the kitchen in search of Zeldah. If she didn't get something to eat soon, her stomach would growl, and that would never do.

* * *

Sophie waited in the kitchen until Adèle came in. She was dying to know what had happened, but she wasn't about to risk her parents' wrath by entering the sitting room. Instead, she sat impatiently in the kitchen with Zeldah. It took her a while to notice Zeldah's nails bitten to the quick. Looking at her face, she saw the dark circles under her eyes, her cheekbones more prominent than ever. Zeldah could eat whatever they ate, so why did she look half-starved and upset?

"Are you all right, Zeldah? You look upset today."

"I'm fine."

Zeldah's red-rimmed eyes begged to differ. Sophie pulled her old friend down to sit beside her at the kitchen table.

"Tell me what's wrong. Maybe I can help."

Zeldah's eyes darted to the closed door. "Your mother doesn't like it when I get too familiar."

Since when did the younger girl worry about Sophie's mother? Maybe papa's outburst about the Jews had affected her worse than she'd realised. She hadn't been paying attention to the younger girl, too caught up in grieving over Jules, worrying about the hospital and everyone else.

She held Zeldah's hand. "My mother isn't here. So, tell me, what's wrong?"

One tear made its way down Zeldah's cheek. "Oh, Sophie."

She put her arms around Zeldah and held her as she cried, her shuddering shoulders almost breaking Sophie's heart. What had happened?

When Zeldah seemed to have spent her tears, Sophie stood to get the coffee pot, glad for once that her father had contacts on the black market and insisted on real coffee. She poured two cups, one for herself and one for Zeldah, despite the girl's protests about not being allowed to drink it.

"Don't be ridiculous. Maman didn't mean you couldn't have coffee. She just said we all needed to use it sparingly."

That wasn't the whole truth, and they both knew it, but ignored it for now.

"I dislike what I am hearing about my people. Things have been bad for them in Germany since that devil Hitler came into power. But..."

"But?" Sophie's heart sank. She hoped Zeldah hadn't heard the same things she had, the horrible stories that came by word of mouth from the streams of refugees that passed through on their way to the unoccupied zone.

"Sophie, the news coming from Poland is even worse. It's beyond believable. They are moving entire villages into ghettos. Why would they do that? Forcing people to leave their homes and jobs and move into the bigger cities." Zeldah held a hanky in her hands, screwing it up as she spoke. "My grandparents wrote to say they had to leave their house in the countryside. My grandfather was born there! He hates the city, being an animal lover. But the Germans, they came and threw him out. No notice. They ordered him and Grandmother to move to Krakow to the Jewish quarter. His letter took over a year to reach us." Zeldah buried her face in her hands, tears streaming down her cheeks.

Sophie wondered how their maid had received a letter... There was no post any more.

"I'm sorry."

"What will happen to them? They are old and have little money. They could have made some if they sold the farm, but it was all taken. Everything. Even Grandmother's wedding ring. We wouldn't know anything about it but a friend of theirs smuggled their letter into France when they crossed the border. They took a great risk, but for nothing. We can't help, can't even write back to them."

Sophie clamped down the fear and revulsion building inside her. What sort of men treated vulnerable old people so harshly? She sought to reassure her friend.

"Don't worry. Your mother is safe and so are you. That won't happen here. You are as French as I am. The Germans have behaved well. It will be fine."

"What will be fine, and why is Zeldah snivelling?" Adèle asked as she walked into the kitchen.

Zeldah stood up and moved to the kitchen sink, rubbing her eyes while keeping her back to Adèle.

"Adèle, be nice. Zeldah has had bad news about her grandparents. They live in Poland."

Adèle briefly glanced at Zeldah but didn't offer sympathy. In true Adèle style, she sat down and complained about her stomach. "Oh. Zeldah, I need coffee. Is it hot? Is there any bread?"

"Yes, madame. It will take just a minute to heat," Zeldah replied. She didn't turn around.

Sophie wanted to slap her sister for her obvious lack of empathy, but she knew it was pointless. Adèle would never change. Zeldah insisted on addressing Adèle formally, calling Adèle "madame" even though Sophie thought it ridiculous.

Zeldah didn't look up as she asked, "Would you not prefer to eat in the dining room, madame?"

"No, it's freezing in there. I'm avoiding maman; I don't need another of her boring lectures."

"Adèle..." Sophie had enough. Adèle wasn't in the slightest bit worried about the effect of her actions on her family. "Maman was up all night, worried sick about you. We all were. Why didn't you come home?"

"Jean-Pierre insisted we stay at a hotel. He is such an old woman."

Sophie caught the dirty look Zeldah sent Adèle, but thankfully her sister was too busy examining her nails to see it. She spoke up for her brother. "He is not. He must have thought you were in danger. What happened?"

Sophie couldn't believe her ears when her sister told her about the encounter with the Germans. She didn't know what was worse: that her sister had come so close to danger, or she seemed to believe she was the only one affected by what happened. All Adèle seemed interested in was her manicure.

Sophie tried to stay patient. "Where did Léo go?"

Her twin waved her hand in dismissal. "I don't know. He told me to go with Jean-Pierre." Her chin jutted out as she added, "He'll be sorry. I won't be friendly to him for at least a week."

"Adèle! Sometimes I could slap you. Léo is a lovely man who was protecting you. Why are you so selfish?"

"Oh, don't you start." Adèle turned her back on Sophie. "Zeldah, is that food ready yet? I'm so hungry I could eat a horse."

Zeldah didn't say a word as she put the plate in front of Adèle. Embarrassed when her sister didn't acknowledge the servant, Sophie thanked her on Adèle's behalf. Zeldah pursed her lips but didn't comment on the rudeness. When they were all youngsters playing out on the Bélanger country estate, Zeldah often called Adèle spoiled and bad-tempered. Back then, she could say what she thought. The children believed they were equals. But as they grew older, the differences between them became clearer, and not just in looks.

Zeldah was as dark as Adèle and Sophie were fair. Sophie thought she was gorgeous, with her emerald-green eyes and jet-black hair. Her skin had a faint tan all year round, not just in the summer. She was as beautiful on the inside as she was on the outside. She had hoped for a career in nursing, but her father wanted something more appropriate for his only daughter. Then Zeldah's parents had had an accident; her father died, and her mother was left with severe injuries. Zeldah had taken over her mama's duties as their servant, giving up all hopes of nursing.

Hospital! Oh, now she would be late. Another thing to thank Adèle for.

"I have to go. I will be late for my shift."

"Ugh, I can't believe you're serious about being a doctor. I thought that was just a phase. All those nasty germs."

Sophie lost what little patience she had left. "Sick people,

Adèle, need care and understanding. I want to be the best doctor I can be. Dr Murphy thinks I have potential."

"He would. He thinks you walk on water. But then so does everyone else."

Hurt, Sophie turned away, not wanting Adèle to see the effect of her harsh tone. But then she was surprised to find herself wrapped in her sister's arms.

"Forgive me. I'm sorry for being such a cat. I need sleep."

Sophie returned the embrace. "You do. See you later." She could never stay annoyed with Adèle for long. She gave Zeldah a quick hug, too. "I will call to see your mama later."

"She would love that. Thank you, Sophie."

Sophie smiled before hurrying to find her mother to say goodbye. She hoped the métro was running on time and she could find a space. Since the Germans had taken their supply of petrol, more French used the métro than ever before, leading to overcrowding and delays.

NINETEEN

"That didn't hurt too much, lady – I mean, Doctor," the RAF pilot said. His face was only marginally more colourful than the surrounding sheets.

"You will be fine, Pilot Officer Cullen. Just do what the nurses say."

The young man's eyes filled with tears. He turned his head. She guessed he didn't want her to see him losing his grip.

"We'll do our best to get you home."

"I don't mean to be a sissy, but you should have seen them. My mate. He put his arms up and surrendered. They didn't care. They... I thought they had to treat us properly."

Elizabeth had told her how the Germans had found the crashed plane. The pilot had been thrown clear and was rescued by a farmer close by. They had to hide and watch the Germans torture his co-pilot. The other man had refused to give up his friend, telling the Germans the pilot died in the crash. He had paid the ultimate price.

"They should have. Your friend was very brave. When you get back to London, you can tell his family that. For now, you must rest. I will give you something to help you sleep."

He nodded. It didn't take long for the drugs to take effect. She glanced up in time to see Dr Murphy watching her. He came closer.

"Good work, Sophie. Thank you for taking over in my place. I'm sure those fly boys preferred seeing a pretty face to my ugly mug."

"My pleasure." Sophie smiled at her mentor before turning her gaze back to the young pilot, who was now sound asleep. "He's just eighteen and saw his friend murdered. Will we be able to get him out?"

"I hope so. It's becoming more difficult, but we have some good friends in high places. You look tired." He took her arm and led her away from the ward. "You shouldn't cover for me again, though. The less involved you are with that ward, the better."

"Because they are all escapees? I am not afraid. I want to help. It makes living a little easier."

"Jules would be proud of how you are coping." His gentle tone and the pity in his eyes were too much to bear.

Sophie shook her head, her eyes filling up. She forced herself to concentrate on his words.

He scratched his chin. "We have to get more supplies for the hospital. Our priority is feeding the two hundred and fifty patients under our care. Even with the best efforts of our amazing kitchen staff, that is proving difficult."

"Yes, I know, but what can we do?"

"I don't know, but we must do something. The Germans cannot expect people to survive on twelve hundred calories a day. It is just madness. As for the elderly, what an insult. Those people have worked all their lives and now, when they should rest and enjoy their twilight years, those savages want to starve them. Nobody can survive on eight hundred and fifty calories."

Sophie didn't answer. What could she say? He was right. But the Germans weren't likely to change their minds, and even if they did, where would the food come from? They had stripped the shops bare. It was as if a field of locusts had descended on Paris, devouring every morsel in sight.

Dr Murphy stood tall and straight-backed as usual, but his eyes were dull with large black circles under them.

"Why don't you go home to your family? We can manage here."

"Thank you. I think I will do just that. But first I must give blood."

"You can't. I insist, as a doctor." Her boss had been thin and pale even before the war had started, but now he looked gaunt. "You gave blood yesterday, and I suspect two days before that. You are vital to the well-being of this hospital and I refuse to let you risk your health. You could pass out during surgery and put our patients at risk." She knew she had to frame her concern in terms of the patients to make him listen. "There are others who can give blood. Now go home."

"Yes, ma'am." Dr Murphy saluted her, a grin on his face, then he turned and left. He was an amazing individual, doing all he did for everyone in need, especially since, being American, he and his family could have left for safety long ago. She had always adored him, not least as he had championed her efforts to become a doctor. In a country where she wasn't allowed to vote, it was nice to encounter a professional who believed she could become a doctor. She took a seat and began writing up her notes on each patient.

Footsteps interrupted her.

"What are you doing back?" Sophie looked up from her work and smiled. "I thought I told you to go home." Her smile died at the pallor of his face. "What's wrong?"

"What are your plans for tonight?" he asked.

"I'm on duty for another two hours." She didn't have time to say another word as he interrupted.

"Make sure you go straight home. Don't go near the Arc de Triomphe. There's already been trouble."

Sophie's skin chilled and her stomach felt heavy. "But we always march to celebrate the anniversary of the end of World War I. Why would they stop us?"

"The Germans have banned any demonstrations. The morning was fairly quiet; the German military police presence was enough to move most people along. Mainly students and whatnot. They arrested one of my friends. Someone just told me he had a rosette in the colours of the French flag pinned to his jacket. He's a science teacher, for goodness' sake, not an agitator. He had left his flowers at the Tomb of the Unknown Soldier and, on his way back to school, met some of his students. The police arrested him. They seem to think he was encouraging the youngsters to riot."

"Was he?"

"Not from what I heard. In fact, he seems to have done the opposite. One of his students told me Caullé told them to lay flowers if they wished but to go home."

"Why did they arrest him?"

Dr Murphy looked sheepish. "Caullé may have given the Germans a lecture on what it means to be French. I believe he was, shall we say, slightly less than polite. Basically, he told them it was his patriotic duty."

"And they arrested him? What will they do to him?"

Dr Murphy looked grave. "Hopefully, they won't make an example of him. There are more protesters gathering as we speak. I cannot risk having you or any of the hospital staff caught up in that mess. We do not need any more attention. It's too dangerous."

He looked so earnest, she couldn't say no to him.

"I will go straight home, I promise. Now, will you please go home to your family?"

"I hate to give you orders but we must protect the hospital from all suspicion."

Sophie agreed, feeling ill at how close she had come to getting caught up in the trouble he expected. She had planned to meet Jean-Pierre and attend the march. She would keep her word to Dr Murphy, but even though he had good intentions, she would be lying if she said it did not bother her being told to go home. This was her country, not Germany, and she should be allowed to honour France's war dead.

Maybe Dr Murphy was fussing over nothing. The Germans had been pleasant so far. They wouldn't hurt a group of students. Then Elizabeth claimed her attention and Dr Murphy's warning was pushed to the back of her mind. Her annoyance fled as she immersed herself in looking after their patients.

* * *

Adèle woke her the next morning coming into her bedroom, dressed in her silk bedgown, hair flowing over her shoulders, marks of her pillow still evident on her face.

"Have you heard from Jean-Pierre?"

Sophie pushed herself out of bed in response to the worried tone in Adèle's voice.

"No, why? I assumed he was in bed."

Adèle pulled her robe tighter around her. "There was lots of trouble last night. Madame Garnier just told me when she dropped the post up. I'm surprised you didn't hear her at the door ... and where is Zeldah?"

Sophie dismissed the jibe over Zeldah being late. "What did the concierge say?"

"The Germans stopped the march and arrested over one hundred students. You don't think he'd have been caught up with them, do you?"

A shiver crept down her spine, but she kept her fears to herself. "Of course not. Jean-Pierre is more cautious than that. He's probably gone to work. Anyway, you know what Madame Garnier is like – she always sees the worst in everything."

Adèle didn't look convinced, but Sophie made her excuses about having to get to the hospital.

She hurried there, and found the talk was all about the previous night's events. It was true, the Germans had arrested some students who'd taken part in the peaceful march. They had released some without charge. But they had transferred others to the Fresnes, La Santé and Cherche-Midi prisons. Rumours circulated that the student prisoners had been beaten and threatened with execution by firing squad.

Oliver's nephew, Victor, was holding court in the canteen. A group of nursing staff, including Elizabeth, clustered around his table. "I was there. I saw everything. Us young people had no chance."

"What do you mean?" Sophie asked.

"We started singing 'La Marseillaise' and people were shouting 'Vive la France' and stuff like that. The gendarmes made no effort to stop the manifestation. They were not in uniform.

"But then people noticed these covered trucks. They had parked around the area of the Tomb. All at once, German soldiers armed with fixed bayonets charged the crowd. I tell you, I saw them for myself. Aiming them at the youngsters. The young people split in all directions, but when one of those Germans started hitting a girl, two or three of the boys turned back. They gave that soldier the kicking of his life. I wanted to join in, but I kept hearing Dr Murphy telling me not to bring attention to the hospital."

"He also told you to stay away from the march," Elizabeth said.

Victor didn't skip a beat. "They dragged the students off to different prisons. I made myself scarce. But a friend, she works as a cleaner at Cherche-Midi, she said they were treated like criminals. They had to stand in the rain all night before the Germans really started on them. They beat them up, but it seems not one student gave out any names. I guess it wasn't an organised demonstration, was it? I mean we march every year. It's our duty as Frenchmen."

Elizabeth raised her eyebrows. "And women."

"Naturally." He dismissed her comment with a wave of his hand.

"What will happen now?" someone asked. "To those youngsters."

"You can't walk on the Champs-Élysées any more, nor in the Latin Quarter. You must have a permit and that is only given to those who live there."

"Oh *merde*," muttered someone. Sophie didn't want to hear any more.

A nurse looked up. "Anyone still thinking the Germans are pleasant?"

Sophie couldn't answer. Her thoughts were on Zeldah and what she had said about her grandparents, Yvette and her experiences at the farm, and the night Adèle had been involved in an altercation. Maybe Sophie had been naïve in thinking things would soon return to normal.

Troubled, Sophie sought to distract herself from the bad news by checking on her patients. One female patient, whose visitors had just left, was distressed. Sophie sat by her bed.

"My grandson is in Fresnes Prison. Marc is a good boy; he did nothing. What will they do to him?"

"I am sure they will release him soon. He will be back in university before you know it." Sophie crossed her fingers as she sought to reassure the old woman.

"Haven't you heard? The Sorbonne is closed, and the students must report to the Germans every day, or maybe it was every second day." The woman picked at her bedcovers, her agitated state making her more confused. "What will they do next?"

Sophie didn't want to think about the answer to that question. Elizabeth came over to help calm the patient down, then insisted Sophie have something to eat.

"That poor lady, worrying about her grandson." Sophie's heart was racing, her legs feeling weak with fear. Every person seemed to have a worse story to tell. Elizabeth didn't help.

"She has reason to be worried. My niece was arrested too, but they sent her home. She has to sign in at the Kommandantur every morning."

"Why?"

"She is a hostage. The Germans have told her, if Frenchmen kill any of their men, they will kill twenty of the hostages."

Sophie's stomach was rock-hard. "Oh, my goodness, you must be going out of your mind. Can't Langeron do anything to help her get to the free zone?"

"I thought about it, but she won't go. If she doesn't sign in, they will come for my brother and his wife. But I have another plan."

Sophie didn't question her friend. She was still reeling. The Boches had just given them a glimpse of what they were prepared to do to keep the population in check.

* * *

Sophie bought a newspaper on her way home, but there was nothing in it about the students. You would think people had imagined the whole thing. She hoped Jean-Pierre was at home by now. Her brother wasn't a student, but he was a patriot and had powerful feelings about the occupiers. She pulled her coat closer around her shoulders. The tense atmosphere in the métro didn't help. Nobody was talking, just staring at a space somewhere above the heads or at their shoes. She bit her lip, trying to keep her emotions under control. She didn't want to cry in front of anyone.

Once home, she took a deep breath and pushed the door open. Her mother was sitting by the fireplace, knitting, her needles clicking away, but her mind was obviously elsewhere. She didn't look up and started when Sophie leaned in to kiss her on the cheek.

"Chérie, you gave me a fright. Oh, you are so cold. Let me ring for Zeldah to make you something to eat and a hot drink."

"No, maman. I can look after myself. How are you? You look troubled." Sophie assessed her mother with a professional eye. She had lost weight, but so had everyone in Paris. But it wasn't that. It was the expression in her eyes. A mixture of fear and bleakness. A chill ran down Sophie's spine.

"What's wrong?" Sophie asked, not wanting to ask if Jean-Pierre was home, in case he wasn't, for fear of adding to her mother's pain.

"Nothing for you to worry about, my darling." Her mother's smile was forced, but Sophie had learned long ago not to push her mother when she didn't want to talk. "I haven't told you in a long time: Sophie, I'm proud of you."

That worried her even more. Her mother never complimented her children.

"Can I get you something, maman? A coffee?"

"No, thank you, darling, I think I will go to bed. You should too, after you've eaten. You look tired. Papa and Adèle have gone out." The word "again" was left unspoken.

Sophie rearranged the perfectly straight cushions on the sofa. "What about Jean-Pierre?"

"He's in the kitchen, I think. Zeldah made him something to eat. He said he was too busy at work today to eat anything. I worry about that boy. He's out at that museum all the time. He would forget his head some days."

Sophie smiled, but a voice inside her head wondered if it was work that had kept her younger brother occupied all day. She said goodnight to her mother and made her way towards the kitchen. The warmth of the room was wonderfully inviting, but somehow, she felt like she was intruding. Zeldah and Jean-Pierre were sitting at the table, chatting intensely, when she opened the door. They stopped as soon as they saw her and then Zeldah jumped up, offering to make her something to eat.

"I wasn't expecting you home, Sophie. I thought you would be at the hospital all night. What with the problems yesterday." Zeldah spoke much too quickly, as if to cover the awkward silence that had descended with Sophie's entrance.

"Please sit down and continue your conversation. I can look after myself. Jean-Pierre, I am so glad to see you here. I was worried."

"I can look after myself, big sister."

"I know you can, but the stories I've heard today... They were just awful."

"Yes, we were talking about that, weren't we?" Zeldah nudged Jean-Pierre. Sensing they'd been discussing something more private, Sophie made an excuse and left, her appetite having disappeared.

TWENTY

Shattered, Adèle snuggled under her covers, but she couldn't sleep. Every time she closed her eyes, she relived the events of the night of the party. It had been over two weeks since she had heard from Léo.

He was taking this too far. The least he could do was send a note or call to say he was all right. It was most inconvenient of him to play games right now. She was surprised to find she missed him. At first, she thought it would be nice to upset her father by dating an ordinary worker. Léo made her laugh and she loved the fact he was no pushover. Not that she ever told him. She liked the men in her life to fight for her affections. It kept them on their toes.

What if Léo was in trouble? No, that couldn't be it. Jean-Pierre would have heard something and told her.

She tossed and turned before giving in and getting up again. Maybe it was time for her to visit her grandmother, but that meant going to Lyon. It would show Léo that she wasn't hanging around waiting for him to show up.

The old lady had moved to Paris when she'd married, but after Grandfather had died, she'd spent more time in Lyon and moved there permanently in June. She'd said being in Paris with the Germans around would depress her. Odd, given that mémé herself was German.

Adèle checked her mother's bedroom and the kitchen before finding her sitting, writing in her journal at her desk in the living room. The fire was set but unlit. "Maman, there you are. I have been searching everywhere for you."

Her mother cocked an eyebrow. "Nonsense. Our home isn't a mansion. Must you always be so dramatic?"

"Sorry." Adèle picked up a piece of paper, moving it from hand to hand. She should just write that on her forehead. She didn't seem to say anything else these days. "I thought I might visit mémé."

Her mother took off her glasses; she only wore them if she absolutely had to. She hated admitting to getting old. Her piercing blue eyes assessed Adèle, immediately making her remember the time her mother had caught her under the kitchen table, eating an entire *pain de mie*. The soft bread made with milk was her favourite snack but she'd still pretended to be Sophie. Her mother had seen straight through her back then, just as she suspected her now. "Why?"

"What? I want to see her. Do I have to have another reason?" Adèle liked her grandmother, who behaved as if she were royalty. The old lady didn't care what other people thought of her or her opinions. She was honest to the point of bluntness, such fun to be around provided Adèle wasn't the focus of her outrage, and an insatiable supply of gossip. As she thought of her grandmother, she realised she genuinely wanted to see her. She frowned. She was fed up with being on her own. Sophie and Jean-Pierre were busy every day but she was twiddling her thumbs at home. It would be a pleasant distraction from the tension in this household, and Adèle would just put up with Lyon for a few days. She could imagine the look on Léo's face when he came to see her, only to find her out of town. Maybe then he would be more considerate of her feelings.

Her mother stood up, almost knocking over the chair. Her hands gripped it, replacing it at the desk, her white knuckles in stark contrast to the dark wood. "Don't be impertinent, Adèle." Maman snapped before she wiped a hand across her forehead. Only then did Adèle notice the dark circles under her mother's eyes, the slight shake of her hand. "Your grandmother hasn't been feeling very well for a while now. Not since she moved to the small apartment. You should let her rest."

"But, maman, that means I should go see her. I could help her."

She took a step back at the dirty look her mother threw her.

"How? Your nursing skills are laughable. You will only put pressure on the household, expect the servants to cater for your every whim."

Adèle wanted to protest, but her mother hadn't finished.

"No, you need to stay here."

Adèle couldn't understand the fleeting look of terror on her mother's face. But she didn't have time to push for an answer. Just then, they heard the apartment door opening and footsteps in the hall. Her mother froze, staring at the sitting room door until it opened, admitting her father and brother. Both looked grim.

"Noël, Jean-Pierre. What's wrong?"

Adèle studied their faces for the reaction to her mother's question. Her father walked over to the cabinet and poured himself a drink, which disappeared in one gulp. Jean-Pierre sat in a chair, one hand rubbing his forehead as if he had a headache. His eyes weren't focused on anyone, but clouded with fear. Adèle's heart beat faster, wanting to hear the answer to her mother's question but yet at the same time trying to ignore the urge to run and hide in her bedroom.

Her father looked at a space above his wife's head. "We found Léo. The Germans arrested him."

Her mother paled as she fell into the chair, biting her clenched white knuckles. Adèle glanced at her mother. They couldn't both fall apart. She forced herself to speak confidently. "For what, papa?"

He turned away and poured another drink. "Assaulting a German officer. The night of the party."

"But he didn't assault anyone! That was someone else, and it was the soldier's fault," Adèle protested. "The German pushed into the Frenchman." She addressed her brother. "Did you tell them that?"

He stood up before replying. "They know, but they don't care. They want Léo to tell them the names of the friends he was with. But he won't."

A knot formed in her stomach. "Why? He is being silly. I shall get my coat and tell them myself."

Adèle gasped as her mother grabbed her arm. "You can't do that."

"Why not?" Adèle noticed the atmosphere, the undercurrent. Something else was going on and she wasn't sure what. Her parents exchanged a look before her father shook his head. She turned her attention to Jean-Pierre; he just stared back at her. He knew. Whatever it was, she was the only one in the dark.

Resisting the urge to stamp her foot, she repeated, "Why not?"

Her father crossed his arms. "Leave it alone."

"I am not a child. What is going on?"

Her mother slapped Adèle across the face. "A child would behave better! Your selfish, self-centred behaviour has put us all at risk, you stupid girl! If you'd behaved like the widow you are and not like a, like a..." She pressed her fist against her mouth as if trying to prevent a horrible name from spewing out.

Adèle reared back from her mother in shock. Her mother looked like she hated her. She didn't approve of Adèle spending time with Léo, but this was something more.

Papa looked at her sternly. "Leave us. Go to your room."

Adèle's cheek burned but she wasn't running away. At least not until she knew what they were talking about. "No, papa. I want to know what is going on. Anyone would think you were hiding something." His refusal to meet her eyes caused her stomach to turn over. What could be so awful? She gave her brother a beseeching look.

Jean-Pierre walked over to the fire. "You might as well tell her. She won't listen otherwise."

Despite the early hour, there was a chill in the air, and the small fire was not giving out much heat. Since the Germans had come, it was almost impossible to find fuel. Her father had resorted to buying it on the black market, but the family still had to be careful about how much they used.

"Adèle, sit down."

"Papa?"

"Don't upset your mother more than you have already."

Adèle sat. Her mother was crying, not noisily but in a dainty, ladylike way. The tears terrified Adèle. Her mother never cried. She considered public shows of emotion to be vulgar.

"You cannot get involved in helping Léo, at least not publicly. We cannot risk drawing attention to ourselves." Her father spoke without looking at her.

"Why not? What have we to be afraid of? It's not like you have done anything against the Germans." Even as she asked, she knew it was ridiculous. Her father wouldn't put himself out for another person, let alone la belle France. He hadn't fought in the first war. He had blamed ill health for that, although he had never been sick a day in his life. What could he have to fear?

"Afraid of the Germans? Don't be absurd." Papa looked to the picture of Pétain hanging over the fireplace. The silence became uncomfortable, broken only by the sobs from her mother. Jean-Pierre stared at the floor.

She prompted, "So why?"

"Because your mother has discovered she is... Well, it appears she isn't what she thought she was."

Adèle glanced at her mother, but she had buried her head in her hands.

"You are not making sense." Adèle stared at her father with wide eyes and fought to keep her voice steady. Her stomach roiled with the undercurrents in the room. Something bad was happening, but she didn't understand what. Jean-Pierre looked up and held her gaze.

"She is a Jew."

Adèle forced her knees together to stop her legs from shaking, her body turning cold. She couldn't have been more stunned if her brother had announced that their mother was a man. "What? How?"

"Your mother has withheld information from us. Your grandmother came clean last June. She's been living a lie. Your grandmother was born—" papa stopped speaking.

Adèle looked at her father, who sounded like he was reading from a newspaper. There was no emotion in his voice, no anger or distress. That scared her even more.

"I am Jewish." Her mother's voice, weak at first, grew stronger. With a rebellious glance at her husband, she continued. "At least according to the rules of my mother's religion."

"Why keep it a secret until now?" Adèle couldn't believe her beloved grandmother had lied to her.

"Is that why she left Paris?" Sophie asked. "Because of a lie?"

Adèle turned at the sound of her twin's voice. She hadn't noticed her come into the room.

Their father nodded before saying, "Someone, a so-called friend, called upon her a few months ago to remind her that her Jewish background wasn't so secret. She decided rather than pay this 'friend' the extortionate amount she was asking, she would just come clean and tell your mother. Your mother told her to go and live in Lyon. She didn't seem to think it was her duty to tell me."

Adèle ran her hands through her hair. "She should have just paid the friend off." Papa had to be wrong. She would know if she was one of them.

Sophie put her arm around her mother's shoulders. "Poor mémé must have felt so alone with pépé dead."

Adèle kept her eyes on their father until her mother spoke. Her voice wavered.

"The Germans may have records. Everyone knows how organised they are, and she assumed they could unmask her. Your grandmother says she told us now so we could protect our family." Her mother fidgeted with her hands, her gaze locked on her husband. Adèle thought she looked afraid, but of what? She glanced at her father.

His lips thinned as he forced the words out. "She became a Catholic when she married your grandfather."

"She loved pépé, and he worshipped the ground she walked on," Sophie said. "They were happy together."

Adèle couldn't believe her sister was harping on about love. Not when their lives were being thrown upside down.

"Maman can't be a Jew," Adèle protested. She wasn't sure what made one a member of the Jewish race.

Jean-Pierre ran a hand through his too-long hair. "According to Jewish law, she is and so are we."

Adèle folded her arms. "I am not a Jew. Don't you ever say that again. I have nothing against those people, but I am not one."

Jean-Pierre rolled his eyes but didn't respond.

"Adèle, stop being horrible," Sophie said. "When I think of how nasty you were to Jules and Yvette – and you, papa, maman? You knew this, and you didn't tell me?"

"I knew nothing. Your mother swears she didn't either. At least, not until June." Their father didn't even look at his wife when he spoke.

Adèle couldn't bear it. "Papa, there has to be some mistake. We would have known, felt something."

"There is no mistake. Your grandmother moved to Lyon for her own safety. I want you and Sophie to join her."

Adèle glared at him. "A few minutes ago, maman told me I had to stay here. Now you want me to go to Lyon. Why?"

"We didn't know about Léo until now. People may come to question you. They know you and he were friends."

Adèle would have laughed at her father calling Léo her friend, but for the seriousness of the situation.

"I am not leaving Paris for that very reason. I have to speak to Léo. Sophie won't leave either. She loves the hospital too much."

Her comment earned her an angry glare from her sister, but she jumped when her father banged the table. "You will both do as I tell you."

Sophie seemed indifferent to their father's rage, her voice calm but firm. "I am staying in Paris, papa. I am needed at the hospital. This changes nothing. I must go. I will be late for my shift." She kissed their mother on the cheek and walked out of the room without a backwards glance. Adèle knew her twin was furious with her, but so what? She had bigger things to worry about.

"What about maman?" she asked.

"My place is here. By your father's side."

Adèle saw her father scowl at his wife's comment. He didn't want her here. Was he embarrassed, or afraid for her safety? Adèle feared it was the former.

Adèle had to get her father to reconsider. He couldn't force them to go away.

"Papa, you work in the government. Your high profile will protect us. For goodness' sake, everyone knows the Bélanger family; they won't allow anything to happen to maman."

Jean-Pierre's lip curled. "You think money will protect you? What good did that do for the Jews on Kristallnacht?"

"Don't speak to me like I am an idiot, Jean-Pierre." Why did her family always dismiss her opinions? "What do we know about being Jewish? We are Catholic, and I am staying in Paris. I will see Léo."

"You cannot. I forbid it." Papa's tone was harsh and final. She was an obedient daughter, but this was far too important. She had to go to see Léo.

"If I don't go, it will look suspicious. As you said, enough people saw us leave the wedding together. I'll tell them what happened. They'll believe me."

Adèle left the room, bracing herself for the task ahead. Jean-Pierre followed her.

"Adèle, wait."

"Don't you try to stop me."

"I won't. I will go with you."

Adèle stared at her brother. She loved him but kept him at a distance. He found fault with her. If she were honest, she was jealous of Sophie, whose relationship with Jean-Pierre was cosy. Perhaps if she proved herself as competent as her twin, Jean-Pierre would respect her too.

"No, I will go alone. It's too dangerous for a man. They won't arrest a girl."

"Adèle..."

"I said no. I am going alone or not going at all."

Jean-Pierre shrugged. "Okay. You win."

They stood in silence, and then Adèle had to ask. She

needed to know the answer, even though her head said she wouldn't like it.

"How does papa feel about having a Jewish wife?"

Jean-Pierre didn't look at her.

"So, I didn't misinterpret his reaction. It's a wonder he hasn't shipped her off to Lyon to live with her mother."

"Not for the want of trying. Maman won't go."

"I wouldn't either. It's all right for a brief visit to see mémé, but to live there?" Adèle shuddered. "It's a nasty place, full of foreigners and..."

"Jews! Go on, you can say it. Those people you despise. Our people." Jean-Pierre looked like he wanted to throttle her.

Adèle swept down the hall to her room. She was not a Jew. She didn't care what the Germans said, or that horrible little Austrian. They didn't have the power to change her entire identity. She wouldn't let them.

* * *

Adèle sat facing her mirror, the brush in her hand. Who ever heard of Jews having blonde hair and blue eyes? They were wrong. She didn't look Jewish. She twisted around, looking at her profile. The door to her room opened, admitting Zeldah.

"Sorry, madame, I thought you were out."

"You heard it all, didn't you?" Adèle wasn't in the mood to play games. "Did you come here to gloat?"

"Why would I do that? I am proud to be Jewish. I don't wish you to be Jewish any more than you desire it. But facts are facts." Zeldah's voice softened. "You are brave to go to see the Germans. I like Monsieur Léo. Is there anything I can do for you? Would you like me to help you with your hair?"

Adèle swallowed her initial thought that she would rather go without grooming. Zeldah was trying to be nice. She handed her the hairbrush.

Zeldah brushed Adèle's hair in silence before styling it.

"Why are you being nice to me? After everything I said. I mean, you know I wasn't speaking about you. I was talking about the foreign—" Zeldah's eyes lit up with anger; Adèle stopped talking.

"Do you think Hitler and the Germans care where a Jew was born? Do they care if they are Polish or French? Male or female? They only care if they have assets. If they are rich, it gives them, the Germans, a way to line their pockets. The best Jews in their eyes are the dead ones."

"Zeldah! You can't speak like that. The rumours of what happened in other countries are only stories. Made up by—"

Zeldah interrupted, "Jews, so they can steal the riches from France. I hear how your father speaks. I know what he and his type say about my people. We make up these stories. But have you asked why? Why would anyone talk about old men and women, children and babies being starved to death? Moved from their homes into ghettos. Losing everything they owned. What reason would we have to tell these lies?" Zeldah glared at Adèle in the mirror. Adèle met her gaze but was the first to look away.

"You are intelligent, Adèle. You can tell yourself anything you want to make yourself feel better. Why did your grandmother run? Why did your mother keep it a secret from her husband? Why? Answer me that."

Adèle had had enough. She wasn't about to explain herself to Zeldah. The maid. She stood up. "Leave. I want to change. I won't talk about my family with you."

Zeldah put her hands on the back of the chair, her knuckles whitening. "You can hide behind that act all you want, but you forget. We grew up together. One time we played as sisters, you, me and Sophie. We were equals once. I know you, Adèle Bélanger. *I know you.* They scare you. I do not take pleasure in this. Only a fool would not fear the future." Zeldah hesitated for a fraction of a second, taking a deep breath. "Hide behind your cold exterior, tell yourself your beauty will protect you. You don't look like a Jewess, but there will come a time when nobody will care what you look like. You can wait until they come for you, or you can do something. Jews who look like you can help save those who stand out in a crowd. Your brother doesn't stand by when people need help. Your people need you." Zeldah held her gaze via the mirror. "France needs you."

"Get out!"

The maid put the hairbrush back on the dressing table and strolled out of the room. Zeldah's control of her temper made Adèle seethe even more. Of all the nerve.

But despite her anger, Adèle knew Zeldah was right, and the knowledge terrified her.

TWENTY-ONE

Shaking off her encounter with Zeldah, Adèle checked her appearance once more and, satisfied with what she saw, she walked out of their apartment intent on calling a taxi. *Old habits die hard*, she teased herself, as she looked at the empty streets. She refused to get on one of those awful charcoal buses. It would have to be the métro.

As she walked, two soldiers passed her, both nodding slightly while grinning at her. One even attempted to say 'good day' in French. Instead of acknowledging their greeting, she ignored them. How dare they come and try to change her world?

She walked down the steps into the métro, taking care not to touch the handrail with her gloves. Out of habit, she headed for the middle first-class car but at the last minute remembered. She turned on her heel, but an officer was standing behind her.

"Please, madame, take a seat. We don't bite." The expression in his eyes, half admiring, half challenging, infuriated Adèle. She stood up to her full height and, in fast, fluent German, told him to take a long walk off a short pier.

Without waiting to see his reaction, she moved to the next car. A Frenchman walked in after her.

"Well done, madame. I do not understand what you said, but I wish I had a camera to take a picture of the officer's face."

Adèle didn't acknowledge the man. She wanted to run away from this horrible, new, confusing, hateful world.

"You should be more careful. You might say something to the wrong man. These occupiers are not the gentlemen they pretend to be. It would be a pity if they were to ruin such a beautiful face."

Adèle glared at her countryman. Was he threatening her or trying to be nice? Either way, she didn't have the patience to engage with him.

A picture of her grandmother came to her mind. Adèle sat ramrod-straight and stared ahead, pretending she was alone in the carriage. It worked; the man didn't speak to her again.

She exited the métro one stop early and walked to the German headquarters. It gave her time to stop her heart from racing.

Adèle swallowed hard, gripping her purse to conceal the shaking of her hands. It was one thing to announce to her family she would see the German officers, but quite another to stand outside their headquarters at 72 avenue Foch. The sheer number of uniformed men was overwhelming. She couldn't yet differentiate between the different insignia signifying various units.

She caught one man giving her an insolent stare. How dare he treat her as if she were a common tramp! Straightening her back, she dismissed him with a frozen glare and walked right up the steps into the building as if she lived there.

"Mademoiselle, can I help you?" a man in uniform greeted her, his words contrasting with his dismissive gaze.

She stared at a point above his head, determined not to

show fear. This was her country, not his. "I wish to see the person in charge."

His lip curled. "On what matter?"

The man's French was appalling. Tempted to speak in German, something told her that would be a mistake. She addressed him in French, speaking slowly.

"My friend, Léo Favreau, is being held on some ridiculous charge. I demand you release him."

The smile on the man's face did nothing for her nerves, nor did the way his gaze kept lingering on her chest.

She tried again. "My name is Adèle Bélanger. Perhaps you have heard of my father?"

"No."

"But I have."

Adèle turned towards the voice behind her. She hadn't seen the senior officer approach. The surrounding men stood straighter, highlighting his importance. He was smiling, but only with his mouth, and his cold eyes appraised her with a look that suggested he could read her thoughts. She was glad her gloves hid her sweating palms.

"What a pleasant surprise, Mademoiselle Bélanger." He clicked his heels as he addressed her in excellent French with only a hint of an accent. "Oberführer Mueller. How may I assist you?"

She held out her hand in greeting, pleased to see it didn't shake. *He's a man and you know how to deal with them.* Flattery went a long way. He bent over and kissed the air above her hand, but she had to resist the urge to clean her glove on her skirt.

"You have an excellent command of our language." She held his gaze as she smiled, tempted to lay a finger on his sleeve. That might be a little too forward. "As I was saying, you arrested my friend. It's all a silly misunderstanding and I want you to set him free."

"Why don't we go to my office and discuss this in comfort?"

Adèle wasn't at all sure she wanted to be alone with this man. Despite his courteous manner, the hard look in Mueller's eyes was intimidating.

"I wouldn't wish to intrude. You must be very busy."

Adèle hoped Mueller couldn't feel her trembling as he took her hand and guided her up the steps.

"May I offer you some refreshment, mademoiselle?"

She should correct him, the appropriate term of address was 'madame' but she decided not to. She tried declining, forcing a smile as she shook her head. "This won't take long."

"*Please* have coffee with me."

Adèle smiled in acknowledgement. As polite as he was, she understood it was a command.

When they reached his office, Mueller picked up his phone and ordered coffee, pastries, and the file on Léo. He had turned his back while talking, giving Adèle a chance to look around his office. The obligatory framed painting of Hitler took pride of place on the wall behind his mahogany desk. A fire roared in the fireplace, making the room hot despite the high ceilings. No fuel shortage here. She wondered who had occupied this building before the enemy had rolled in. Where were they now?

"So, what is your interest in this criminal?"

"Léo is no criminal. He wasn't the one at fault. The soldiers were drunk and bumped into us. Then someone else..." Too late, Adèle realised he had baited her. The smirk on Mueller's face was enough to silence her.

"Carry on."

Adèle's heart raced, but she remained the picture of calm. She sat straighter in the chair, taking control of the conversation.

"Where is Léo? Why hasn't he seen anyone? He should at least have a lawyer."

"Your friend is not being cooperative. Perhaps you should speak to him. Tell him to give us the information we want. Then he will be free to go."

"What information? I told you, it was an accident caused by your soldiers."

Mueller's smile at her words turned her stomach. He contradicted her. "Our men were enjoying a rare night off before being attacked by terrorists."

His tone warned her to be careful, but she was too angry to pay heed to the warning.

"Can you hear yourself? Nobody was 'attacked'. They were boys fighting. Not terrorists. Léo wouldn't hurt a fly."

"You seem to *know* him, *Adèle*."

His emphasis on 'know' and the use of her first name sent shivers down her spine. Papa had been right to stop her from coming here.

"Perhaps you are a terrorist?" His speculative glance pierced her, fixing her to the seat. "Why were you in the streets so late at night?"

Feeling light-headed, she gaped at him. A terrorist? Could he hear himself? Using her most autocratic tone, she answered.

"We were returning from a wedding. We did not break curfew. The last I checked, I was free to walk the streets of my country."

Mueller stood and walked around his desk to perch on the side, facing Adèle. She forced her feet into the carpet to stop her knees from shaking. She waited for him to speak.

"Such spirit." He smirked, pushing out his chest, although whether consciously or not, she wasn't sure. Did he expect her to be impressed? His eyes probed hers. "You know, with your colouring and your attitude, you could be German. Perhaps we should examine your file."

Now she understood the meaning of his words, her blood turned cold. "My file?"

He shrugged, but his look radiated superiority. This was a man used to getting what he wanted. But what was that? She bit her lip as he continued. "Everyone has a file now. People like your friend have ideas. It's my job to snuff out those ideas before they become flames."

Despite his controlled tone, Adèle sensed the German was enjoying toying with her, and by responding, she was giving him what he wanted. She stayed silent.

"Lost for words?" He stood up, leaning over her for a second or two before returning to the other side of the desk, settling back in his chair with exaggerated casualness. She refused to give in to the fear, forcing herself to look at the picture of Hitler hanging behind him. She studied it as if it mattered more than anything the man could say.

"Perhaps you should speak to your friend Favreau?" His friendly tone rang false. "He may listen to the voice of reason coming from an attractive woman."

Suppressing the urge to run and hide behind her parents like a little girl, Adèle tried not to show any emotion. Did she want to see Léo? She wanted to help him, but was her being here going to make things worse for him? It was rather late for her to be having second thoughts.

Mueller stubbed out his cigarette, and, picking up the phone, called for the prisoner. He spoke in German.

"No, not to my office, you fool. Take him to one of the clean interrogation rooms. I shall escort the young lady."

Adèle had understood every word but she couldn't let the *Oberführer* know. She took deep breaths to still her heart. What state must Léo be in, if Mueller didn't want him in the ornately decorated office?

He switched back to flawless French when he spoke to her. "Come. We shall go and see your friend. You can talk some sense into him."

Adèle stood, stumbling as her legs betrayed her.

"Let me help you." He put his hand on her elbow. His touch intensified her urge to run, but she pushed those thoughts from her mind. She had to be strong, to show this peasant she was not a little mouse playing his game. She was a Parisian, and proud of it.

"I apologise. I got up too fast and became a little dizzy."

Adèle sensed he didn't believe her, but that didn't matter. She'd spoken firmly, in the hope he might not realise just how terrified she was.

Every step seemed to take forever, though the room wasn't that far down from Mueller's office. Taking another deep breath, she followed the officer in as he opened the door. The room was empty. She exhaled, looking at him for an explanation.

"You should sit down."

Adèle sat. She didn't have to wait long. The door opened and two guards came in, half-pushing, half-dragging a dishevelled person who bore no resemblance to Léo. His features were a solid mass of open wounds and congealed blood. Adèle gasped. She couldn't believe her eyes. "You animals! What have you done to him?" She moved towards Léo, but Mueller put his hand on her shoulder and pushed her back into the seat.

"What is she doing here?" Léo spoke as if every word hurt. His voice didn't sound like his own, and he stumbled over the words. "She has nothing to do with anything."

"So you say. But why should I believe you? Maybe if I hand her over to Herr Weiss, he will make her say otherwise."

"You pig!" Léo lunged for Mueller, earning him a thump from the soldier escorting him.

"Leave him alone! How can you treat an innocent man like that? I shall tell everyone. We have rules in France. I thought the Germans were gentlemen." The words burst forth before she had time to think about them.

"Shut up."

Shocked, Adèle stopped speaking. No one had ever talked to her like that before. She glared at Mueller but his attention was on Léo.

"Herr Favreau, tell me what I need to know," the officer said. He put his hand on Adèle's shoulder once more. She shook it off.

Léo stayed silent.

Terrified, she let the words flow. "I'll tell you. It was all my fault. Léo wanted to leave on time for the curfew, but I was having fun. He stayed to walk me home. He wouldn't have been anywhere near that square if I had behaved." *This is all my fault.* Adèle knew she was speaking too fast, but it was the only way to keep her voice from shaking. "It's not fair he had to pay the price for my thoughtless behaviour. Your, I mean, the soldiers were at fault. They bumped into us."

"Adèle, shush."

"No, Léo, he needs to know. It wasn't Léo who hit the soldier, but another man in the square. I don't know his name."

Adèle didn't know if the *Oberführer* was listening. He didn't look at them, but suppressed a yawn. His next words chilled her to the bone.

"Interesting. But different from the version your friend has told us. So, which of you is lying?"

Adèle couldn't believe it. She was telling the truth, but Mueller didn't believe her. The one time when she wasn't using her feminine wiles or lying to make her life easier!

"I swear on the Bible my version is the truth. Léo, being a proper gentleman" – she saw her insult had hit the mark, as the officer's eyes widened – "tried to protect my reputation. He did nothing wrong. Now let him go so I can take him to the hospital. He needs medical attention."

Oberführer Mueller moved towards Léo, looking him in the face for a few seconds. Adèle allowed her hopes to rise.

"Take him away."

She couldn't believe it. She'd failed. "No," she squealed. "You can't. He needs a doctor."

"Our doctors will see to him."

Adèle jumped out of her seat and hugged Léo, forcing herself not to wince at his odour.

"Don't come back," he whispered. The Germans tore him away and pushed him out the door.

Adèle sank back into the seat. Judging by the look of triumph on the officer's face, she had made things much worse, though she wasn't sure how. She was even more frightened for Léo than before.

"Now, you shall return home. I may need to question you further. This would not be a good time for you to go on a vacation."

Adèle didn't have the strength to argue, or even to acknowledge, the threat. Fighting tears, she pushed her chair back. Mueller held the door for her and escorted her down the stairs and back to the main entrance. Clicking his heels and bowing, he thanked her.

"You have made my day much more interesting."

Tempted to retaliate with a smart remark, she curbed her tongue. It wouldn't achieve anything. Ignoring him was the best thing to do.

Adèle turned and walked as fast as she could out of the place. Her thoughts were in such a whirl, she was almost home before the tears came.

* * *

As soon as he came home, Jean-Pierre rushed into her room. "What took so long? Did you see him?" Adèle was lying face down on her bed. "What did they say?"

She turned on her side to face him. "I made it worse. Papa was right. I shouldn't have gone."

"How could you make it worse? What did you do, Adèle?" Jean-Pierre's accusing tone made her feel even more despairing.

Adèle got up from the bed and started pacing. "Oberführer Mueller didn't believe me. He told me to go home, and not to leave Paris. He has this crazy idea Léo is a terrorist."

"*Merde!*"

"I'm such a fool. It was my fault Léo was there in the square. Why did I insist on staying at the wedding? It was stupid, thoughtless, and selfish. And now Léo is paying the price." Adèle let the tears fall, not to gain her brother's sympathy. What would they do to Léo now? Every time she closed her eyes, she saw Léo's bruised, bloody face, heard the pain in his voice, and saw the way he had shuffled like an old man. She sat on the bed. Even in agony, he'd sought to protect her, telling her to go and not come back. *Oh, Léo, you deserve much better.*

"They will let him go."

"I don't think they will," Adèle whispered. She raised her head to stare at her brother. "They've beaten him up. He has the bruises to prove it and a nasty black eye. I suspect, from the way he walked, he may have a broken rib. He was panting. The *Oberführer* wouldn't let them bring Léo into his office, for fear he would make a mess. Oh Jean-Pierre, what have I done?"

Jean-Pierre held her as she cried but stayed silent. But then, what did she expect? What could he say when she knew he blamed her for being near the station in the first place? She couldn't argue with his reasoning. If she had left earlier, Léo would have been at home, not in Mueller's hands.

The pressure built in her chest, as her body tingled with dread. "Jean-Pierre, I'm sorry."

"That's easy to say when you are here, and he is in there. What are you going to do?"

Adèle strangled her sob. "Do?"

Jean-Pierre withdrew his arms, standing up, his back to her. What did he want from her? When he turned towards her, the coldness in his face hurt her more than anything the Germans had said.

"You did this, Adèle. Now you must fix it."

Then he left.

But she didn't have a chance. The next day, the posters announced the death of the terrorist Léo Favreau, executed nineteen days after they arrested him.

TWENTY-TWO

APRIL 1941, PARIS

Sophie's stomach grumbled as she moved to each patient, carefully reading their notes and checking their condition. She could only imagine how her colleagues felt after the long, cold winter. They depended on rations. Papa kept his family well-supplied. Sophie secretly donated as much as possible to the hospital, but it was still a miracle Dr Murphy had kept it running. She clicked her tongue. Their job was to help cure sick people, not worry about feeding them.

Dr Murphy strode onto the ward where she was working and called, "Sophie, can you come, please? I need your help with an emergency."

Sophie nodded, handing the patient notes over to the nurse in charge. "I'll be back to check on Monsieur Dufort. Monitor his temperature."

The nurse nodded. Sophie hurried along the corridor after Dr Murphy.

"Sorry, but I have a meeting to go to and can't get out of it. I need you to look after some children." His voice dropped as he glanced around. "They are special guests."

Sophie understood their names wouldn't be on the hospital records, not their real names at any rate.

"What is wrong with them?"

"I suspect typhus." He spoke the dreaded word even louder for the benefit of anyone listening. Sophie stopped at the door to the children's infectious ward. "Elizabeth will explain. Prepare yourself." With that, he left.

Heart racing, Sophie pushed the door open. A boy, only three, turned, his face paling even more as she walked in. She tried smiling to reassure him.

Elizabeth patted his hand. "Sophie is here to help us."

The boy didn't react. Perhaps he didn't understand French.

His arm was bleeding through the fresh bandage Elizabeth had applied. Elizabeth turned towards Sophie. "It needs stitches. It's deep. I cleaned it out and used sulfa powder, but... I think you should have a look. I suspect it's broken in several places."

Sophie ran a hand across her forehead as she concentrated on the job at hand. The child looked at her with big brown eyes, but didn't say a word. He hadn't cried either, which was even more concerning. He'd suffered a deep laceration to his arm and multiple fractures. Most adults would scream in agony, yet the child kept silent.

"Poor thing, he is so used to hiding." Elizabeth ruffled the boy's hair.

"Hiding?"

"He's one of the group from Poland. From what the adults say, they had a lucky escape. We can't keep them here, though. They will have to move somewhere safer."

Sophie felt the child staring at her and looked up into his face. She couldn't speak Polish but spoke to him in German as it shared many similarities to the Yiddish language. "You need to rest, then you will soon run around again. You understand?"

He nodded, his face remaining mask-like.

"You're safe now. Elizabeth will give you something to help you sleep. It will help with the pain too."

The child just stared.

"Where is his mother?" she whispered, even though she knew the child didn't understand French.

"We don't know. She didn't come with him."

Sophie pressed her hands to her breastbone. "He didn't come alone, did he?"

"No, he came with a group. I shall get the girl who brought him to us."

Elizabeth returned with a young girl who couldn't have been over fifteen but could have been younger. Her eyes looked like she had lived a hundred years, but her skeletal frame was underdeveloped.

"This is Hannah. She says the boy's name is Szymon. He lost his parents in a ghetto raid. Hannah and the boy escaped from Poland. They didn't expect to find the Germans in France. They were to go to the free zone, but young Szymon fell. She stayed behind with him and tried to help, then someone told her to come here."

Sophie smiled at the young girl, despite the horror she felt at her appearance. Terrible lip sores suggested a diet poor in nutrition. Hannah had unusual colouring. One eye was green, the other blue. Her long hair was dark brown, matted, and dirty. She needed a bath and some fresh clothes. If Sophie wasn't mistaken, she had lice. "Thank goodness they did, or this child would have lost his arm, and perhaps his life. Do you speak French?" Sophie asked the girl.

The girl nodded. "A little. I understand more than I can speak."

Sophie switched to German. "What are your plans now?"

"We must leave for the free zone as soon as possible. I have heard rumours the Germans will soon take the Jews like they do in other countries."

"Take them where?" Sophie wasn't sure she wanted to know. Her thoughts turned to the story Zeldah had relayed about her grandparents.

Hannah stared at the palms of her hands. "You have not heard of the ghetto, and the other rumours?"

Sophie didn't want Szymon listening to their conversation in case he grew more scared.

Even in shock, children picked up on non-verbal clues. She finished dressing his wound and splinting the fractures in silence. Then she drew the girl away to the other side of the ward. There they sat on an empty bed. Elizabeth went to search for clean clothes for the children and some food. Sophie stood up to lock the door after Elizabeth left before returning to sit by the girl.

"Tell me," Sophie whispered. As the girl outlined her experiences living under the Germans, Sophie's stomach clenched. Her chest tingled as she struggled to listen. She wanted to put her hands over her ears.

"My parents had a gracious home, my mother, she kept it spotless. We had money. Papa was a dentist and worked very hard. Mama insisted I have piano lessons. When the Germans came, it wasn't so bad. But then they moved us out of our homes. They wouldn't let us take anything with us but one bag. Mama tried to persuade them to leave us alone. They shot her. Papa too, when he tried to help her."

Sophie couldn't believe the lack of emotion with which the girl told her horrific story. She wanted to wrap Hannah in a hug, but the younger girl's body language suggested that wouldn't be welcome.

"Our maid helped me. She isn't Jewish, but she's worked for our family for a long time. She would have hidden me, but the Germans already knew my name and had my description. The ghetto was a horrible place. All the Jewish people had to share small spaces. It's one thing to share a room with family, but strangers. I couldn't afford food. Those with money could buy some. The Germans took everything my family had of any value, apart from some diamonds Mama had hidden on her person."

"How did you escape?"

"The maid. She couldn't leave me in that place. She knew people, she must have paid them with her own money. Szymon and I owe her our lives. The Germans took away his father in a truck. Nobody knew what happened to his mother."

Sophie couldn't bear to listen, but she forced herself. The information was invaluable. It was the most detailed first-hand account she had heard about the Germans' abuse of the Jews. If she passed on the details to the RAF pilots they helped to rescue, maybe they could convince London to do more to help.

She would spread the news among her Jewish friends so they could be on their guard. But even as she had that thought, she pushed it from her mind. The Germans wouldn't, they couldn't behave like that here in France. The French people wouldn't stand by and let that happen. Not to their own countrymen.

Hannah said, "We met a priest. He helped us get to France. He knew how bad things were. He was a German, but he was not a Nazi."

"Thank God you found him. How will you get to the free zone?"

Hannah dropped eye contact and wrapped her arms around her body. "Can't tell you that. Friends will help me. I have to leave now, but not without Szymon. When will he get better?"

"Not for some weeks."

Hannah paled, her eyes wide with fear. "We do not have weeks. We must leave."

Sophie knew she had to help Hannah and her young charge. She didn't know how.

"Hannah, you can stay here with Szymon for now. It will be

nice for him to have a friend. I will find you something to eat." Hannah shook her head, but Sophie pretended not to see. "You are too thin, and those sores on your lip will not heal. You look like you haven't slept in weeks."

Hannah looked at the floor and whispered, "I have nightmares. I shout out in Polish. It is not safe." Hannah touched her lip, her hands shaking as much as her voice. "I can't stay here. I don't have papers. If the Germans come…"

Sophie's throat scratched as she held back tears. This undernourished child dressed in rags had more moral courage than most.

"They won't. Please trust me. I would never let them find you or Szymon. If they see you on the street, with those sores on your lip, you will give yourself away. You need to rest and recover before you move south."

Hannah stayed silent, darting looks at Sophie. She sensed how torn the girl was. Who could blame her? She was being asked to give up a chance for freedom to wait for another person who wasn't her family.

"Please stay, for Szymon. He is so little, and he needs you," Sophie pleaded. She hated using emotional blackmail, but sensed it was the only way to keep Hannah at the hospital. The girl wouldn't survive on the streets of Paris.

Hannah didn't argue. Sophie kept talking. "We will give you some clothes. You must pretend to be mute. That way, your accent cannot give you away. I will say you are a maid. Only speak to me or Elizabeth. You can trust her. No one else. You understand?"

"Yes." Hannah looked her in the eye for the first time. "Why?"

"Why what?" Caught up in her plans, Hannah's question caught Sophie off-guard.

"Why are you helping me? You don't know me."

"I am training to be a doctor. It's my job to preserve life."

"Even a Nazi's life?"

Sophie didn't want to answer that question. She had once believed all life was sacred, but after hearing Hannah's story, she wasn't too sure how hard she would work to save a German.

Changing the subject, she asked, "Do you have to tell your friends you won't be going with them?"

"They aren't friends. The boy in charge, he says he will take me and Szymon, but I have to ... be nice to him." Hannah screwed her eyes shut as she spoke.

Sophie wanted to throttle this boy. Hadn't Hannah been through enough? "Hannah, nobody will take advantage of you here. Here, lie down and sleep. I will give you something to keep you asleep for a while. Your body is craving rest."

Hannah stared at her, still wary.

"Please, Hannah, trust me. There are others like me in the hospital. We will not harm you, I promise."

With a sigh, Hannah slipped between the sheets, fully clothed. Elizabeth would have a fit when she saw the filthy girl underneath the snow-white bed linen. Sophie thought about telling her to get undressed, but the girl was already asleep.

Sophie watched her for a little while, wondering how anyone could live through so much terror. And she suspected Hannah had only told her a fraction of what had happened since the day the Germans invaded Poland.

* * *

Elizabeth volunteered to sit by Hannah's bed for the evening, so the girl wouldn't wake alone. Sophie felt guilty about her earlier assumptions. Elizabeth had cried when she heard Hannah's story.

"We have to keep her safe, Sophie, her and that poor child."

"Yes, we do. I just hope we can," Sophie replied, wondering how they would make good on the promises she had made.

TWENTY-THREE

That night, Sophie trudged home, her feet dragging. When she reached home, all she wanted to do was fall into bed, but she heard her parents shouting as she opened the door. They had never even argued in front of their children, let alone raised their voices. She hurried towards the noise, through the open door to the sitting room, and couldn't believe the scene in front of her. Pieces of her mother's favourite Wedgwood china decorated the floor. Her mother sobbed as her father roared at her, red-faced. Adèle was in the room with them, looking frozen to the spot.

Sophie's stomach churned. "Papa, stop it! What's happened?" She rushed to her mother's side, kneeling down, careful to avoid the broken china. She put her arms around her mother's shoulders. "Can't you see how upset she is? Stop shouting at her."

Her father seemed to deflate right in front of her, sinking into a chair, his shaking hand running through his greying hair. Sophie stood and faced her sister.

"Adèle, take maman to her room. Now."

Adèle didn't argue, but helped her mother to stand and ushered her out of the room.

Sophie turned to her father. "What's happened?"

"They took Jean-Pierre."

"Who? Where? What do you mean?"

Her father wasn't listening. He had his hands over his face and was mumbling to himself.

"Papa!"

"It seems your brother got himself involved with something at the museum."

Jean-Pierre? What could he do at the museum?

"Someone tipped off the Germans that Jean-Pierre and his friends were printing the newspaper *Résistance*. He had just walked in the door when they arrived to arrest him. He didn't have time to run. Your mother was here alone. She threw a china pot at one officer. She's lucky she's still here."

Sophie swallowed hard to stop her stomach from emptying its contents. The Germans had taken Jean-Pierre, and her mother had fought to protect him. A wave of pride ran through her. Then her father stood up again and began pacing the room.

"What did I do to deserve this family? Can't she understand my position? It's bad enough we found out about her past, but this? How is this going to look to my boss?"

Her father's ravings cut through her thoughts. She stared at him, as if seeing him for the first time. The pompous, self-opinionated man who insisted on the best of everything, even while the rest of Paris starved. He didn't care who he got into bed with, figuratively or literally, if recent rumours were anything to go by. Her anger and disgust boiled over.

"Do you hear yourself? The Boches have your son, they threatened your wife, broke into our home, murdered Adèle's friend, and all you can think about is yourself?"

Her father turned crimson as his eyes bulged. He raised his

arm, but she didn't move a muscle. His cheeks reddened even more as he lowered it again.

"Don't speak like that. Show respect."

"People earn respect." Sophie walked from the room without looking back. She couldn't believe her ears. *Not Jean-Pierre.*

Her hands shook as she walked towards her mother's closed door. Leaning against it, she took a few seconds to compose herself. Jean-Pierre's face flashed into her mind, smiling, having played yet another joke on Adèle. Her poor brother. What would those animals do to him?

Knowing she had to be strong, Sophie took a deep breath before walking into her mother's room. Adèle had helped their mother into bed, and she lay motionless. That scared Sophie more than the sobbing.

"Adèle, where is Jean-Pierre? What has he done?" Sophie asked.

Adèle's swollen eyes filled with tears. "I don't know. Do you think he would have trusted me with anything?"

Sophie couldn't cry. She couldn't think. Jean-Pierre in the résistance? It made little sense. Her brother hated violence.

"You must find Boris. He will know what to do." Sophie whirled at the sound of Zeldah's voice behind her. She hadn't realised she was in the room.

"Zeldah, what do you know about this?"

"Nothing." Zeldah's overbright emerald-green eyes shimmered with tears, her teeth biting her bottom lip.

Sophie sensed Zeldah was lying, but she couldn't ask why. Not in front of her mother.

After checking on her mother, Sophie asked Adèle to stay with her, then followed Zeldah to the kitchen. She shut the door behind them.

"What do you know, Zeldah?"

"Nothing, Sophie." Zeldah wouldn't look at her.

"Stop lying to me. The Germans have my brother. I must do something. Tell me."

Zeldah eyed her for a few moments, but Sophie stood there, determined not to leave until she knew more.

"You have heard of the newspaper *Résistance*."

Sophie forced her face to remain impassive. What on earth had her brother got involved in? "Yes."

"Jean-Pierre wrote some articles for the paper and he has been helping to print and deliver it. The Boches must have followed him."

Sophie groaned. Speaking out privately, amongst family, against the regime was one thing, but active resistance?

"He's so young."

Zeldah misinterpreted her words and sprang to his defence. "Maybe in years, but not in his mind. You don't know the truth of what he is capable of. He has been doing more than working for the paper, too. He helped to get downed airmen to the free zone and back to England. Some came from your hospital – from Dr Murphy."

Sophie didn't want to believe what she was hearing, although she noted the pride in Zeldah's voice. Her brother had been working with Dr Murphy and she hadn't even known about it. Why hadn't they told her?

"Why did he tell you and not me?" Sophie realised the answer almost as soon as she spoke. "You are in this, too, aren't you? Don't deny it, I can tell. Oh, my goodness, Zeldah, get out of Paris. If Jean-Pierre talks..."

"He won't betray me. Us." Zeldah unconsciously stroked her stomach. Sophie's eyes followed Zeldah's hands as understanding dawned.

She looked Zeldah in the eye and asked, "How long?"

Zeldah bit her lip and then admitted, "Three or four months. We are in love. Jean-Pierre said we would go to Argentina, to his friend from the museum. We were all set, but now..." She rubbed her eyes. "I hate them. Do you hear me? I hate them! I wish I had been here when they came. I'd have told them I was in on it too."

Sophie caught the girl as she broke down crying.

"What are they going to do to my beautiful Jean-Pierre? He has such a soft heart. He couldn't just stand by and do nothing. I know I should admire his bravery. But I love him; I wish he had stayed out of it."

Sophie agreed but knew it would have been impossible. Her brother had always been the same, ever since they were little. He'd been quiet and studious, but with a sunny disposition that made him popular with everyone. If a child was being bullied, Jean-Pierre would make friends with the child and protect him against anyone, even those older and stronger than himself. It worked, too. He had a way of commanding respect in other people, from his peers to the adults around him. Jean-Pierre was special. As soon as he knew someone needed help, he'd have been the first to volunteer. She kicked herself for not having guessed what he was up to.

Zeldah's feverish, overbright eyes roamed Sophie's face. "Your father? Doesn't he have contacts?"

Would her father help? Even after everything he'd said and the arguments he'd had with Jean-Pierre, he was his flesh and blood. Would that matter?

"Who else is in the group? Think." Sophie urged the maid to speak. She would ask Dr Murphy, but she couldn't tell Zeldah that. Had Jean-Pierre shared all his secrets with the girl?

"I don't know. Jean-Pierre said it was better, safer, if I didn't know. I can't help him." Zeldah buried her face in her hands, her shoulders shuddering. Sophie held her close as she sobbed.

After the girl had quietened down a little, she asked, "How long has it been going on between you and Jean-Pierre?"

"Two years. Since the summer before this dreadful war

started. He loves me, and I love him. I can't live without him."
The tears flowed again.

She let Zeldah cry for a while. When the sobs subsided,
Sophie took charge.

"You must think of the baby. We must be strong. Now dry
your eyes and carry on as normal for now. Don't go home. Stay
here. If anyone asks why, tell them I said my mother needed the
company."

"Where are you going to do?"

"Tomorrow, I will go to see some friends. Please trust me
and don't leave the house. I will come back to tell you what I
find out as soon as I can. In the meantime, you are safer here
than anywhere."

Zeldah looked so young and scared. Sophie hugged her.
Despite the pain in her chest, she remained calm. Someone had
to protect her family. Would they mistreat Jean-Pierre, beat him
or subject him to torture? He wouldn't betray his friends, not by
choice. Her heart thumped and she counted backwards to try
and calm herself. Who could help them?

For a few seconds, Sophie considered telling Adèle of the
extent of Jean-Pierre's involvement, but then reconsidered. The
fewer people involved, the better.

* * *

After a sleepless night, she went first to the hospital to find Dr
Murphy in his office. He listened to her story, a grave expression
on his face.

"Sophie, I'm sorry. You know I will do all I can, but you
must prepare yourself for the worst. Jean-Pierre is likely to end
up in prison in Germany."

"I can't just stand by and do nothing. I'll go to the museum."

"No. That's the last place you should go. You need to keep a
low profile. They have arrested Boris and the rest of the

museum team. There is an informer, but nobody knows who it is. You cannot trust anyone." Dr Murphy changed his tone. "We need you here. We're short of staff and cannot give you time off. I'm sorry."

She knew he was trying to keep her safe and loved him for it, but she still felt powerless.

"Why didn't you tell me my brother was helping you?"

Dr Murphy didn't reply. She knew the answer: for the same reason he hadn't told Jean-Pierre she was helping airmen. To protect them.

"We can bribe the guards to release him. Or break him out?" Even as she put her ideas into words, she knew she was being ridiculous. "He's my baby brother."

"I can't imagine your pain, but you must think clearly. You will be under suspicion too, as Jean-Pierre's sister. Any actions you take could jeopardise our work here at the hospital. The best thing we can do is to follow our usual routine. It's what Jean-Pierre would want. Do nothing rash." Dr Murphy's eyes begged her for understanding. He was protective of the hospital and those that depended on them. Patients, pilots and other soldiers, children like Hannah and Szymon.

Sophie didn't want to get the hospital into trouble, but neither could she abandon her brother.

The wards were busy. It didn't stop her thinking of her brother, but for now, she had to help those around her.

* * *

That evening, just before her shift ended, Elizabeth found her in a ward checking notes. She beckoned Sophie to follow her into an empty room where they could talk.

Elizabeth whispered, "Sophie, Dr Murphy told me. See Inspector Lavigne."

Sophie recognised the name. "But he is a policeman. They answer to the Germans."

"Not all. Go on, tell him I told you to speak to him. He is my cousin; he won't betray you."

Sophie knew Elizabeth believed what she said, but what if her friend was wrong? She stared at Elizabeth as she tried to get her thoughts under control. What alternative did she have? She had to do something for Jean-Pierre. What if Elizabeth was right, and there was a senior policeman who still answered to France?

She didn't take long to decide. Jean-Pierre needed her help. It was too late to do anything after her shift ended. They would catch her out after curfew. Attracting more trouble wouldn't help anyone, so she would go first thing in the morning.

When she got home, Zeldah was fast asleep, curled up on a chair in the kitchen, waiting for her to come home. She drew a blanket over the girl. There was no point in waking her. The morning would come soon enough.

* * *

The next morning, Sophie chose a formal outfit. She twisted her hair into a chignon just as Adèle slipped into her bedroom.

"Where are you going?" Adèle asked. Her pale face was a testament to the fact she was finding sleep difficult too.

"Best you don't ask questions, Adèle."

"Don't shut me out too, please. You know how I feel about what happened to Léo, now Jean-Pierre! I want to do something. I want to help."

Sophie softened and took her sister's hands in hers. "You can, by looking after maman. She needs support right now."

Adèle pulled away. "I want to do something useful."

"Looking after our mother is useful," Sophie said. "You must persuade her to leave Paris."

"Leave! Why?"

"Are you as stupid as you sound? They have shot your friend for being a terrorist, now our brother is in Fresnes or somewhere. Who do you think will be next on the Germans' list?" Sophie hated spelling out the danger, but her sister had to deal with reality.

"Not maman."

"Maman, you, me. We are all Jews and, according to the occupiers, we have family and friends in the Resistance."

Sophie hesitated and hated herself for doing so. Should she tell Adèle about her work at the hospital? Would Adèle approve of the efforts to hide downed airmen and help them escape back to Britain? Did she trust her sister enough to tell her?

She felt someone watching them. Looking up, she caught Zeldah's eyes wide with fear. She looked back at her twin.

"How long do you think you can watch from the sidelines? It's decision time, Adèle. Are you with us or not?"

Adèle didn't answer.

Sophie didn't have time for her twin today. With a spray of perfume and a scarf, she left the house. She walked to the police station, not trusting her ability to cycle. Her knees shook. Was she doing the right thing? Or was she inviting more trouble?

TWENTY-FOUR

She arrived before nine. The station was quiet, with only a few disinterested gendarmes hanging around. Walking up to the front desk, Sophie asked to see Inspector Lavigne.

The bored gendarme didn't look up from his desk. "Do you have an appointment?"

"No, sir. I would like to speak to him regarding a sensitive matter."

Sophie handed over what looked like a note but was a bribe. The policeman took it without commenting, then picked up the phone to announce her arrival.

"Take a seat. Someone will be down in a minute."

Sophie had barely settled on the cold, hard bench when they called her name. She stumbled as she stood and put out her hand to steady herself. Touching the grimy, off-white walls made her thankful she was wearing gloves. The man escorting her waited, his glance of disapproval making her more nervous. Her hands sweated inside the leather as she followed the man up the stairs. The walls got whiter as they moved up through the building, but the windows remained barricaded. She shivered, and not from the cold.

The man in front of her came to a sudden stop, and she collided with him. She waited as he announced her and then retreated without a second glance in her direction. Taking a deep breath, she walked into the room. The plush carpet was soft under her feet, and there was a roaring fire under the imposing picture of Marshal Pétain, the smell of real coffee making her mouth water. No sign of rationing here.

"Some coffee?" the man asked her when her gaze acknowledged him.

"Yes, please."

"Sugar?"

Sophie nodded, her eyes roaming the room and taking in every detail. Again he waited until she looked at him, before nodding at a seat beside his desk. He sat on the other side.

"A bitter day outside, too dreary for a pretty girl like yourself to be out so early. What can I do for you?"

"Your cousin, Elizabeth, suggested I speak with you. My name is Sophie Bélanger."

He stirred his coffee. "Yes?"

Was it a good sign he didn't recognise her name? "The Germans arrested my brother, Jean-Pierre Bélanger."

"On what charge?"

Sophie wanted to take the spoon out of his hand, but she couldn't. "The SD picked him up."

That got the man's attention. He sat back in his chair, his expression no longer friendly.

"I have nothing to do with them."

Sophie held out her hand. "Please help me. I don't know who to turn to. My brother, he is not a terrorist. An idealist maybe, a scholar definitely, but he would never hurt another soul." Her voice shook, despite her best efforts to keep calm.

"You make him out to be a saint."

"Not a saint, no. He has lots of faults but is not a fighter. He works at the *Musée de l'Homme*."

"Ah, the museum." He leaned away from her. "That explains a lot. The less I know the better. I cannot understand why Elizabeth would send you. What can I do?"

Plenty, thought Sophie, but he would do nothing. Still, she had to try.

"Please, if you could find out where he is being kept, how he is, a way for us to see him... They won't tell us anything."

He studied his nails for a moment before asking, "What age is your brother?"

"Nineteen."

The man stared at her before standing and walking to the fire. "Why me? Your father could pull strings."

"You know my father?" Sophie asked. Why hadn't he shown any sign of recognising her name?

The man turned to face her. "Most of Paris knows your father."

His sarcastic tone irritated Sophie into snapping, "Then you will know he will do nothing. It doesn't matter that Jean-Pierre is his only son. My father, he..."

Sophie couldn't continue. No matter what he had done, he was her father.

"Your father is a coward. He won't put his neck on the line for anyone, not even his own son. Yet you expect me to help?" His ramrod-straight body matched the man's bitter tone.

Sophie wished Adèle had come with her. Adèle had a way of charming the most difficult of men. Although they looked alike, they couldn't be more different when using their feminine charms.

"Please don't be angry. I love my brother and would do anything to help him." She despised herself for begging, but it was all she could do.

Was it her imagination, or did his eyes soften? He walked back to his seat, sat down and pulled the chair in as close as possible.

"Mademoiselle, the best thing you can do is stay away from this whole mess. Otherwise, you will compromise your position and the safety of the hospital."

He knew about the airmen and refugees they helped! Or was it a trick? Sophie didn't speak.

"Look at my desk, Mademoiselle Bélanger, and tell me what you see?"

Files and papers covered the desk. What was he asking her? She rubbed her chin as she stared at the mess.

He chose a file from a pile of similar-looking ones. "Here, look at this."

She took the file he handed to her, holding it carefully in both hands as the bulging contents threatened to spill out. Glancing at his face to make sure he meant for her to open it, she took a deep breath and read the first page.

"I don't understand what you are showing me. It's a letter about the black market."

"And the next? And the one after that. They are all letters written by concerned French citizens who feel they must inform the authorities about their neighbours."

Sophie let the file fall back onto the desk in her haste to distance herself from it. "Why?"

"Who knows? Greed, envy, or some other motivation. Some may believe it is their duty. Stress brings out the true nature of people. You cannot trust anyone. No one. I am not the only one to hold such files. We get so many denunciations, it is difficult to keep up with our actual job of policing this city. Who knew so many held petty grudges against their neighbours?"

Sophie couldn't respond. She didn't know what to say.

The man stood, dismissing her. "I will do what I can to find out where your brother is being held. Don't worry so much. Your brother is only a boy. They won't execute someone so young."

"I hope you're right," Sophie answered.

"I hope so too, or God help us all."

Sophie stood. "Thank you for the coffee and your help."

Monsieur took her outstretched hand. "Mademoiselle, consider leaving Paris. Your mother and sister, too. Things will get worse for your people before they get better."

Sophie challenged him. "'My people'? Are you not a Frenchman, monsieur?"

The look he gave her told her everything. Somehow, the policeman knew her mother was Jewish.

* * *

Adèle paced back and forth in the sitting room. She picked up a picture of Jean-Pierre, tracing his face with her finger. What was happening to him right now? Where was Sophie and would she get their brother released? Her father had gone out just after curfew ended, refusing to speak to anyone. Her mother hadn't got out of bed.

All Zeldah could do was sit in the kitchen and cry. Adèle glanced out the window but there was no sign of Sophie. She twisted her hands together, sitting down and picking up the paper before discarding it unread. Hearing the front door open and close again, she stood up but at the last minute decided to wait for Sophie to find her. She wanted to talk without their mother or Zeldah listening.

Sophie walked in, her face ashen, her body shaking. Adèle rushed to her side, taking her hand and leading her to the couch to sit.

"What did they say? Where is Jean-Pierre? When is he coming home?"

"They don't think he will come home."

Adèle gasped, her stomach hardening. "You don't mean... They couldn't shoot him." A picture of Léo swam in front of her eyes. He'd been innocent, while Jean-Pierre was a Resistant.

Sophie shook her head. "Jean-Pierre will end up in a prison camp in Germany. He won't be shot because of his age."

Adèle sagged back against the couch. "Prison. He's too soft for that. Why can't they just let him go with a warning? Tell him not to write any more newspaper articles."

Sophie didn't seem to hear her. "The gendarme I spoke with advised me – us – to leave."

"They think the Germans will arrest us? Do they believe we wrote articles too?" Adèle stood up and paced once more.

"None of this has anything to do with writing articles."

She felt light-headed; what on earth was Sophie talking about?

"Jean-Pierre and others were involved in more than the paper. The Germans believe they helped Allied prisoners escape to the free zone and beyond. Someone betrayed the group."

"He wasn't working at the museum?" Adèle stuttered over the words, ignoring the twinge of jealousy that her twin knew about their brother's activities. Why had nobody told her? *Because they didn't trust you.*

Sophie stood up, her hands clasped together, a determined expression on her face.

"Don't worry about that for now. You must leave."

"Leave? But where will we go?"

Sophie's piercing look warned her she wouldn't like the answer. "I am not going anywhere, but you, my darling sister, have to take maman to Lyon."

"I can't run away and leave you here alone."

"You can, and you must. Take Zeldah with you."

Adèle bit her lip in an effort not to lose her temper at her twin's officious tone. She wasn't a child. She was tempted to ignore the request; her curiosity won. "Why Zeldah?"

"Because she is pregnant with Jean-Pierre's child."

Her younger brother was going to be a father? *Jean-Pierre and Zeldah. Papa is going to love that.*

She ran her hands through her hair, pulling it back from her face, trying to calm the flood of emotions through her body: anger, sadness, but most of all frustration.

"Oh, for goodness' sake. What is happening to this family? Papa refuses to speak to any of us, Jean-Pierre's in prison, maman in her bed, the servant is pregnant, and you are behaving like de Gaulle died and left you in charge."

Sophie smiled at the reference to the Free French leader, but then looked serious again. "You've heard the rumours. We should believe them. Zeldah told us about her grandparents and I have seen things at the hospital. You need to get out of here while you still can." Sophie put her hands on her sister's shoulders, her tone grim. "Jean-Pierre was right when he told you not to go to avenue Foch. Your visit to the Germans didn't go unnoticed, not if what you told me about that *Oberführer* is true."

She shrugged off Sophie's hands and marched over to the fireplace. She didn't want to leave. Palpitations hit her chest, making it more difficult to breathe. She wanted – no, needed – Sophie's strength, her guidance on how to deal with this changing world. She thought of her brother stuck in a prison after what Léo had been through...

Adèle flexed her fingers. She'd refuse to go. "You haven't thought this through. We're better staying here with people nearby that we know."

"Like who? Do you think one of your German friends will ride up on a white horse to rescue you?"

Why did her sister have a way of penetrating her skin like no one else?

Ignoring the jibe, she spat back, "It's not like I can just get on a train and go to Lyon. We need papers, and we can't ask for them. That would put the cat among the pigeons."

Her sarcasm just bounced off Sophie.

"Don't worry about that for now. Just get packed. One suitcase each. We will tell people you will visit mémé, as she is not well. They will believe that. Zeldah must go with you to help look after maman. We will say she is ill."

Adèle protested, "Travelling with a Jew will only put us in more danger." The disgust in Sophie's eyes made her wish she could retract her words.

"I won't respond to that comment. Zeldah is going with you. She can sew some of our jewellery into your clothes, your needlework skills being non-existent."

Adèle let the silence linger until it became uncomfortable.

Sophie surprised her by walking towards her and taking hold of her hands. "Do this. For our family. Maman and Zeldah are even more devastated than we are. They need your strength." Sophie's eyes glittered as she squeezed her hands. "I'm asking you to do this. Please."

Overcome with emotion, Adèle pulled her sister into a hug.

Her mother and Zeldah needed to get out of Paris, and she was the only one who could take them. But she was coming straight back to Paris. No ifs or buts.

She released her sister to walk over to their mother's writing desk. Running her fingers over the woodgrain, she pressed the hidden button opening the secret compartment. Fingering the cache of French francs her mother held for an emergency, she hesitated for a fraction of a second before removing them. She turned and handed them to her twin.

"I can sew just fine. Take this. You go back to the hospital. I will sort things out here. I know where papa hid the loose diamonds he recently bought. They'll be easier to hide."

Sophie eyed her. Irritated, Adèle snapped, "What now?"

"Do not tell papa of our plans."

Adèle tapped her foot, the sound of her heel against the wooden floor competing with the soft clink of dishes coming from the kitchen. "He wouldn't betray us, and besides, he can help us. We need money, and lots of it. Neither of us have a bank account and even if we did, we couldn't take out large sums without alerting the authorities."

"I'm serious. We can't trust him."

Adèle's heart fluttered. Papa? No, he wouldn't. "He's our father."

"He's a collaborator first, our father second."

TWENTY-FIVE

The next evening, Adèle took advantage of Sophie being at the hospital. She sent her mother and Zeldah to bed before dressing in her green Jeanne Lanvin dress, fingering the material as she remembered Jean-Pierre's reaction when she'd bought it.

She'd never worn it until now, but it suited her. She wore her hair down to look younger and replaced her usual Chanel perfume with a lighter fragrance.

She set the table for dinner, decanting a bottle of her father's favourite red wine. Hearing his footsteps outside the apartment door, she lit the candles and ran her eyes over the table once more.

"Evening, Adèle. You look beautiful, if somewhat over-dressed." He glanced at her suspiciously. "What's the occasion?"

She ignored the butterflies in her stomach as she gave him a kiss on the cheek.

"Can't I spoil you just because you're my father? Do I need a reason?"

Helping him out of his jacket, she then poured him a glass of wine, indicating he take a seat.

"Does my darling daughter need new dresses?" Her father took out his wallet. She should act insulted, but she needed the money.

She took the bundle of francs, giving him another kiss on the cheek. She went to the kitchen and hid the money in the cupboard before returning with his favourite foods.

She listened as he talked about his day, asking questions as if she was hanging on every word. Under her eyelashes, she observed him closely, trying to read him. He loved her, didn't he? What if Sophie was right? Would he betray his family? Her?

He wouldn't hand his child over to the Germans. What about Jean-Pierre? Maybe he was trying to help him but keeping his actions secret so as not to raise their hopes.

When they finished, he raised his glass to her. "That was delicious, thank you. You should marry again. I know several eligible men who would appreciate your skills as a hostess."

She clasped her hands together under the table to still the shudder running through her body. Married? No thank you.

"Papa, what do you think will happen to Jean-Pierre? He won't be shot, will he?" *Like Léo.*

Her father sat back in his chair, rubbing his lips with his napkin before taking another drink. "Jean-Pierre must help himself. If he provides the Germans with answers, they will reward his loyalty."

Ignoring her rapid pulse, she leaned in as if having trouble hearing him. "Answers?"

"A youth of nineteen can't be the mastermind of the operation. It's very simple. He gives them names; they give him a deal. He'll probably have to serve a spell in prison, but that will pass."

The hairs on her arms stood up as he spoke as if discussing the weather. He wanted, no *expected*, his son to turn traitor. To give up other men and maybe women to the enemy.

Do not tell papa of our plans. Sophie's words swirled in her head together with memories of her father bringing them places during their childhood, his joy when Jean-Pierre was born, a son at last.

"He won't agree to that. My brother has too much integrity."

Her father pushed his chair back, the wooden legs scraping against the floor.

"You speak to me of integrity. Your brother cheated and lied. He disobeyed Pétain's orders."

"He's fighting for France, for our freedom. You want the Germans to leave..." Her heart stilled at the look on his face. "You don't care, do you?"

Her father turned away, walking over to the drinks cabinet to pour a cognac before moving to take a seat on the couch. "Why would I expect you to understand? Women are too emotional."

She fought the urge to shake him. Could he hear himself? She had to convince him.

"He's your son. He..."

Her father's head snapped up. "He made his choices. Thank you for the lovely meal, but now I'd like to read some papers I brought home from work."

"But..."

"Go to bed."

TWENTY-SIX

Elizabeth used her contacts to get the travel permits. Sophie gathered money together for her family by selling some of her mother's jewellery. The hospital's black-market contacts came in useful. She needed to avoid alerting the Germans to the sale of a considerable amount of gold. The Germans had implemented a tax on jewellery, which they collected in a percentage of gold or other valuable metals.

When everything was ready in terms of money and papers, Sophie spoke to Zeldah alone, outlining the plans. They sat on the same side of the kitchen table, whispering although they were alone.

"You need to try to get to America. I've heard there are some ships leaving from Marseille, but you will have to wait in Lyon until I can find a way to get you on the ship's manifest. You and the baby will be safe. Dr Murphy has given me the names of some people who may act as a sponsor for you." Sophie handed Zeldah a list and a letter of reference. "Hide this on your person. The letter may help you if you do get to America. He's also going to try to smuggle some letters out via the embassy."

"Your doctor friend is a kind man. But..." Zeldah's lips tightened, her green eyes flashing. "I won't leave without Jean-Pierre."

"Yes, you will, for the sake of his baby. When Jean-Pierre gets out, he can join you both. Now take this." Sophie handed her a diamond and ruby cluster ring.

Zeldah put her hand out in wonder but refused to do more than just touch the ring.

"I can't take it; it's too valuable."

"You can. Jean-Pierre would have given it to you as your engagement ring. Don't wear it. Hide it. If you need to, sell it to get away. Don't stay in France. You can come back when the war is over."

"Mama isn't fit to travel."

Sophie took Zeldah's hand, caressing it. "Your mother wants this for you. She wants you to be safe. You know she doesn't have long left. The cancer has spread too far."

Zeldah broke down, sobbing. Sophie's tears trickled down her face. "I will look after your mother; she'll be admitted to the hospital and kept out of pain."

"I must stay with her. I can't leave, not now."

Sophie shook her head. "You have to escape; your mother deserves to die in peace."

Zeldah paled and stared at her in silence, the tears flowing unchecked down her cheeks.

Sophie swallowed, trying to stem her panic. More people connected to the museum had been picked up by the Germans. What if they found out about Zeldah? Zeldah bowed her head. Sophie whispered, "Do it for my brother. For his child. Your baby."

"If you think it's best... But you will tell Jean-Pierre where I am, so he can join us?"

Sophie blinked to clear the tears from her eyes. She didn't want to think about Jean-Pierre and the baby he was unlikely to see. She refused to share her fears for Jean-Pierre with anyone, not even her twin. If she did, her family wouldn't leave Paris. Zeldah would insist on staying, too.

She couldn't help Jean-Pierre, but she would not let the Germans take his lover and their child too.

"Take this." She pressed some francs into the girl's hands. "Just in case you get separated from Adèle." Sophie choked out before wrapping her arms around the girl. "Don't let Adèle boss you around."

Zeldah couldn't reply as her tears streamed down her face. They returned to the room where her mother and twin were waiting. They were both crying, too. Sophie reassured them all that she would follow soon, but first, she had to find someone to replace her at the hospital. That was the excuse she stuck to. She was more determined than ever to carry on with her role in the resistance. Nothing was going to stop her helping those who were working against the occupiers.

* * *

Adèle didn't sleep all night. As soon as she heard her father leave the apartment, she went through his desk, taking every franc she could find. They had to leave today. He wasn't going to change his mind, and every day they remained in Paris made their situation more precarious, according to Sophie. She didn't bother arguing with her twin; she'd been right about their father.

Walking over to her mother's writing desk in the sitting room, Adèle picked up a photograph of the whole family. They were all smiling; her father had his hand on Jean-Pierre's shoulder. When had it all gone wrong? Was it just the war, or had the cracks been there all along?

She threw the photo down on the desk, ignoring the shattering glass. Struggling to contain her tears and furious at her own weakness, Adèle snapped at her mother.

"Stop crying. You'll be arrested for causing a scene. Remember who you are. We are the proud Bélanger family."

Adèle caught Sophie's look of approval but ignored it. Her twin would not join them. She knew that look, the pursed lips and determined expression. No, Sophie was staying in Paris. It was all very well for her. She wasn't putting her neck on the line escorting a pregnant Jewish girl out of Paris, not to mention having to stay in Lyon.

Madame Garnier waited at the bottom of the stairs; she must have heard them leaving the apartment.

"You're going away?" The concierge didn't try to hide her curiosity.

Adèle was tempted to walk past her but Sophie stepped forward. "Maman isn't feeling well. Adèle is taking her to Versailles for a little rest. You know my twin isn't a good nurse so it's a good job Zeldah is." The concierge squinted at their luggage, the small bags confirming Sophie's story.

To Adèle's ears, Sophie's laugh sounded forced but the concierge didn't seem to notice. She didn't suspect Sophie of lying, nobody would.

"And you, Sophie, are you going?"

"I wish, but I'm needed at the hospital and someone must look after papa. Can't leave a man on his own."

Madame Garnier nodded in agreement. "Bon voyage." The telephone rang in the *loge*.

Adèle walked out onto the street and flagged a vélo-taxi. Despite the telephone call, Adèle spoke in a low voice so that the concierge wouldn't hear their destination.

When their vélo-taxi arrived at the Gare de Lyon, it was bustling. Adèle fingered the tickets in her pocket. Behind her, Zeldah and Sophie spoke in whispers. Adèle tried to stifle the jealous feelings consuming her. Sometimes it seemed as if Zeldah and Sophie were sisters.

Sophie kissed Zeldah and hugged her before embracing their mother. Then she held Adèle.

"Look after them; you're the strong one."

Adèle gripped her sister, not wanting to let her go. Sophie hugged her and then pushed her back. "I must go home. Au revoir." Sophie's eyes glistened with unshed tears as she walked away toward the métro.

They walked up to the gates, her mother faltering at the sight of the grey-green uniforms patrolling up and down the concourse.

"Ignore them, maman. You have the right to be here; they don't." Adèle took her mother's arm and led her along to the train.

Adèle handed the ticket inspector their travel documents, putting her shaking hand back in her pocket as soon as she could. The supervising soldier smiled at her, so she forced herself to be civil. Sophie had warned them not to do anything to bring attention to themselves.

The inspector waved them through. They'd passed the first hurdle.

As they approached their train carriage, Adèle spotted four men, all wearing long leather coats and trilby hats. The SD. Honestly, for a secretive organisation, could they make themselves any more obvious? She watched as people shuffled past them, looking guilty even if they were totally innocent. Her mother stiffened as she spotted them.

"Think of Jean-Pierre. Treat them with the same contempt you would give to a beetle," Adèle whispered in her mother's ear. Her words worked as her mother straightened her back and walked past the men as if they were invisible. She put her hand on the door of the train car, completely sure they would pounce at any second, but nothing happened. She climbed the steps, leading the way into the right compartment and finding their numbered seats. They were still empty, which, given the amount of travellers, was unusual. Adèle saw it as a good omen. She sat by the window with her mother taking the seat next to her.

Zeldah placed the smaller bags on the seats opposite before putting their suitcases onto the luggage net. A man jumped up to help her. They all waited in silence for the train to move off. The train was freezing despite the number of passengers. Adèle buried deeper into her fur coat, closing her eyes briefly and thinking of her father. Her gut twisted with hurt, remembering the conversation after their dinner.

Zeldah stared white-faced out the window while maman had her eyes closed. The atmosphere grew tense as the train failed to move. What was the delay? Adèle tapped her fingers on her lap.

A hiss of steam and they were off. This was it. She closed her eyes, squeezing them to stop a tear from escaping. She'd come back to Paris just as soon as she'd delivered maman to Lyon.

The motion of the train must have sent her to sleep as she woke with a jolt to the screech of brakes. Zeldah's face whitened, and maman looked as if she was frozen with terror. Adèle patted her mother's hand. "Everything is going to be fine. Close your eyes and rest." Her mother nodded like a child and closed her eyes. Adèle caught Zeldah's gaze and smiled, but Zeldah didn't respond. They heard shouting. The train had stopped at a station but nobody could leave.

Adèle rooted in her pocket for her papers, trying to take reassurance from the fact a control taking place inside the train was better than one where the passengers were forced out onto the station platform.

The door slid open and a grey-green-uniformed soldier walked in. "*Papieren.*"

No attempt at pleasantries. Adèle waited until the men seated next to her mother had been dealt with before handing both her and her mother's papers over. The soldier gave an appraising glance, but she ignored him. He threw her papers back at her before turning to Zeldah. She heard his audible intake of breath before he muttered, "*Jude.*" The other passengers turned to stare at Zeldah. Adèle expected Zeldah to break down, but she stared back at the soldier, a defiant expression in her sparkling, emerald eyes. In that instance, Adèle saw the beauty and character that had attracted her brother. The soldier spat out several disgusting remarks in German. Adèle knew Zeldah didn't speak the language, but the meaning could still be interpreted. Zeldah just adopted a haughtier expression, which incensed the soldier. He put a hand out to take Zeldah's arm when Adèle intervened.

"Take your hands off her. She's a French citizen with the correct papers and has the right to travel."

Whether it was the fact Adèle addressed him in his own language or the imperious tone she used, the soldier blushed. He jumped back from Zeldah as if she was contagious.

Adèle stood up.

Placing a hand on his sidearm, he glared at her. "Where do you think you are going?"

"To find your superior. How dare you manhandle my friend – and her pregnant? You have no right behaving like an ill-mannered lout. You make me ashamed to have German blood."

The man blanched at the word 'superior'. Enjoying herself, Adèle said to Zeldah, "Just wait until Helmut hears about this when he returns from Berlin. Have you noted his number?"

The soldier nearly fell over his own feet, trying to get out of the compartment, spewing apologies to everyone. Adèle stood until he closed the door behind him before falling back into her seat.

"You were quite marvellous, young lady." An older man lifted his hat and nodded to her.

Shaking, Adèle gave him half a smile before clenching her teeth, hoping her last meal wouldn't make a reappearance. Zeldah mouthed "thank you" before turning to stare out of the window. Maman snored gently. Adèle believed she'd slept through the whole thing until her mother squeezed her hand under the fur coat Adèle had draped over her to keep her warm. Her mother had been acting too.

Soon afterwards, the *douanier* came into the carriage. "Avez-vous quelque chose à déclarer?"

Adèle wasn't about to declare the money her father had thrown at her, nor the diamonds sewn into her clothes. The customs inspector moved closer and asked for her papers. Everyone else stared at the floor, willing him not to pick on them or search their suitcases. He held out her papers and when Adèle reached out for them, looking up to catch his eye, he winked and smiled. Then he left.

TWENTY-SEVEN

The next morning, they finally spotted the *Notre-Dame de Fourvière*, the large Catholic cathedral taking pride of place overlooking Lyon. As the train pulled into the station, Adèle looked out the window but didn't spot any men in trench coats. Were the SD even active in the free zone? She dismissed the thought as soon as it entered her mind. Of course they weren't. There'd been German spies in France long before war was declared but no military patrolled the free zone. She needed to relax.

The man in the hat lifted down their suitcases from the luggage net and Adèle carried them as she negotiated the steep steps from the train car. Her mother's arm was tucked into Zeldah's with the maid helping her.

"Let me help you."

A porter took the suitcases and escorted them down the concourse and out of the station to a *gazogéne*-powered taxi. She was desperate to get to her grandmother's house and have a wash and a sleep. She tipped the porter generously. Once her mother and Zeldah were seated, she joined them, giving directions to the taxi driver.

It didn't take long to reach her grandmother's as the roads were almost as empty as those of Paris. A wave of relief washed over her as she spotted her grandmother standing at the door, her hair pulled back into the bun she always wore, her make-up done and dressed in a nice, fitted dress. She wouldn't look out of place at a Parisian café.

"Thank God!" Mémé ushered them inside and tipped the taxi driver to carry the cases inside. She waited for the man to leave before asking, "Did you have any trouble?"

"Adèle was magnificent, mama. You should have seen her tackle a horrible soldier who was very insulting to Zeldah. She ate him up and spat him back out. I was so proud of her."

Adèle's eyes filled up at her mother's compliments. She dropped into a seat, her legs feeling shaky. "I lost my temper. I couldn't believe the dreadful things he said to Zeldah."

"I'm used to it." Zeldah stood, her suitcase in hand, a strained expression on her face.

"Zeldah, please make yourself at home in my house. You have blossomed into a beautiful young woman. No wonder my grandson is so taken with you."

Adèle stared at her grandmother. How did she know about Jean-Pierre and Zeldah?

Zeldah's eyes glistened. "Could I please use the bathroom?"

The old woman put her arm around Zeldah. "Put that case down. Adèle will take it to your room. You need to look after yourself and my great-grandchild. The bathroom is through here and I shall show you where you will sleep. You make yourself comfortable."

Zeldah protested, "I should help you."

"Nonsense. I remember how tired I was when I was carrying my daughter. And that was without having to deal with the Boches. Adèle will help me."

Open-mouthed, Adèle watched as her grandmother pampered their maid. The world really had turned on its head.

* * *

When Adèle walked into the kitchen the next morning, Zeldah was sitting at the table.

Adèle picked up the coffee pot, looking around for a cup. "Where is my mother?"

"In bed. She doesn't want anything to eat." Zeldah's flat tone and black circled eyes suggested she should be in bed too.

Her grandmother walked into the kitchen. "Good morning, girls. Did you sleep? You didn't tell me: how is Paris coping with the occupiers?"

Zeldah answered, "The people are hungry. They ration everything according to age and race. Elderly people have fewer rations than the ordinary French, and us Jews have even less. Some shops forbid Jewish people from entering. There are several soup kitchens set up to feed people."

Adèle leaned forward. "Papa doesn't seem to have a problem finding food." She lifted another piece of bread before liberally applying her grandmother's home-made jam.

Her grandmother grimaced. "Your father is a collaborator. He'll be dealt with when the war is over."

Adèle stared at her grandmother but didn't comment. What was the point of arguing? Everyone hated papa now. Even Sophie. He hadn't done anything to help Jean-Pierre, that was true, but he had looked after them when they were younger. He'd indulged her, taking her side when she wanted to socialise and her mother insisted she play the grieving widow. Even at their last dinner before it turned difficult, he'd given her money for dresses. Was he motivated out of love for her?

"I have friends coming to lunch. They will help us get Zeldah out of France."

Zeldah's lips thinned in response to mémé's comment. "I don't wish to leave. I want to be near Jean-Pierre."

"My grandson will be lucky to be sent to Germany. It is his

wish you and his child are safe. If you love him as much as you say you do, you will abide by his wishes."

Zeldah bit her lip, one tear escaping down her cheek. Adèle swallowed. "Sophie's contact, a gendarme, said they would go easy on him due to his age."

"The police are under the control of the Germans. I don't think we should pay much notice to what they say." Her grandmother's shaking hands belied the cold-sounding words. She loved her grandson and was plainly terrified for him but trying to hide the fact from Zeldah. "Now, I have some shopping to do. Coming, Adèle?"

"No, thank you. I'm going back to bed. The trip has me exhausted."

Her grandmother's eyes hardened. "You need to consider getting a job."

"Me?"

"Yes, you. Who is going to pay for your keep? I don't have the same contacts as your father."

"I can work." Zeldah stood and cleared the table.

"Zeldah, you will stay indoors and rest to build up your strength. This may be the free zone but the Vichy crowd could teach the Germans lessons on being anti-Semitic. It's better if you stay here. I shall be back soon."

She put on a small hat, set it at a jaunty angle, and left the house. Adèle ignored what her grandmother had said. Get a job? It was ridiculous. She wasn't staying in Lyon. She was going back to Paris as soon as she could.

TWENTY-EIGHT

Sophie paced up and down the hospital lobby. She'd finished her shift but was waiting for Elizabeth. Her friend had contacts all over Paris and had been busy trying to find out what was happening to Jean-Pierre.

"Sophie, sorry." Elizabeth hurried to her side, putting on her coat. "I didn't mean to keep you waiting, but it took me longer than I thought. Walk with me." She allowed Elizabeth to take her arm and together they walked down the street. People passed them but nobody lingered, all keen to get home.

"Did you see Jean-Pierre?"

Elizabeth stopped and turned to face her. "No, but I spoke to a contact at the prison. The whole group are being held in solitary confinement; they aren't allowed to mix with the other prisoners. He's in good shape: hungry, cold, but otherwise well."

Sophie watched Elizabeth's face closely for signs her friend was lying but she didn't appear to be. "What does it mean, this solitary confinement?"

"He's being kept on some sort of punishment watch. He's not allowed visitors, books, or food parcels. It appears they are all being treated like that, including the women. Maybe it's the Germans' way of breaking them."

Sophie hoped that's all they did, but she wasn't about to put her deepest fears into words. She couldn't admit to the nightmares she'd been having where Jean-Pierre was tortured. Adèle's story of Léo's beating had left its mark.

"Sophie, have faith. Boris Vildé and some of the others are well known; they have some good contacts. Keep your chin up."

Elizabeth hugged her and they separated at the métro, going in opposite directions. Sophie travelled home, her mind occupied with her brother and her twin. How she missed them both. She was losing everyone she cared about. She thought of Jules and blinked rapidly to stop any tears from falling. She wasn't going to make a spectacle of herself on the street.

She opened the door of their apartment, the silence taunting her. She didn't want to be alone but was thankful her father was out again. Not that she spoke to him when their paths did cross.

She headed to bed without eating.

* * *

The next morning, she had a day off and decided to visit Yvette. She'd put the visit off for too long, and it would get her out of Paris for a while. She'd visited the prison, trying to find out word about Jean-Pierre, but each time she'd been turned away. It was better to keep busy, and a trip to see her friend was a distraction, at least.

Shivering, she put on one of Jean-Pierre's old sweaters, though it was not as cold as it had been. One thing to be thankful for. She took the electric train, storing her bicycle in the baggage car.

Her mood lifted as she left Paris, the occupiers and their red flags behind her. Out here in the countryside, you could pretend France was free. It took just over an hour to reach the town and another ten minutes to cycle to the small farmhouse.

Spotting her friend in the back yard at the vegetable patch, Sophie leaned her bicycle against the stone wall of the house and called out.

"Morning, Yvette."

Yvette jumped, but then, seeing who it was, came running.

"What on earth are you doing here?" Despite her question, Yvette looked delighted to see her. "Look at you, you are too thin, and those eyes. You look like you haven't slept in a year. Your heart is as broken as mine."

"I'm so sorry, I should have come earlier but I just … couldn't. I wanted to see you, but you remind me… And then they came for Jean-Pierre." She saw the shock register on her friend's face. She hadn't known. "Oh, Yvette."

Yvette shushed her. "It doesn't matter, you're here now. Come inside and explain what you mean about Jean-Pierre. What do you mean they took him? Who? Why?"

"I am so glad to see you." Sophie pulled her friend close and hugged her. The tears, once they rolled, wouldn't stop. Yvette led her into the house, into the front room.

"The Germans came and took Jean-Pierre away. They've accused him of all sorts including writing resistance papers." Sophie sobbed. "Adèle and my mother went to stay in Lyon."

"I'm so sorry." Yvette held her while she sobbed, before pushing her away, looking into her face. "And your father? Was he arrested too?"

"Papa? Don't make me laugh. The Boches love him, and vice versa."

"Sophie Bélanger, that is no way to speak of your elders."

Sophie hadn't seen Madame Stein sitting in one of the darker corners of the room. Why was she sitting in the dark?

"Good morning, madame." Sophie greeted her friend's mother, but she wasn't about to apologise for her remarks about her father. He disgusted her. "Papa has made his choice. He refuses to help his only son. I do not believe he deserves respect."

Madame Stein gaped at her.

"Maman, Sophie is right. What sort of man would turn his back on his own son?" Yvette said. "Why don't you come to the kitchen and help me with the déjeuner? Maman likes to eat early."

Sophie saw Yvette wanted to speak to her in private. She excused herself and followed her friend to the kitchen.

"We don't have coffee. But I can offer you warm milk." Yvette heated some milk before pouring it into a cup.

"Thank you." Sophie took a deep drink of milk, the cream clinging to her lips. "It tastes better than the finest wine."

"Couldn't you move here, and stay in Paris on those nights you have to work?" Yvette had her back to Sophie as she cut the bread. "It would be nice to have you close. You couldn't live with us, as you are not Jewish."

"But I am."

Yvette whirled around to face Sophie, her face ashen. "What?"

"I am Jewish, at least according to your religion. We've just discovered that my grandmother converted when she married my grandfather. But that doesn't matter now."

Yvette came over and took her hands in hers. "How I wish you'd known you were Jewish when you and Jules were together! My parents were wrong to prevent you two from getting married. The world has turned upside down."

Sophie hugged Yvette as the tears fell for their brothers, friends, and themselves. At last Sophie pushed Yvette away so she could look her in the face. "You need to leave here and go south."

"I can't."

"But why? Your mother won't leave?"

"No, she would, but I can't." Yvette's chin jutted out like it always did when she'd made her mind up about something. "People depend on me. That's all I can tell you."

Sophie couldn't believe her ears. "You must go. The police officer I begged to help Jean-Pierre, he warned us to leave." She told her friend about her visit to the police, and also about Hannah and Szymon. "Please think about what I've said. Adèle has taken my mother and Zeldah to Lyon to stay with my grandmother. Zeldah is pregnant with Jean-Pierre's child and they are working on getting them out of France."

"Pregnant? Poor girl, she must be so upset with what's happened to Jean-Pierre."

"She loves him so much. The news upset my mother because Zeldah is a servant, papa because ... well, let's not get into that."

"I can imagine your father's reasons. Poor Zeldah. I remember her as being beautiful. No wonder she stole Jean-Pierre's heart." Yvette smiled before the smile faded and she asked, "How is Adèle?"

Sophie tried not to react to Yvette's tone.

"I would say she was the same as always, but it wouldn't be true. Don't look at me like that. She has changed, well, somewhat. Losing Léo like she did. Then Jean-Pierre being arrested." Sophie shrugged.

"She is and always will be a selfish brat." Yvette laughed.

Startled by Yvette's laugh, Sophie asked, "What?"

"Given her opinions about Jews, I would have loved to see her face when she realised she is one of us."

Sophie didn't respond. She couldn't blame Yvette. Adèle had been beyond rude when she'd met Jules and Yvette for the first time. Her sister could have been reading from *Mein Kampf*, given her disgusting views. There was nothing she could say in defence of her twin, so she changed the subject.

"Please think about leaving. I couldn't bear it if you got hurt or worse." Sophie's eyes filled with tears. She wished Jules was here to talk sense into his sister.

"To think we were almost sisters." Yvette swallowed hard, making a half-sobbing sound. Sophie hugged her, being careful not to lose the grip on the glass in her hand. Their tears mixed as they fell.

"In my heart, we are. Yvette, whatever you are doing, please be careful. It was horrible losing Jules. I couldn't bear it if I lost you too."

At her words, Yvette pushed her back and looked into her eyes. "We had a letter. They said Jules was shot trying to escape."

Sophie's glass slipped to the floor and shattered. It was empty, but the glass fragments went everywhere.

"Oh, I am so stupid. I didn't mean to blurt it out like that." Yvette appeared horrified at her bluntness.

Sophie mumbled, the pain in her heart almost physical. "He was trying to get back to us?" Oh, why hadn't he just stayed where he was? At least he might still be alive.

Yvette lifted an eyebrow, cocking her head to one side, her eyes not leaving Sophie's.

"What?"

"Does that sound like Jules to you? He would have stayed with the men, seen to the injured at least until they were repatriated. I don't believe it. I think they shot him because he was Jewish." Yvette's voice shook. "They'll pay for it too."

Oh, Jules. She could see his face, his chocolate-brown eyes filled with love for her. If she concentrated hard enough, she could almost feel him standing beside her. Tears flowed down her face, her hands and legs shaking so much, she had to sit down.

"Jules loved you so much. He told me he would marry you despite what our parents thought. He planned to ask you to go to America, believing Dr Murphy would help you both."

Sophie struggled to regain her composure. Jules would have wanted her to help his family.

Yvette prepared something to eat while Sophie went to wash her face.

When she came back downstairs, she sniffed the air, the tantalising scent making her mouth water. Yvette looked up. "It's rabbit. I have plenty. Rabbits are so easy to rear. You should take a couple back to Paris with you. In no time, you would have an entire load of them." Yvette kept talking, but Sophie couldn't concentrate. What had Yvette meant when she said people depended on her? Was she doing a similar job to Jean-Pierre?

"Sophie, be brave. Jules wouldn't want you to be sad. He is—"

Sophie cut her off. "You and your maman should go to Lyon. My grandmother will help you. The Germans could come looking for you." Sophie looked Yvette in the eye. "Please think about it. I couldn't bear it if the Germans took you away. Lyon is safer. For now."

"You are a fine one to talk about safety. Why are you still in Paris? Why didn't you go with Adèle to Lyon?"

"The hospital needs me." Sophie had to tell the truth. "Or rather I need the hospital. I've lost everything else. I want to be near Jean-Pierre to help him if I can. But you might be safer in Lyon."

Yvette threw up her hands. "For how long are we safe? I listen to the BBC, yes, I know it's forbidden, but I have to know what is going on. The British are losing. Hitler will order his troops into the rest of France despite what that puppet Pétain thinks."

Sophie agreed with Yvette, but they couldn't anticipate what would happen. All they could deal with was today. If Yvette and her mother got to the free zone, they might be closer to whatever rescue efforts there were for the Jews of France.

"Maybe, but then you could go to Spain. At least in the south, nobody knows you. You could get false papers."

"With this face, nobody would bother to look at my papers." Her fatalistic tone worried Sophie, but she knew from experience that when Yvette dug her heels in, nothing would change her mind.

And Sophie couldn't argue about her friend's appearance. Yvette was beautiful, but her dark, curly hair, black eyes and tanned skin marked her out as being Jewish.

She wasn't about to give up trying to keep Yvette and her mother safe. The Germans had taken enough.

Sophie set the table. "What are you doing here that is so vital?"

Yvette's face settled into a closed expression.

"Come on, talk."

"No, it's best you don't know and ask no more questions."

"But, Yvette—"

"I have work to do here." Her firm tone told Sophie that she had made her mind up. "I am fighting back in my own way. Jules didn't die in vain."

* * *

During the meal, they talked about their brothers when they were younger. They laughed and cried. It was cathartic for both of them.

"What is Paris like now?"

Sophie took a second to collect her thoughts. "Quieter. But more dangerous. It is hard to explain. There are hardly any cars or people on the streets, yet the métro is packed. There is an air of tension as if something is about to explode."

"You mean as in people resisting?"

"I don't know. There have been a few isolated incidents, but in reality nothing more than people whistling the anthem or drawing the victory sign on walls. A friend from work went to the cinema. We are used to people sneezing and blowing their noses."

At Yvette's look of confusion, Sophie hastened to explain. "Sorry, I forget you don't know what it is like. There are always propaganda films being played. I haven't been in ages, but there was quite a famous one about a French pilot being imprisoned by the British. Can you imagine it? The audience sends a message to the authorities they don't believe it by sneezing or snorting. The usherettes add to the noise by telling people to be quiet; the result is nobody gets to hear the movie. It made the Germans very cross."

"That is resistance!"

"You don't live in Paris, my friend. They can arrest you for the slightest thing. They arrested one lady for using her face powder. It seems the Germans thought she was being disrespectful to the newsreader. I'm serious. It's like a tinderbox."

Yvette shuddered. "Maybe it is a good thing I am not there."

Sophie nodded. "You would hate it and not just because you are Jewish. We have to be polite no matter how they behave. But sometimes people fight back. I saw a soldier ask for a light at a café. The Frenchman said he didn't smoke, all the while blowing rings of smoke into the German's face." Sophie fell silent for a second before mumbling, "Sometimes we are unkind."

"What do you mean?"

"Not all Germans are the same. There are real nasty people, but you get those in every country. You should see some of papa's French friends. They would put Hitler to shame. I think a lot of the German soldiers stationed in Paris are lonely. Can you imagine walking around a city where you don't understand the language and everyone hates you on sight? They must miss home, their families, their sweethearts."

Yvette rested her elbows on the table and put her head in

her hands. "Sophie, Sophie, what will I do with you? You want me to cry over these men? They don't belong here, so tell them to take their tears and go home."

Sophie didn't bother trying to convince Yvette. She felt bad enough even thinking of feeling sorry for the Germans. The same ones who'd killed Jules and now had her brother in prison. She didn't need a doctor; she needed a psychiatrist.

"I'd best get back home."

"Why don't you stay the night? I have a bottle of wine. Maman goes to bed early and we can stay up and drink the whole thing. Please say yes."

Sensing Yvette was just as lonely as she was, Sophie nodded. She could go back to Paris and reality tomorrow.

"Great. Now, how good are you at catching rabbits? Let's see if we can catch a couple for you to take home. You can put them in your basket and tell whoever you meet they are pets for your cousin's children."

"I don't have any cousins with children."

"So what? They won't ask you to produce them. Don't think about the risks; think about your patients eating warm rabbit stew." Yvette poked her tongue out. "I will even give you my mother's recipe so long as you don't tell her."

There was no fear of that. Madame Stein said only two words to Sophie before retiring to her bed.

* * *

Sophie left early the next morning with a headache and four baby rabbits. Yvette had also given her a box of herbs to fill the window boxes in the hospital. Some had medicinal uses and others could help flavour the plain meals the patients had to eat.

"I wish I could give you some chickens, but you wouldn't get those past the soldiers. Maybe next time, I will have more eggs."

"You have given me plenty. I love you. Please take care of yourself."

"I will, and you too. And for goodness' sake, stop feeling sorry for the occupier. You need to toughen up, my friend."

* * *

Rather than go home to an empty apartment, or – worse – her glowering father, Sophie left the train station and cycled to the hospital. She didn't have any issues with soldiers and arrived complete with the bunnies. If only she had had a camera when she presented them to Elizabeth.

"What are they for?" Her friend held the basket at arm's length as if it contained a poisonous snake.

"In time, food, but for now, they can keep the children amused. Yvette packed some other things for us. We need to put up some window boxes and use these plants to grow more herbs. We can use them to help eke out our medical supplies. It will be fun." Sophie fought hard to keep her voice jovial. She busied herself sorting the plants into medicinal and culinary.

"How is Yvette? Did you have a good time?"

Sophie was about to say yes, but she caught the look of concern on Elizabeth's face. She gave up all pretence. "Yvette had a letter saying Jules was shot trying to escape. Can you believe it?"

"We know Jules would have tried to get back to you and his family. He's – was – an honourable man."

"And leave behind his wounded patients?" Sophie shook her head. "They're lying, but I don't know why." Sophie twisted her hands, before confiding, "Yvette has changed. I mean, in some ways. She's as lovely as ever, but she's full of hatred for the Germans. She said they will pay. I'm worried. Thank God she isn't here in Paris, but I wish she would go to Lyon or even further. Oh, Elizabeth, I can't believe Jules is dead, Jean-Pierre is in prison, and now Yvette is … well, I don't know what she's involved in; she won't tell me." The tears rolled down her cheeks as her legs gave way and she took a seat at the table.

Elizabeth moved to put her arms around Sophie's shoulders, her voice trembling. "You have been through so much. Yvette is a grown woman and must make her own choices. Blast this war."

Together, the women cried. After a few minutes, Sophie pulled a hanky from her pocket and dabbed at her eyes. She had to keep busy; it was the only way to survive. She stood up.

"Is Dr Murphy here?"

Elizabeth mopped her own eyes before coughing. She reached into her pocket, taking out a cigarette and lit it with shaky hands. Sophie went over to close the door just in case a busybody saw a woman smoking and reported her. Not that it was illegal to smoke, but with the rations cut, it was unusual for a woman to have cigarettes and she didn't want anyone asking awkward questions.

"Yes. But he's with a patient, one released from prison about two weeks ago. She isn't doing so good."

"These will help fill her up." Sophie unpacked some fresh butter and some early peas.

Elizabeth sniffed the peas. "I've hated these all my life, but you can't imagine how good they smell now." She took another drag of the cigarette before licking the tips of her fingers and putting it out. Then she placed it back in the packet in her pocket. "Help me take these things to the kitchen and you can fill me in on the nicer parts of your visit."

* * *

Later, Sophie met Dr Murphy's patient. Blinking rapidly, she stared in horror at the sleeping figure. The young girl had what looked like cigarette burns on her forehead and on her chest.

They were inflamed and the red-raw skin looked even worse against the snow-white hospital sheets.

Catching her gaze, Elizabeth swore under her breath. "They became infected. She was lucky she didn't die."

"What happened to her? She looks so young."

"Lucie was a student. She lied about being at the demonstration back in November."

"And they picked her up now? That was months ago."

"She's been in prison since November. Her family didn't know where she was. The German secret police found some anti-German content in her journal. They tortured her. Kept in solitary confinement for months. I don't know how she survived without going mad."

Sophie's blood roared in her ears. If they treated an innocent girl like this, what were they doing to Jean-Pierre? Chills flooded her spine.

"They did this because she said she didn't like the Germans?" Even as Sophie spoke, she could hear Yvette telling her to wise up to the Germans and not be so soft. She stared at the young girl, so small, against the hospital bed. "She's only a child. Like Jean-Pierre."

"I doubt your brother would thank you for referring to him as a child." Elizabeth turned back to her patient. "Lucie will survive but will always carry the marks, both the physical and mental. I swear it gets more difficult to keep my thoughts to myself. The papers should print these stories, not that trash they give us. Can you imagine if everyone knew the truth? Then the resistance would rise."

Would it? Sophie wasn't sure. She didn't think many would care what happened to youngsters like Lucie or Jean-Pierre. It seemed all they cared about was themselves and their survival. Maybe that was how the Germans were winning. By keeping the citizens of Paris half-starved, queuing up every day, walking on eggshells in case they fell foul of some new rule or regulation, they reduced their spirit to nothing. They became like sheep following along although the road they were on led to disaster.

"Sophie, what are you thinking about? The look on your face would scare Hitler himself."

Sophie looked at the floor. She wasn't about to admit her thoughts. Even if they were only partially true, they were too scary to face.

TWENTY-NINE

14 MAY 1941

Hearing whispered voices and what sounded like crying, Sophie pushed the door of the ward open carefully. This ward wasn't used, so someone was in trouble and she was keen to help.

Noémie sprang up from the bed she was sitting on. Another nurse was still sitting on the bed; she seemed frozen in place, her hands clutching a green ticket.

"What's wrong? I thought I heard crying. What can I do?" Sophie directed the question to Noémie but continued to stare at the other nurse. She couldn't remember the girl's name.

"Eliana's mother got a signed letter from the police commissioner. She's to present herself with a family member on 14 May at seven in the morning. The letter says to bring her ID, which will then be verified." Noémie moved closer to her friend, putting a reassuring arm around her shoulders. "I've tried telling Eliana it's just a formality, but she's worried."

Noémie continued. "Eliana was born in France but her mother is from Czechoslovakia. She married Eliana's father, a Frenchman, but he died in the last war. It's only the two of them."

Sophie moved to the girl's side. "I believe you are right to worry. Perhaps it would be best for your mother not to turn up."

"She can't do that." Eliana's face paled further. "The police have our address. Mama believes it would be better for her to go but she refuses to let me go with her. She says it is best for her to go alone. I am needed here." Eliana's hands trembled as she looked down at the piece of paper. Sophie took it from her and read through it. It seemed innocent enough, a requirement to have papers checked wasn't in itself unusual, but a sixth sense warned her this wasn't a good thing.

"I have a friend with the police. I can ask him what he makes of this. In the meantime, please dry your eyes and don't say a word to anyone."

"Why? Everyone knows I am Jewish. It's not like I've hidden it. Mama refuses to let me work on the Sabbath. Dr Murphy has been so good to me." Eliana's voice trembled even more. "I can't let Mama go alone, but I don't want to let the hospital down either."

"Please, Eliana, don't fret. Noémie, why don't you take her to the canteen and make a hot drink. Eliana, wash your face and try to pretend everything is okay. For now. I will come and find you soon."

Sophie went to find Elizabeth. With her contacts, she was bound to know what this green invitation really meant. She walked to the infectious ward and donned a new apron before entering, making sure she hadn't been followed.

Elizabeth looked up from Szymon's bed. The young boy's arm was recovering well but he had not yet spoken.

Hannah sat on her bed beside Szymon's, little resembling the girl who'd arrived two weeks ago. Her long brown hair gleamed in the sunlight streaming through the window. Her lip sores had disappeared and while she was still very slender, she didn't look so different to the adolescents in Paris after a hard winter with little food available. She smiled shyly at Sophie, but the wariness and distrust hadn't completely left her eyes. After what the girl had seen, Sophie wasn't sure it ever would.

"Elizabeth, could I have a word?"

Elizabeth nodded before securing the new bandage on Szymon's arm. "Hannah, can you read him a story while I speak to Sophie?"

"Oui, I need to practice my French."

"What's up?" Elizabeth whispered as she led Sophie to the far end of the ward.

Sophie handed her the green invitation, watching Elizabeth's face closely. Her friend wasn't surprised.

"Yes, I've seen them. They've been issued to all the foreign Jews who registered under that census they did in 1940. The one we told them to ignore. But they didn't listen." Elizabeth shook her head. "They believed in France. So many told me they had to obey as it was the law. But it was a trap, Sophie." Elizabeth returned the green invitation, her hand trembling. "This is how it started in Poland and elsewhere, Jews summoned and then transferred to ghettos."

"We don't have ghettos here."

"No, but we do have camps." Elizabeth glanced in the children's direction. "I don't know where they intend sending these people but my cousin told me to tell my friends to ignore the summons. Whose is it? I don't recognise the name."

"A friend of Noémie, a nurse working with her called Eliana. She doesn't have one; this is her widowed mother's. She's Czech. Eliana, an only child, was born in France. She wants to accompany her mother but is worried about letting the hospital down. Her mother wants to go alone."

"Her mother shouldn't go at all."

"I told Eliana the same, but she says her mother is terrified of disobeying the rules. People believe in the law, as you said. So long as they abide by the regulations, they will be safe."

Elizabeth's face flushed, her eyes glittering as she spoke, "I could kill that miserable old git Pétain, and his friends. This is their doing."

Sophie agreed, but they couldn't do anything about those in power.

"What shall we do about Eliana?" she asked.

Elizabeth glanced at the children. "We need a nurse to escort them to the free zone. And a doctor."

"You mean me?"

"You could travel to see Adèle and your family. You speak German so you can communicate with the children and the authorities. Can Eliana speak Yiddish?"

Sophie shrugged. "I suppose so. She said her mother stopped her working on their Sabbath so that would suggest she is religious. What about papers? Eliana's even more Jewish-looking than Yvette and that's saying a lot." Had Yvette and her mother got the green invitation?

"We'll think of something." Elizabeth took Sophie's hand. "Are you sure you are up for this? It will be dangerous. Especially now they have Jean-Pierre. They may be still watching you."

"They can watch. They murdered Jules and imprisoned my brother, terrified my grandmother and my mother. I won't let those innocent children fall into their hands. Not if I can help it."

Elizabeth patted her hand. "That's the spirit."

Sophie told Hannah and Szymon she would be back soon before she set off to find Eliana. Then she would visit the Litwaks, her Jewish neighbours in their apartment.

* * *

That evening, Sophie gathered some coffee, sugar and a couple of tins of sardines, and walked up the stairs to the next floor. She heard talking as she approached the apartment. She knocked, the talk stopped, but nobody answered the door.

Knocking again, she called out, "Forgive me for calling so late – it's Sophie from downstairs."

The door opened slowly, Monsieur Litwak cautiously peering out. He was wearing his coat despite it being after curfew. When he saw she was alone, he smiled, his eyes filled with relief. "Forgive my manners, Mademoiselle Bélanger. Come in, please."

Sophie entered. The apartment had a similar layout to theirs, but that's where the similarities ended. It was freezing and looked rather empty. She bit her lip, trying not to shiver and embarrass the man. "Please go straight through. My wife is in the kitchen. My girls, they are in bed."

"Thank you." She walked over the bare oak parquet floors, the darker shading of the walkway compared to the surroundings suggesting a rug was missing, past the furniture bare of ornaments and darker patches of wall paint suggesting missing frames. She pushed the door open, walking into the kitchen where a worried, frail-looking woman stood by the table, her hands clasped together. An older man wearing a kippa sat at the table. Sophie smiled at his nod of acknowledgement before turning to the woman.

"This is for you, Madame Litwak. We have so much papa thought we should share with our neighbours." Her father would die rather than share, but she preferred a white lie than for the woman to think it was charity.

Sophie passed over the parcel of food. She handed the cigarettes to Monsieur Litwak. "We had an unexpected windfall and thought the men might appreciate a little gift."

Monsieur Litwak gave the cigarettes to his father, who turned the packet over and over in his hands.

Madame Litwak opened the package. Her eyes widened as

she took in the coffee and the sardines. "Thank you, you are very kind."

"Please sit down. We don't get many visitors. I apologise but we couldn't find coal." He held up his hands. "We have tried burning wet paper. It makes it last longer, but it doesn't give out much heat."

"I won't stay long. I wondered if you had received a green ticket?"

Madame Litwak gasped. "You got one too? We thought it was just..." Face flushed, the woman stopped talking.

Sophie shook her head. "One of my colleagues did. Or at least her mother did. Eliana's parents were born in Czechoslovakia."

The man took a seat and sighed heavily. "We were just discussing the invitation. It is for my father but says to bring a family member. There is only me. My brothers live in America and my mother died some years ago. I can't leave my family, but I don't wish my father to go alone. Who knows how long he will be away?"

Madame sobbed at that comment. Monsieur Litwak took his wife's hand and patted it. His father spoke up.

"I told you I am going with my friends. I can look after myself. Your place is with your family." The old man's stern tone expected no argument. His eyes met Sophie's. *He knows it's something more than a way to check the records.*

"I'm going to see my grandmother; she lives in Lyon. I wondered if you and your family might like to accompany me?" Sophie didn't know how she'd get papers for them all, but she'd worry about that later.

He shook his head. "Thank you for your thoughtfulness. I'm French and I am a law-abiding citizen just like you, mademoiselle. We would not get an Ausweis. If we went without and were caught..." He let the silence speak for itself.

Sophie stood up again. "I can bring you more cigarettes; they are useful as ... bribes."

"You are very kind, but we will be fine. God will protect us. Thank you for the thought and for your kindness." He indicated the food.

Sophie nodded to the family and walked to the door. Monsieur Litwak followed her outside, closing the door over behind him. "You believe this is not another census?"

Sophie nodded again. She couldn't leave without saying more, without trying to persuade them. "I don't know what to believe any more, but I have reason to think that those who present themselves with their card... Well, they may find themselves in grave danger. That's why I hoped you might come with me. Zeldah, she told us stories from her family in Poland..."

He shook his head. "Yes. I have heard the same stories. But perhaps that is what they are. Just gossip. I bid you goodnight and thank you again."

She nodded, unable to speak for fear her voice would tremble and she'd cry. She walked back down the stairs. Families were being torn apart and for what reason?

* * *

A week later, on the evening before they planned to make the trip, Elizabeth got the papers and miraculously an Ausweis each. Eliana and Sophie persuaded Eliana's mother to pretend to be very ill. The old woman was so nervous, they gave her a mild sedative.

Elizabeth patted Eliana's arm. "It will keep her sleepy on the journey but won't do any lasting harm."

"Maybe I should take some too?" Eliana tried to joke, but Sophie was half inclined to agree, given how the nurse jumped at every noise and they hadn't yet left for the station.

"Dr Armand will meet you at the train. He is an actual

doctor so there won't be a problem with the patient transfer."
Elizabeth's eyes twinkled with amusement. "Trust him, Eliana.
He and I served together in the last war."

Eliana nodded. Elizabeth trimmed Hannah's hair before
braiding it, making her look younger than her years. Using her
father's money, Sophie had purchased some new clothes for the
children and gave Eliana some of hers. Her feet were smaller
than Sophie's, but they had stuffed the shoes with newspaper.
They were all very well dressed in the hope the Germans would
be less likely to suspect they were runaways.

"Hannah, you are deaf and mute. So just stare at my face if
anyone asks a question. I will answer questions."

Hannah nodded, her eyes wide with terror. Sophie
squeezed her hand. "You need to pretend you are going on a
holiday, otherwise they will suspect something. You can't look
so scared."

"I'll try."

"I'm terrified too, but your story has helped me realise we
have to do this." Eliana pushed a strand of hair back from
Hannah's face. "We will be together."

Szymon still wasn't talking, so they didn't have to worry
about him.

They took a vélo-taxi to the station, not wanting to risk
taking the métro. At Gare de Lyon, Sophie's heart raced. There
seemed to be more green uniforms around than before.

Szymon squeezed her hand as they walked up to the inspectors. The man took her papers, but his eyes fixed on Eliana. He
barely glanced at Sophie's papers, singling out Eliana for questioning.

"Mademoiselle, your name?"

"Eliana Rossi." Eliana lowered her eyes rather than holding
his gaze. Sophie had coached her on how to act when questioned by anyone in uniform. *Treat them as if they were Hitler
himself and it can't hurt.*

"Nationality?"

"French, monsieur."

Sophie held her breath, willing Eliana not to get too defensive. It was one thing to be a slightly outraged French citizen having to answer such a question, but being too disagreeable could provoke the bear.

The man scrutinised Eliana again. "You look Jewish."

"Jewish? How dare you?"

His head jerked up with surprise at her tone. Sophie held her breath.

"Because I have dark eyes and tanned skin? Haven't you ever been to Italy? Both my parents grew up on extensive vineyards before they moved to Paris to establish their wine business."

The man shrugged, his expression disbelieving, yet he hesitated. Eliana didn't look like she was poor and starving, unlike most Jews in the occupied zone, having been on slashed rations and unable to work. Sophie moved forward. "Can you please hurry? My patient needs her medication. Without it, she is likely to have another seizure right here." Sophie dropped her voice to a loud whisper. "She'll start thrashing around and foaming at the mouth. It isn't a pleasant spectacle."

As if Eliana's mother heard her, the older woman drooled and made funny noises. Sophie would have laughed at the man's horrified expression if it weren't for their perilous position. "Go ahead. The porter will help you with your bags."

They moved ahead in silence, with Eliana holding on to her patient's arm. Szymon held Sophie's hand in a vice-like grip but Hannah walked straight-backed as if she travelled by train all the time.

Sophie tipped the porter, entered their carriage and closed the door of the compartment behind her. Eliana looked fit to cry. She moved to the bathroom, leaving Hannah to help Sophie get Eliana's mother settled. Szymon sat in the corner, clutching a teddy bear Dr Murphy had given him.

Sophie wondered if the SS would get on and check their papers, too. She willed Eliana to return so that they were all together. The train's whistle blew just as the nurse walked in the door, a tight smile on her face.

"Thank you, Sophie, I think..."

Sophie shook her head. She didn't know who was in the next compartment and how far their voices would carry. Eliana caught on quick.

"I feel better now. I shouldn't have eaten those truffles. They've never agreed with me."

Sophie grinned at Eliana. If anyone French had overheard her, they would assume they were collaborators. Nobody got to eat truffles these days.

* * *

Their journey passed without incident. Even the *douanier* was pleasant. As they pulled into Lyon, Sophie whispered, "Remember, you might not see German agents, but they are all around you. This is the free zone in name only."

Hannah and Eliana nodded. Szymon had fallen asleep and Madame Rosi was out cold. Sophie was a little worried she had given the lady too much sedation.

At Lyon station, she was pleasantly surprised to be met by a doctor who was waiting for her at the train car door, rather than outside the gates as she had anticipated. "Dr Armand, at your service. Thank you for transferring Madame Rosi to our care." The doctor clicked his fingers at the porter to take the baggage. "We have a long history of dealing with her family. I believe you are her private nurse?" He directed the question to Eliana, who, after glancing at Sophie, nodded.

"Dr Bélanger, I have an ambulance waiting outside for my

patient and her nurse. There is a taxi waiting to take you and the youngsters where you need to go."

"Thank you, Dr Armand." Sophie turned to Eliana, who she wanted to hug and wish the best. But that wouldn't be appropriate. "Thank you for your help. Be sure to greet those Italian boys with a kiss from me. Make me jealous and send me a picture of the vineyard."

Eliana smiled, her lips trembling. "Thank you for everything. I won't forget."

* * *

Sophie took the children with her to her grandmother's. She wasn't sure what she was going to do with them, but trusted Elizabeth had more connections who would help her.

"Sophie, my darling girl. And who are these young people?" Her grandmother didn't seem a bit surprised to see the children. Sophie wondered just how far Elizabeth's network stretched.

"This is Szymon. He doesn't speak. He owes his life to this brave young lady, Hannah."

"Welcome, children, come in, please. We have plenty of space as there is only Sophie's mother here."

Sophie's heart almost stopped as her body chilled. "Zeldah? Adèle?"

"They have gone to Marseille." Her grandmother ushered the children inside and towards the kitchen. "I have some bread, jam, and café au lait on the table." She indicated the table set against the wall. "Help yourself."

Szymon wouldn't let Sophie's hand go until she promised him she'd be back. Hannah helped him with his coat while Sophie followed her grandmother to the kitchen.

She stood watching her grandmother as the woman prepared coffee for them both. "Why did Adèle go to Marseille? Did something happen? I thought..." She hesitated, not sure how much her grandmother knew. "... a friend was taking Zeldah."

Her grandmother reached over and patted her hand. "The *friend* was otherwise detained. I suggested Adèle go, it will do her good. She may see how unfortunate and precarious life is for some and actually do something about it." Her grandmother blinked away tears. "Your mother doesn't leave her bed. Have you seen Jean-Pierre?"

Sophie choked her own tears away as hope and fear clashed on her grandmother's face. She shook her head before asking, "Do you know what will happen to Hannah and Szymon?"

"A friend is coming later. We will know more then. For now, come here." Mémé opened her arms and hugged her. "I've missed you."

"Me too, mémé, me too."

THIRTY

Adèle helped Zeldah from the train carriage, the pregnant girl looking very green. She hadn't suffered from morning sickness at the start of the pregnancy but the worry about Jean-Pierre had affected her badly, leading to regular bouts of vomiting. That and the crowds on the train had increased their discomfort. Adèle summoned a porter to help with their bags.

"Can you find me a taxi, please, to take us to the Hôtel Splendide?"

"I can find you a taxi but that hotel, like everywhere else in Marseille, is full. The place is teeming with refugees, from Spanish to German to Jews." The last word was spat through thin curled lips, his gaze focused on Zeldah. "They all run here in the hope of getting away, but the net is tightening."

Beside her, Zeldah shuddered but from fear or feeling ill, Adèle couldn't tell. Adopting her most superior tone, she addressed the despicable porter. "Mind your manners if you expect a tip. Now take these bags through and find us a taxi." She took Zeldah's arm and escorted her through the police check and outside. The porter had a word with the taxi man but to Adèle's surprise, the taxi man spat on the ground, just missing the porter's shoes. The porter muttered a curse before disappearing back into the station.

With a warm smile, the taxi man came towards them, took the bags and turned to Adèle. "There are no hotels with rooms in Marseille but if you permit me, I will take you to stay with my sister. It's not the Ritz, but it is clean and" – he lowered his voice – "safe." He looked around before adding, "We have friends who can help you. And you will not have to register like you would at a hotel."

"Help?" Adèle pretended not to understand.

"Madame, people dressed like you accompanied by a beautiful Jewess only come to Marseille for one thing. To leave. Now come before our porter friend returns. I'm worried he could make trouble."

The taxi driver helped Zeldah into the vehicle before holding out his hand to Adèle. He gave hers a light squeeze. "Smile, madame. Most of us remain French, and believe in freedom and rights of all."

They drove through the crowded streets, which were worse than Lyon. "Every building is full to capacity and still desperate people keep coming." The taxi driver pointed to various buildings their windows open to allow the occupiers to carry on conversations with the people standing on the streets. They heard all accents, from rough Spanish sailors through to the German and Austrian Adèle usually associated with her nights out at Maxim's. Only these people didn't wear a uniform, unless you accepted their expressions as one. Fear and desperation were the one defining feature on every face.

The driver drove down a tree-lined avenue and stopped near the end. Taking their cases, he set them down on the road before helping Zeldah from the car and saying, "Follow me." He led them through the garden gate and up a long path to the house. It was much grander than Adèle had expected. For a moment she hesitated, wondering whether they were walking into a trap. Were they going to be robbed or murdered?

"My sister, Agathe, lives here now. The owners, her very good friends, have already left. They asked her to stay in the hope they can return one day and still have a home." He knocked on the door, three short knocks and one long one. A short, older woman opened the door, her eyes widening at the sight of her visitors.

"Come in, Louis, don't stand on the step." She came out to greet them, her eyes glancing left and right as if expecting someone to jump out on top of them. She closed the door behind them before looking to Louis, waiting for an explanation.

"My new friends need a place to stay. They had an unfortunate experience at the station."

"The gendarmes?" the woman asked.

"No, the porter, Charles."

The woman muttered furiously. Adèle and Zeldah exchanged a small smile as their host called upon the devil to take his own off the streets of her city.

"I only have soup. Plus some old bread. I haven't been out today." The woman held out her hands in apology.

"Please don't worry, it will be fine, thank you for taking us in," Zeldah replied. Adèle swallowed back the request to be taken to a restaurant.

"Louis, you take these ladies into the dining room. I shall bring in the soup. We can then discuss your plans. Would you like to freshen up?"

Zeldah nodded, so the woman escorted both her and Adèle to the first landing. "My friends, they were wealthy in assets, but they had very little cash after paying for tickets and other things. You shall sleep and eat in comfort, even if the food is scarce."

Once more, Zeldah moved to reassure her. "We are very

grateful to you and your brother. Thank you."

Adèle took in the once-luxurious surroundings, the wallpaper brighter in patches, no doubt where paintings used to hang. The carpet sank under her feet and the large bed had clean-looking sheets. There were no ornaments on the shelves or on the dressing table. She picked up a sole photograph of two young women.

"My best friend and I." Agathe's voice broke. "It was taken after the last war. Now she is gone and I've no idea where. I bought her house when the government said no Jews could own assets, but I couldn't pay her much. We thought she could hide here, but..." The woman's eyes glistened as she squeezed Adèle's arm. "You must make your memories with your friend before she must disappear too."

Adèle opened her mouth to protest they weren't friends but stopped. Zeldah was more than their ex-maid, and she was going to give birth to Jean-Pierre's child. Her niece or nephew.

Once Adèle had used the facilities, they wandered back downstairs, following the sound of low voices to the dining room. The conversation ceased as they entered.

Adèle took out a small bundle of francs. "This is to help cover the cost of our stay."

The woman crossed her arms. "Non – you need that to get out of France."

Adèle pressed the money into her hand. "Please. We would have paid to stay at a hotel. Zeldah needs nutritious food and the rest, you can use it for whatever you wish. We have some more." Though not as much as they would have if her father had helped. She dismissed his face from her mind. He was dead to them now. "How will Zeldah get out of France?"

Zeldah pushed out her chin, a desperate look in her eyes as she wrapped her arms around her stomach. "I don't want to leave. I want to stay here. At least until they decide what to do about—"

"Everything." Adèle interrupted quickly. The couple had treated them well but they were strangers and didn't need to know of Zeldah's connection to Jean-Pierre.

Zeldah threw her a dirty look, no doubt thinking Adèle didn't want to acknowledge her relationship. But that wasn't it. She was trying to keep Zeldah and her baby safe. The couple ignored her question, the woman indicating they sit and eat while the soup was hot.

After their meagre lunch, Agathe insisted Zeldah rest, muttering something about swollen ankles. She escorted the girl upstairs, leaving Adèle alone with Louis.

"You asked earlier how we will get your friend out of France. You are not going too?"

Adèle shook her head. "No. I must go back to Lyon. Our family, some of them are..." She stopped as the self-preservation instinct kicked in.

"You are wise to keep your own counsel. In this city, the walls have ears. The Germans, they do not occupy us yet, but their spies are here. There are some Vichy officials who would gladly hand your friend over on a plate. It's a pity she is so beautiful. She will attract a lot of attention."

"Do you know people who can help? You said something in the station." Adèle hesitated before adding, "My sister's friend in Paris is trying to get her an American visa."

Louis didn't blink. She guessed many people travelled to the port on the promise of a visa. "Yes. I know people. Good people. Monsieur Fry, he's an American. He is helping, as are some others. Will I take you to see him?"

"Please. I'll just go and tell Zeldah."

She ran up the stairs to find the Jewish girl sobbing in the bed. Was it the baby? Agathe had mentioned swollen legs but was that a problem? Adèle didn't know much about pregnancy apart from thinking it was a grotesque experience – losing your figure and then having to have the baby. She took a breath before asking, "What's wrong?"

Zeldah tried to sit up. "I don't want to go. I want to stay here. What if they release Jean-Pierre and he finds out I deserted him? He'll think I don't love him."

"No, he won't. He'll believe you loved him so much you had to do everything you could to save his child. You're overtired and run-down. You need rest. Stay here with Agathe; she's a good woman. I will be back soon."

Zeldah grabbed her hand in a vice grip. "You will come back, won't you? Don't leave me alone."

As if she would do that. But before she could protest, the voice inside her head answered for her. She would have done. Not long ago. She'd been so selfish.

"I promise I'll be back. Now rest. Think of my niece."

"Not your nephew?"

"Pah! Boys are too much trouble." Adèle forced a smile. A boy would remind her too much of Jean-Pierre, who she may never see again.

* * *

Adèle picked up their papers and her purse before heading back down to where Louis waited. She followed him out of the house but they walked past his taxi. "It is better not to arrive in a taxi; it brings too much attention. This way we can mingle with the crowd."

She was glad of his hold on her arm as the streets were swarming with people, some selling personal items, others pleading for help, some searching for family members – and all the while the gendarmes stood watching. She kept her purse tight to her side, not wanting to lose the monies her grand-mother had pressed into her hand.

* * *

Louis introduced her to a group of gentlemen, but Monsieur Fry was unavailable. Her questions as to his whereabouts and when he would return were left unanswered. A small woman, about five foot, came forward and took her to a side room. There she asked her for the truth about Zeldah.

"Why must she get out now? She is French, yes?"

"Yes, but Jewish."

"Like all of Marseille. Why does she need to leave now, and why the United States?" The woman held her gaze, making Adèle squirm on her seat. "The truth, please. We can't help you otherwise. Is your friend's name on a list?"

"List?"

"The Germans helpfully make lists of those they would be interested in detaining. Under Article 19, Vichy are obliged to hand over any person they request."

"For what? I mean where do they go?"

"Not somewhere pleasant. Now, back to your friend?"

"Zeldah isn't on any list, not that we know of. She is my brother's fiancée and pregnant with his child. My brother was involved in the résistance in Paris; he's currently awaiting trial."

"A trial? The Germans don't normally waste time with those." Despite the woman's sardonic tone, her eyes were full of pity.

"He is only nineteen and we are hopeful he will be sent to Germany to a prison camp. But if the Germans find out about Zeldah, they may use her to get him to talk. He refuses to name those he was working with."

"A brave man." The woman shuffled some papers on her desk. "We will need a wedding certificate and new papers for your friend just in case her name is on any German list. She can revert back to her real identity when it is safe. Do not tell anyone, even the people working here, more than they need to know." The woman stood up and shook Adèle's hand. "I hope we will meet again when France is free. Your family must be proud of your brother. It is an honour to meet you."

Adèle coughed, not realising she'd been holding her breath, and only then took the woman's hand. She wanted to protest she wasn't worthy of the praise. It was Jean-Pierre, Zeldah, and Sophie who made the family proud. And her grandmother.

* * *

It took every franc she had but, finally, she was in possession of a ticket on a ship to Martinique and from there to New York. Louis drove her back to the office that Fry and his friends were using. He waited outside as she went in to see if Zeldah's papers had come through.

"Your friend has some powerful people vouching for her." The young man spoke with what she thought was a Spanish accent, although as his cigarette was still in his mouth, it was difficult to tell. "There is an American visa waiting for her, in her real name, in Martinique. She's a nurse and will look after the children travelling alone."

Why were they going alone? Where were their parents? Adèle wanted to ask but it was better to pretend she knew the arrangements. Sophie's Dr Murphy must have told his friends Zeldah was a nurse to get her an American visa.

Despite there being no postal service, some post made it out in the diplomatic pouches. A secret everyone knew, but nobody admitted to.

The man thrust the paperwork into her hands. "Tell your friend to keep her head down and mouth shut. Say nothing until she's on the ship to New York and Martinique is but a blip on the ocean."

Adèle nodded, too caught up with sorrow to say anything else.

"Are you sure you don't want to escape with her? They say it's only days until the *doryphores* invade us too."

Adèle wasn't running away. This was her home. "No, I'm staying here. The Germans will not push me out of France."

* * *

The day came for them to say goodbye. They gathered at the port with the other people being helped by Varian Fry and his friends. There was a strong police presence but no obvious signs of any Germans. Despite this, Adèle knew Fry was concerned the Nazi spies were watching. The tension in the air was reflected in the pale but determined faces of the people standing by. She saw the children travelling alone, some of them so young, each one holding hands with another one. She assumed they had been paired up to avoid anyone going missing. Zeldah stood to the left of the group of children, pale-faced but with a determined look in her eyes. "Please say thank you to Sophie and your grandmother for me. Tell Jean-Pierre I love him. I wrote this for him. If you get to see him, will you give it to him please?"

She passed the note to Adèle, who put it in her bag, trying to ignore her shaking hands. She had to keep it together.

"Try to write or send a telegram to Monsieur Fry. He can get word to us."

Adèle rubbed away the tears on her face. She realised she'd miss Zeldah and her fierce love for Jean-Pierre. Zeldah rubbed a hanky over her face; it was sweltering, and the crowds were making it worse.

"If you see him, tell him I love him and will do forever."

"I will. Look after you and the baby. Let those women spoil you." Adèle indicated some matronly women also waiting to board. They kept looking over their shoulders as if expecting the Gestapo to pounce any second. "Don't wear yourself out looking after the children; let the others help you." Adèle pulled Zeldah into a hug, surprising both of them. "Keep safe."

Zeldah held her gaze. "You are so much more than a beautiful face, Adèle Bélanger. Help your people. They need you."

THIRTY-ONE

"Nurse, I can't believe it is June already. Seems like it was only Christmas a few weeks ago."

Sophie forced a smile for the benefit of the patient. Inside, she stifled a scream. To her, every day lasted a year. She was lonely without her family, desperately worried about Jean-Pierre and still mourning Jules. Every night, she cried herself to sleep. Some mornings, she woke up thinking Jules was alive and then reality set in.

The ward nurse walked up to her. "Sophie, Dr Murphy wants to see you and Oliver."

"Coming," Sophie replied as she checked the last patient. By the time she arrived at Dr Murphy's office, Oliver, the head porter, was already there, along with Elizabeth, and the conversation was in full swing.

"We have to do something, Dr Murphy. We don't have the resources to feed the patients." Oliver didn't hide his frustration. He worked more hours than anyone else, and was often found at patients' bedsides, telling them stories or giving them special treats. Sophie thought he would have made a wonderful doctor if circumstances had permitted. He was a firm favourite with all the staff.

"Then we must find them," Dr Murphy said.

"Where do you expect us to look?" Oliver had exhausted his reserves of patience. "We have already traded our wine rations for potatoes. There is nothing we haven't thought of."

"I know people in the countryside who might help us," Sophie volunteered.

Dr Murphy discounted her idea. "You can't ask the Stein family for help. It may compromise them."

Sophie ignored his protest. "It may, but Yvette wants to do something, and she has a lot of contacts with the farmers. She may know people who can help us. They can't help us with bread, as the Germans told Yvette they would collect her harvest, but they might be able to provide us with vegetables. Her idea about the rabbits worked."

They couldn't argue with that. The rabbits she had brought back from Yvette's farm had multiplied and provided a stew a few times. One nurse had skinned the animals and used the fur to make mittens for children. They had used every piece of each unfortunate animal.

"But what about transport? We don't have any petrol," Oliver pressed, but she could tell he was interested.

"I can cycle out there and find out if they can help. If they can, we can worry about the transport then. I wanted to check on Yvette and her mother, anyway. This is a perfect excuse. I will stay overnight as it's my day off. It will be nice to get a change of scene. I will go tomorrow and come back on Friday in time for the late shift."

"I don't know, Sophie, it's perilous. What if they catch you?" Dr Murphy asked.

"Doing what? Going to see an old friend? That isn't a crime. At least not yet," Sophie replied, trying to sound more confident than she felt. "If Yvette and her friends can help us, it's worth asking."

"If they can, you must make them aware of the risk. They may see it as black-market dealing," Elizabeth said.

"Only if money changes hands. Anyway, the Germans don't want to target an American hospital, do they?" Oliver replied with a big grin on his face. He loved getting one over on the occupiers.

Oliver had a point. With America not in the war, the Germans were more polite to the Americans left in Paris.

"Yvette will consider it payback for Jules." Sophie stumbled over his name but recovered. She didn't look at her colleagues' faces. If she saw pity, she would lose her promise not to cry. Tears belonged in her bedroom. "Madame Stein hates the Boches more than me. She blames them for taking her husband and her son. If she gets involved, she could move mountains with one glance."

Her friends laughed, as had been her intent. She caught Dr Murphy's eye, his expression troubled. She wished she could ease his concerns, but suspected he hadn't shared half of them.

* * *

Sophie cycled with a large basket on the front of her bike to Jules's country house the next morning. This time there was no sign of any wheat in the fields, which lay bare. Instead of many chickens, she saw only two rather sorry-looking hens. There was no sign of Yvette. Sophie put her bicycle against the wall. Looking around, she made her way to the front door. It was hanging off the hinges, as if it had fallen off and someone had tried to mend it. Someone with little expertise. She called for her friend, but there was no answer.

Her heart beat louder. Pushing open the door, she stepped inside. The room was in darkness. It took her a few minutes to realise the shutters were still closed and there was no fire in the grate. Not that you would expect one in August. Even so, she shivered.

"Yvette? Madame? Are you home?"

She walked through the house, seeing signs of life in the kitchen. Pushing open the back door, she spotted Yvette.

"Yvette!" She couldn't keep the relief from her voice. The woman dropped what she was holding and ran towards Sophie, throwing her arms around her.

They hugged, and Sophie could feel her friend's bones through her clothes. Her heart sank. All thoughts of finding food for the hospital disappeared.

Her friend looked older than her years. Sophie looked around, astonished by the empty barn and sheds. Last time she had visited they had been full of sheep, goats, horses and other livestock, but now, apart from one cow, it all stood empty.

"The Germans!" Yvette spat as she caught Sophie looking around. "They came again, like last year, but this time they took not only the wheat, but everything else not nailed down. We are lucky they left the cow, but even that was only because we told them she had run dry. It's the same cow you doctored. She had a severe case of mastitis, but they were too stupid to know that."

"They took everything? But how are you supposed to survive?"

"They don't care about that. They laughed when I complained and told me to keep pigs! Insinuated I would find them good company. Maman was nursing two hens back to health, and she could save them too. We manage with the forest and good neighbours. Everyone shares what they find."

"Did they visit every farm?" Sophie's voice quivered as she held Yvette's hand, her gaze not believing what she was seeing.

"Most. They hit some worse than others. The Jewish ones. Some got to keep everything."

Sophie raised an eyebrow.

"Collaborators," Yvette confirmed, a twisted expression on her face. Then she took a loud breath. "You shouldn't be here, Sophie. It is too dangerous. Every day, we face new threats." Yvette looked around as if expecting the German army to pop up from behind the gorse hedge before ushering Sophie inside.

"Where is your mother?"

"Maman is ill." Yvette filled a glass of water for Sophie. "Not too bad now. She had me worried. The doctor from town is a good man. He came to see her. Gave her what he could."

"Would you like me to check on her?"

"In a while, maybe. You know maman. She is not the best patient."

Sophie heard the unsaid words. Madame had no interest in seeing Sophie.

"How is Paris? Any news of Jean-Pierre? How are Adèle and your mother and grandmother?"

"Adèle took Zeldah to Marseille but has now returned to Lyon with my mother and grandmother. They send those three-sentence cards. It is difficult, but trying to get papers to visit them is next to impossible. A friend warned me not to make too many trips to the police. Not while Jean-Pierre's case is still pending."

"Do you have a court date yet?"

Sophie shook her head. She changed the subject. "Yvette, I know we spoke last time about you leaving. Now you have to leave. You can't live like this. The front door, the lack of food."

"They kicked the door. It was open, but they enjoy breaking things. Maman shouted at them. It terrified me. I thought they would shoot her. Her outburst seemed to amuse them rather than annoy them. They inferred she had lost her mind. Maybe they are right."

Yvette looked away, but not before Sophie saw the tears. She pulled her friend into her arms and let her cry, her whole body shaking.

"It was horrible, Sophie. Awful. They brought a smell of fear to this area that was never here before."

"Please take your mother and go to Lyon. My grandmother will look after you. You know she will. Things are happening in Paris. Horrible things, much worse than this, and this is bad." Sophie hesitated, wondering how much she should share. She wouldn't tell Yvette about Lucie.

"Just last week, during the *rafle du billet vert*, French police arrested almost thirty-six hundred Polish Jews. Not the Germans; it was our own men. The old man who lived upstairs in our apartment had a green ticket. His family haven't heard from him, nobody seems to know where they went." Sophie's voice trembled. She wanted to grab everyone she loved and run away. Terror kept her awake at night. She wasn't just worried for her friends, but for all the Jewish people. For France, too. What had happened to religious freedom?

She felt Yvette's body stiffen. "I heard rumours about that, but it won't change my mind. Sophie, what happened was horrible, but they were foreigners, not French people."

Sophie shook her head. "You are wrong, Yvette. That is just what the papers and government want you to believe. There were French people, too. I know some of their families. The children were born in Paris. That didn't stop the police from taking their fathers and mothers."

Yvette didn't answer, a mulish expression on her face.

Sophie ignored it and kept talking. "I took two children to mémé. Hannah, she's a girl who escaped from a ghetto in Poland, and Szymon, the boy she rescued. Mémé knew people and now they are out of danger. You and your mother could be too. Mémé said there are several orphanages for Jewish children. The people running the orphanages could use your help, and they will find a hiding place for your mother." Sophie looked Yvette in the eye. "Please think about it, Yvette."

"I love you for trying to help us, but I won't leave. Please don't ask me to explain. Just respect the fact I have my reasons."

Sophie couldn't refuse Yvette anything. She nodded, although she kept her fingers crossed. She wouldn't stop persuading her friend to move to safety.

"Sophie, it's always lovely to see you, but what prompted this visit?"

Sophie hesitated, not wanting to make Yvette feel bad.

"I didn't know you were having trouble, too. I thought you might help us." Sophie explained the severe food shortages in Paris, including the fact that butchers' and other shops often just closed for days on end.

Rather than laugh at her, Yvette cocked her head to one side, as she always did when she was thinking.

"So, you want to find someone to supply food to the hospital? I am not sure there is anyone who can do that. Before the Germans came, we could have helped, but now..." Despite her reply, Yvette still looked like she was trying to think of a solution.

Sophie interrupted again. "I don't want to get anyone into trouble, but I thought we might work out how to get extra potatoes and other vegetables. The odd rabbit if one landed on your table." Sophie continued. "I know it's asking a lot, Yvette, with how you have all suffered at the hands of the Germans. But our patients are starving. Not just the ones from the British camps, but the elderly, too. They can't survive on eight hundred and fifty calories a day."

"I will see what I can do for you. But now let's eat. Then we will fill bags with items from my little garden. I think the plants are growing to spite the Fritz." Yvette laughed. "You can tell the Boches it is a present from your in-laws. Maybe I should give you some poisons and you can make a drink to share with them."

Although Sophie knew Yvette was joking, Sophie shuddered at the thought of murdering anyone, even a German.

THIRTY-TWO

JUNE 1941

Sophie was second in line at the baker's. Surprised to find the baker in a sunny mood, she returned his smile.

"Morning, Mademoiselle Bélanger. Did you see the papers? The war is over."

"What?" She couldn't hide her shock. Was it all over? *Jean-Pierre will be released.*

"Well, not over yet, but Hitler has made the biggest mistake of his life. He invaded Russia."

It took everything she had to keep smiling as the baker kept chatting. "So now he is fighting on both fronts. I tell you, Mademoiselle Bélanger. This is it. Our time under the beetles will soon be over. It may take three or four years, but victory will be ours."

Sophie didn't argue with the baker. She couldn't find her voice. Not that it would have mattered. He had already moved on to the next customer. She moved out of the shop, listening to similar comments being made among the women waiting. Invading Russia? Hitler and Stalin had a non-aggression pact. What was his motivation for entering a war with the Soviets? What would this mean for Jean-Pierre? Was it good news?

She hurried home, but her father wasn't back. The empty rooms taunted her. She'd planned on spending the day doing laundry and reading. But the encounter had changed her mind. She wanted to see what her colleagues thought of this news. Changing into her uniform, she went to the hospital. They could always do with another pair of hands.

On the streets, there was a distinct atmosphere. Nobody was celebrating, but a few people were smiling. The newspapers didn't mention Russia, at least not on the front pages. But she spotted a couple of signs stuck to windows. *French people, the Red Army is fighting to free you.*

She watched as two German soldiers pulled the posters down, but hurried along when she realised she'd been staring.

She wasn't in the hospital's door before a member of staff hugged her. "Isn't it wonderful? That idiot Hitler doesn't know what he's done. Even the great Napoleon couldn't fight through the Soviet winters. This will be a terrible decision. Good for us, but bad for the Hun."

Sophie kept her feelings to herself. She felt someone watching her, but told herself it was her imagination. She walked towards Dr Murphy's office, where she found him, Elizabeth, and two other trusted members of staff, Oliver and his nephew Victor, discussing the recent development. 'Discussion' was the wrong word. They appeared to be arguing.

Elizabeth acknowledged her presence with a smile, but then looked back at Dr Murphy.

"I am not saying it's not a good thing. I just think any show of support for the Russians is too early. The Germans won't tolerate it," Dr Murphy insisted.

"Yes, but there are so many more wanting to fight now." Victor jumped to his feet. "This is the moment we've been waiting for. Comrade Stalin has called us all to fight. We can't wait much longer. We must show them."

"Victor, I appreciate your willingness to fight for France,

but it is not the right time. Your comrade Stalin is in Moscow; we are here. The Germans will wait to see what happens. They have their spies. They will break up your communist rings and shoot the lot of you. And a load of innocents while they are at it."

Victor snarled as he sat back down. "What do you want us to do? Knit?"

Dr Murphy ignored his sarcasm but spoke to the group. "We need to use this news to our advantage. The unions will be keen to help. Get your contacts to find us train drivers and attendants who will help us. We need transport. Not just to get our visitors out, but to get food and supplies into the hospital. I'm more interested in feeding our patients and curing them than murdering Germans."

Victor stood up. "I can't listen to this. I want to fight." He left before anyone could stop him.

Oliver apologised for his nephew and moved to follow him but Dr Murphy put a hand on his arm. "Let him be. He is young. He needs to cool off. Go back to work, everyone. Sophie, what are you doing here today? It's your day off."

"I know, but I had to come." She waited until Oliver and Victor left leaving her alone with Elizabeth, and Dr Murphy. "I went to collect the bread earlier, and the baker feels the same as Victor. In fact, if a German had come in, I think he would have assaulted him there and then. This news, I don't know what it will do." She looked at her mentor for an explanation.

"Cause problems for us. That's what it will do." Dr Murphy took a sip from his glass. "Don't misunderstand. It's great that Hitler has spread his armies. He has underestimated the task in front of him. But the Russians are not our friends. I can't say that in front of Victor. Comrade Stalin! What has he done to help his people so far?"

Sophie shrugged her shoulders. She knew nothing about Russian politics. If Jean-Pierre was here, he would be able to answer. She tried to hold on to her earlier optimism, but it was hard.

"So, you don't think this development will help my brother and the rest?"

Dr Murphy's head swung up. "Oh, my dear Sophie, forgive me. That would be the first thing on your mind. I don't know, maybe? We can only hope so."

Elizabeth spoke up. "My concierge has a sister in the south of Paris. She said, when she asked two of her German guests what it would mean for them, they burst into tears. Grown men. They are being sent to the Eastern front."

Sophie tried to feel compassion for the two men, but she felt nothing.

Dr Murphy spoke. "We will have to be on our guard. What Victor does not see is that many Parisians have no love for the communists. They may now side with Hitler and help him win the battle against what they call a common enemy."

"They couldn't, would they?" Elizabeth asked.

Dr Murphy's lips thinned. "They already have. My sources tell me they have formed a new unit. The LVF, a legion of French anti-Bolsheviks who have volunteered to fight alongside the Germans against Russia."

Sophie couldn't believe her ears. French men fighting with Hitler. The world had turned on its head.

"Why haven't the papers mentioned it?"

"Pétain will announce it in the next couple of days. Or at least his office will."

Elizabeth paled. "The victor of Verdun championing the cause of Frenchmen fighting with Germans. Who'd have thought we would see that day?"

"I don't think we have seen anything yet. I just hope those youngsters in the Sorbonne and elsewhere keep their heads. Friends, there is nothing we can do now but pray. I need to do my rounds."

They took the hint and left but, at the door, Sophie turned back. "You will be careful, won't you? I don't think communists like Americans too much."

"Nobody likes us now. The Allies think we have forsaken them, and the rest... Who knows what they think?"

Sophie closed the door behind her and went to find work to keep herself busy. She headed for the children's ward. She needed the innocence of the children to offset the ugliness of the real world.

* * *

Later, she came across Elizabeth crying in a ward.

"What's wrong? Come with me." She took the head nurse away from the prying eyes of their colleagues. They went to Dr Murphy's office, knowing that he was out at a meeting.

"Here, sit down." Sophie handed Elizabeth a hanky. A block of ice encased her heart. "Have you heard something? Is it Jean-Pierre?"

Elizabeth shook her head, her hands trembling as she held the hanky to her nose.

"No, not him. But a member of the same network. They arrested her on 18 June but I've just found out."

"A museum worker?"

"No, Sophie. Sister Marie-Laurence, the nun who you met once. The Irish lady."

Sophie sat. "She was working on the escape line. So she knew Jean-Pierre. That's what she meant by my family being brave."

"Yes. Mon Dieu, what will they do to her?"

"The Germans won't torture her. She's from a neutral country. Don't worry, they'll release her and say it was all a mistake."

Elizabeth held her gaze. "We both know that's naïve. We'd

better pray she doesn't break under interrogation and lead the..."

"... them right here. Elizabeth, you must go away. Dr Murphy is American. He's protected, but you are French."

"So are you."

"Yes, but they'd have picked me up already if they suspected me."

"I'm not going anywhere. I wasn't crying for myself but for my friend. She worked through the first war, you know, nursing at the front. She treated German casualties too. Maybe that will help her."

Sophie didn't think so but she didn't say anything. Speculation was pointless. "We should contact the Irish embassy to alert them."

"That's been done." Elizabeth's defeated tone suggested she didn't think it would help.

"Nothing is going to be achieved by us sitting here crying. All we can do is continue her work and pray they will be merciful."

Sophie hoped her words would bring some comfort to Elizabeth. But with the nun's arrest, if her link to the museum came out, wasn't it more proof to the authorities that her brother and his friends were doing more than publishing a newspaper?

* * *

A few days later, there was more bad news as Dr Murphy's words came true. The press made a tremendous fuss over the formation of *Légion des volontaires français*, or LVF as it became known. Posters appeared all over the streets, showing a French soldier side by side with his German counterpart. Sophie read the account on the métro. It said fifteen thousand people attended a rally at the Vélodrome d'Hiver.

Sophie brought the paper into work, but Elizabeth gave her the unofficial version.

"The police say less than ten thousand people showed up and a quarter of those were women. There weren't standing ovations or anything that you are reading about. Sophie, don't even try to understand the LVF and their followers. They argue between themselves all the time. Their leaders hate each other."

"I know, but I can't believe Frenchmen volunteering to fight alongside the Germans."

"Look at the reaction. There are more V for victory signs being chalked onto walls. Métro tickets shaped into the cross of Lorraine cover the streets. The Resistance is growing. Even if these people won't do what we do, they are protesting in their own way."

Sophie knew her friend was right. She wished it raised her spirits, but she could only think of Sister Marie-Laurence and all the others behind bars, especially her brother.

Elizabeth read her mind. "Have you been to see Jean-Pierre?"

"Yes, well, to the prison. They won't let me see him." *No matter how many ways I try to bribe them.* "I saw this on the ground outside. There are copies of it all over the place."

She handed Elizabeth a copy of the latest poster signed by Otto von Stülpnagel. "They have banned the Communist Party. It forbids all communist activity in France. They will sentence those found guilty to death."

"Wonder what they don't consider a crime – breathing? Did you hear they arrested the students over in the 5th arrondissement for wearing French colours and whistling 'La Marseillaise'? Those youngsters believe themselves to be invincible."

"I wonder what it will take to convince them otherwise?" Sophie didn't expect an answer. The German reprisals would be severe, of that she knew. But she believed it wouldn't stop young people from expressing their feelings.

THIRTY-THREE

END OCTOBER 1941

Sophie walked down the street to the hospital. The Allies were losing the war. Even if the collaborationists wrote the papers, they couldn't make up the news. Britain was fighting alone. How long would they last?

On arriving at the hospital, she went looking for Dr Murphy. Determined to continue her studies, she wanted to assist him in theatre. Knocking and entering, she found Elizabeth with him, both poring over some paperwork. Dr Murphy pushed it to one side.

"Sophie, I wasn't expecting you this early. How are you?"

Sophie caught the look between him and Elizabeth. They were hiding something, but what?

"I was fine, but you two are up to something. What?"

"We were just talking about bed shortages," Dr Murphy answered at the same time as Elizabeth said, "Food shortages."

Sophie frowned. She hated being treated like a child.

"What are you hiding from me? Tell me." She made a move for the papers Dr Murphy had been reading.

"Sophie, sit down. We heard some bad news."

Her heart hit the floor at his answer.

He blurted, "It's not about Jean-Pierre."

"The Germans shot ninety-eight hostages over the last two days," Elizabeth said, taking Sophie's hand. "Jean-Pierre wasn't one of them. They were Jews or communists."

"But why? Where? How can they just shoot people? Why wasn't there a trial?" Sophie knew she was babbling, but her brain didn't want to deal with the implication for her brother. The Germans would shoot ordinary French citizens. Her brother and his group had committed crimes, at least in the eyes of the occupiers.

"It's the fault of those idiots who think killing random German officers will achieve something." Elizabeth shook her fist. "Ninety-eight Frenchmen in retaliation for the shooting dead of Colonel Karl Hotz in Nantes on 20 October and Hans Gottfried Reimers in Bordeaux the next day."

"But neither of those events took place in Paris. Why would they kill Parisians?" Even as she asked, Sophie knew her question was stupid. The Germans didn't need excuses. "Why were you trying to protect me? Do you think this makes it worse for Jean-Pierre? He is having a trial. They will follow the legal process."

Dr Murphy sighed. "You might as well tell her, Elizabeth; she will see it for herself."

"Tell me what?"

"This." Elizabeth picked up the paper and handed it to Sophie, who skimmed it. The tears blocked her vision.

"But they can't." Sophie handed the paper back to Elizabeth.

"It's not the fact they've announced they will kill the men who help anyone escape and send the women to concentration camps. We all expected that. Well, most of us." Elizabeth looked at Sophie with concern. "I'm most worried about the offer of money for information. Ten thousand francs is a lot of temptation, and we all know there are those who will betray us for a lot less."

"They will give informants that much money?" Sophie asked. She didn't believe it.

"Sometimes they have offered more. How do we fight this? That is what Dr Murphy and I were discussing when you came in."

"Pay them more."

Both Dr Murphy and Elizabeth stared at Sophie. Elizabeth recovered first. "You can't be serious. We don't have that budget."

Sophie knew they didn't, but they had to do something. "What can we do? I am almost tempted to kill von Stüpnagel myself."

Elizabeth surprised her. "He is not to blame. Don't look at me like that. I have no love for the man, but I have it on good authority that Berlin wanted one hundred men shot for each officer. Von Stüpnagel said no. He doesn't believe in shooting civilians."

Dr Murphy nodded. "I believe that. He didn't hide his anger when those SS idiots bombed the synagogues. It doesn't matter, though. They will replace him. Berlin doesn't share his ideals. They will send someone worse."

Sophie put her head in her hands, not wanting her friends to see her tears.

"Sophie, do you want to go home? Be with your father?"

"No, I don't want to go home." At the look of hurt on her friend's face, she forced herself to calm down. "I want to get those ... those people out of France. How dare they try to make us live in fear? I told you I wanted to help more. I don't care about the cost, financial or otherwise. They won't defeat us with their threats or their money. They don't know what they are dealing with."

"Sophie, I am ordering you to take today off. I appreciate

your sentiments, share them even. But we will achieve nothing by acting hastily. You least of all. Your family is already under suspicion. Go home, speak to your father."

"He's the last man I want to speak to."

"Reconsider. He could help us. Maybe not willingly, but he may provide information."

"On? Sorry, I don't understand." Sophie wondered if her friend had hit his head. Her father was a collaborator, a threat to the hospital and everyone in it.

Dr Murphy spoke slowly, as if she was a child. "He has dinner with Nazis and their friends. He must hear things."

"Yes, but he won't help. He won't even visit Jean-Pierre. His only son." She had to make him see the truth.

"He won't help by choice. But you know him. You can make him talk without him realising what you are doing. You could even accompany him on some of his visits. See who is going to these gatherings. I have my suspicions about some of our contacts. Somebody betrayed Jean-Pierre, Boris, and the group. Until I can prove something, we must suspect everyone."

"So, you worked with my brother?"

Dr Murphy glanced at Elizabeth, who gave a slight nod.

"Jean-Pierre was one of our couriers."

Elizabeth took over. "He escorted almost one hundred airmen out of Paris. He had his contacts in the free zone. We knew some of them, but they have already arrested most. The rest are in hiding. We are trying to build up a new network. There are some who seem a little too eager to get involved. We need someone on the inside, so to speak."

Sophie turned on Elizabeth. "You want me to behave like Adèle, after everything you said about my sister."

Elizabeth flushed, but with shame or anger, Sophie wasn't sure. Dr Murphy intervened.

"Feelings run high when it's our families. Your sister is not a collaborator; she just made some, shall we say, unorthodox choices. We won't ask you to do something you can't. It is up to you."

"I can't go to dinner with papa. I don't trust myself to stay quiet. It's not about the risk to me, but I could put Jean-Pierre in more danger. The Germans killed my future. Jules would be alive if it wasn't for them. I would love to help more, but this is not the way, not for me. Papa doesn't trust me."

Dr Murphy sat forward in his chair. "Make him. You can do this, and you are our only chance. We believe there are a few people who move in similar circles to your father, who will help us. But we can't just ask them. We need you on the inside. It will only be for a few weeks."

"Other Frenchmen who appear to be collaborators are on our side?" Sophie's head felt like it would burst.

"No, or at least none we know of. Some Germans are, shall we say, sympathetic." Dr Murphy smiled. "You look surprised, yet your mother is half-German. Nothing is ever black and white, my dear Sophie, especially in times of war. Now go home and think about what we have said."

"I would prefer to stay here and keep busy."

Elizabeth stood up. "Stay and work then. It is best we all keep to our regular routines. We must practice caution and be vigilant. We should appear to work as normal. I have a few patients with nasty bedsores I could use some help with. Ready, Sophie?"

Sophie needed Elizabeth's silent strength beside her.

"Lead the way, Nurse Elizabeth."

THIRTY-FOUR

Although she kept busy, Sophie's mind turned over what Dr Murphy and Elizabeth had said. She wanted to help, they'd given her a perfect way, yet she'd turned them down flat. She visited Lucie and seeing the girl's appearance made her mad. She was recovering physically but the scars those animals had burned into her body would never heal. Nor would her mind. Jean-Pierre was still in solitary, and what were the Germans doing to him? Was he being tortured?

She took her métro home. Opening the apartment door, she heard laughing. Her father had company over. She stilled. This was her chance.

She glanced in the mirror. *Act like Adèle. You can do this.* Taking off her coat, patting her hair into place, she forced a smile and walked into the living room.

"Good evening, papa. You look well." Sophie ignored the surprised look on his face and turned to his guest, a woman not much older than herself.

"Oh, I love your dress, that colour is so fabulous on you. I'm Sophie." She held her hand out as if she was used to meeting strange women in her father's company.

The woman flushed and shook Sophie's hand. "Aimée. Thank you, this dress is my favourite. It's new." She flashed a flirtatious look at Sophie's father.

Sophie inhaled and walked over to the drinks cabinet. "Can I refill your glass?" she asked, thankful her tone remained calm and conciliatory.

"Yes please." The woman held out her glass but her father shook his head. He stared at her, a suspicious look on his face.

Aimée said, "You should invite Sophie to the party this weekend, Noël. Gustav was complaining earlier he didn't have enough female guests."

Heart hammering, Sophie took a seat. "Tell me more. I love parties, but my work means I don't get out much."

"Your beau must be very patient." Aimée took the seat beside her.

Sophie put her drink on the small table beside her. An image of Jules filled her mind but she was doing this for him. She couldn't falter. "Tell me more about this party."

Aimée pushed her hair behind her ear, bending in towards Sophie, her low-cut dress exposing more skin than was polite. "Everyone will be there. It's a birthday party for one of the bigwigs; I can never remember their names. You should come, shouldn't she, Noël?"

"Would you be able to get me an invitation?" Sophie used her sweetest tone, thinking how much Adèle would laugh if she was observing this scene.

"Of course he can." Aimée blew a kiss at Noël before turning back to Sophie. Her desperateness to be friends was off-putting but Sophie forced herself to remain seated. "Now tell me more about your work. It must be incredibly exciting."

Her father drained his drink. "Aimée, we must go, our table is reserved for ten. Goodnight, Sophie, darling." His kiss aimed at her cheek landed mid-air. She wasn't as lucky with Aimée, who kissed both her cheeks, leaving a trail of red lipstick.

Sophie walked them to the door and then stood staring at her reflection in the mirror. Could she keep this act up at a real gathering?

Turning, she walked back into the sitting room and downed her glass in one go. She picked up a photograph of the family taken before the war had started. She would do anything to get Jean-Pierre out of prison and back home where he belonged.

THIRTY-FIVE

Sophie fiddled with the top of her dress, wishing she'd worn a nun's habit. She smoothed down imaginary creases as the black car drove her and her father along the Champs-Élysées. The Wehrmacht-uniformed driver stared straight ahead and appeared uninterested in the occupants of the car. Her father, wearing a brand-new tuxedo, smiled at her.

"You look so feminine and beautiful, Sophie. Just perfect."

She wanted to tell him to go and play with the traffic but instead Dr Murphy's words reminded her to play nice. She needed her father – or more precisely his contacts. They needed someone on the inside of the Nazis' inner circle in Paris.

She closed her eyes, picturing Jean-Pierre. He would be horrified if he heard she was swanning around in a German car on her way to a black-tie function. His reaction would be the same as those of the few French people on the streets who'd glared in her direction as the car drove past. They assumed she was a willing collaborator. Still, if that was what it took to avenge Jules and secure Jean-Pierre's release, she'd sleep with the devil if she had to.

* * *

They were caught in a traffic jam consisting of a line of black cars, many sporting the Nazi flag. She spotted the red carpet ready for their arrival. She watched as the car in front divested its guests, a fat man wearing a general's uniform; the skinny brunette clinging to his arm could have been his granddaughter. Shivering, she focused on the image of her brother's face. She was doing this for him and others like him.

When their turn came, the valet held the door open. Her father exited first before holding out his hand to help her manoeuvre out of the car. She allowed him to tuck her arm in his as he walked her into the enormous house. As they entered, a maid stood forward to take her wrap while a man dressed in servant's livery did the same for her father. A chill ran up her spine as she handed over the small piece of satin that had covered her shoulders. It hadn't offered much cover, but it was a small barrier between her and the guests she was about to meet.

"Sophie, this way." Her father propelled her gently in the direction of the main reception area. The luxury carpet sank under her high heels, her eyes taking in the silk wallpaper and exquisite paintings decorating the walls. A glance inside the room as they approached highlighted the size of the ensemble. This was not an intimate gathering, but a large party. She swallowed, the butterflies in her stomach becoming more frenetic by the minute.

"This way." Her father escorted her across the room, her heels now clacking on the wooden floor. Tall tables for guests to gather around dotted the room, covered in black cloths with floral centrepieces. The scent of fresh flowers competed with expensive perfume and cologne. Everyone seemed to shout rather than speak, the noise giving her a headache. She took a glass of champagne from a passing tray.

With every step she took, her satin dress slid against her

skin, her earlobes protested the weight of the diamond earrings her father had insisted she wear. She hadn't recognised them as belonging to her mother. She hadn't asked where they came from, not wanting to know the answer. A quartet of musicians played in the background. She recognised Wagner, purported to be Hitler's favourite music.

Her father stopped at a table where his friends greeted him with wide smiles, their eyes flickering over her with interest and speculation. She pulled her shoulders in, feeling undressed and wishing once more for her wrap – or better yet, her bed at home.

She waited for her father to make the introductions, but he seemed to have forgotten. Or did he want his friends to think she was his date? She turned away, looking for an escape route, her gaze being drawn to a picture of Hitler high on the opposite wall. He was the reason Jules was dead and Jean-Pierre was in prison. She took a step forward, almost walking into a younger woman, breathtakingly gorgeous, dressed in a silk gown that accentuated her perfect figure.

"The artist took rather a lot of liberty with the painting, don't you think?"

Sophie didn't know how to respond. Was she being tested? "You've met Monsieur Hitler?"

The woman's eyes danced with mischief. "He and I are well acquainted."

Was she laughing at her?

"Haven't we met before, Mademoiselle Bélanger? I think we stayed in the Hotel Albion in Berlin at the same time, maybe two, no, three years ago now."

Sophie shook her head, clasping her champagne glass tight, her knuckles whitening at the stranger's use of her name.

"No, but you may have met my twin sister, Adèle. She travelled more extensively than I did."

"You are the doctor in the family?"

The tone of the woman's voice made Sophie hold her gaze.

Was she trying to reassure her she knew of her task or was she spying on her? She took a sip of the champagne, letting her gaze roam around the room.

"You speak French very well."

"Please call me Inga. Yes, my parents sent me to school in England. I seem to have a gift for languages: French, Spanish." Inga shrugged her shoulders. "It comes in useful sometimes."

Sophie didn't disclose her own fluency in German and English. She pretended to be overawed by the glamour of the party. Champagne flowed freely as elegantly dressed women paraded around the room on the arms of uniformed men. Titbits of conversation highlighting outrageous flirtations made her skin crawl, the women worshipping the men like they were gods, when they were murderers. She drained her glass, willing the night to end. She'd almost forgotten the woman by her side.

"Awful, isn't it?" Inga followed her gaze and raised her eyebrows. "The number of older German men with young French women." Sophie stayed silent, prompting Inga to add, "Maybe I shouldn't criticise; it's just at twenty-one, it would be nice to have some partners my own age."

Sophie didn't comment. She wasn't going to fall into such an obvious trap.

"Please excuse me, I see my father is looking for me. Nice to meet you."

Inga just nodded but the hairs on the back of Sophie's neck stood up as she made her way across the room to speak to her father. She forced herself to smile at the man her father was speaking to.

"Sophie, my dear, are you having fun?" Her father turned to his companion. "My daughter is new to our gatherings."

The man clicked his heels and bowed, before taking Sophie's hand and kissing it. "Your beauty leaves our other guests in the shade. I look forward to getting to know you better."

Sophie forced herself to keep smiling although she wanted to rip her hand from his and run to the bathroom to wash his touch away.

* * *

The night dragged on. She saw Inga dancing, expertly of course as she glided across the dance floor, with various men in uniform. One she recognised as Canaris himself. Inga seemed to favour one gentleman over all her suitors. With him, she seemed to relax, be more natural – or was Sophie just imagining it? She wished whomever Dr Murphy felt was important to their work would make himself known. She had a pain in her face from forcing a smile and if one more *gentleman* tried to hold her closer than was polite when dancing, she'd grind her stiletto into his ankle.

She slipped away from the main room, taking time to tour the rooms open to the guests. There were no personal photos displayed, the only ones on show being those of Hitler with various Nazi bigwigs. She walked into the library, the tips of her fingers running over the huge selection of books on the walled bookcases, then moved to the far end of the library to the baby grand covered in photo frames. Someone should tell the owners to move the adornments elsewhere and leave the piano to sit in its own glory. Her eyes roamed over the photos, recognising Goebbels, Göring, Himmler, and one man whose eyes frightened her. She picked up the frame, examining it closer. Was it just the light or were his eyes really soulless?

She jumped when a man's voice broke into her thoughts. "He's the ideal Aryan, blonde and blue-eyed. Is he your type?"

She quickly put the photo frame back on top of the piano. "Sorry, I shouldn't have touched it. I was..."

"Don't worry, Heydrich would be thrilled to see a beautiful woman admiring him. Although he should be used to it; everywhere he goes women throw themselves at him. He's married of course, but ... well, I shouldn't continue. Doesn't sit well to talk badly of those who are favourites among the party faithful." The man strode over to the cabinet near the fireplace.

Sophie's pulse beat faster. Was this her contact?

"Please sit and talk to me if you don't mind. I've had my fill of political badgering and watching my words in case our SS friends take offence. Would you like a proper drink?" He lifted a bottle of whiskey from the selection of bottles displayed on a cabinet in the corner of the room and took her silence for assent, pouring two glasses. "Do you play?"

Sophie fingered the keys of the Steinway baby grand piano. She'd love to sit and play but it wouldn't be appropriate in this setting, not least as the guests in the other room wouldn't appreciate her music choices.

"Not very well, and certainly not at the level this instrument deserves. The owner or his wife are very lucky to live in such a beautiful house."

The man frowned. "The SS moved in here, shortly after the armistice was signed. I'm not sure where the former owners went, but they didn't wait to pack up their things. They sensibly put a higher value on their lives."

He didn't look away as he spoke, even though his words could be considered treasonous by some. Surely that meant he was her contact... She moved closer to him.

"Did they leave in the *exode*?"

"No. I believe they left a few hours after the armistice was signed, ran during the night." He handed her a small tumbler of neat whiskey before taking a seat and a sip of his own drink. "Why don't you sit down and tell me a little about yourself. I know your father, by reputation. I didn't know he had a daughter who worked. I rather imagined his children would be living a life of luxury, waiting to get married." He glanced at her hand.

She wanted to protest that if his kind hadn't arrived, she'd be married now.

"What is it you do, Mademoiselle Bélanger?"

"I'm a doctor. At least I will be. I'm in my fourth year of study."

His eyebrows rose. "A doctor. I can't imagine that made your father happy. He seems quite traditional in his views."

"Yes, papa is old-fashioned; he believes there is nothing for a woman to do but grow up and swap a domineering father for a husband."

The man laughed, a nice sound, not the one she'd expected given his uniform.

"The Führer shares your father's opinions. In Germany, motherhood is a virtue to be rewarded with medals and other favours. Ugly, fat, and continuously pregnant would be Hitler's wish."

"I don't live in Germany." Sophie put a hand over her mouth. "Forgive me. I spoke out of turn."

"There is nothing to forgive, I like intelligent women who continue to use make-up to enhance their beauty." The man took a sip. "It's forbidden, you know, and if you want to please the party heads, you should wear a dirndl and plait your hair above your head." He stared at her for a few seconds. "Even dressed in our national costume, you would be stunning."

She blushed under his admiring gaze.

"You work at the American Hospital?"

Was this it? This was the contact Dr Murphy had hoped for. She took a step closer.

"Sophie, what are you doing hiding in here? Everyone keeps asking where you are, they want to dance..." Inga came to a stop. "Hello, Dietrich."

"Inga."

The room temperature fell several notches, the tension palpable between the two people. Sophie took another sip of her whiskey, wondering why. Both seemed like nice people – if you ignored the fact they were Germans at a party given in Hitler's honour.

The uniformed man stood up, clicked his heels and bowed. "Au revoir, Mademoiselle Bélanger. I look forward to chatting with you again. Soon."

He turned and, without a look in Inga's direction, strode out the door.

Inga sank into the chair he had just vacated.

"Thank God Weiner saw you heading this way. He knew Dietrich was in the library. What did he say to you?"

"Nothing." She wasn't about to repeat his flattering comments, nor his depreciating remarks about Hitler's ideals.

She put her unfinished drink on the cabinet. "I should go; it's late and I have work tomorrow."

"Wait, Sophie..." Inga whispered as the sound of breaking glass interrupted her. Inga jumped; for a second, she looked scared before she recovered her composure. "I will walk with you to the cloakroom."

Sophie couldn't say there was no need as that would be impolite. "I have to find my father first."

To her relief, her father was standing on the edge of the main room, and he agreed it was time to go home. With a brief wave at Inga, Sophie collected her wrap and allowed her father to escort her to their ride.

She feigned tiredness so she wouldn't have to speak to him and once home retired to her bedroom. But she couldn't sleep; the events of the evening were too disturbing. Who was her contact and how would she ever get to speak to them in private?

THIRTY-SIX

Two days later, after her father had gone to work, there was a knock on the door. Sophie opened it to find Inga with a large bouquet of flowers and a box of pastries.

"Inga. What are—"

Inga put a finger to her lip before saying loudly, "I'm so sorry I'm late. You've no idea how late it was when I went to bed last night. I slept in. Your lovely Madame Garnier allowed me to come right up; I hope that was convenient."

Sophie held the door open, allowing Inga to walk in while she was still talking. Looking behind her guest, Sophie didn't see Madame Garnier but she knew the woman was listening.

"It was so kind of you to take up my invitation. Wasn't the party wonderful..." Sophie closed the door with a heavier hand than normal. "What are you doing here? My father is at work."

Inga's smile lit up her face. Her eyes, nose and chin were so perfectly proportioned, it was easy to see why men had fallen over themselves to dance with her the other night. Today she wore a beautifully tailored jacket and matching skirt with high heels. Her baby-pink silk blouse flattered her slightly rosy cheeks. But Sophie got the impression there was a lot more to this young lady than expensive clothes and good manners. Her eyes locked with Sophie's; she was a woman on a mission. "Good. Then we can talk. Properly."

Inga pushed the pastries into Sophie's hands and threw the flowers on the hall table. She took off her gloves and set them and her bag beside the discarded flowers.

"Do you have coffee? I could murder a cup."

Lost for words, Sophie directed her guest into the living room. "Wait here and I'll go and make it."

Inga walked around the living room, looking at the different family photos. "Ah, that's what you meant by I must have met your sister. You're identical twins. Where is she now? And who is this? Your brother?"

Sophie put the pastries down and removed the family photo from Inga's hands, returning it to its place on the mantelpiece.

"My sister is in the free zone and my brother is sitting in Fresnes, courtesy of your countrymen."

Inga's look of sympathy surprised her even more than the visit.

"I'm truly sorry. What did he do?"

For a second, Sophie got the impression Inga knew all about Jean-Pierre, but that was ridiculous. He wasn't well known.

"He wrote an article for a newspaper. He's younger than you."

"In our struggle, age is meaningless. I shall pray for your brother. I'm sure they will be lenient if *all* he did was write some articles."

Sophie didn't like the inflection on 'all' but she remained silent.

Inga prompted. "So, will we have a coffee and talk?"

Sophie walked towards the kitchen with Inga picking up the pastries and following her. "I know you Frenchwomen don't eat anything, but I love your pastries so I intend having one even if you don't." Inga placed the box on the table before looking around. "Where do you keep your plates?"

"Please sit down and I will get them for you."

Inga sat. Sophie's mind worked frantically as she prepared the coffee and put plates out for the pastries. What was this woman doing here? More importantly, what did she want?

Inga took a sip of coffee and a bite of her pastry before smiling appreciatively. Sophie couldn't taste the coffee, never mind bring herself to eat.

"I don't mean to be rude but what are you doing here?"

"Isn't it obvious?"

Sophie shook her head. "Not to me."

"I want to help. We're on the same side and the men we both work for want us to get to know one another better."

Sophie put her coffee cup back on the table, the contents spilling over the rim. "You? You're the person I was supposed to talk to? I thought it was... Never mind."

"You didn't think it was Dietrich, did you? Was I in time to stop you putting us all in danger?"

Eyes flashing, Sophie clenched her teeth, struggling to maintain control of her temper. "I wasn't about to trust him. He's German."

"So am I and, if what I've heard is true, so are you."

Sophie's mouth fell open.

"Yes, I know your grandmother was born in Germany although she has been living in France since the last war. My contact told me I was to work with you. What did your contact say?"

Was this still a trick?

"Please trust me. I know your brother is in prison because he was caught running an escape line. He's been active in rescuing Allied personnel since the armistice. He helped move downed pilots to Marseille to a man known to the Gestapo because of a mole they planted in the network."

"You know who betrayed my brother?"

"No, not yet. We know the SS and Gestapo have infiltrated several escape lines."

"Why should I trust you?"

Inga picked up her coffee and drained its contents. "The man you spoke with in the library is a career Nazi despite the fact he doesn't sport a party badge."

"But he spoke about Heydrich in the most disparaging way … and also of what Hitler expects from women."

"He's good at what he does. What better way to gain someone's confidence than to tell them what they want to hear? He's no fan of Heydrich's, but that is because he's jealous of the attention that devil gets." Inga took a second before saying, "It doesn't take a mastermind to work out that you being a young single woman who happens to be training as a doctor would object to a role that dictated you have several children for the good of the state."

Sophie put her head in her hands. "I've been so naïve, haven't I? Some spy I'd make if I'm so easy to read."

Inga took Sophie's hands in hers. "Nobody is asking you to be a spy. You and I want to help the same people and hopefully bring an end to the horrible regime in some way. You did well. From what you say, you didn't fall for his deception."

"I did. I was just seconds away from asking him whether he was the person who would help us when you burst in."

"I don't believe that. I think you would have been more cautious. You weren't giving me any tells that you were anything other than a very bored French woman. Although you might want to work on your acting skills for the next function. You're supposed to want to be partying with us, you know."

Inga smiled and Sophie found herself liking the young woman. She was just as beautiful as the other night, even without the silk dress and dazzling jewellery, but there was sincerity in her eyes.

Sophie picked up the pot and poured another cup of coffee. "How did you get involved with all this?"

"My parents brought me up to believe in equality for everyone. They protected me. I hate Hitler with every ounce of my being. I was lucky; my father saw what was happening in Germany. That's why he sent me to be educated in England. He thought if I remained in Germany I would be indoctrinated and become a Nazi. That's what happened to lots of young people: they were raised to be full of hatred."

"I think that's an excuse. They can still think for themselves; they know it's wrong to persecute a whole race of people or those with disabilities, or other minorities. They could fight back."

Inga smiled sadly. "It is so easy to say such things standing on the sidelines. You cannot imagine what it is like to live in Germany. Long before the war began, Hitler and his friends were imprisoning, torturing, and murdering those who disagreed with him. Courageous men and women stand up to him – but at what cost? Their entire families are held accountable. It is one thing to be a brave individual but when the price of your bravery could be the life of your child..."

Sophie nodded. She understood what Inga meant, but it was the same for those resisting in France. There were posters all over Paris outlining the consequences for helping the resistants, yet so many men, women and in some cases children had worked against the occupiers. All the families that had sheltered the Allied soldiers left behind after Dunkirk, those that offered shelter to the refugees that had flooded the country after the Nazis came to power.

"Anyway, we are not here to talk about my countrymen. You have need of travel documents for some friends. Yes?"

Sophie eyed Inga warily. It was one thing for her to put her life in her hands, but to give her names of those they needed to save... She looked at Inga closely. All she saw was innocence and willingness to help.

"Yes, but how do you get these papers?"

"The less you know the better. That way, if you are caught and interrogated, you won't be able to reveal anything under torture."

Sophie pushed down the nausea that threatened to overwhelm her. This twenty-one-year-old spoke like torture was as guaranteed as darkness falling at night.

"You must be careful, Sophie. Not everyone who hates the Austrian does so because of Hitler's racial policies. Many don't care about the Jews or anyone else. They despise Hitler because he's not German, he's not one of them. They want to dispose of him and either continue in his place or put their own person in charge."

Inga stood up, smoothing down her dress as she asked, "What about that woman downstairs? Is she just inquisitive, or dangerous?"

"Madame Garnier. She's nosy like many concierges in Paris but she's not dangerous, at least not to me. I did her a favour a while ago. It keeps her on my side."

"Shall I give her the remaining pastries?"

Sophie smirked. "Yes, and some flowers. She loves both and a few words of flattery will work wonders. Madame Garnier adores my father. She lives in hope he will see the error of his ways and take up with her."

Inga laughed. "From what I can see, your father prefers his women a lot younger." She clapped a hand over her mouth. "Good grief, how rude of me. I'm sorry, Sophie. I shouldn't speak of him like that."

"You can't say worse things about him than I have. My father can't be trusted. He won't even intervene to help Jean-Pierre."

Inga didn't meet her gaze.

"You're going to try to help him, aren't you? With your contacts?"

Inga shook her head. "I'd love to, but I can't. We can't. We have to be very careful to look and play the part of loyal followers. Your brother's case ... it is too high-profile. I'm so sorry. I wish I could. He's a brave man."

Sophie couldn't speak for the lump in her throat.

"Get me those names, Sophie. You can give them to me at the next party. It's for Jürgen's birthday, the grey-haired old goat with the wandering hands."

"What about Dietrich? What shall I do if he seeks me out?" Sophie didn't want to think of how close she'd come to disaster.

"He won't. He's been recalled to Berlin." Inga winked, gave her a kiss on the cheek, gathered the pastries and flowers and left with a loud, "See you soon, darling."

Sophie sank back onto the chair. What had just happened?

La Toussaint came and went without Sophie seeing her father. She had spent All Saints' Day at the hospital rather than sitting in her empty apartment, missing her family and Zeldah. What a difference one year made! This time last year, they had all been together. Now she didn't know where Zeldah was, and her brother was still languishing in prison.

She had been to see Yvette several times since finding out about Jules. She hadn't given up on persuading his family to move to safety, although how long they would remain safe under the Vichy regime was anyone's guess.

She sat at the table in the canteen, stirring the liquid in her cup aimlessly.

"Sophie, thank goodness you went to see Yvette. Her tisanes are much nicer than that awful drink they insist on calling coffee. I have been using her lemon balm tisane on the ward, and it is helping to calm the patients' nerves. You must ask her for more when you..." Elizabeth stopped talking. "Sophie, what's wrong?"

The tears slid down Sophie's face. She couldn't help it.

"Sophie? Did something happen to Jean-Pierre? Your family?"

"Don't mind me, Elizabeth. I was just thinking of last year. We were all together on La Toussaint, and now look at us. I can't believe so much has changed in twelve months. And it is only going to get worse. When will this war be over?"

"Oh, my poor dear friend, you are overtired. No wonder, with the hours you have been putting into this place. You should go home and sleep." She sat down beside Sophie at the table and lowered her voice. "Or are you avoiding your father? I take it the strain of pretending everything is all right between the two of you is difficult. Dr Murphy and all our friends are so grateful; your contact at the party has worked out even better than we thought."

Despite Elizabeth not naming Inga, Sophie still glanced around in case someone was listening. She cared about the German woman and the risks she took on a daily basis delivering papers and other items were breathtaking.

Elizabeth put her hand on her arm. "Talk to me."

Sophie glanced at her friend. "You know what he is, Elizabeth. He has proved over and over he doesn't care about anyone other than himself." Sophie put down the teaspoon. "I asked him again to use his contacts to visit Jean-Pierre but he won't even let me talk about my brother. I hate him."

A tear escaped. Sophie brushed it away.

"He is still your father, and perhaps there is time for him to see the error of his ways. He isn't the first Frenchman to side with the occupiers, and he won't be the last. There is someone I've been trying... There may be a way to get you a pass to visit Jean-Pierre. Leave it with me." Elizabeth gave her a hug. "Have you had any news from your mother?"

"She writes sometimes. But thirteen-line postcards aren't the same, are they?"

Elizabeth didn't answer. What could she say? They both

knew Sophie had to stay in Paris. Her connection with Inga and others in the resistance network was now a vital part of the work they were all doing to free France from the occupiers.

* * *

The rest of the day passed in a blur but just before the end of shift, Elizabeth came looking for her, a wide smile on her face.

"Come in here." Elizabeth pulled Sophie into the stock-room. "I have something for you." She handed Sophie a small piece of paper.

"What is it?"

"Permission to see Jean-Pierre. You can go on Friday."

Sophie's eyes filled as she fingered the piece of paper. "Really? Oh, Elizabeth, you've no idea how much this means." She threw her arms around her friend's neck. "Thank you."

Elizabeth coughed, her eyes shimmering with tears. "Give him our love."

* * *

When she got home, there was no sign of her father, for which she was glad. She went to bed, wondering how the day had passed for Jean-Pierre.

The next day, her father appeared as she was having her breakfast.

"Papa, I got permission to visit Jean-Pierre. Will you come with me?"

He poured himself a coffee, lighting up a cigarette as he took a seat. "You shouldn't go, Sophie. People are watching."

"What people? I'm going to see my brother. He's your son; you should come too."

"There's nothing to be achieved by my visiting him." Her

father drained his coffee. "Excuse me while I change. I have a work lunch to attend."

Sophie stared after him, open-mouthed. She couldn't believe him. He'd dismissed his son as if he was meaningless, worthless.

She swallowed her anger. She couldn't afford to fall out with her father now, as going to the same parties as Inga was a good cover.

* * *

When Friday came, she gathered together a parcel of food and some warm clothes for Jean-Pierre. She added some writing materials in the hope he'd be allowed to write and she could send the letters on to her mother and Adèle. As she approached the prison and joined the queue of other visitors, her stomach churned. What would Jean-Pierre look like? Would he be scared like Lucie, the patient at the hospital?

A guard scrutinised her permission slip. Fearing he was about to deny her, she passed him a bar of chocolate. She opened the parcel for Jean-Pierre, biting her lip as the guard went through every piece. She was tempted to ask him if he thought she'd smuggled in a file.

"I will give it to your brother, not that he deserves it."

Sophie saw the speculative gleam in his eyes. He'd sell the contents on the black market. Her brother wouldn't benefit at all.

"Thank you so much. I will make sure there is extra for you every time I come here with some francs for your trouble." And with that she secured his service.

The guard indicated she follow him to some cubicles covered with chicken wire. He pointed at a seat, waiting until she sat. Then he rang a bell and the door at the opposite end of the cubicle opened. She stifled a gasp as Jean-Pierre shuffled into a cubicle. His hands and feet were manacled. She choked back the tears as her eyes locked with his. He'd aged a thousand years in the months since she'd last seen him. He'd been starved and tortured, his cheekbones pointing out of his face, a mass of discoloured bruises decorating his face and arms. And his hands... She put a hand to her mouth. Dear God, what had he endured?

He whispered rather than spoke. "Thank you for coming, Sophie, but you shouldn't. This isn't the place for you."

"It's not the place for you either. Dear Lord above, what have they done to you?" She barked at the guard, "You're a Frenchman, for goodness' sake, how can you stand by and do nothing?" The man glared at her but turned back to the newspaper on his lap.

Jean-Pierre shook his head. "Sophie, don't come back."

"I will. I'll come as often as I can. I left food parcels for you. We've got an arrangement." She indicated the guard with a jerk of her head. "I tried to get papa to..."

"Don't talk to me about that man. You have no idea what ideas he had for me to get out of here."

Sophie knew then that her father had spoken to his son, and that he expected Jean-Pierre to help himself by giving up other people. God forgive her, but a small part of her wished their father had been able to convince her brother to turn traitor. Then he wouldn't look like this, be stuck in this horrible place.

"Have you spoken to your lawyer?"

Jean-Pierre rubbed the manacles on his hands. "He says I will go to Germany due to my age. But he hasn't even read my file. He's not interested, Sophie."

"I'll go and see him, speak to him."

Jean-Pierre shook his head. "Stay away from him. I don't trust him."

He held her gaze until she nodded.

"Do you have any news of Z ... my family?" Jean-Pierre's voice broke.

Sophie could only shake her head, her ability to speak choking over the lump in her throat. "Adèle got them to safety. That's all I know."

"Thank you and Adèle. Look after yourselves; you will need each other. Be strong."

She inched forward, ignoring the guard's glare. "Jean-Pierre, stop it. You can't think like that. They will send you to Germany. You're so young."

"They'll shoot us. You and I both know that. I love you, Sophie, but please don't come back."

He struggled to get to his feet when the guards came for him. They screamed abuse at him, one lashing out.

Automatically she moved forward but the guard on her side stopped her.

"You'll make things worse. Listen to your brother and go home."

* * *

Sophie fell asleep listening to the BBC. It was banned, but she listened whenever her father was away. The broadcasters speculated it wouldn't be long before the Americans joined the war. That night she dreamed of American soldiers breaking into Fresnes, releasing not only Jean-Pierre, but all his friends.

THIRTY-EIGHT

DECEMBER 1941

America's entry into the war was a cause of celebration for most. Everyone Sophie spoke to said that surely the Allies would now win the war. But for those at the American Hospital, life became even more difficult. They were cut off from all communication with America, and perhaps more importantly the funds in their Swiss bank accounts. The Germans had stopped the couriers from carrying money across the border, at least those operating legally. Now they were dependent on smugglers to bring in funds, which meant amounts were smaller and more prone to not arriving due to the dangers of being caught.

Meanwhile, expenses were rising, given the increasing cost of heating the building and feeding the patients and staff, never mind the cost of the medicines the patients required. Still, no one was ever turned away, whether they could pay or not. Sophie enjoyed tending to the old British soldiers who had stayed in France after the last war, and were now kept prisoner by the Germans at Neuilly. Because of their age, they were not sent to prison camps in Germany, but as anyone who nursed them could see, the conditions at Neuilly weren't luxurious. The prisoners suffered from starvation and a host of illnesses including but not limited to frostbite, dysentery, and festering open wounds. Dr Murphy's rule about never having a German treated by their hospital had been followed. Now they had a perfect excuse – every bed was filled.

She found it difficult to be pleasant to her father when they were alone. In company, she could put on an act, but when they were alone, she ignored him.

One morning, he walked into the kitchen, where she had taken to eating breakfast rather than join him at the dining table. "Paul sent us an invite to his Christmas party."

Sophie pushed her breakfast away. As secretary general of the *Institut d'étude des questions juives*, Roger Desrosiers and his friends were responsible for the anti-Semitic propaganda exhibition that opened in Paris last September. Her father had been on the guest list and had the gall to ask her to come with him. She stood up. "I'm not going to that party and you shouldn't either."

She took her dishes to the sink. Her father waved the newspaper in her face.

"You should be more careful with your opinions. Your American friends are in the war. Won't be so nice for them now, will it?"

Sophie ignored her father, who had taken to life as a single man with relish. Aimée had only been one of many women to visit their apartment.

"Sophie Bélanger, listen to me. I am still your father. I want you to leave the hospital. You can't continue working there without it being noticed."

"Noticed by whom? Your friends?" Sophie couldn't even look at the man she called Father. She looked at him but saw Jean-Pierre sitting in manacles, starving and tortured both physically and mentally. "I would rather work at the hospital or in the surrounding streets than be involved in anything to do with you. You have tainted our family name."

Her father roared at her. "How dare you accuse me of tainting our name? Your mother did that when she lied to me. Your grandmother had no right polluting the blood of the Bélanger family. I shudder to think what Roger would say if he knew." Her father paled, too late realising what he had said.

Oh yes, Roger would love to find out his close friend was married to a Jew.

"Yes, I could tell him, and believe me, if I thought the only danger would be to stop you taking advantage of people, I would. But I won't do anything to put maman and Adèle at risk."

"Not to mention your precious hospital."

"Papa. Don't push me. I think it's rather ironic how friendly you have become with Roger Desrosiers. How long would that friendship last if that man or his friends were to know your wife was Jewish? Your children too."

"You wouldn't dare."

Sophie wished she could wipe the smug look off her father's face, but he was right. She wouldn't tell the despicable Desrosiers anything. She couldn't bear to be in the same room as the man, let alone talk to him.

"I won't say a word to your precious friends."

He visibly relaxed.

"There is a price for my silence. I need some items. Things you can find easily. I expect you to provide them for me without question."

"Bribery? You, you..." He raised a hand as if to hit her, but she stood her ground and he backed down.

"From now on, you will not bring your women home here. You can stay with them if you wish. But this is my home and I won't entertain your trollops."

"Sophie..." He clenched his teeth.

"You should be proud of me. I'm learning from the best. Do what suits me and only me." She poked him in the chest. "You are the master of that."

He pushed her hand away.

"I will use your contacts to help raise monies for us to feed those in need at the hospital." At the darkening look on his face, she continued. "The hospital staff can sell the coffee – the genuine stuff – cigarettes, and whatever other delicacies you can conjure up on the black market and use the proceeds for food. Oh and, let me think, ten bottles of the best red wine available. Don't pass off the cheap stuff you use to entertain your less important guests."

She wanted to ask for a steady supply of fresh fruit and vegetables and decent meat too, but even her father had limits to what he could source.

By the look on his face, he didn't know how to take her. She turned on her heel and left the room, feeling pleased and disgusted at the same time. Adèle would have been proud of her. Her twin always knew how to turn a situation to her advantage.

* * *

A couple of days later, she surprised Dr Murphy and Elizabeth with a cup of real coffee.

Elizabeth held the cup in her hands, sniffing the contents. "I swear I've died and gone to heaven."

"My father can be very generous." Sophie tried to keep a straight face, but failed miserably. But she couldn't bring herself to tell her friends the truth behind the gift. She made up some excuse about helping him make an impression on some woman.

Elizabeth's expression told her she knew Sophie was lying, but thankfully her friend didn't pursue it. Dr Murphy was too preoccupied with his hospital to even consider if Sophie was lying.

"Papa also donated a dozen bottles of red wine. The good stuff. I thought they might make useful gifts."

Dr Murphy's smile lit up the room. "Perfect for bribes."

* * *

Inga had been at her apartment; she saw the pile of chocolate and other luxuries sitting on the table. Going into her bedroom, she checked the secret compartment where Inga left the paperwork for her, the false identity papers, Ausweise and whatever else she could provide.

She'd given the girl a key so that she could come and go when Sophie's father wasn't there. It was safer to leave the papers for Sophie rather than meeting to hand them over. And if anyone suspected anything, they would assume her father and Inga were having an affair. Inga always paid Sophie's father a lot of attention when they were at their parties.

Inga was almost as passionate about helping people as Sophie was. She provided false documents for Jewish refugees. Inga had proven over and over she had powerful friends, providing Sophie with several Ausweise, the travel pass required to cross the demarcation line into the free zone.

Her friend was a firm believer in Wilhelm Canaris, the chief of the Abwehr. She said she had proof Canaris was working with the Allies to bring about the end of the war. Inga's beau worked closely with Canaris and thus could provide practical and financial help to those in the resistance, though Inga wouldn't contribute to the purchase of arms or back any attacks on the Germans.

Sophie wasn't convinced at first that anyone high in the German military intelligence, the Abwehr, could be anti-Hitler.

She assumed they were of a similar mind to the SS. Inga proved she was wrong.

THIRTY-NINE

21 DECEMBER 1941

Sophie finished her ward round before heading to Dr Murphy's office. He sat behind his desk, chatting to Elizabeth.

Elizabeth indicated the chair beside her so Sophie sat down, her heart beating so fast she was sure her friends could hear it.

"The women – Agnès Humbert, Yvonne Oddon, and the others – were moved to Fresnes."

"What does that mean?" Sophie hated the way her voice shook.

Elizabeth took one hand in hers. "It means the trial will proceed, probably in January. My contact in the prison is trying to find out more. But it's difficult." Elizabeth hesitated but after exchanging a glance with Dr Murphy, she continued. "It seems our friends, your brother included, have made life rather difficult as they refuse to confirm any facts. They haven't given up any information either and the Germans are losing patience."

Sophie inhaled sharply. What did that mean for Jean-Pierre?

"They must hold a trial, Sophie. Have faith a little longer. There's still hope." Dr Murphy held her gaze. "We must have hope."

Sophie stood up, brushing her hands down her uniform. They still shook.

"Are you going to the New Year's Eve party?" Dr Murphy asked.

"Yes, Inga asked me to be there. It's the last thing I feel like doing."

"Go, Sophie. You may hear something that could be useful."

She nodded although she doubted she'd hear anything. What could help her brother now?

* * *

New Year's Eve

The crystal chandelier glittered, sending shards of light over the assembled guests. Sophie stood by, idly watching the guests chatting or dancing in the room. She couldn't see her father but for that she was thankful. There was no sign at this party that the Germans were concerned about the entry of America to the war or the fact that the Soviets were proving difficult enemies on the Eastern Front. You would think these people, including those dressed in uniform, hadn't a care in the world.

"Sophie, you must consider leaving Paris. It is becoming more dangerous," Inga said as she handed her another full glass. Inga was even more beautiful tonight in an elegant black velvet gown, the front cut low but with a veil of lace artfully protecting her dignity. Her hair was styled like a crown on top of her head, set off by a diamond tiara matching the diamond drops in her ears. Only close up could you see the lines of exhaustion on her face, the underlying hint of fear in her eyes.

"I can't leave now. People need me," Sophie replied in a soft voice, glancing over her champagne at a French woman draped all over a German soldier.

"I'm leaving. Werner has asked me to marry him. We are going to Hungary." Inga's voice dropped as she moved closer. "I think I am being watched, and I know I am under suspicion. I have to get out now, while I still can. If I'm being watched, you may be too." Inga took a sip of her champagne before laughing gaily as if she had just made a joke. She glanced around, nodding at a couple of people. "Sophie, trust me and leave Paris."

Sophie felt a shiver of fear but she didn't argue. She wasn't leaving, not while Jean-Pierre was still in prison.

"Why Hungary?" she asked.

Inga smiled and tipped her glass against Sophie's. "Where else can I find such wonderful parties?"

Sophie couldn't help but laugh at her friend. She hoped the authorities wouldn't catch up with Inga. She also hoped the people Inga had helped would stand up for the German woman when the end of the war came. She might look and act the part of a German socialite, but she saved many lives. It was impossible to determine how many.

"You should go home. Your expression will make the champagne go flat. Take care, my sweet friend. And please, leave Paris. Things will get nastier. Believe me."

With that, Inga was gone, her heavy floral-scented perfume trailing in her wake.

* * *

That had been the last party Sophie had attended. She couldn't bear to smile and act the part of Daddy's little girl as her father fawned over his new friends.

The only time she and her father spoke now was to argue. The recent spate of government rules, and the actions of Sézille and his compatriots, made life almost unbearable for the Jews living in Paris. More than half had no means to sustain themselves as they were unemployable. Families were going hungry. Some argued all of Paris was starving, but while life was difficult for the average French household, with women spending hours queueing for meagre rations in the stores, it was a thousand times worse for the Jews. They were prohibited from shopping early in the day when there was a better chance of finding something nutritious. They stopped the children from playing in the parks, they could not change addresses, and they confiscated their radios, among other measures.

Her father's connections meant Sophie could help her neighbours. She shared his cigarettes and wine with the hospital. She gave his white bread, caviar, and other delicacies to her Jewish neighbours. They could use the produce to swap for food, and fuel for their fires. It gave her a certain satisfaction to hand out gifts from known anti-Semites to her starving neighbours and friends, although she knew if she got caught, the joy she was feeling now wouldn't last for long.

FORTY

Jean-Pierre's trial began early in January. Sophie prayed her brother and his friends wouldn't be condemned to death. She wished she could be there at the trial but it was forbidden. Elizabeth had described the set-up to her: four German officers sitting behind a large table draped with a red cloth adorned with the black swastika. She'd gone to sleep but nightmares about bloodbaths had woken her, leading her to head to the kitchen to get a glass of warm milk. She spotted a light on in the living room.

She pushed the door open to see her father sitting staring into the fire. Hope flared in her chest. He did care.

"Papa, you have to help Jean-Pierre."

"What do you want me to do? Your brother knew what he was getting into. I blame that maid."

"Zeldah? That's absurd. Jean-Pierre met the other members of the Resistance group at the museum. It had nothing to do with Zeldah."

"It has everything to do with her. My son wouldn't be in this situation." Her father hurled his glass into the fire and went out of the room, slamming the door behind him.

Sophie didn't follow but sat in the room until daybreak. Then she got dressed, picked up her coat and left the apartment. She went to the nearest church, where she lit some candles and prayed. The priest came to sit beside her.

"Can I help you?" he asked.

"Can you? I don't think anyone can. My brother's trial starts today." For the first time in a long time, Sophie started talking and couldn't stop.

"Father. They must understand it was a different time back in November 1940 when Jean-Pierre and the others were writing their papers. The street protests and assassinations weren't happening. At least not on the French side."

Sophie kept quiet about her brother's role in getting airmen out of France. She didn't know what the priest's political views were, and it was best to keep that information quiet.

"Your brother and his friends are patriots. I pray too they will be judged mercifully. You must prepare yourself. Jean-Pierre is likely to be sent to Germany. He is very young. The judge will take that into account."

"Do you really think so?"

"Yes, I do. The Germans aren't monsters, my dear, although some may behave like they are. Let's pray the judge has compassion and understanding in his heart."

Sophie prayed with every bone in her body. Thanking the priest, she returned to the hospital. She didn't bother with a paper, not wanting to read any of the lies the Germans would be spreading about her baby brother.

* * *

Elizabeth kept her updated as to how the trial was progressing. She had an informer in the jail that could get close to one of the female prisoners. She told her how, out of the four German officiators, Captain Ernst Roskothen appeared to be a caring and considerate man. Unlike Captain Gottlob, the Nazi prosecutor, he didn't have a flair for dramatics and was as civil to the prisoners as he was to anyone else.

"From what my contact says, Roskothen is trying his best to run a correct courtroom. He uses a civil tone. I think he is a good man. The prisoners have spoken up for him when they get back to the prison."

Coming from Elizabeth, that was high praise indeed, but Sophie didn't like what she'd heard about the prosecutor, Gottlob, or the other two old officiations.

Jean-Pierre was being tried as a spy as well as for aiding escaped prisoners and spreading enemy propaganda. There were nineteen members of the so-called museum group being tried with him.

"How does Jean-Pierre look? I'm sure he is terrified but hiding it."

"He is thin, grey-faced from being locked up for so long. But from what I hear, he is holding his own. He stands as tall as the rest of them, Sophie."

Sophie bit back tears, wishing again, with all her might, she could find a way to get him out of there. She wondered where Zeldah was; had she had the baby yet? Did Jean-Pierre have a daughter or a son?

* * *

The trial continued day by day with Elizabeth updating her whenever she had more news. Sophie prayed for Jean-Pierre and the others.

"My contact says the women believe *Le Gosse* – as they call Jean-Pierre – will be sent to a prison camp in Germany. The others, they believe they will be shot."

Sophie ran a hand through her hair. "How can they know

anything yet? The prosecution is still continuing their case and the defence hasn't even begun."

"Sophie, you have to be prepared. The evidence is damning. They didn't just publish resistance newspapers but they ran rescue lines. They helped the Allies and other people wanted by the Germans to evade capture."

Sophie rounded on her friend. "Now it sounds like you think they deserve to die." Immediately she regretted her words. "Ignore me, Elizabeth. I'm sorry, I didn't mean that."

"I know you didn't, but all this waiting and hearing what's going on in fragments isn't doing you any good. Couldn't you go to Lyon? See Adèle and your mother?"

Sophie wanted nothing more but she couldn't leave her brother. "I mightn't be able to see Jean-Pierre, but at least he knows I'm close by. I have to be here for him."

FORTY-ONE

17 FEBRUARY 1942

Sophie sat in the canteen, her hands crossed as if in prayer, but she was out of those. She couldn't think, couldn't feel. She knew Elizabeth was watching her closely but she couldn't find the energy to react.

"Sentenced to die by firing squad." Elizabeth's words swirled around her head. It couldn't be. Not Jean-Pierre. He was too young, too full of life, too ... what? Brave.

"Sophie, try not to give up. From what I've been told, the German judge was pale reading out the sentences. He didn't want to do it, that much was obvious."

"Then why did he?"

"It was the only punishment allowed for their crimes. The men and three of the women were sentenced to death. But Vildé made a passionate appeal for Jean-Pierre's life. He said he was entirely responsible for your brother's actions. He said Jean-Pierre had no idea what or who he was taking into the free zone."

Sophie raised her head. "As if anyone would believe that. My brother may be young, but he's not stupid."

"Still, it may help."

Sophie stood up. Her heart was cold now, her insides chilled to the bone.

"There will be an appeal." Elizabeth's desperation carried over into her voice.

"I'm going home," Sophie said to nobody in particular. She walked out of the hospital and kept walking, marvelling as all around her people carried on with their usual routines. They walked, some laughed, some joked, a man even whistled at her, but inside she was dead; she couldn't feel anything.

* * *

She couldn't bear to go home in case she bumped into her father. He could have helped her brother, but had chosen not to. She worked all the hours she could, falling into bed only when her body demanded rest. She slept in a ward they had used for contagious cases in the past but was now empty. Not that she could sleep as her mind turned over, trying to find a way to help Jean-Pierre. He had to be entitled to an appeal; they couldn't just shoot him.

* * *

"Sophie, where are you?" Elizabeth's raised voice woke Sophie. What now? She had just worked eighteen hours straight. But she immediately felt guilty. Elizabeth would only wake her if there was an emergency. She jumped out of bed, having fallen asleep in her clothes. She brushed the sleep from her eyes.

"In here. What's the matter?" she replied.

"Sophie, you need to sit down. I have some bad news."

Sophie's heart beat faster, making it difficult to breathe. *Don't say it, please don't say it.*

"Sophie, it's Jean-Pierre." Elizabeth took her hands and held them tight. "He's dead. The Boches executed him and the others yesterday at Fort Mont-Valérien. I just got word. I am so sorry."

Sophie snatched her hands back. "No, they can't have! We were to appeal. The women, some of their sentences were commuted. Someone made a mistake." Even as she said the words, Sophie knew it to be true. She sobbed, trying to draw breaths and making herself cough instead. She didn't want to believe it. Not Jean-Pierre.

After a few minutes, she could take a deep breath. "Can I go to him?"

"No," Elizabeth whispered. "I'm sorry. You must be brave. They have already buried them."

Sophie rocked back and forth as the pain cut through her heart. Her adored brother dead, her family destroyed. The urge to die too almost overtook her. First Jules, now Jean-Pierre. How would she survive?

"Is there somewhere you can go?" Elizabeth hesitated before adding, "Perhaps you would like to see your father?"

"He is dead to me. He could have helped, but he refused. Because of him, Jean-Pierre is dead." Sophie stood, wiping her hands down the front of her dress. "Thank you for telling me."

"You can't go back to work. You have had a shock. You need to take some time."

"I'll go to Lyon. Can you get me an Ausweis? I need to be with my family. What's left of it."

FORTY-TWO

FEBRUARY 1942, LYON

Adèle returned to the small apartment, thinking how much she missed the social life in Paris. Lyon just didn't compare.

"There you are. I was worried about you."

Adèle looked sadly at her mother. The woman bore no resemblance to the family matriarch she had once been. The imprisonment of her son, combined with the separation from her husband, had aged her. Her hands shook with fear and her face bore signs of tears. This from the woman Adèle had seen cry maybe four times in her lifetime, prior to the arrival of the Boches.

"I am fine, maman. Nobody even looked twice at me."

The scathing look she earned from her grandmother did nothing for her spirits. Adèle put the basket containing her purchases on the kitchen table. Her mother had insisted on employing a maid, which was just as well since Adèle's cooking abilities hadn't improved. Zeldah's face popped into her head. Had she had a boy or girl? Had she told her uncle and aunt she was married? Being an unwed mother wasn't any more acceptable to an American Jewish family than it was in France.

Zeldah had promised to write, but since America was in the war too, there had been no letters.

Maman hadn't reacted well to the news of the baby. In fact, she had been extremely rude to Zeldah, accusing her of seducing Jean-Pierre. Her grandmother had been the opposite. She had welcomed Zeldah into the family and given her some money for the journey to America.

Her grandmother's view was that Jean-Pierre had made a good choice, a woman who would make a wonderful mother. It was so frustrating. Living away from Paris, deprived of letters from home, Adèle did not even know whether they had yet sentenced her brother.

"Adèle, stop pacing. You are upsetting your mother. What is the matter with you?"

"Nothing, mémé," Adèle said as she threw herself down in a chair. "I am just bored."

Her grandmother looked at her over the top of her glasses. "Bored. The world is at war and my granddaughter is bored."

Adèle's mother stood up; she was still wearing her dressing gown. She rarely got dressed, and never put on make-up or did her hair.

"Mama, leave Adèle be. She is not a boy who has to go and fight the enemy."

Adèle and her grandmother both stared at maman in surprise. She never corrected anyone these days, least of all her mother.

"I am tired, and I have a headache. I will go to bed," maman said. "Please do not fight. I cannot stand it any more."

Adèle gripped the handles of the chair she was sitting in as her mother walked out of the room.

"So, when are you going to do something worthwhile like your sister?"

Stung, Adèle glared at her grandmother. "What would you have me do? I am not a doctor."

"No, but you have a brain and a pretty face. A lethal combination when used properly. You must do something, Adèle. If everyone in France behaves like you do, the war is already over."

"The war for France has been lost. The Germans are crawling all over the country, in case you haven't noticed."

The crack across her face came swiftly; she hadn't even seen her grandmother step towards her, never mind raise her hand.

"Don't take that tone with me. My daughter may be too weak, but her children aren't. I will not sit by and let you waste your life like this. You will help. Go to de Gaulle."

Rubbing her cheek, Adèle wondered if the older woman had lost her mind. De Gaulle had called for Frenchmen to join him in London in the fight against the Boche, but she wasn't a soldier.

"Haven't you heard of Edith Cavell?"

Adèle shook her head.

"She was a nurse in the last war. She helped run an escape route for injured soldiers to get back to France and England. She was eventually shot by the Germans."

"So you want me to be shot?"

"Yes. Better that than do nothing."

Adèle couldn't reply. Her grandmother sat down abruptly, looking suddenly old.

"Can't you see they will come for us, eventually? Do you want to walk to your death like a sheep, or will you fight back?"

"You are crazy. Nobody is going to kill me. Why would they?"

"You're Jewish. You have read the stories in the papers, heard the news."

"Propaganda," Adèle replied. But even as she said the words, she wasn't sure she believed that any more. Would the Quakers have been sending children to America unaccompanied if they didn't think the threat was real? "And I am not Jewish. I told you before, I am French."

"French and Jewish are not mutually exclusive."

"You are Jewish, and maman is, because of your parents. I am not. Neither are Jean-Pierre or Sophie. The Germans have been clear on that matter." Adèle rubbed a spot on the table.

"Listen to you. The Germans don't decide who is Jewish. You are Jewish if your mother is Jewish. It is part of our religion."

Adèle rounded on her grandmother. "You converted and now you lecture me?"

"You are full of pride and foolishness. I hope you are spared, but I believe you will find out the hard way that I am right. I cannot stand to be in the same room as one with such a selfish heart."

Mémé pulled herself to her feet, looking frail, as if she had lost all her energy to fight. She walked slowly towards her bedroom without a backwards glance. Adèle stared after her, frustration threatening to overwhelm her. Just what did the old woman expect her to do?

She stood up, deciding it was time to find some fun. She took a bath and dressed quickly in one of her favourite outfits. It was slightly old-fashioned, but what would have been noticed in Paris wouldn't be commented on in Lyon – one benefit of living in a backwater place. She sprayed her perfume rather liberally, despite the bottle being almost empty. Maybe she could find a friend who would provide her with some more. Her female relatives had written her off. Why not just use her assets and make her life as comfortable as possible? There were plenty of rich and powerful men in the Vichy regime who would be only too glad to have Adèle Bélanger grace their arms.

With one last glance in the mirror, she took her bag and left the apartment behind, determined to change her life.

FORTY-THREE

She headed into a hotel, making her way to one of the unoccupied tables. A few years, even months, ago, a young woman from a good family wouldn't sit at a table alone, but those days were gone. She asked for a glass of wine and a menu. Then she sat back to people-watch.

"Adèle? Is it really you?"

She looked up, pleasure filling her body as she gazed into the face of Auguste Citerne, looking more tanned than he had that time in Maxim's. He'd changed his glasses as well; these ones suited him better. He looked more distinguished.

"Auguste, what a pleasure."

"The pleasure is all mine, Adèle, but what are you doing drinking alone? In Lyon? Why have you left Paris? Your father must—"

She interrupted, "Father doesn't care." She hesitated for a split second but continued before she could think about it too much. She had to talk to someone. "Jean-Pierre was arrested, and I was told to get my mother out of the city. She and my grandmother are staying in Lyon, so I am stuck here too. I came out because I just couldn't stand talking to two old women any longer. I am going mad."

Auguste chuckled. "Still the same old Adèle. Glad to see you haven't changed, and still believe the world revolves around you."

Stung, Adèle was about to retaliate, but then saw he was teasing her. Slightly mollified, she sat back in her chair. "Will you join me? Please say you have time. I am dying to hear what it is like in Paris. I miss it."

Auguste glanced at his watch. "I have a couple of minutes before I have to meet someone." He took a seat and gestured to the waiter to bring him a coffee.

To break the silence, she prompted him to talk. "So how is Paris? I haven't seen you since..." She flushed, remembering that horrible evening in Maxim's.

Auguste shrugged. "I can't say you're missing anything. Most of our friends are no longer around, having escaped via Dunkirk or ended up in camps. Others like your father have taken a liking to the enemy and are profiting from the war."

Adèle blanched. She knew her father wasn't a saint but surely he wasn't as bad as that. Sophie's voice echoed in her mind. *Don't trust papa. He loves himself first and last.*

She ignored the reference to her father. "I'm so glad you came to Lyon. I've been worried sick about Jean-Pierre."

Was it her imagination, or did he look away when she mentioned her brother's name? She was being ridiculous, her thoughts running ahead of her.

"Adèle, I apologise but I must be going. I will be late for my next appointment. Try to keep your chin up."

"Must you go?" She caught the surprise in his eyes. "I'm sorry, but I am just so bored. My grandmother is sick of me; today she suggested I go to de Gaulle."

She expected him to laugh or at least smile. Instead, he moved closer as if to kiss her cheek.

"Why don't you help us?" he whispered.

Frustrated, she threw her hands up. "People keep telling me that, but what? What can I do?"

"You may be surprised." He straightened up. "If you wish to find out more about Jean-Pierre, I know someone you can speak to, a good friend of mine. She's an American, a reporter."

Adèle gasped. "That ancient, badly dressed woman who was so rude to me in Maxim's?"

He rolled his eyes. "I don't remember it being her that was rude. That was Dolores. She's gone home, I believe. The lady I suggest you meet is Catherine White. She's a correspondent for the *New York Post*. She's well connected and may find out information for you. I must go. Bonne journée."

And then he left, leaving her with the distinct impression she should contact the journalist as a matter of urgency. She wondered where she would find the woman.

Her worries soon fled as a well-dressed, charming man greeted her, asking if he could join her. They quickly established that they had mutual acquaintances, and Adèle spent a pleasant, if rather dull, afternoon and evening in the company of her new friend. He insisted on seeing her home, but she deftly avoided his advances. She played the overprotective mother card and, being French and knowing all about mothers and their daughters, he ran.

FORTY-FOUR

The next morning, her grandmother woke her with a coffee and a note. "Someone pushed it under the door. It's addressed to you."

Café Lucie at eleven. She looked at the back to see if there was a signature but it was blank. She lifted her eyes, meeting her grandmother's.

"What is it?" mémé said.

Should she tell the older woman she might get news of Jean-Pierre or should she pretend it was an assignation? She opted for the latter.

"I met someone; he's asked me to coffee this morning. I'd best get changed or I will be late."

Her grandmother's look pierced her. "I wasn't born yesterday. What are you up to now?"

"Nothing, mémé, I promise."

She had a quick bath before dressing in a flattering light blue chiffon dress with a matching bolero-style jacket. She pulled out her black shoes, thinking wistfully of the delightful matching blue shoes she'd left behind in Paris. A touch of lipstick and a quick spray of perfume and she was ready.

Her mother and grandmother scrutinised her as she prepared to leave.

"You're meeting a new man, aren't you?" Her mother's lip curled. "I hate to think what Nicolas's family would say."

"They aren't here, are they?" She bent to kiss her mother, her lips touching the air near her cheek.

Her grandmother pulled her into a hug, whispering in her ear, "Be careful and make me proud."

Adèle couldn't resist giving her a small smile. Her grandmother may be old, but there was no hiding anything from her.

She closed the door behind her and set off in the direction of the café. It was only a ten-minute walk but she didn't want to be late.

When she arrived, she spotted Auguste sitting with a blonde lady, in her mid-thirties, holding a newspaper. Auguste looked up as she approached and stood waiting to greet her.

"Adèle, always a pleasure, and this is my friend Catherine." Auguste bowed slightly.

"Charmed to meet you." Adèle tried her most sincere smile but the effect was wasted as the other woman didn't even look up. "I have been looking to make your acquaintance. I was wondering if you had news of my brother."

"Your brother?" The woman looked at her over the top of her newspaper.

"Jean-Pierre Bélanger. They arrested him for writing the newspaper *Résistance*."

The woman's eyes widened slightly. She knew Jean-Pierre, or knew of him. She folded her paper, then looked around her before speaking softly. "They did more than publish a newspaper."

Adèle nodded, though she wasn't sure exactly what the group had done. She wasn't about to admit that Jean-Pierre hadn't trusted her with the details.

Catherine's eyes narrowed as she appraised Adèle. "You haven't heard?"

Chills ran through her. "No, mademoiselle."

"Adèle, please sit down." Adèle found her arm in a tight grip as Auguste almost pushed her into a chair. "You must be brave."

Swallowing hard, Adèle looked from one to the other. "Tell me. Please."

Catherine spoke, almost whispering. "Jean-Pierre is dead. The Boches shot the entire group."

"Dead?" Adèle repeated, her throat closing, her breath choking her. "No, that can't be right." She glanced at Auguste, begging him to tell her a different story. "They said they would send him to Germany." She clutched at his arm. He took her hand, patting it awkwardly.

"The judges condemned the entire group to death, including the women. But at the last minute, the women were given a reprieve and sent to Germany. The men..." He shrugged. What else could he do?

She stared at his face, her gaze focused on his nose. She had to breathe slowly, or her heart might burst from her chest. She couldn't cry. Not here in a public place. That would never do.

She desperately wanted him to say that perhaps he had made a mistake. "Are you sure?"

"Yes." He held her gaze but she didn't want to see the sympathy on his face. She looked down at her shoes. This morning she'd worried about not wearing the right shoes and her brother was dead.

"But ... nobody told us." She hated the way her voice broke.

Catherine folded her hands in her lap. "Your father didn't send word? He was aware."

Adèle balled her fists. He hadn't even had the decency to contact his wife to share details of their son's fate! Why hadn't Sophie come to tell them?

"My parents are estranged. I must go. I have to tell maman and mémé."

Adèle stood up, her legs shaking. She gripped the side of her chair for a few seconds.

Auguste jumped up. "Adèle, wait. I must talk to you."

Catherine glared at him. "Let her go. Now is not the time."

"What?" Aware of an undercurrent she didn't completely understand, Adèle looked from one to another. She sat back down, slightly relieved she hadn't fallen. "Tell me."

Catherine pursed her lips but Adèle ignored her. She stared at Auguste until he spoke up. "How do you feel now? About doing something more than drinking fine wines with strangers."

"You've been watching me?" she stuttered.

"It's not important what we were doing. Are you willing to avenge your brother?"

Adèle couldn't meet his gaze. She wanted to kill the person who had killed her brother, but was that what he was asking?

"Let her process the news." Catherine addressed Adèle. "Go home. Tell your mother. Grieve. Come back in two days' time if you wish to speak to me about what you can do for your country." The woman's decisive tone sliced through the confusion reigning in Adèle's head.

Adèle didn't respond. She took her gloves and stood up, then walked slowly home. She had no idea who she saw on her way. The world carried on as normal. People laughed, shouted, and haggled, their lives just the same as they had been that morning. Yet hers was over.

Her darling brother was dead, murdered by the Boches. She had killed him just as surely as if she had held the gun. She had brought the attention of the Germans to her family with her egotistical belief that she could save Léo. If only she had listened to Jean-Pierre, and left the wedding on time, none of this would have happened. Her family would still be living in Paris, not scattered all over France.

Or dead.

She pushed the door to the apartment open slowly. Her mother and mémé were in the sitting room. She could hear them talking. Dread made her retch, and she raced to the bathroom just in time. After a couple of minutes, there was nothing left. She took a sip of water and pushed her hair out of her eyes. She had to tell them now. She couldn't bear it if someone else broke the news.

She entered the room, and the look on her face was enough to stop them both in their tracks. Her mother paled, but her grandmother's mouth drew into a thin line. She knew. Somehow, the old lady had guessed. A look of understanding crossed between mémé and Adèle before she turned her attention to her mother.

"I have some news. It is not good."

"Tell me. Did they send my poor boy to Germany?"

"They didn't send him to prison. They ... they took him with the others. They shot him."

"Shot him? What do you mean, they shot him?" Her mother raised her voice. "Who?"

"The Germans. They killed Jean-Pierre and Boris, and all the men they arrested. They sent the women to Germany. He's gone."

Her mother stared at her, her face white with shock, but it was the lack of tears that alarmed Adèle most. Her grandmother stepped forward, guiding the grief-stricken woman into a chair.

"Adèle, go for Dr de Guelis now. Go on, I will stay with your mother."

FORTY-FIVE

Adèle didn't wait to be asked again. She moved as fast as she could, passing their startled maid, who had obviously overheard the conversation, as she stood crossing herself. She opened the door and raced down the stairs to the street outside. The clinic wasn't far, and the doctor was in when she got there. She quickly explained what had happened and he took his bag and returned with her. By the time they got back, mémé was trying but failing to bring her mother round from a faint.

"Move out of the way please, madame. I will see to your daughter." The doctor administered some smelling salts, bringing her mother around with a fit of coughing.

"Adèle, do you have any brandy? Wine, even?" the doctor ordered, before turning to her mother and saying, in the softest of voices, "Come now, madame. We will take you to your room. I will give you something for the shock."

Adèle fired off instructions to the maid as she watched the doctor move her mother, who appeared to have aged twenty years. She went to follow, but mémé stopped her.

"Let them be. Your mother will speak to the doctor better if you are not there. You should sit, Adèle. You have had a shock too."

"It's all my fault. I killed Jean-Pierre. I stayed late at the wedding, got Léo in trouble and then I went to see the Germans..."

Mémé grabbed her by the shoulders and forced her to look at her. "You did not do this. The Boches did. You must not take the blame for this."

"I was so selfish. I didn't think," she protested.

"You were young and carefree, spending time enjoying yourself in your own country. Nobody could have foreseen this. Now I don't want to hear you speak like this again. Lay the blame at the feet of those who deserve it."

"But..."

"Yes, you are selfish and stubborn, and too invested in how you look. But you are not a murderer. Believe me." Her grandmother's fingers dug into her upper arms. "You are not to blame, chérie." Adèle collapsed against her grandmother and sobbed. She couldn't stop, even when the doctor returned. He helped her to sit down before taking a seat himself. The maid poured them all an ersatz coffee before retiring to the kitchen. Only when she left did the doctor speak.

"Those murdering animals. Shooting innocent men like that. What is the world coming to?" Agitated, the doctor lit a cigarette, the match shaking in his nicotine-stained fingers.

Mémé said, "It will get worse before it gets better. We only need to listen to the news to know that. The things they are doing in Poland and elsewhere will be done here."

"No, you cannot say that. This is France, the land of freedom." The doctor shook his head. "We would not let such things happen here."

"You are a fool if you believe that. There are already men, women, and children in camps. Laval has seen to that."

"*Mémé.*" Adèle was astonished at her grandmother's rudeness. "Doctor, I apologise."

"Don't apologise for me. I mean it. Anyone who believes the Boches will behave better here than elsewhere is in denial. Nothing will save us. Nothing but ourselves. Can't you see?"

"I can see that if you were a younger woman, you would fight with de Gaulle." The doctor's admiration for the older woman shone through in his voice. "We must do what we can to stop them, but in the meantime, life must go on. I have so many patients, I must get back to the clinic. Adèle, come for me again if your maman needs me, but I suspect she will be fine. She is a strong woman underneath it all. She must be, with a mother like this."

The doctor said his goodbyes, and the maid showed him out, leaving Adèle and her grandmother alone. They sat in silence for some time before Adèle spoke.

"Do you really believe it will get as bad here as in Poland and other places? For your people, I mean?"

"My people?" her grandmother clarified, her arched eyebrows conveying a coherent message.

Adèle shifted in her chair. "You know what I mean. The Jews."

"Darling, I am Jewish. Your mother is Jewish, and therefore you are Jewish, too. To answer your question, yes, I believe it will get worse for our people. Will there be ghettos in Lyon? No, I do not think so. But they will move people to the camps where the foreigners are being held now. The Boches have shown their true colours on several occasions, and this time it has hit our family hard. Jean-Pierre died a hero. He believed in his work."

"You knew about it?"

"Yes, I knew. I supported him fully. Maybe I should have talked him out of it when he came to stay. Instead, I gave him money and my jewellery to help fund the cause. But it is too late to think along those lines now. We must remember: he saved lives. He told me they had rescued fifty or more airmen. Men who would have been shot or transferred to prisoner-of-war camps. Instead, they got back to Britain, to fight again."

Adèle didn't want to hear about the men her brother had saved. She wanted Jean-Pierre alive. She didn't care about the others.

"Do you know what Sophie is doing? Where she is?" Adèle asked. "I haven't heard from her in a long time. Not since she wrote to say she was going to come and visit."

"No, child, I know nothing more than you do. But knowing your sister, she will be as involved as Jean-Pierre." Her grandmother stared at her. "The question is whether you will pick up where Jean-Pierre left off. People need help. We must try to do what we can. Otherwise, we might as well start goose-stepping and hailing Hitler."

"What can I do? I am not a doctor or a writer. I don't have the brains that Jean-Pierre and Sophie have."

"Yes, you do. You have just never had to use them. I am sure if you think about the people you have met recently, you might see there could be a reason for them all being in Lyon at the same time."

Adèle sat straighter. "You mean they are in the résistance?"

"Unless Lyon has suddenly become the place to be seen. Why would people you know from Paris appear here? And in the company of an American journalist? Something doesn't add up."

Could her grandmother be right?

"I have to go and find Citerne."

"Wash your face and change first. Hold your head up high. We are not beaten yet."

Overcome with admiration for the old lady, Adèle asked, "When did you become so brave?"

"Ha. Brave is delivering a thirteen-pound baby with no pain relief. The Boches are but an inconvenience compared to that."

Adèle stared at the older woman for a moment, then they both laughed. She hugged her grandmother impulsively, despite knowing she didn't like displays of affection. Then she went to do what she was told. She would find Citerne and do something. Anything but sit here remembering Jean-Pierre's face.

FORTY-SIX

She walked to the place Bellecour, hoping Citerne was having dinner in the same restaurant as last time. The maître d' recognised her and could direct her to Auguste's table.

"I apologise for interrupting you," she said as she approached.

He looked up and smiled. "Don't. My meal will improve with such delightful company. Can I get you something?"

Adèle was still queasy from the shock of finding out about Jean-Pierre. She couldn't face eating.

"No, thank you, but I hoped we could talk. In private. I have told my family the news. My grandmother suggested I take up Jean-Pierre's cause." Adèle took a seat opposite Auguste at the table.

Auguste sat back, using his napkin to dab at his mouth. For a second she was distracted by how surreal this all was. Auguste was a thirty-odd-year-old gentleman, from his manicured nails to his well-fitting, expensive clothes. He didn't fit the popular image of a resistant.

He surveyed her in silence until she grew uncomfortable. She opened her mouth to speak, but he forestalled her.

"And you? Are you here because she sent you, or because you wish to avenge your brother?"

"Both." She decided she might as well be honest. "I am not sure what I can do. I don't have Sophie's doctoring skills or patience, and I am not a writer."

"You have other talents. Don't underestimate yourself. France needs men and women like you. But we must proceed with caution. There are many who do not see things the same way. They would sell their grandmother down the river for a few francs."

Adèle glanced around the room at his words.

"Stop it. You are making it too obvious. You must be discreet. As far as anyone knows, we are old friends from Paris. Lovers, maybe."

Adèle was about to protest that he was too old for her when she realised he was teasing.

"How can you do that? Tease me at a time like this?" she asked.

"The Boches have taken many things, but I refuse to let them take the joy from my life. Now, let me get you a coffee. Then we will finish our meal and take a walk. Only then can we talk in private."

Adèle nodded and, as they chatted, she drank her horrible coffee, despite having had one at home.

Auguste paid the bill and escorted her out of the restaurant. They walked in silence for a while.

"It is easy to see how this area got its name, isn't it?"

Surprised at the change of topic, she looked at him blankly.

"La Croix-Rousse, named for the reddish-brown stone cross erected in the sixteenth century. This area was one of the centres of the silk industry, hence the high ceilings from which the looms hung. The *traboules* are covered, allowing the silk merchants to transport valuable material from building to building without it getting wet in the rain."

She couldn't believe what he was saying. She wasn't interested in a history lesson. She didn't plan on staying in Lyon. She was going back to Paris to avenge Jean-Pierre. She tried to interrupt his monologue, but he continued walking and talking as if they had all the time in the world.

She fiddled with the cuffs of her coat as they walked, trying but no doubt failing to hide her impatience. They followed a maze through the *traboules* before finally stopping to sit for a while.

He glanced discreetly around them before putting his hand on the back of the bench, across her shoulders.

"You will work for me. I insist on strict safety precautions. You will not know the others who work with me. If you are taken, you cannot give them up."

"Taken? By whom? The Germans aren't here yet," she protested.

"There are spies everywhere. Do not believe for a second you are free. There are many just waiting to put the Germans into power." He looked around and then stood up again, offering her his arm.

"Never assume nobody is watching or listening," he murmured under his breath. She looked around her but couldn't see anyone who seemed out of place. Certainly, nobody was paying them any attention.

They walked along in the evening sunshine, Auguste holding her arm as if they were a courting couple. She smiled and laughed as if they were flirting, while he told her of his orders to set up a resistance unit.

"I must speak to my superiors. I will call to see you and your grandmother tomorrow evening. To pay my condolences to your mother."

Adèle nodded, then kissed his cheek goodbye.

When she returned to the apartment, it was in darkness, but

as she listened outside her mother's bedroom door, she could hear her sobbing for her son. She ached to comfort her, but Adèle knew that there was nothing she could do to ease her pain.

FORTY-SEVEN

Auguste called to see them, as promised. He greeted her grandmother as an old friend. Adèle was surprised; she hadn't realised they'd known each other so well back in Paris. They sat and exchanged news until maman went back to bed. Then the actual conversation began.

"Adèle, how serious are you about helping us?"

"Very."

"I mean are you prepared to risk everything, including your life? The reason I ask is: I have to return to England and I want you to come with me."

"England? But I want to fight the Germans."

"Yes, and you will, but first you must be trained. The English believe French-speaking women can help the war effort. They are willing to train them and then return them to France. You are ideal, being French and having a knowledge of both Paris and Lyon."

"You mean I would work as a secret agent?"

"Yes." He turned to address her grandmother. "The risks are high. If Adèle is caught, she is on her own. The Germans won't care that she is a woman. They will torture her."

"I am still here, you know," Adèle interrupted, but both ignored her.

"Are they really recruiting women?" her grandmother asked, her face bright with curiosity, making Adèle believe she would have volunteered had she been forty years younger.

"Not officially. Churchill believes the British public would be horrified. The general view is women are too fragile."

Her grandmother made a very unladylike sound in response to that remark, but Auguste continued as if he hadn't heard her.

"Unofficially, it is recognised that women have several advantages. Young men of Adèle's age stand out, as they are possibly former French soldiers. They are more likely to be stopped, questioned and possibly picked up by the Boche for transfer to work in Germany. Women have greater movement and are less suspicious. There will always be those who believe the fairer sex are not as capable as men. Having seen some women in action, I know that is a lie. But it works to our advantage, as hopefully the Boche will believe it too."

Her grandmother nodded her agreement.

"What would I have to do?" Adèle asked.

Auguste didn't answer her immediately. "Adèle, you will find out if you are selected. Until then, you don't need to know."

"But they will teach me to kill? I want to avenge Jean-Pierre's death."

Auguste met her gaze but stayed silent.

"Auguste!" She had to know the answer.

"Yes, but don't be too eager to cross that line. Taking a human life – and the Germans are human, even if that seems a contradiction in terms – is not something to be considered lightly," he admonished gently.

Adèle didn't agree, but she wasn't rude enough to say so.

"How do I get to England? It is not as if I can step onto a boat."

"Well, not one advertising that journey," Auguste joked.

Then he became serious. "I will take you. I have been ordered to return to London. I told my boss I had met a potential new agent. He suggested I bring you with me."

"When?"

"Tomorrow afternoon."

"So soon?"

"Are you with us or not? You must make that decision. There is no time to waste."

"I am."

"Good. We will pretend to be a couple taking a romantic trip. We shall take a train to Perpignan and from there we will go over the mountains."

"The mountains?" she asked incredulously.

"Yes. You are young and healthy. You will be fine. Just pack warm clothes and find some hiking boots. I will leave you to make your arrangements. You must come up with a story for your maid, your neighbours, and your mother."

"I cannot tell maman the truth?"

"Nobody can know. It is risky enough that your grand-mother knows, but she has proved her loyalty."

Adèle couldn't believe it. Was he telling her that her grand-mother was in the résistance? She couldn't be. She was old.

It was as if he could read her mind. "Underestimate no one. That is the first lesson you will learn. Now I must go. Till tomorrow afternoon." He made his goodbyes and left, her grandmother seeing him out.

Adèle sat and waited. She had committed herself to crossing the Pyrenees, and yet somehow it seemed like a game.

"You knew he was involved?" she said when her grand-mother returned, not really expecting an answer.

"He came to see me one time in Paris with Jean-Pierre. Must have been a few months after the war started. They said a lot of things."

"Mémé, stop patronising me."

"Yes, I knew. I have been following the rise of Hitler since he first came into power. I helped several individuals escape from Germany before war was ever declared. I may be stuck in this old body, but my mind is young."

"You did?" Adèle knew she sounded rude, but her grandmother had seemed like every other well-off Parisian. At least until recently. "What did you do?"

"A little of what you will do, I imagine. We, a couple of my friends and I, went to Germany and smuggled out some artworks, money, and jewels for those who were being watched. We set up bank accounts in Switzerland to help fund the bribes to secure their release from the camps and, ultimately, their visas to leave Germany. The persecution of my people, and that of anyone who said no to Hitler and his friends, began long before the Germans marched into Poland."

Adèle stared at her grandmother, not sure what to say.

"My involvement with the rescues gave me access to first-hand accounts of how my people were treated. To the fact that the Germans are true monsters."

"Is that why you told papa the truth?"

A pained expression crossed her grandmother's face so quickly, she almost believed she'd imagined it.

"They left me with no choice. Someone who I thought was a close friend tried to blackmail me. She believes, like many others, that Hitler is correct. I decided your father would be told, given the circles he moves in. I wanted to be the one to do it." Her grandmother sighed. "I cannot travel any more, so I do what I can. With money and such. I warned them about your father."

"Papa?"

"He is a traitor, Adèle. Not just to your mother for his behaviour. But to France. Never trust him. Do not expect him to put his blood before his own well-being."

Adèle didn't argue, but she didn't believe her grandmother.

Her father was a lot of things, but he adored her. He would never give her up.

"You do not believe me, that much is obvious. But I speak the truth, much as it pains me to say it. I liked your father, as did your grandfather. Thank God he is not alive to see the man he has become. Anyway, we must prepare for your journey. We will tell your mother you are returning to Paris to look for Sophie. She won't question that. You will find some of Jean-Pierre's clothes in the wardrobe in my room; they might fit you."

"You want me to dress as a man?"

"I do not want you to freeze to death before you reach England. Now, my little one, you must rest. It will be some time before you sleep in a comfortable bed once more. I know it will be difficult, but you will do it."

Adèle choked up at the look her grandmother gave her. Was that pride in her eyes?

* * *

Her mother took the news calmly, suggesting it would be nice if Adèle could talk Sophie into coming to Lyon.

"Tell your sister I need her here. You can stay in Paris if you wish. If you hadn't behaved so selfishly at the wedding and brought the attention of the Boches to our family, Jean-Pierre would have been safe."

Adèle kissed her mother's cold cheek goodbye, trying not to let the hurt show.

Her grandmother gathered her close. "Ignore your maman. She doesn't really blame you. It is the grief."

With one last look at her family, Adèle left.

* * *

She hurried to the rendezvous point near Auguste's favoured restaurant. Nobody seemed to be watching her; everyone seemed preoccupied with their own business. She had packed a pair of Jean-Pierre's trousers in her case. She couldn't walk through the streets of Lyon wearing them, but they would be useful to cope with the temperatures of the mountain.

"You ready for this?" Auguste asked her as he kissed her on both cheeks.

"Yes," Adèle said, surprised to hear that she sounded more confident than she felt.

"Do you mind if we walk to the station?"

It was at least a thirty-minute walk, and ordinarily she would have insisted on taking the bus or, prior to the war starting, a taxi, but these were different times. It would be good training for the journey ahead.

"Not at all. Some parts of Lyon are beautiful, and we might as well take advantage of the sunshine."

His glance of approval showed that she had passed her first test. A thrill of excitement flushed through her. At last she was doing the right thing. She could contribute to the war effort. She hoped wherever Jean-Pierre was now, he would be proud of her.

FORTY-EIGHT

"We will make our way out via Andorra. I have friends there. Being situated between France and Spain, almost every family has someone who knows the mountains intimately. They are doing good business at the moment, first in helping Spaniards get away from Franco and now French leaving France."

Adèle didn't answer. She'd given no thought to the plight of Spanish refugees before. Never imagined a day may come when she had to flee in a similar fashion. She sat straighter. It wasn't the same; she was coming back to help free her homeland.

Most of their journey was by train. Auguste made light of the trip, making her laugh and proving to be an interesting companion, but she didn't fall for his nonchalant act. His entire body remained in a state of alert, his eyes checking out each station and the passengers who joined or left the train.

Auguste whispered at one point, when the carriage they were in emptied at a station, "From now on, pretend you don't know me. Just in case. We'll continue by train. Our contact is a priest, Abbé Roo at L'Hospitalet. It's the last village near the border. He has many contacts. If something happens, make your way there. Tell him I sent you."

Adèle's pulse raced. "What do you mean? Did you see something?"

"Relax. There's nothing wrong; we've had a good journey. But just in case our luck doesn't last, I want you to be safe." He leaned closer, his voice dropping to a murmur. "I could be recognised. It's not my first journey through here. Just do as I say."

She nodded and sat still as he moved farther down the carriage. She hadn't realised how much of a distraction his chatty presence had been. Alone, her thoughts raced to Jean-Pierre. How terrified he must have been: all those months in prison, hopes rising, falling and rising again, only to end up in front of a firing squad.

* * *

At the last station, they left the train separately, Adèle falling behind Auguste so she could catch up with him when he was further up the road.

She didn't speak and he seemed distracted until they reached the church. Then she smiled.

"What?" Auguste asked.

"I was just thinking how unusual it is to be going to a priest for an introduction to a smuggler."

The priest welcomed them into his vestry and indicated they take a seat near the warm fire blazing in the fireplace.

"Are you hungry or would you like to rest first?"

"Hungry," Auguste confirmed with a grin at Adèle. "Is that roast pork?" He sniffed the air appreciatively.

"Yes, a member of my congregation donated half a pig. My housekeeper knows we're expecting guests so she has been busy."

"Guests?" Auguste's chin clenched but the abbé didn't seem to notice.

"Yes, a pilot – nice fellow – he's Polish, and a German Jewish gentleman, Monsieur Blau, with a passion for mathematics. They are both upstairs but shall join us for dinner."

Auguste relaxed, the priest turning his attention to Adèle. "Are you ready for this, young lady? The mountains, while beautiful, are harsh."

"I'm ready."

"Don't worry, Monsieur l'abbé, Adèle is stubborn; she'll be fine. She's stronger than she looks."

The abbé shrugged but was stopped from commenting further by a knock on the door, admitting an older gentleman with wire-rimmed glasses and a young man who for a second made Adèle's heart squeeze. He had a look of Jean-Pierre: the blonde hair and twinkling brown eyes. Despite the circumstances, he seemed to be excited rather than afraid.

He insisted on kissing both her cheeks. "Like a Frenchman." His accent was surprisingly good. "My mother, she made me take language lessons. My father arranged for them to be with a very pretty young French lady."

Adèle ignored his flirting and turned to the older man. "Monsieur Blau, I assume?" What on earth had this man been through? His skin was almost translucent and his hair white although he wasn't that old. She held out her hand, wincing as he grabbed it.

"Now I have hope I can climb too. If a little lady like you can do it, I must be brave. Yes."

Adèle agreed too quickly, trying to hide her dismay. His desperation worried her. She glanced over at Auguste but he didn't take any notice. He was deep in conversation with the abbé, his fingers pinching the top of his nose. What was going on? Whatever it was, the pair seemed to realise they had a witness and stopped talking. Auguste flashed her a quick smile before turning to hold his hands out to the fire, thus preventing her from seeing his face. How convenient.

"Come, let's eat. Monsieur Blau, would you like to say a blessing? My housekeeper cooked extra vegetables. She's embarrassed, but we couldn't get chicken or lamb."

Monsieur Blau waved his hands. "Please don't apologise. I will eat what you have, for strength for this trip. My days of keeping kosher or avoiding pork are long gone. Now, I eat whatever I get. Who knows when the next meal will happen?"

Adèle gripped her fork. His speech, delivered with grave passion, touched her in a way she hadn't expected. Tears pricked her eyes as she imagined what he had been subjected to.

The abbé nodded his approval, before laying his hand over his guest's. "God will understand."

They all bowed their heads as Monsieur Blau led the blessing, asking for a successful trip and giving thanks for the food. Despite his words, Adèle noticed the man didn't eat but one slice of meat. She guessed the ingrained teachings of his youth were too much to overcome.

On the other hand, it had been so long since Adèle had tasted roast meat, she thought she was in heaven.

The young pilot flirted and joked with her. He was on his way to join the RAF. She was almost sorry when the smugglers turned up, each man dressed in rough clothing and carrying a rucksack. She'd thought they were staying with the abbé for a couple of nights but obviously plans had changed. The men didn't hold back as they heaped their plates high with meat. They each drank from their own casks. Adèle declined the offer to taste whatever alcohol they contained.

"How do you know you can trust them?" Adèle whispered to the priest beside her. It wasn't just their lack of table manners but the fact they wouldn't have looked out of place in a jail. Her life was in their hands.

"Faith. These men hate the Germans as much as you do. Plus, they get paid to do their job."

Adèle had no option but to trust the priest's recommendation. She wasn't going to get over the mountains on her own. As if reading her thoughts, the younger of the two guides gave her a disdainful look before returning to his meal.

* * *

As they waited for dawn to come so they could set off, an argument erupted between the two men, and could have turned physical but for Auguste's intervention.

"What's wrong?" Monsieur Blau's voice shook as his eyes jumped from one smuggler to the other.

"Something about his wife." Adèle lied to the older man. She didn't think his anxiety would abate if he knew they were fighting over the amount they'd been paid. The younger man wanted more and argued that they must have gold secreted on their persons. He'd suggested stripping them, starting with Adèle. Auguste set him straight. Soon after that, the pilot passed Adèle a pocketknife. "I will keep an eye on you, but just in case."

Adèle accepted it gratefully, although what use it would be against a burly man was debatable. Still, she felt better with it.

Dawn broke and it was time for them to start. The abbé wished them all a safe trip, withdrawing into the warmth of the vestry almost before they reached the gate to the property. She didn't blame him; it was freezing.

She had believed herself to be fit, but as the mountain slope became steeper, her leg muscles cramped in protest at the pace set by their escorts. They strode as if walking through a flat field, joking with Auguste and the Polish pilot as they went. It was all right for them. She swore silently as she tripped over another rock.

Monsieur Blau was also suffering. He winced as he used his hands to prevent himself from slipping back down the mountain slope. She understood his pain; her own fingers and palms were already covered in open blisters. They were only allowed short breaks with the smugglers threatening to shoot them if they were too tardy in moving.

"They don't mean it." Auguste reassured her, though the men's expressions suggested otherwise.

When they stopped for a longer rest, and Auguste together with the pilot and Monsieur Blau moved away to answer the call of nature, the younger smuggler made his way over to her. She eyed his approach warily, her hands fingering the knife in her pocket. What did he want?

"Mademoiselle. I think you are very brave. Put this on your hands and feet. It will make the blisters get better faster."

He handed her a small jar of evil-smelling cream. She was tempted not to obey him, but he waited to see that she did as she was told.

"Why are you being nice to me? Last night you wanted to rob us."

He grinned at her, not a bit put out. "I didn't think you understood us. We take great risks; it is fair we are paid well. Isn't it?"

"You are helping France. Isn't that enough?"

"That is what you think? If so, why are you running away?"

He didn't let her reply but stalked off.

The next morning, her blisters weren't as raw. She approached the young smuggler. "Thank you," she said when he looked at her enquiringly. He nodded but didn't say anything.

"What was in that cream? My sister is a doctor, or at least she will be. I'm sure her patients could benefit from a similar salve."

"It is best you do not know. Women get funny about these things."

The other smuggler snorted with laughter, and Adèle decided to ignore them. She pushed on, determined not to slow their group down although the boys were not joking and laughing either, now. They were finding the going tough too.

* * *

They soon reached Andorra. There their guides left them, with instructions to find new guides for the rest of their trip – but only after the young smuggler grabbed Adèle and stole a kiss. Too shocked to reproach him, she just watched as he set off with a wave of his hand.

Auguste teased her. "Still leaving broken hearts in your wake. Come on, Mata Hari. We still have a long way to go."

She bristled at the reference to the First World War spy who'd been shot, but she didn't have the energy to argue back. All she could think of was a hot bath and a proper bed. Crossing her fingers in the hope their hosts would oblige, she set after Auguste and soon they came to a small holding, a dog barking to announce their arrival.

A woman came out, her hand stilling the dog by her side. Adèle judged her to be in her late sixties; she had only two front teeth and grey hair, but her voice was younger. "Welcome. You're late; we were worried."

Auguste embraced the woman warmly. "My beautiful Françoise, you are as young as ever."

Laughing, the woman waggled her finger at him. "You tell lies so smoothly, not even your mother would know." She turned to smile at the rest of the group. "Please come inside. There is hot soup and bread for all."

Adèle gave up all thoughts of a bath as they crossed the threshold into a large room that seemed to be the entire living quarters. A large bed took up one corner of the room. The whole place smelled of wet dog overlaid by the delicious scent of the dish simmering over the fire.

"*Escudella*." Auguste sighed. "Wait until you taste it, Adèle. Françoise is a master chef."

The woman poked Auguste in the ribs with her elbow. "Stop behaving like a child. It's warm, filling, and full of energy. Sit please."

She gestured at the large table on one side of the room, opposite the bed. Adèle sat on the backless stool, struggling to remain upright. She just wanted to sleep. Françoise dished everyone up a plate of pasta, pulses, some green vegetables and was that a pig's trotter? Adèle winced, catching Monsieur Blau's eye across the table.

A young girl walked in with some eggs. Françoise took the basket from her. "My daughter, Viviane."

Adèle watched as Françoise deftly cracked the eggs into a skillet and produced an omelette almost without blinking. Putting it on a small plate, she handed it to Monsieur Blau. "I think you would prefer this, no?"

"Oui, gracias. Thank you."

Everyone smiled as the German tried to pick the right words. Françoise beamed, her glance moving to Adèle's empty plate. "You too would prefer just eggs?"

"Yes please." Adèle held out her plate, suddenly famished. Again, the woman worked at speed and soon Adèle was enjoying the lightest omelette she'd ever tasted.

"Madame, you will sleep with me and my daughter. The men can take the barn."

"I don't want to be any trouble." Adèle ignored Auguste's strangled cough as he smothered a laugh.

"We wait for the guides. They may take a day, two, or perhaps a week. They are a law unto themselves, those Spaniards." The woman was still smiling. "You will stay here and I will find you a guide."

* * *

On the second day, Auguste said, "Adèle, I must check something with Françoise. You stay here with the others and rest. You are safe so long as you don't take any trips."

She was too tired to argue. Auguste disappeared with Françoise, but when they didn't return after forty-eight hours, the Polish pilot got restless.

"Why wait? We can find a guide in the next village. Everyone up here will know how to cross the mountains; they live here."

Viviane, who hadn't spoken two words since they arrived, shook her head. "Certain men will try to exchange your money for old republican pesos. They are worthless."

Adèle thanked her and, following her recommendations, waited for Auguste and their host to return.

Five days later, they walked in, having enlisted the services of a former republican fighter.

Over the next few days, he led their group down narrow goat paths to Spain. Adèle had to close her eyes more often than not, and couldn't look down.

Finally, their guide told them they would cross into Spain the next morning.

On the last night, Adéle asked "Why are you helping us?"

"There are more than one hundred and thirty thousand of our people – Spanish republican refugees – in Vichy. Your government sends them to work in Germany. If the Germans triumph in France, our chance to beat Franco will never come. Spain will never be free. This is why I help."

She nodded, but he hadn't finished.

"I'm willing to die for my country." He patted a small submachine gun slung across his chest and asked, "Are you?"

Adèle didn't answer.

They crossed the border the next morning. Thankfully, Auguste had the right contacts, and they avoided being detained in Spain. Adèle had heard enough about Spanish jails to be grateful.

FORTY-NINE

Sophie couldn't believe she had missed Adèle. Her mother said she had gone to Paris to see her, but her grandmother had privately told her the truth: Adèle had gone to England to join in the resistance.

Adèle, her self-centred twin, had finally decided to fight for France.

Sophie was torn between feeling proud of Adèle and wanting to tell her to stay in England where it was safe. Well, safer than being an agent in France, anyway.

She spent some time with her mother and grandmother before returning to the hospital where she was needed. In the months before her trip to Lyon, she had become even more involved with resistance activities. In addition to her duties at the hospital, she carried messages around the city, and took downed airmen and other refugees to the demarcation line.

Sophie liked spending time with Angela, Dr Murphy's wife. She was also heavily involved in the résistance. Sophie couldn't believe how bold she was, running a group from their little apartment situated right in the middle of the Germans' favourite Parisian street. But anytime Sophie mentioned her fears for the little family, Angela just reminded her that it was easier to hide in plain sight.

This afternoon, it was Angela who was worried about Sophie.

Angela chatted as she prepared another meal from a variety of vegetables. Sophie swore that once the war was over she would never eat another rutabaga again.

"Sophie, it's time for you to get out of Paris. It's far too dangerous for you to continue living here, never mind working at the hospital."

"I can't just leave, Angela. What about my work?"

Dr Murphy's wife looked at her with understanding and pity. "Things are changing, becoming more dangerous. That new Nazi has a fearsome reputation."

SS Major General Carl Albrecht Oberg had arrived in Paris on 7 May. Oliver insisted the general had scouted out the American Hospital on a previous visit to France before the war, but nobody else remembered seeing him.

"We don't know anything about him. It's all just rumours."

"Sophie, you know better than most not to discount those rumours. Not only is he SS, but he worked closely with Heydrich. You can't imagine he'll hesitate to inflict the same barbarity on France."

Sophie closed her eyes. The Germans seemed unbeatable. Every day the news came of them invading more countries: Romania, Yugoslavia, Greece, and they were advancing in Russia too. Some said Moscow would soon fall.

Talk at the hospital was all about the defeat of the Free French Forces by Rommel. Japan seemed to be winning the war against the Americans in the Pacific, and Germany appeared to be doing well in Russia.

Were the Allies going to lose? Sophie refused to believe they would. They had to keep fighting. They just had to believe Hitler and his friends could be beaten.

* * *

Sophie's uneasiness increased when a law introduced in June 1942 instructed all Jews over the age of six to wear the Jewish star on the left side of their chest. She hated seeing her friends and neighbours wearing the yellow star with the word '*Juif*' inside. She was tempted to join them by wearing a star too, but her work meant it was not a good idea to draw attention to herself. Still, she loved seeing how many Catholic priests, vicars, students from different backgrounds, and other people wore a star in protest.

Late one morning, on her way back from night duty, she encountered Arlette Litwak, her seventeen-year-old neighbour, standing against the wall in the apartment's hall building with her younger sister, Minette.

"Morning, Arlette, how are you? And your parents?"

When she didn't get an answer, Sophie looked at the girls more closely. "What's the matter? You've been crying. Can I help?"

"Maman isn't home." Minette hiccupped. "This was the first day we went out wearing our stars." Minette pointed to her coat at the ugly *Juif* star. "Maman collected them from the police station yesterday. I can't have a new dress because we had to use our clothing ration for these."

Sophie reached out to the young girl, knowing it wasn't the lack of a new dress that had her so upset.

"It's bad enough we can't go to the park or the cinema, and we can't find food to eat because we are only allowed to shop in the afternoon when the shelves are empty, but today..." The younger girl's voice broke as she sobbed.

Sophie pulled both girls closer to her as they cried, her mind filled with horrible thoughts. What else had these poor children been subjected to?

Arlette found her voice. "We got on the métro to go to

school. People shouted at us for being in the wrong car. Jews are supposed to travel in the last one, but we didn't know. They pushed us off. Minette fell over and scratched her knee. Some of our old friends saw but instead of checking on her, they walked past us and left her lying on the platform. Why would they treat us like that?"

Sophie couldn't answer. She didn't have the words.

"Why, Sophie? Others were laughing at us. Nobody tried to help. Why do people hate us so much?"

"How could they hate such lovely girls as both of you? Now, why don't we go to my apartment? I will fix up your knee, Minette, and then we shall all have breakfast. You can clean your faces too, so your mother doesn't worry."

"We can't take your food."

"You can and you will. My father had friends over for a party; there are leftovers. He won't miss them." And Sophie didn't care if he did. She would not let these girls go hungry after such humiliation.

"But you should keep it for yourself. Everyone is hungry these days."

Sophie winced at the girl's words. She was well-fed compared to many, thanks in part to her father's dealings.

"I have plenty. Now come on, girls, let's get you fed and back to your own apartment before your mother comes back from her visit and worries." Sophie chivvied them along the stairs until they came to her door. Her father was out, so they had the place to themselves.

"My father's friends brought him some sardines and some potatoes. I have a little bread, so why don't we make up a picnic for your parents too."

Sophie bathed Minette's knee before sitting both girls down, then made them fresh coffee.

"I can't believe we are having real coffee," Minette said. "It's like it was before the war."

Sophie smiled at Minette, but her eyes met Arlette's. They both knew the worst wasn't over.

* * *

After the girls had gone back to their own apartment with a small bag of presents for their family, Sophie tried to rest. But she couldn't sleep.

The knock on the door didn't wake her, but her heart hammered as she went to open it. Who would call on her during the day? She opened the door carefully, half-relieved, half-alarmed to find the Litwak girls' father at her door.

"Monsieur, is everything all right? The girls?"

"My girls are fine, thanks to you. I wanted to thank you for being so kind, mademoiselle. You have a big heart."

"There is no need for thanks. It was only something small." Sophie hesitated. "Have you had any news from your father?"

At his pained expression, Sophie wished she'd kept her mouth shut.

"Nothing, but maybe there is no paper?" The man looked at his hands, his shoulders slumped.

"I'm sorry, I shouldn't have asked."

He smiled at her. "You have been so kind to us. Not just with your little gifts but also for treating my girls like people."

"They are people."

He sighed. "That view is not held by as many as one would wish. It has been some time since anyone else showed us kindness. It does not bother me so much, but it causes my wife and children much pain. I wanted to tell you I will repay your humanity someday."

"Please, monsieur, it was nothing. My father has rich friends. You should be careful, though. I have heard..."

"Yes, I know. I have heard the same. But how can we live

our lives based on rumours? We have to take each day as it comes, yes?"

Sophie nodded, her eyes tearing up at the bravery of this man standing at her door.

"It may be bad here, but it is not as bad as it was where my family lived. There you could be killed for being Jewish. My family escaped a pogrom to come to France and I was born here. Thank you again, mademoiselle. My family is in your debt."

The man nodded before shuffling back upstairs to his apartment. Sophie closed the door and sank to the floor, her head in her hands. She knew they weren't safe, but what could she do?

Something dreadful was happening but Sophie wasn't sure what. Two of the most dedicated nurses the hospital had, Noémie Rosenberg and Maria Weitz, hadn't turned up for work. Being Jewish and therefore not allowed on the official payroll, they were both volunteering at the hospital. In return, Sophie and others provided them with food when they could. Nothing would have kept them from coming into work, unless it was outside their control.

Sophie pushed past the crowd of people gathering around the hospital, hearing titbits of conversation about the round-ups.

"I can't believe it. What do they want all those people for? The men can work, but what will they do with the women and children?"

"Where are they holding them? Why are they putting them in camps? Making them wear yellow stars is one thing, but holding children in open-air prisons, that's not right."

Sophie couldn't believe her ears. She kept searching for Dr Murphy, and finally found him in one ward set up for the elderly British patients. She got his attention and beckoned him over, not wanting to cause panic on the ward.

"Noémie and Maria didn't turn up today. Is it true? Have they arrested over thirteen thousand people?"

"Yes. The French police arrived at the houses of known Jews early this morning. I hope our nurses got a chance to hide before they turned up. The women and children are being held in several camps. Most are held at the Vél d'Hiv, but some men have been taken to Drancy. I've sent some ambulances to bring back those who are ill."

"I'll go to them."

Dr Murphy caught her right hand, pulling her back to face him. "You? Have you lost your mind? You can't walk into one of those camps. Someone could denounce you."

She was about to interrupt, but he kept talking.

"It's not about your being Jewish. People know you have been helping your neighbours. You haven't been subtle about it. Most know you have given out food, but some know you are the one to go to if they need a false passport."

"They won't turn their back on me."

"Sophie, you can't think that way. When people are desperate, they do some awful things. I don't know what I would do to save my son or my wife. Do you?"

She knew what he was saying was true, but she still had to go.

"We might never get you back out. The best thing you can do for everyone is go into hiding. For your protection as well as ours."

Sophie didn't like arguing with her mentor, but this was too important.

"Noémie and Maria are my friends. I have other friends, too, who may be there. I can't just walk away. I know you mean well, but don't you see? I can't abandon them."

"But—"

She didn't wait to hear his argument. "I can't just stand by and do nothing. I'm not registered as Jewish; nor was my mother. It will be fine."

Dr Murphy didn't look convinced.

"I have to do something. Please give me your blessing."

His eyes searched hers, but she refused to back down. His face fell as he realised he couldn't change her mind. He pulled her close and kissed her forehead.

"I would be proud to have you as my daughter," he whispered before releasing her. In a gruff voice, he said, "Go, but be careful. Wear your uniform. Make yourself known to the police as a French nurse."

"Thank you." Sophie reached up to kiss his cheek. "I will be careful."

* * *

Sophie took the bus to the Vélodrome d'Hiver. It should have only taken thirty minutes, but after less than ten minutes she got off. It would be faster to walk, due to the roads being cordoned off. When she arrived she met with some initial resistance from the gendarmes guarding the perimeter. They wouldn't let her into the building.

"You should go home, mademoiselle. Nothing for you here."

"I am a nurse," she replied, not wanting to say 'doctor' in case they asked for proof. Female nurses were less conspicuous. "There are sick people here. I am needed." Sophie spoke confidently, not prepared to show any fear.

"But they are Jews," the man responded. "You don't need to get your pretty hands dirty dealing with vermin."

"In the eyes of God, we are all are one people, monsieur." She touched the cross she wore around her neck. "Let me through or I will complain to your superiors."

He scowled but let her pass. She pushed her way into the building, then stopped in her tracks as the heat and stench combined to make her retch. The glass roof, painted blue to hide it from bombers, gave off a glaucous light, making the inhabitants look green.

"Nurse, help me, please! My baby is dying!"

"Nurse, over here. My mother, she is not breathing."

"Nurse, nurse!"

Sophie couldn't move. The screams of the children mingled with the silence of the adults. There were so many people all crammed into the space. In the distance, she heard a sound like gunshots. Had someone tried to leave? She moved further into the middle, staring around her as more and more people streamed into the already crowded space. Old, young, men, women, children and babies. Some wore suits while others were dressed for bed. A few clutched battered suitcases. Some women held their handbags under their arms, their eyes wide with shock. Children ran crying for their parents; others stood as if frozen to the spot.

A commotion, coming from up above her and to the right, caused her to look up. She was just in time to see a man tear himself away from two gendarmes and make a dash for the balcony. He would jump, but couldn't he see he wouldn't survive? Even as she thought it, she watched in horror as he came closer to the edge.

Someone shoved her, and she would have fallen if not for the same person grabbing her. A thud, then silence. She looked back to see the body on the ground, the head bent at an awkward angle. He was dead, but still the man who had saved her – she guessed he was a doctor given his white coat – moved forward to check.

The middle-aged man, his hair covered with a kippa, examined the victim, closing the man's eyes and muttering what could have been a prayer. Sophie knew he had to be sure, although there was no way anyone could have survived the blunt force trauma.

She glanced at the people staring at the body in silence, waiting for some reaction. A few seconds ticked by before a woman screamed, one fainted, and a few men held their coat sleeves to their mouths. A couple of women covered their children's eyes, and more pulled the youngsters away from the grisly scene.

"You finished gawking?"

She hadn't realised he was now standing beside her, his anger palpable despite his cool tone.

"Sorry, I just... Thank you for saving me," Sophie said. "I'm here to help; what can I do?"

The doctor pushed his glasses further up his nose. One lens was cracked. The same side as the nasty bruise on his cheek. Someone had hit him. She forced herself to focus, despite her stomach churning at the view behind him. Why didn't someone move the body?

"Did you bring food or water?"

Sophie nodded. "A little, but it was taken from me as soon as I entered. I can ask for more."

"Don't waste your breath. They won't help us."

"But they aren't Nazis. They're French," Sophie protested. The doctor looked at her with a pitying expression. She didn't like it.

"Who do you think rounded up these people? The gendarmes were only too happy to help." The doctor picked out a route through the mass of people. When Sophie didn't reply, he answered for her. "Yes, the French police told them to leave their homes with a blanket, sweater, pair of shoes and two shirts, and then they dumped them here. Into this cesspit. There are ten toilets. Five are boarded up and the other five are overflowing, so be careful where you walk. The children need the most help; some are alone."

"Where are their parents?" Horror made her stomach clench. She did her best not to bump into anyone as she followed the doctor. Should she be even following him? He didn't seem to welcome her presence. There were plenty of others she could help, but she sensed he knew a lot of these people.

"Some men believed they could protect their families by hiding elsewhere. Nobody, not even in their worst nightmare, imagined they would take the children." The doctor stopped in front of a very pregnant lady clearly in advanced labour.

"Please rest easy, madame. You cannot stop the course of nature," he said. Despite his gentle tone, Sophie could see by the way he examined the patient that he was concerned.

"Can I help? I have delivered a few babies," she said, desperate to prove she was useful. "My name is Sophie and I work at the American Hospital."

"As a nurse?"

"For the moment. I was due to sit my final exams to qualify as a doctor when war broke out."

"Do your best to save her." He leaned in closer to Sophie so the mother-to-be wouldn't hear him. "The baby won't live," he whispered.

Sophie nodded.

"Madame, this is Sophie. She will stay with you and help you. She has lots of experience. You will be safe with her."

"Please, Dr Levy, don't leave me."

The doctor spoke very quietly to the distressed woman. He touched her stomach gently as he gave her a reassuring smile. Sophie couldn't hear what he said.

"But, Doctor, it's not due for another two months."

The doctor exchanged a look with Sophie before moving on. Sophie kneeled on the ground.

"Let me try to make you more comfortable," she said, wondering what she could do without water, food or medical supplies. She rolled up the woman's discarded jacket, putting it under her head.

"My baby can't come yet. It is too early. He will die." The patient spoke through the contractions. "I have two girls, but my husband, he wants a son. To carry on his name."

Sophie tried to keep the lady calm. She refused to lie to her and tell her everything would be fine. The woman wasn't stupid. There was no way a baby born so early would live, even in the best of circumstances, and this situation was far from that.

It took nine hours for the labour to progress. The woman finally gave birth, but the baby was already dead. Sophie wrapped the child in a small blanket the woman had, before placing him in her arms. She tried her best to clean the newly delivered woman but without fresh water, it was pointless. A surge of anger flooded her; this woman and her child deserved better. Sophie wanted to stay and comfort the woman but she was needed elsewhere. Reluctantly, she left the poor unfortunate lady crying, cuddling her bundle.

FIFTY-ONE

Sophie toiled for hours, but no matter what she did, nothing seemed to help the poor wretches around her. Then she heard someone calling her name. She looked up.

"Arlette, Minette, what are you doing here?" Sophie stared at the girls. They were French. She'd been told the round-up was for foreign Jews only. Their father and mother might have been on the list, but not the girls. It was their father who had protested that he was a law-abiding citizen. She wondered where he was.

"We were forced to come by the police. We can't find maman and papa," Minette answered.

"But you shouldn't be here. You are French."

"They won't believe us. I tried to argue, but then they wanted me to come outside with them, so I ran. I was scared," Arlette answered, terror making her eyes far too big for her face.

Sophie hugged the girl close. She didn't want to imagine the ordeal the girl had probably avoided. "Stay close to me." She took off her armband with its red cross and handed it to Arlette. "Put that on. If anyone asks, you are a nurse."

Arlette took the band uncertainly. "What about Minette?"

"She is too young to be a nurse. She will stay beside you here. Now, can you hold this lady's hand and wash her face? She has a fever." Sophie glanced up and spotted someone she recognised and needed to speak to. "Be kind and don't move. I will be back."

She went to leave when Minette grabbed her arm, her grip so tight Sophie knew it would leave marks.

"I promise I will be back. I won't leave without you." Sophie gently pried the girl's fingers loose.

She made her way to the gendarme she'd recognised.

"What are you doing here, Fabien Berger? It's a shameful day for France."

He flushed bright red, his eyes darting everywhere, as if by avoiding her gaze he could pretend to be elsewhere.

"Well?"

"I have my orders." Fabien flushed even more deeply, something Sophie would not have thought possible.

"Some orders are meant to be ignored," Sophie reprimanded him. "What do they intend to do with all these people?"

"They are going to work camps in the east."

Sophie stared at him, then looked towards an old man in a wheelchair, his grandson or great-grandson sitting on his lap.

"They are to be workers for Germany?" she asked, not bothering to modulate her sarcastic tone.

Fabien didn't comment but stared at the floor.

"You have to make this better," she said in a more persuasive voice.

"Me? How? I can't release them. I would be shot."

"Do something." Sophie didn't feel an ounce of pity for the policeman. If everyone had refused to obey these orders, they wouldn't be standing here. But he continued to stare at the floor.

Sophie took a risk. Some people became brave when they were given exact instructions. She hoped Fabien was one.

"The Litwak girls are with me. One is wearing my armband. I want you to take them to my home."

"Leave here with two Jews? That's impossible," he protested. Something in his tone made her fight harder.

"You have known them since we were all children. For goodness' sake, do I have to remind you about the flowers you once picked for Arlette?" The man's neck turned bright red, matching his face. "Take them to my apartment. Father is away, so it is safe. For the moment. And then come back for more. It's time to stand up and be counted, Fabien."

Sophie walked away. She prayed she had convinced the man. It took a few seconds, but he dutifully followed her.

In the bad lighting, Minette's face seemed to turn even greener when Sophie came back with a policeman.

"Girls, you remember Fabien. The sergeant will escort you to my home, where you will find medical supplies, and food and water. He will help you parcel it up. You will return as soon as you can," Sophie instructed loudly, in case anyone was listening. Minette was about to protest, but Arlette took her sister's arm.

"Yes, Nurse," Arlette replied. Sophie could see by the look on the girl's face she knew something was up but wasn't sure what.

Sophie winked at Arlette, hoping to reassure her, and gave the terrified girl her key. "My father is away on business, but if you see Madame Garnier, tell her I gave you the key. Don't engage in any conversation or explanations; you know how nosy she is. If she gets difficult, imply Fabien will get his colleagues to search the apartments above yours. She'll do anything to avoid that." Arlette gave her a half-smile but she didn't know if the girl knew the concierge's son was in hiding.

She turned to Fabien and commanded, "Take them." She walked away like one who expected to be obeyed. When she looked back, they were gone.

* * *

Sometime later, the policeman returned alone, carrying a bag for Sophie. "Arlette said you might need these."

Sophie spotted her armband, and some bread and water. There was a small package of bandages too.

"Thank you, Fabien."

He passed her the package, gripping her hand in the process. "No, thank you" – he looked at the floor before staring back into her face – "for reminding me of my values." Releasing her hand, he stood straighter, legs apart, his voice more confident. "What else can I do?"

Sophie glanced around the area. There was so much to be done but so little help. "Can you help clear an area for the sick? The doctors and nurses are so few; perhaps we could help more if we were all in one place."

The confident stance disappeared, as he shuffled from one foot to another, avoiding eye contact.

"What?" Her voice rose to a bark, her patience running out.

"I wouldn't do that." His eyes stayed on the floor as his neck flushed. "It will only help the Germans decide who are the weaker members."

Her scalp tingled as he verbalised her own thoughts from earlier that day. "So, you don't believe the 'working in Germany' story either."

This time he stared into her eyes, and she saw the fear and disgust warring in his.

"I don't know what to believe any more. That is the God's honest truth." He walked away, his shoulders slumped in defeat.

Sophie didn't have time to go after him and console him. She had too many people who needed her.

* * *

She worked day and night for four days, grabbing sleep where she could. She couldn't leave, or find any way to get word out to the hospital, but she knew Dr Murphy and the team there would understand.

The conditions deteriorated with each passing day, yet most of the people remained resilient, believing in France. As she moved among the crowd, she heard snippets of conversation.

"France offered the Jews a home when no one else wanted us. They won't desert us now."

"My son fought and died for France, as did his father in the last war, and his grandfather lost a leg in the war before that. They will realise they have made a mistake, won't they, Nurse?"

Sophie didn't respond. She couldn't lie, but she didn't want to dim anyone's hopes either. She checked the woman's heart again.

"How long have you had heart trouble, madame?"

"A few years now, but it is not serious. I take the tablets the doctor gives me. I am fine."

"Do you have your tablets with you?" Sophie asked.

"No, I forgot them. It was silly, they were on the bedside table, but I had to leave in such a hurry. Once I get home, I will be fine. The air in here, it is too hot."

Sophie left the woman sitting down as she went to find Dr Levy, telling him the lady was in severe danger. "She needs her tablets. Can we not get some?"

"Are you still that naïve? They refuse to give us water or food, and you think they will worry about medicine?"

Sophie flushed at the doctor's tone. She wasn't used to being spoken to like that.

He saw and apologised. "Forgive me. I shouldn't have taken my temper out on you."

Sophie returned to the woman, but she had fallen asleep. The end would at least be quick for her; given her weakened condition, she would soon die in her sleep.

She moved on to the next patient, a young child whose mother had jumped from her apartment balcony in her attempt to avoid arrest. The mother had died, a neighbour told her, but the four-year-old child had survived with a suspected broken arm. His name was Samuel. The neighbour didn't know where Samuel's father was.

"My name is Sophie. What's your name?"

"Samuel." The child clutched his teddy in his good hand.

"Samuel, can I have a look at your arm?"

The child nodded. Sophie worked as gently as she could. It wasn't broken, but badly sprained. His mother's body must have protected him. What possessed her to jump with a child in her arms? She turned to ask the neighbour to look after the child so she could tend to other sick people, but she had disappeared. Sophie couldn't believe she had left Samuel behind. He had nobody.

Sophie bandaged Samuel's arm properly.

"Do you know where my papa is? He left us before the gendarmes came," he said. "Does he know Mama died?"

Sophie didn't know what to say. She stayed silent.

"Will my arm be fixed?"

"It will be just fine, mon petit," Sophie reassured him. He beamed with happiness, his smile making her tear up. What would happen to a small child all alone? She couldn't leave him here. She had to get him out.

Once more she approached Fabien, carrying the child in her arms. He looked at her warily. "A child?"

"His name is Samuel and he is about four years old. His mother died when she jumped from their apartment balcony." Sophie cuddled Samuel closer, avoiding his bad arm. "She was holding him in her arms, and her body cushioned his fall. He has a badly sprained arm."

Fabien looked around himself, a terrified expression on his

face. "I want to help, I do. But I can't take a child out. They will question me."

She glared at him and he couldn't hold her gaze.

"I am not a brave man," he mumbled.

"Yes, you are. You got the girls out, didn't you? Fabien, he is just a child."

Sophie saw the hesitation in his eyes. She had to get past his fear.

"Tell them he needs an operation, and you are under orders to take him to the local hospital." Sophie spoke firmly, not wanting to waste time arguing. She didn't want to draw attention to them either.

"But what if they don't want him?"

Sophie wondered if Fabien ever thought for himself. "Take him to the American Hospital. My colleagues will look after him for now."

"But—"

"Can you just take him? I don't have time to answer all your questions right now." Immediately she apologised. "I'm sorry. I know you want to help me. I just ... it is so hard. So many need so much, and I have nothing."

She barely heard him, he spoke so softly. "You have more than most. You still have your heart. Come, Samuel."

She tried to hand the little boy over, but he clung to her neck with his one good hand. "Samuel, mon petit, go with this man. I can't keep you here and I can't leave. You will be fine."

"He understands French?"

Samuel cuddled his head closer to Sophie's chest.

"He does. He was probably born here, just like a lot of these people."

"But they said it wasn't French people. They said they were only sending foreigners back."

"They say a lot of things!" Samuel wiggled in her arms. She couldn't afford a scene. "Fabien, speak to him, please. He doesn't trust you. Your uniform is frightening him. He said the gendarmes came for his mother."

Fabien spoke to the boy gently until he finally agreed to go, but only after Sophie promised to come and find him later.

"I will see you soon, Samuel. Be good," she said. "Bonne chance, Fabien."

FIFTY-TWO

On the fifth day, Fabien approached Sophie. She could tell by the look on his face that he didn't have good news.

"You need to leave now." Taking her by the arm, he pulled her towards an exit. "The buses have arrived to take these people to their allotted camps."

"But—"

"Go now, Sophie. I don't think the Germans will want any witnesses to what happens here. Don't take any chances. Go. *Please*. You have done enough." He leaned in closer as if to kiss her cheek, but instead whispered, "I took a couple more young women to your apartment. They need you. They are terrified."

She wanted to congratulate him for overcoming his fear to help someone without her bullying him into it. Instead she asked, "What about you, are you in danger?"

"Me? The gendarmes are safe. The Germans need us." Fabien's tone was bitter. "For the moment at least."

Sophie nodded and left reluctantly – the guilt of leaving people behind eating at her heart.

She walked down the street towards the métro, wondering at the lack of German soldiers; all she could see were French policemen. Walking into the subway, she glanced at her fellow passengers, hoping to see a look of sympathy or understanding or even anger at what was happening a few streets away, but there was nothing but a few crinkled noses and unkind comments about her smell. After five days working in the grimmest surroundings, they wouldn't smell too fragrant either.

* * *

Wearily, she forced one foot in front of the other until she reached avenue Kléber and her apartment. She walked straight by the open door of the *loge*, ignoring Madame Garnier's greeting. She didn't care if the woman thought her rude. She trudged up the stairs and, opening the door of her home, let herself inside. Despite the silence, she knew the girls were waiting for her; she could sense the fear.

"It's only me."

Arlette and Minette greeted her with a warm smile but the other three girls stared at her warily, fidgeting with their hands, wiping them on their clothes.

"Sorry, we didn't know where to go. You didn't say what to do, so we waited for you to come home," Arlette explained. "I hope that was the right thing to do."

"It was." Sophie reassured the girl, hating the fear in her eyes. "My father didn't come home, thank goodness."

"Your father? No. We have seen no one, not even the concierge, which is a good thing, as she would have recognised me and Minette. We ate some of your food. We were too afraid to go outside."

Sophie was grateful they hadn't ventured out. She didn't want to think what the consequences for everyone would have been if they'd been found and traced back to her apartment.

"I must have a bath, then I will speak to some people about finding you some proper shelter. You cannot stay here." Sophie caught the strangers exchanging a glance, and hastened to reassure them. They didn't know her like Arlette and Minette did. "It is not that you are not welcome, but it is dangerous, for you and for me. My father, well, he and I do not always agree on politics."

The girls looked at one another before each nodded their understanding.

She thanked her lucky stars her father hadn't come home, but it was pure luck. She hadn't thought ahead when she suggested the girls use her apartment. Why hadn't her father been home? Was he with his mistress?

"I'm sorry about the need for secrecy but the less you all know about each other's families, the better for all of us. If you are captured again..." The girls gripped one another's arms. "... the less you can tell the Nazis. But we will do our best to make sure you reach the free zone. So when I've finished, you all need to take a bath and change. Pick what you want to wear from our closets but think practically. You will be travelling a lot so you should be dressed for comfort." She gestured for Minette to come closer. "Pick something and Arlette can cut it down for you. Zeldah left some of her sewing materials in that room." She pointed towards another door. "Nothing about your appearance can testify to the ordeal you've endured over the last week."

* * *

Sophie headed back to her bedroom. As if hot water and new clothes would erase those memories. She wouldn't forget, not if she lived to be a hundred.

She washed, ignoring the temptation to stay in the bath forever. After dressing in clean clothes and gulping down the food Arlette had prepared, she left again, telling the group not to open the door until she came back. "No matter who you think it is."

FIFTY-THREE

She headed to the Catholic church. Monseigneur Patrick had been fairly outspoken in his sermons, and critical of the Germans. Would he help her? There was only one way to find out. Sophie joined the queue for confession. Once inside the box, she whispered her need to speak to him urgently and in private. He agreed to see her after he finished hearing his parishioners' confessions.

In the meantime, she took advantage of the opportunity to pray. She knew she needed all the help she could get.

After a rather long time on her knees, she felt a tap on her shoulder, and the priest instructed her to follow him into the sacristy at the back of the church.

"Now, mademoiselle, what can I do for you?"

She quickly outlined the events of the last few days, not holding anything back. She spoke of the suicides, rapes, shootings, and cruelty she had witnessed. She also told him of the bravery of the people and the acts of humanity that had brought tears to her eyes.

"I shall pray you gain relief from your memories. I shall also pray for all those who remain incarcerated. But I sense you have come for more practical help, am I correct?"

Sophie nodded. This was it. She was putting her life, and the lives of those who had trusted her, in this man's hands.

"A policeman helped me rescue some young women from the Vél d'Hiv. I only managed to help one child."

"You did more than most. What can I do? Where are these people?" the priest asked. He took a seat on one side of the desk, indicating she take the one opposite.

"The girls are in my apartment. I can't keep them there. My father ... he does not share my views. I worry he will return at any moment. I have other contacts, but they cannot help a group of young women. I thought you might know someone."

Across the desk, the priest took her hands in his. "I am so glad you came. Yes, I can help. I know people just as outraged as you about the treatment of the Jews. What is your home address?"

Sophie reeled off the address, noticing the priest's eyes widen in recognition.

"What is it? You know something about my building?" she whispered, her heart beating louder. Had the girls been discovered? No, she'd have heard the German trucks on her way over here.

The priest hesitated. "A couple, Monsieur and Madame Litwak, from your building, are safe, for now. Do you know them? They were separated from their daughters in the confusion."

Sophie restrained herself from hugging him. "Arlette and Minette are safe. Can you get a message to their parents?"

He looked doubtful. Perhaps it wasn't safe but at least she could tell the girls their parents were in hiding somewhere. Or should she? What if they were caught and tortured for information?

"It is best to keep such information to ourselves for now." The priest patted her hands.

"How will we get them from my apartment to your friends?" Sophie knew that task would be difficult, not least due to the number of ordinary French people who would consider it their duty to report the hidden Jews.

The priest took his time, considering how to answer her question. Sophie waited, feeling her eyelids dropping as fatigue took over.

Finally he spoke. "You look dead on your feet. Go home. I will send someone to you. You can trust that person, though you may be surprised when you see who it is."

Perplexed, Sophie wanted to ask for more details, but he gave a shake of the head to silence her. The priest's housekeeper had walked in without Sophie having noticed, tiredness lowering her guard more than usual.

"So that's where you have been hiding, Father. Monsieur Henry is expecting you to call to their house to discuss their baby's christening."

"I completely forgot, Madame Perrin, I am on my way. Sophie, thank you for coming to see me about your forthcoming marriage. I would be delighted to marry you and your young man when he returns from Germany."

Sophie stood up, thanked the priest, and walked out of the room.

* * *

Back at her apartment, she briefed the other women, telling them they must be ready to leave at a moment's notice. The group seemed more on edge than they had been, and not just due to her news.

"What's wrong?" she asked.

"Your father called. I answered the phone thinking it was

you." Looking terrified, Arlette apologised. "Sorry, Sophie. I told him I was your new maid."

"What did he want?"

Sophie couldn't believe he had chosen today to call. What if he got suspicious of her having a new maid? She would have to go back to the priest and tell him to hurry.

"He said he was worried about you."

Sophie's lip curled as she tried to hide her contempt for her father. The only person he was concerned with was himself. She obviously didn't do a good job of hiding her disdain as Arlette stumbled over her next words.

"I told him you were putting in extra shifts at the hospital. He said you are not to work too hard, that he will be away for the next few days and will return the first weekend in August."

Pressing her hands to her stomach, Sophie smiled. "That leaves us a little more time."

Arlette's eyes widened, huge in her pale face. "So you don't believe he will rush home after a stranger answered the phone?"

It struck her then how different her father was from Arlette's. Monsieur Litwak would do anything for his girls, including race to their rescue if he was free to do so. Her father hadn't cared enough about Jean-Pierre to help him, although he could have. Sophie would never forgive him for turning his back on his son.

"No, he will stick to his own plans. My father's priority is his own comfort."

At least her father was one less thing to worry about, she thought, before she finally went to bed.

FIFTY-FOUR

The next day passed slowly. Sophie prayed the priest hadn't gotten into trouble. She tried to rest, but her nerves wouldn't let her. She sat and exchanged stories with the women, who were also waiting nervously.

Elizabeth brought Samuel from the hospital, standing at Sophie's door and thanking her loudly for taking care of the child while his mother recovered. Sophie hoped her nosy neighbours would fall for Elizabeth's story.

Samuel was in good spirits, seeming to believe this was all a big adventure. His arm was healing nicely, and he never spoke about his mother or how he had got injured. Sophie didn't think that was too healthy, but now was not the time to probe.

He and Minette bonded quickly, Minette fussing over him like a mother hen with her chick. Sophie found it difficult not to ease the Litwak girls' concern for their parents, but it was safer for everyone. Hopefully, the family would be reunited in the free zone.

Night fell without anyone coming to see them. Sophie tried to hide her anxiety but Arlette cornered her in her room just before she went to bed. The others insisted on sharing, meaning

Sophie had her bedroom to herself. Sophie was saying her prayers when Arlette came in, quietly shutting the door behind her.

"Is it bad that nobody came?"

Sophie took her hand and drew her down to sit beside her on the bed. "We must have patience. My friends will not want to cause suspicion by acting hastily."

"You trust them? These friends?"

Sophie ground her teeth. After all the risks she had taken, the girl was questioning her.

"I'm sorry, forgive me. I didn't mean to ... but it is just so frightening. People we have lived beside for years stood back when they took us. Nobody stepped forward to help. At least not until we met you. Why do they hate us so?"

Sophie pulled the girl into her arms, shushing her. "People are afraid. Some are weak, and others are too caught up in their own problems. Nobody hates you, Arlette. You are a strong, beautiful young woman with a big heart. Look how well you care for Minette and the others. They look to you with respect for your bravery. Be strong, my friend. Someday this madness will be over."

Arlette met Sophie's gaze. "France will never be my home again. Not after this." She stood up but Sophie stayed on the bed.

"I will go and let you rest. No matter what tomorrow brings, I thank you, Sophie Bélanger, for everything you have done for my sister and me."

Arlette walked out of the bedroom, leaving the door slightly open. Sophie buried her head in her pillow to mask the sound of her tears.

* * *

The next morning, Sophie climbed out of bed and dressed quickly. She would go to the priest to find out what, if anything, would happen. She couldn't take another sleepless night.

The girls and Samuel were in the sitting room. Judging by their pallor, she wasn't the only one who hadn't slept. The sudden knock on the door made them all jump.

"Police! Open up."

Heart hammering, Sophie opened the door. She recognised the man in front of her: Elizabeth's cousin, Inspector Lavigne.

"I have information you have been dealing on the black market. I have a warrant to search the entire building, starting with this apartment." He spoke loudly, and his voice carried. Sophie was startled at first that he was not being discreet, but she soon realised what he was doing. 'Hiding in plain sight' was the term Dr Murphy had used. The police officer was banking on the fact that the other residents would rush to hide their own black-market produce, and thus be less likely to pay attention to what was happening in Sophie's place.

She led him inside. The women stared at him silently, suspicion written all over their faces.

"He is a friend. He will keep you safe," Sophie whispered. "Go with him and do everything he says."

"Are you certain? It was his kind who took us to that place." Arlette's words echoed the thoughts of the others, as they nodded in agreement.

"We share the same uniform, but not the same beliefs, mademoiselle. Now please, we must go. I have sent men to knock on other doors. The neighbours will be busy for a few minutes. We have to leave."

Sophie kissed each of the young women, leaving Samuel and Minette for last.

She bent down to kiss the boy goodbye, whispering into his ear, "When you are bigger, come and find me."

He kissed her goodbye but didn't let Minette's hand go. Minette kissed her too. "Thank you for saving us."

She watched through tears as the policeman led the group downstairs and into the police van, which soon drove away. She closed the door of her apartment and sagged against it, then jumped when the knock came. Opening the door, she frowned at the concierge, the worst gossip in the building.

"I came to see if you were all right. One policeman told me your maid was conducting black-market trading from your apartment."

Sophie would bet money that the woman was lying. Her nosiness would have made her give any excuse to question Sophie.

"No, they were mistaken. I asked my maid to put together some parcels for the hospital, and she asked her friends to come and help. The police thought we were buying and selling. It is all sorted now, but thank you for your concern." She could see that the woman didn't believe her, but she didn't care. She tried to close the door.

"But they took away a group. And I thought I recognised..."

Sophie straightened her back and faced the woman, holding eye contact. "It is just paperwork. They wanted to check all was in order. The ladies, none of whom you know, will be back with their families before nightfall. Now if you will excuse me, I must shower and return to the hospital. Patients are waiting."

"I don't know what your father will think of all this."

"I am sure he will be delighted to discuss it with you on his return. You can tell him about your bribes to the police so they turn a blind eye to your son's escape from the prisoner-of-war camp while you are at it." Sophie took a second to deliver her next blow. "My father is on friendly terms with the head of police. Perhaps he will put a good word in for you when they come to arrest you."

The woman's face paled as she glanced upward towards the

attic. Sophie was thrilled that her dig had hit the mark. How ungrateful madame had been at the time, but at least now, Sophie had a weapon to keep the concierge in check. She hated blackmailing the woman but in these desperate times, it was necessary.

* * *

She closed the door and leaned against it again, letting the tears come freely for the first time since she had entered the horror at the Vél d'Hiv.

FIFTY-FIVE

APRIL 1942, LONDON

Adèle stared at the devastation in London, the missing buildings, the piles of rubble and the people continuing about their business as if there weren't large craters on the roads. The parks she remembered from their year of touring London were unrecognisable with what looked like vegetables planted all over them. Then there were the barrage balloons on the skyline. Someone told her they were to stop the Luftwaffe getting too close if they came over again. She couldn't imagine her beloved Paris looking like this.

Shuddering at the thought of Maxim's lying in a pile of rubble, she picked her way past the sandbags and up the steps into the building where she was lodging. That was another thing: nobody had prepared her for the difficulty of finding suitable accommodation in London. She should have got more money from her father, told him she needed to buy a whole new wardrobe, then she would have stayed in a hotel. Instead, she was stuck sharing a flat with Charles Bergin, a friend of Auguste. She scowled, not wanting to think about him. He'd dumped her almost as soon as they arrived in London with some story about how he had so many people to see, things to do.

She stomped up the stairs, her stomach churning at the smell of grease. Opening the door of the small flat, she took a deep breath.

"If that's you, Adèle, come in. Your chips are getting cold."

Fish and chips again. She plastered a smile on her face and stopped in the old kitchen, the dark brown walls doing nothing for her depression.

"You're wet. Why didn't you bring an umbrella?"

"It wasn't raining when I left. I can't believe this country; everything is damp. How can you bear it?"

"What? There's nowhere like England. You have another bad day?" He watched her, a smile on his face, but his eyes were wary. A twinge of guilt hit her; it wasn't his fault she was fed up. He was stuck recovering. He said he'd been hit by a car in the blackout.

"I just don't know what's taking so long. We've been here two weeks already and Auguste hasn't been in contact." *I need to go back home, not hang around here getting wet and –* eyeing his supper *– fat.*

FIFTY-SIX

22 JULY, PARIS

Two days after the girls and Samuel had left her apartment, Sophie turned up for her shift at the hospital. She was told Dr Murphy wanted to see her urgently. She met Elizabeth in the corridor and together they walked to Dr Murphy's office.

"Leave," Elizabeth whispered. "We had a tip-off; they know what you have been doing."

"I can't leave," Sophie protested. "I have too much to do. There are so many depending on me, and not just here." She pushed the door open.

Dr Murphy had heard her response to Elizabeth as they walked in. "You must. You are putting everything at risk. Can't you see that? Things have changed, Sophie. I don't want you to go. I want to keep you safe right here. But that's not possible."

Sophie looked from Elizabeth to Dr Murphy and back. "What happened? Tell me."

Her friends exchanged a look before Elizabeth mumbled, "One of the girls staying at your apartment was Noémie's friend. Dr Levy got Noémie out of the round-up and we sheltered her here at the hospital. Noémie was on her way to a safe house in Nice and saw her friend at a train station. She thinks

the girl must have panicked as she approached the train platform and then turned back. Noémie thinks she saw the SS
soldiers at the barrier."

"Oh, for goodness' sake. That's the first rule, never turn
back." Sophie's frustration boiled over. "What of Noémie, was
she caught too?"

"No. But she came back here instead of making her way out
of Paris. She is worried about her friend telling the Gestapo
about you and Fabien. She doesn't know about Inspector
Lavigne."

"She can't implicate Fabien. She doesn't know his name. He
will be fine. What about your cousin?"

Elizabeth shrugged. "He can say he arrested her and she's
being spiteful. Don't worry about him. You are the one in
danger."

"Not only are you putting yourself in danger, but all the
patients we have here. Get out of Paris." Dr Murphy's voice was
firm. "Go to Yvette, take her with you and get to Lyon. Now,
while you still have a choice."

Sophie wanted to argue, but she couldn't. She didn't care
about herself any more, but she cared about the people in the
hospital, in particular Elizabeth and this man and his family.

"Okay. I'll go. How much time have I got?"

"A few hours. Noémie said her friend was one of many
picked up at the station. Maybe they will just send them to a
camp, but if the girl thinks she can save herself, she may be
tempted to give the Boche information."

"Is Noémie going to be all right?"

Elizabeth handed her two Ausweis. "She will be fine, we
have sent her out by a different route."

With tears in her eyes, she hugged Dr Murphy, then Elizabeth. There wasn't time to say goodbye to the others.

Dr Murphy touched her arm. "Hurry, you must go."

* * *

Despite everything she had learned, she took the risk of going home, where she packed up some of her father's cigarettes, sardines and soap in her bag. They would come in handy for bribes. She took whatever money she could find. Her father could afford it.

She couldn't avoid taking the train to Yvette's house. Thanking God for Elizabeth's connections, the soldier barely looked at her Ausweis before telling her to move on.

She saw Yvette's house in the distance but as she cycled, – a farmer, judging from the dirt on his clothes – ran into the road just in front of her. She swerved and would have come off her bike, but the man reacted quickly.

"Don't go to the Steins'. Come to my house," he said, looking around, agitated. Sophie wondered if he was drunk – but where would he get the alcohol? She thought of screaming for help, but some instinct told her it would be a bad idea.

She tried to move her handlebars as she said, "Thank you, but I need to see Yvette."

"Mademoiselle, you must come to my house now."

The man didn't give her a chance to argue; he grabbed her bicycle and forced her off the road. She tried to fight for control, but he was too strong. Shocked, she couldn't stop shaking, wondering if her fate was to end up raped and murdered by one of her own countrymen.

"Please move quickly. Yvette was my friend too."

His use of the past tense made her follow him. What did he mean *was*?

He led her down a path, the overhanging trees making it difficult to see, but soon they came to a small farmhouse. He pushed her roughly through the door.

"I'm sorry about that, but you cannot go to the Steins' house. The Fritz were here this morning – they took Yvette away. They left two men at the house waiting to see who arrived. I've been watching the roads to make sure nobody falls into their hands."

Sophie stared at him. She couldn't believe how close she had come to disaster.

"Thank you." She couldn't look at him, ashamed of what she'd thought he had planned for her. "What about Yvette's mother? Did they take her too?"

The man didn't answer, and the feeling of dread in Sophie's stomach increased.

"She's dead, isn't she?" she whispered.

"Yes, those murdering scum shot her. May they rot in hell."

Sophie closed her eyes, saying a quick prayer for Jules's mother and for Yvette.

"Do you know why they arrested Yvette? Was it because she is Jewish?"

The man shook his head. "It would be better if that was the reason. They lock up the Jews, but they do not bring them to the Gestapo. The man who took her, I have seen him before. In Paris. He works for Oberg."

All the breath seemed to leave Sophie's body in one go. Her darling friend Yvette was in the hands of that monster. She couldn't speak or breathe. She should have tried harder to convince Yvette and her mother to go to Lyon, to stop whatever her friend was doing and leave.

"You must go away. You cannot stay around here. It is much too dangerous for everyone. Some turncoat must have informed. I tried to warn Yvette. She was too trusting, but she didn't listen. She helped so many people, but wouldn't help herself."

Sophie could just imagine Yvette telling this man to get lost, exactly as she had done when Sophie suggested Yvette go to her grandmother. Hopefully, that stubbornness would help her face the horrors ahead.

"You're that doctor friend of hers, aren't you?"

Sophie nodded. She didn't ask how he knew.

"She said you were beautiful, blonde hair and blue eyes. Just what the Germans like. They are likely to know about you. You will need a new identity. Have you contacts to get new papers?"

"No."

The man cursed before going upstairs. He came back with a heavy black dress and shawl, both stinking of sweat. "You must change. A beauty like you will stick out around here. Mess up your hair and try to look older."

"Whose are these?" Sophie took the clothes, trying to conceal her distaste as her nose wrinkled at the smell.

"My mother. She does not need them now. She is bedridden. You can change in the storeroom. Be quick. There isn't much time." He picked up her bag, but as he did so, some things she had packed rolled out.

"Cigarettes and sardines?" He investigated the contents of her bag, his expression changing from friendliness to suspicion. "Are you sure you are not with them?"

"They are my father's. He has lots of contacts on the black market. I am a doctor, not an informer."

"Prove it."

"How? I can tell you I am Jewish."

He stared at her blonde hair, disbelief written all over his face.

"I don't know what to tell you to make you believe I am telling the truth. I was in love with Yvette's brother; I loved Yvette as a sister and wanted her to move out of harm's way. Yvette wouldn't listen. I thought these might help her in her work. You know, as bribes."

The man studied her for a few minutes.

"Yvette told me her brother's girl was like a sister to her. I'm sorry. It's just – well, you never know these days, and I can't remember the last time I had a cigarette. A real one, I mean. You shouldn't have them, though; don't you know? Women lost their cigarette rations months ago."

"You take them, then. Use them for bribes or whatever you like. That's why I brought them."

He grinned, taking a cigarette and lighting up. "Thank you, Doctor. Now go and change – quickly, please."

Sophie changed, giving the man her own clothes. He dug a hole and buried them, along with the rest of the clothes she had brought with her.

"Do not speak to anyone. You must walk to the next village. Go to the church – not the Catholic one. Speak to no one but the rector. Tell him you need papers. Do not tell him you were here at my farm. He should know about Yvette – we spread the word – but just in case the messenger got rounded up, tell him again."

"Yvette won't betray anyone."

He looked at her sadly. "I admire your loyalty to your friend. But you are stupid if you believe that. Everyone talks. Eventually. Now go. We are wasting time."

* * *

Sophie walked in the direction the man had suggested. Thankfully, it wasn't too warm a day. She smelled so bad, most people kept their distance. Those who stopped to ask her anything, she ignored, hoping they would believe she was an eccentric older woman. She walked to the Catholic church and was up the steps before she remembered it was the wrong church. Turning, she walked away, wishing she could buy a cool drink. But the farmer had warned her not to go anywhere but the church.

It was late afternoon by the time she reached the right church. She walked inside, thankful for the coolness after being in the heat. The building was empty. Panic filled her.

How would she find the rector? She didn't even know his name.

She took a seat and prayed the man would come soon. Looking around, she wondered at the similarities and the differences between this church and the one she had been brought up to attend. There was no lingering smell of incense here, nor any pictures or statues of Mary. She wasn't even sure if she should kneel or whether her head should be covered.

She didn't know how long she sat there; every second felt like an hour. She kept expecting to hear a car draw up outside and the crunch of boots on the steps.

"Can I help you?"

She looked up into the kindly face of an older man who appeared to be in his late fifties.

"Are you the rector?"

"Yes, madame. You are new to my church but welcome."

"My name is Sophie. I was told to come here for help. I am a friend of Yvette Stein."

"I am sorry, but I don't know any Yvette Stein."

Sophie panicked. He was being cautious, thinking this was a trap, and she had no way to prove who she was.

"I could do with some water. Is there somewhere we could talk?" As he glanced around the empty church, she whispered, "Somewhere more private."

He looked at her again before nodding. "Follow me."

She walked behind him, wishing again she could have borrowed different clothes. He must be close to vomiting with the smell – she was.

"Thank you, Rector. I'm sorry; I do not know what to call you." He didn't answer. "My name is Sophie Bélanger. I am a doctor – third-year medical student, from the American Hospital. Yvette's brother Jules was my..." Sophie faltered before whispering, "beau." She choked the tears back. "Yvette was picked up by the SS early this morning."

The rector stared, the colour draining from his face as she outlined what had happened.

"They shot her mother and left people at the farm to wait for any of Yvette's visitors. Warn your people."

"Why would you come?"

"I know you are trying to be discreet, but honestly, do you think I would wear these clothes because I like them? I am sorry, I mean no disrespect, but do you want to keep talking while we wait for the black cars to show up or are you going to warn your contacts?" Sophie's patience had run out.

The man glared at her but turned away. He picked up the phone.

She listened as he asked for the doctor to come and see an old lady who had collapsed, possibly from sunstroke.

Sophie sipped her drink, waiting while the rector walked back and forth.

"How many people did Yvette know?"

"I don't know. I warned her to be careful. How do you know it was the SS?"

"The farmer who warned me off said he recognised the cars when they were first approaching. He didn't have time to warn Yvette, but he watched from a distance. He saved my life and I don't even know his name."

"Better that way, given what has happened. What will you do now?"

"I need papers and I wish to cross to the free zone."

"You and the rest of the world."

"I am Jewish."

He looked so surprised she almost laughed.

"I didn't realise. I guess should have, when you said you were Jules's fiancée."

"I didn't know back then. I assumed I was Catholic. It is how I was brought up – I have a genuine baptismal certificate.

But my grandmother converted over forty years ago, and in the eyes of the Nazis that makes me a Jew."

"I am sorry."

"Don't be. I'm not. It changes nothing about me. People are people regardless of their background, religious beliefs, or racial heritage." She almost wanted him to challenge her, but he didn't.

"It is a pity that not everyone believes that – we wouldn't be in this mess."

The doctor arrived, interrupting them. Sophie listened as the rector explained.

"May God help her." The doctor turned his attention to Sophie. "Thank you for warning us. Please excuse me."

Sophie and the rector listened as the doctor made a phone call. He spoke about wanting to check a baby after a difficult birth. The call was short.

"You've warned the others?" the rector asked.

"Yes, word will spread quickly." The doctor pushed his hair back, his hands shaking slightly. "We agreed on the code months ago. The ones most at risk will flee. The rest of us will just have to hope for the best. Thank goodness the group leader insisted on code names. Yvette knows few people by their real names."

The rector nodded. "Yes, but if they are picked up, they will talk too. We cannot be too cautious." The rector focused on Sophie. "You should go now."

"I will, but first I need papers."

The doctor sighed. "Come with me. I have a friend who will help. You also need a bath."

"I know, I stink. It was not my idea – the farmer who saved me suggested it would keep the Germans away."

"I think he was right. No offence, but you smell worse than a *porcherie*."

The doctor picked up his bag and said goodbye.

"Thank you, Rector, for your help. Good luck."

"You too, Sophie. Maybe we will meet again once this is all over."

Sophie followed the doctor out of the church. Given how many people had lost their lives, she wasn't counting on living to see the end of the war. Planning for tomorrow was about as much as she could manage.

FIFTY-SEVEN
JULY 1942, LONDON

Adèle sat in the Lyons' Corner House, not particularly impressed by the drink she sipped. What was the British fascination with tea?

"Cheer up, Adèle, it may never happen." Charles tried to make light of the situation. Adèle wished Charles would disappear. She saw the English girls smile in his direction but his pale eyes and floppy hair, which was neither brown nor blonde, did nothing for her. He had a title, something he was at pains to tell her was a burden, but she didn't care enough to remember what it was. Her foot tapped as they waited for someone to join them. Adèle hated the secrecy. Why couldn't Auguste have just told her where to go for training?

"I know you are suffering my company but you shouldn't act like you know everything. They won't like it."

"Who won't like it? I'm not looking for their approval, Charles. I want their knowledge so I can go home and get my revenge."

"That's another thing, old girl. You can't go around talking about revenge. You will fail the psychological tests for starters."

Adèle could have screamed with frustration but instead she dazzled him with her brightest smile. "I'm sorry for being such a bore. I'm homesick, that's all."

To her horror, Charles took her hand and kissed it. She stiffened, trying not to cringe at the feel of his lips on her skin. "I think you are awfully brave. You should stay here in England where you are safe."

"Never. It's freezing and wet. Does the rain never stop? No wonder English people are so pale and never smile. I shall go mad if I don't get home soon."

"There she is; be nice." Charles stood. "Miss Atkins, thank you for coming. Would you like some tea?"

"No thank you, Charlie. So nice to see you've recovered. Now run along, dear, and leave me with Mademoiselle Bélanger. There's a good chap."

To Adèle's amazement, Charles kissed the woman on the cheek and was gone with barely a glance in her direction. So much for being smitten.

"I believe you cannot wait to see the back of us, Mademoiselle Bélanger."

Adèle shifted in her seat under the woman's unwavering gaze. She scanned the lady quickly, taking in her English tweed jacket, her straight skirt, her slight Parisian accent, although she wasn't French. No, if she had to guess, the woman sitting ramrod-straight in her chair was from Eastern Europe, although she was making every effort to hide that fact. What else was she hiding? She was well groomed but dressed in a way that made her seem older than she was. Her gaze travelled back to the woman's face and she found herself caught like a rabbit in the sight of a shotgun. For a moment, her mind went blank.

Miss Atkins spoke. "Are you finished?"

"I like to know who I am dealing with. You assessed me just as closely." Adèle didn't pretend to be embarrassed. She was

French and going to fight for her country. She wasn't going to be beholden to these people for anything. The English had been all too eager to leave her country, not to mention French soldiers, via the beaches of Dunkirk.

"So what did you make of me? You can be honest. I don't expect you to be coy, madame."

Adèle responded in French. "Although fluent in English and French, neither are your first language. You speak French with a slight Parisian accent. I believe you come from Eastern Europe although where exactly, I am unsure. You are single, married to your job, and for some reason, you wish to appear older than you are."

Miss Atkins smiled. "Very good, excellent in fact. You are one of the few to guess somewhat accurately. Now let's finish our tea and go somewhere we can talk. In private. Walls have ears and all that."

"The walls have ears? This expression I hear all the time in England. You are obsessed with spies."

"You should be too, Adèle, for all our sakes."

Miss Atkins paid the bill and then left, leaving Adèle to follow in her wake. Miss Atkins walked quickly, making Adèle feel like a soldier following a general. She sped up a little so she could walk beside and not behind her new companion. She was her equal after all.

They stopped in front of a nondescript building but once inside, it was evident not only did everyone know Miss Atkins, but they respected her authority.

Adèle followed her up the various flights of stairs before they reached an office. Miss Atkins opened the door and stood back, allowing Adèle to walk in first. She shivered, wondering if the English insisted on being cold to make them appear hardier. Miss Atkins took off her coat and put it on the stand beside the door.

"Would you like tea or coffee?"

"Coffee please, black, no sugar."

Miss Atkins smiled.

"What?" Adèle asked.

"Sugar is in short supply around here. If I was a German spy, I would know you were an agent. It's one of those basic mistakes our agents make in France."

"I'm French. I know how to behave in France." Adèle gazed around her, deliberately not looking at Miss Atkins. How dare the woman treat her like she was a child? She was almost twenty-five, for goodness' sake.

Miss Atkins left without comment. Adèle rooted in her purse for her compact to check her lipstick. She wondered if she would meet the man in charge. Auguste had warned her she needed him onside. She'd paid little attention. Men were easy. A smile, a glimpse of leg and they were mastered. Miss Atkins, on the other hand, would prove more difficult. She had to find another way to endear herself to that one.

Miss Atkins returned alone, the coffee arriving shortly after. The uniformed young woman flashed a smile in Adèle's direction as she left the coffee pot and cups on the table in front of them. She closed the door behind her. Only then did Miss Atkins speak.

"We shall have to get you enlisted into the First Aid Nursing Yeomanry or FANY for short. You have been accepted for training but I guess that won't surprise you."

Adèle took a sip of her coffee to mask her elation; she didn't want Miss Atkins to suspect her reason for returning was revenge. The coffee's rich texture surprised her. She could be in Paris.

"Your brother's execution had as much to do with recent events in Paris. If he had been tried earlier in the war, I expect he would have been sent to Germany."

Adèle hid her shock. How much more did this woman know about her?

"We know more than your mother."

Amazed her thoughts had been read so quickly, she glanced at Miss Atkins.

"Adèle, we are on the same side. We both want to get rid of Hitler and his henchmen. I understand your resentment, believe me, I do. But try to hide it a little better. You might not feel you need anyone but the role you have signed up for is a dangerous, lonely one. Our agents depend on those back in England. I would suggest you make yourself more appealing to those in a position to help you, and not just the men."

Chastened, Adèle nodded. She played with her coffee cup, unsure of what to say.

"I suppose you are wondering what's in store for you."

Adèle didn't reply, so Miss Atkins continued.

"The initial assessment and training will take three weeks and will include a psychiatric evaluation. Once you pass this step, you will then learn about parachuting, explosives, Morse code, and hand-to-hand combat."

Adèle opened her mouth but shut it quickly as Miss Atkins kept talking.

"Each team is made up of three agents, being a courier, wireless operator, and an organiser. You played piano as a young girl?"

"Oui. My mother thought it necessary for young ladies to have certain skills."

"Mothers the world over share similar opinions. It is of benefit to us. Those who have studied piano make better wireless operators."

"You want me to be the wireless person?"

Miss Atkins took a sip of her drink before placing it carefully back on the saucer. "Not necessarily. It will depend on the results of training. The role of wireless operator is by and large the most dangerous."

"I'm not afraid."

"You should be." In an obvious attempt to cool the atmosphere, she continued in a softer tone. "The wireless operators carry incriminating evidence of their guilt should they be stopped by the Germans or French police. It is rather difficult to disguise a radio although our boffins have some interesting innovations. But the success of each network is dependent on keeping in contact with London, so the role is a vital one."

Tempted to interrupt again, Adèle stayed quiet. Miss Atkins took another sip of her drink, making it more difficult for Adèle to stay silent. She had so many questions, but it was best to listen more than speak.

"Given your knowledge of France, its language, customs, people, I believe the role of courier might be more relevant to you. As courier, you would be responsible for carrying messages between members of each circuit or network."

"I would know everyone in the resistance?"

"No, only some of your network. We are learning from past mistakes."

Adèle spotted a look of pain – or was it guilt? – in her eyes before the lady blinked and it was gone.

"Each area of France is covered by a different and totally independent network. If one circuit is betrayed to the Germans, those members cannot endanger the other networks."

"But surely nobody would betray their friends?" protested Adèle, before realising she had rudely interrupted. "Sorry."

At that moment, the door opened and a tall, thin man walked in. Without introducing himself, he took a seat at the table. He'd obviously been listening as he answered her question.

"Everyone who is captured talks eventually. All we ask is that our agents do their best to hold out for forty-eight hours in a bid to give other agents a chance to escape the eventual round-up that will come."

"But—"

The man interrupted her. "Do not underestimate the lengths the Germans will go to in order to obtain information. They think nothing of inflicting pain; in some cases, they seem to do it purely for pleasure."

Believing the man was trying to intimidate her, Adèle switched her attention back to Miss Atkins, who had started talking again.

"As I was saying, women are naturally suited to the role of courier. For one thing, men of military age risk being arrested and sent to Germany as forced labour. Female couriers are less likely to arouse suspicion, particularly when they have a good cover story for having to move around, such as being the local nurse."

"Pick something else for me; I am not nursing material, not good with blood." Adèle closed her eyes for a second, an image of Sophie clear in her thoughts. Her twin relished the chance of practising her operating skills; she had taken delight in telling Adèle the gory details. She missed Sophie.

The man spoke again, speaking over Miss Atkins, who didn't correct him. He must be the head man.

"The organiser must be a man. Men are better at sabotage and engaging the enemy."

Adèle bristled but a look from Miss Atkins told her to hold her tongue. The man didn't appear to notice her reaction.

"Frenchmen hold very traditional views on what roles women should undertake and being their boss is not one of them."

Adèle wondered if he recognised the irony of what he had just said. He wasn't exactly advocating equality for women. She didn't argue, though. What happened on the ground in France wasn't any of their business. Not as far as she was concerned.

"Have you any questions?" he asked.

"Who decides which position I will hold?"

The man looked to Miss Atkins but replied, "Your course tutor will make a recommendation as to which position you are most suitable for depending on what strengths and weaknesses are highlighted during the training."

"When would I start?" asked Adèle.

"You will receive your orders in due course outlining where and when you must make yourself available for duty, but you should be prepared to start a week on Monday." Miss Atkins smiled at Adèle.

"Another week. Why can't I start today?" Adèle replied. The man spoke before Miss Atkins could answer.

"This is not some dinner date, Mademoiselle Bélanger. It is an important mission, not one to be taken lightly."

Adèle opened her mouth about to tell him she had climbed mountains, braved blizzards, slept in a hut with complete strangers waiting to be denounced at any moment, but once again Miss Atkins saved her.

"Adèle, your impatience to help your country is commendable but we need some time to set up your backstory. You will no longer be Adèle Bélanger. She has to disappear, and we will give you a new identity to use on the ground. Your code name will be Claire – this is the name you will use during training. Now, let me escort you out of the building. Your instructions will be delivered to your flat in due course."

Only then did Adèle realise she hadn't given Miss Atkins any personal information, including details of the apartment she was staying at in Clapham Junction. The woman clearly knew all about her. The man hadn't finished with her.

"Mademoiselle Bélanger, remember this if nothing else. The Germans are ruthless, but at least they are the enemy in plain sight. What you must be careful of are the French collaborators."

Adèle opened her mouth to refute this slur on her people but shut it again. Hadn't her own father betrayed his people? The man misinterpreted her silence.

"Before you get all patriotic on me, all communities have those elements who are only concerned for their own survival. They would sell their grandmother into slavery if it bought them some extra money or power. Beware of all contacts you make, including any that you may have had from your childhood. Sharing a common background doesn't mean that their political beliefs or opinions now mirror your own. You need to be wary of everyone and only trust someone when you are completely sure that you could trust them with your colleagues' lives. Remember, if you get caught, you will betray those on your team."

He glanced at her as if expecting her to say something. She wasn't about to argue she wouldn't betray anyone. He would think her naïve. She returned his gaze, thinking she may have seen a glimmer of respect at her silence.

He continued. "Some would-be agents find that they are not suited to the work required of them. Others decide not to proceed for personal reasons. If you have any doubts about whether you still wish to go into the field, then please come and tell us. We are not in the game of sending unwilling operators into danger."

"I won't change my mind, sir. I want to go home. The sooner the better."

But she might as well have spoken to the wall for the notice he took. He left the room with a nod to Miss Atkins, closing the door behind him.

Miss Atkins lit a cigarette. "He takes his job very seriously."

"How can you work with such a man? It's a wonder he didn't have you making his tea."

Miss Atkins laughed. "A gin and tonic I can manage, but tea? Now, let's get you home. I'm sure Charlie is waiting."

Adèle sighed. "Does he have to babysit me? Shouldn't he be doing something more useful for the war effort?"

Miss Atkins's look could have given her frostbite. "Never underestimate anyone, Mademoiselle Bélanger, friend or foe."

With that, she closed the door, leaving Adèle to find her own way out.

FIFTY-EIGHT

JULY 1942, GUILDFORD, SURREY

Adèle tried to curb her impatience as the train was late again. She was to be at Wanborough Manor in Guildford this afternoon. The British people didn't seem to worry about it. When someone complained, they were quickly asked if they knew there was a war on. She stared out the window of the train carriage, the green fields reminding her of parts of France.

She closed her eyes, wondering where Sophie was. Her thoughts turned to Jean-Pierre, seeing him smile as he sat in the armchair by the fire, another one of his books on his knee. He'd been so brave, escorting downed pilots across France while she entertained their father's German friends. She squeezed her eyes, determined not to let a tear fall. Jean-Pierre must have despised her for getting Léo killed by not obeying the rules and then by collaborating. That's what she had done – or at least it could seem like that to outsiders. She hadn't forsaken her father but instead accompanied him on his business dinners. She'd gone out for meals with German officers, worn clothes from shops only frequented by their wives or mistresses, and enjoyed their gifts of food and wine. As their father was still doing. Auguste had warned her that her papa's name was on the list for scores to be settled. He'd told her about papa buying up Jewish businesses at knock-down rates. Not everyone cared he was taking advantage of the Jews, but they did care he was friendly with the occupiers. That was enough to ensure his death sentence.

She urged the train to move faster. The sooner she passed the course and got back to France, the better.

* * *

The house they had instructed her to arrive at reminded Adèle of something from one of Jean-Pierre's books. It was old enough to have belonged to Henry VIII and hadn't seen much restoration since. She left her case at the front door and was directed into what must have once been the dining room. Blackout curtains hid the original red velvet curtains adorning the bay windows. The mantel over the ornate fireplace was free from dust and ornaments. Someone had set the fire, but it wasn't lit. Adèle looked at the other recruits, all men with the exception of one other girl of a similar age. This girl, code-named Gabrielle had the worst French accent she'd ever heard. Adèle didn't understand how the boffins believed Gabrielle could be an agent.

A couple of uniformed Waafs were handing out tea and real coffee, a luxury that Adèle couldn't resist. Adèle joined one of the smaller groups chatting amongst themselves.

A uniformed man with an air of authority strode into the room. "Good afternoon, ladies and gentlemen. I am Major Hunter. Thank you all for joining us. As someone may have already explained to you, there are three elements to the resistance. The first are the saboteurs, those who make life difficult for the occupiers. The enemy have swiftly put the random attacks that have taken place down and the repercussions against the civilian population are harsh. Sabotage will be more important when we get closer to the Allies landing in France." A small cheer went up at that last remark.

The major continued. "The second level of resistance are those managing the escape lines. These extremely brave men and women help our chaps get back to Blighty and many of those around us owe them our lives. But you are not being trained in how to run an escape line."

The major glanced around the room. "We want you to build up networks of trained resistants all over France. You will forge teams of trusted people. Each person you bring into a team increases the risk of penetration by the enemy. We will teach you the security precautions you must take to protect not only yourselves, but also those people around you. But these teams won't take on the enemy, at least not now. The third level of resistance, and by far the most important, is sending back information on the enemy. Espionage is the name of the game and, by the time we are finished with you, you will be able to break into the most secure areas and get us the information we need."

Adèle's stomach churned. She had to accept the best revenge for Jean-Pierre was to help bring about the end of the war with victory for the Allies.

One man grumbled, "I thought we were going in to set Europe ablaze?"

"Patience, Fred. You will all be trained to kill." Adèle flushed as Major Hunter's eyes seemed to single her out before he continued. "Using explosions to derail trains, blow up depots or a garotte to silently kill a man. But if we are going to win this war, we need to know our enemy. It was information coming from resistance circuits in France that saved us being annihilated in the Atlantic. One team fed back information on the mechanics and make-up of the Germans' submarines and a detailed map of the French coast from which the German Navy operates. Another fed back codes that helped to break through the German communications. Both those events have shaved years off the war. We expect you to collect top-level intelligence so that we will know more about their troop movements than they do in Berlin."

Some of the men shuffled from one foot to another, their facial expressions veering from disbelief to rebellion. Major Hunter looked around the room, listening as the whispered grumbles and voices of dissent grew louder.

The major coughed. "Anyone got something to say?"

Fred shuffled his feet; he obviously had an issue with standing still. "When can we get started? We've had the pep talks."

Major Hunter's gaze sliced through the man. "If you are caught spying, the Gestapo will pull out your fingernails, burn you with hot irons, and that's on a good day. Believe me, we are not sending you over there to get a suntan or sample this year's Beaujolais. This is a dirty war, ladies and gents, and it's about to get a whole lot dirtier."

FIFTY-NINE

JULY 1942, MARSEILLE

The doctor was true to his word and got Sophie to Marseille. She'd had plenty of time to think about her plans. She wanted to serve in the resistance, but her priority was to help rescue Jewish children.

She was given her new name – Suzanne Picard – and corresponding identity papers. Her papers said she was a nurse. She was told to go to a café on the rue des Catalans at ten every morning on the days of the week that had an E in them. Her contact, Monsieur Brenner, would approach her.

Marseille was a lively port at any time but now it was absolutely chaotic, filled with refugees from all nationalities, many of them sharing one common denominator – being Jewish. Where the genuine ones were fleeing from persecution, there were those who took advantage of them. The streets were crowded with people of all nationalities, all desperate to escape. But there was nowhere for them to go. Although officially still the free zone, the number of German spies in the area had increased. But it wasn't them Sophie feared. It was the Vichy officials who were all too eager to detain Jewish individuals. Marseille's Hôtel Bompard, an internment centre for women and children awaiting immigration, was home (although 'prison' would be a more apt word) to almost a thousand women and children. She ached to help them but was desperate not to blow her own cover.

Sophie returned to the café a few times, but nobody stopped to speak to her. She sat staring at the sea as she stirred her drink. It took all her patience, but she didn't have much choice. Although Marseille was in the unoccupied zone, she couldn't risk talking to anyone.

She tried to pretend what she was drinking was real coffee as she watched the people coming and going.

A man walking with a cane asked if he could share her table. She agreed, then turned back to stare at the different nationalities walking the street.

"One never knows who one might meet in this old port."

Sophie nearly fell off the chair. The man with the cane was Monsieur Brenner, her contact. His raised eyebrows told her she had made her first mistake by not masking her surprise.

She quickly tried to regain some poise. "Yes. I am looking for my uncle. We got separated, and my mother is worried about him."

"Nice to meet you, at last. I am sorry it took so long, but one cannot be too careful. When I leave, follow me. Meet me at the bookstore near the pier."

Sophie didn't answer as the man left. She waited a few minutes, checking to see that no one had followed her contact before she, too, left the café. She found the bookstore easily enough, but there was no one there, apart from a lady who looked like an assistant but could have been the owner. Sophie looked through the various books, wondering if something had happened.

"You are to go through to the back," the woman said as she beckoned Sophie over. "That book you were looking for was damaged."

Sophie walked through the back door and down the stairs. There she found Monsieur Brenner and another younger man, who introduced himself as Guillaume.

"Sorry about that," Monsieur Brenner said. "I thought I was being followed, so I had to walk a bit out of the way."

"I saw no one at the café." She crossed her arms, feeling a little uncomfortable as the younger man looked her up and down.

"You get a sixth sense about things like this. It never hurts to be careful, these days. So, what can I do for a pretty young thing like you?" Monsieur Brenner asked.

Sophie took a deep breath. It was one thing to resist the occupiers, surrounded by people she knew and trusted. But she didn't know these men and didn't feel comfortable – especially as Guillaume continued to stare at her like a starving man looking at a plate of food.

"I am a doctor and was told you had need of my services." She tried to sound confident.

"Thankfully not now, but in due course your skills will be useful. But for the moment, you need a cover story."

"Put her to work at the hospital as a nurse?" Guillaume suggested.

"Too risky. If she is anything like most doctors, I know she will be too eager to show off her knowledge."

"I want to help. I worked as a third-year medical student at a hospital in Paris. I would like to help Jewish children, but in the meantime, I can carry messages or whatever you need."

"Why are you so keen to get yourself killed, or worse?" Monsieur Brenner asked.

"My brother, fiancé" – that's how she thought of Jules now – "and best friend have all been murdered by the Boches. I was at the Vél d'Hiv." He glanced up, their eyes meeting. He'd heard about what happened. She continued. "Don't treat me like an idiot, or I will leave and find someone else who needs my help."

"Settle down, Mademoiselle Picard. We are all friends here."

Sophie didn't apologise for her outburst. She didn't see them as friends and they seemed to think she was a hindrance, not an asset. She'd had enough of playing the nice girl.

"She will go down well with the soldiers. What about Marie's?" Monsieur Brenner asked Guillaume.

"As a waitress or a companion?"

"I will waitress, but I am not becoming a prostitute for any cause."

Guillaume shrugged his shoulders. "It was worth a try."

Sophie glared at the younger man, who stared back at her with an insolent expression on his face. She didn't like him. The feeling was no doubt mutual.

"Guillaume, leave us. You are not helping." They watched him walk away before Monsieur Brenner tried to apologise. "Forgive him; he has an odd sense of humour. His suggestion has merit; as a waitress you could be privy to certain conversations. We need to get one step ahead of the Germans."

"Show me where I need to go."

"Patience, mademoiselle. First, you will need papers. The ones you have are out of date and poor forgeries. You are lucky you haven't been picked up already. Do you have any weapons training?"

"No." Sophie wished she had gone to Lyon to her grandmother. But she couldn't risk involving her family; they had paid too high a price already.

"We can remedy that."

"I don't need any. I will not take a life. It's against my principles as a doctor."

The man stared at her as if she had just announced she was Hitler's mistress.

"You have to be kidding me," he said.

"I do not joke about life and death."

"You will be no use to us if you are captured."

"I won't carry a weapon."

"Don't tell me you think the Germans would take pity on you because you have a pretty face."

"I will not kill another human being," Sophie said. "If you find that a problem, pass me on to another circuit. I am not sure I am compatible with yours."

The man laughed, but she sensed he wasn't laughing at her. "You have spirit, that much I will say. I believe your views will change. For now, I will go along with your wishes." He opened the drawer of the desk, removing a pack of cigarettes. "You must be vigilant. Despite being the so-called free zone, Abwehr spies are active in the area. You cannot recognise them. They blend in with the population. They could be the waiter or the old woman walking her dog." He paused to light a cigarette. "But the worst are the agents of the Sûreté Nationale. They use every trick in the book to find their suspects and tell the gendarmes to make the arrests." He took a long drag of his cigarette. Sophie wondered was he waiting for her to speak before he added, "I've been doing this a while now and they nearly caught me last week. Two men called to the office I was working at. Thankfully I was walking down the stairs as they were coming up. They stopped to ask me where Monsieur Brenner's office was. I told them it was on the sixth floor and walked out as they walked up."

"You were lucky."

"Yes, and some day that luck will run out. Until then we must be cautious. Do not trust anyone but me or Guillaume, no matter what they say or who they purport to be."

Sophie nodded.

"Where did you work as a doctor?"

Sophie wasn't sure how much she should tell him. "At a Paris hospital."

"With Dr Murphy? He is a good friend of mine. A saint of a man – although to be honest, I think his wife is the saint. How is young Philippe?"

"Thriving. He is the image of his dad, although he has some way to go before he catches up to him in height." She stopped talking as she caught his grim expression. "What?"

"You told me your whole life story. I gave you a few crumbs of information and you talked."

"But you said he was a friend."

"Yes, and that is exactly what the agents of the Sûreté Nationale will do."

"That's not fair."

"Suzanne, or whatever your name is, life isn't fair. It was hardly a leap to believe that an American doctor still living in Paris would be involved in the résistance. I know Dr Murphy, though not well. We only met in passing and he mentioned his son."

Sophie glowered at him.

"I am sorry. I didn't trick you to be mean, but to show you how easy it is to let your guard down. A careless mistake and you will be caught. Not only you, but also those you know after they make you talk. Trust no one. I mean it. Not even your closest friend. Since the war, nobody knows anyone any more."

Sophie didn't respond. He had been in the résistance a long time, so perhaps he was right.

"The less you know about the people you work with, the better, for everyone's sake."

Sophie tried her best to curb her impatience. This man was behaving as if she was a liability to those in the résistance.

Monsieur Brenner poured a glass of water and sat at the table in silence. She wasn't sure if he even remembered she was there.

"Having given it some consideration, I think we would be best sending you to Mary Elmes and her people. They aren't in a résistance circuit – their primary focus is to save Jewish children. They need doctors."

"Are you afraid I will betray you?"

"You have shown spirit, and are intelligent and a quick learner. But your priority, as you said, is to help people, not kill them. I think it is best for everyone if you go to Perpignan. We can find a hundred couriers, but doctors – they are a rarer commodity."

He stood up. "I know a girl who can take you tomorrow. In the meantime, go back to your hotel and settle your bill. Tell them you are going to someone, a grandfather or something. It doesn't matter. The girl will come in the morning. Her name is Chloé, and she will carry this book."

Sophie nodded.

"Now leave. Bonne chance, mademoiselle."

Sophie nodded once more in thanks and left, not trusting herself to speak. As she walked back to her hotel, she tried to hold the tears back. She missed the hospital, her home, and her mother. Most of all, she missed Adèle. She hoped her sister was behaving and staying out of trouble.

* * *

The next morning, a girl about Sophie's age arrived and introduced herself as Chloé. They quickly shook hands, and she explained they would make the rather long trip by train and whatever lifts they could find.

"My papers? Your boss didn't like them."

"He suggested using your real ones. Said you could tell anyone who asked that the hospital in Paris sent you to the Red Cross to work in the camps."

"Good plan. My name is Sophie Bélanger. Nice to meet you."

They travelled by train and on foot, and at one point rode in a horse and cart driven by a farmer, who gave them apples to munch on.

"What will I be doing?" Sophie asked Chloé.

"The camps need doctors. I was talking to Mary Elmes last week, and she said the conditions are deplorable."

"What camps?"

Chloé looked at her in surprise. "The camps have been here for years. First, they were used to house the Spanish refugees, and now they are also used for the Jews."

"What type of place is it?"

"Best I show you rather than try to describe it. The camp commandant at Rivesaltes is on our side, although you wouldn't know it from listening to him talk. He sounds like a perfect Pétain pet monkey."

Sophie laughed as Chloé did a good impersonation of a monkey. Despite the circumstances, it was nice to have a girl her age to talk to.

"You will get to meet Mary and her friends too. Mary's Irish so she could have left, but she stayed to help." Chloé clearly worshipped this Mary woman.

Chloé described how Mary had worked in Spain during the Civil War, and helped to house the refugees from that period when they came to France. Now she worked tirelessly, helping the Jewish children and their parents. "She brings in food and clothing. Just seeing her is enough to boost the adults' spirits." Chloé hesitated, giving Sophie a sideways glance.

"What?"

"I just hope Mary and those like her work faster. Rumour has it, the Germans are going to invade the free zone. If that happens, God help us all."

SIXTY

GUILDFORD

Their training began immediately. They started with a physical exercise class in the pouring rain. As Adèle crawled across the mud, taking care to avoid the rope barriers and other obstacles, the words *it's about to get dirtier* rang in her ears.

Both men and women trained together and the class tutor expected both sexes to complete similar exercises. Next, they were due to learn to handle many different firearms, from revolvers through to light automatic weapons. But the tutor's attention wasn't on the weapons; he was in deep conversation with other members of staff.

"What's going on?" Adèle asked.

"The Germans have marched into the free zone."

Adèle gasped. Her grandmother and mother lived there. Sophie could be there too, maybe.

The man looked at her in concern. "You have family there?"

Adèle couldn't answer, not because she was being discreet but because her voice wouldn't work. She stared at her shaking hands before shoving them into her pocket. She couldn't fall apart now. There was even more reason to return. Their instructor returned.

"As you may have heard, the news from France is grim. We can't do anything about that but train as hard as possible so we get you lot over there to sort them out. Agreed?"

"Yes, sir."

They had to learn not only how to fire the different guns but how to break them down and put them together. Adèle learned quickly and impressed her trainer by being the quickest in the class.

"Have you done this before?"

"No." She was determined to be the best agent they had seen.

* * *

Adèle excelled in many aspects of her training, but her marksmanship skills were remarkable.

"Hard to believe you never shot before, Claire. Anyone would think you had been taking out pigeons for the last twenty years."

Adèle beamed at the compliment. She didn't know why other people found it hard to hit the target; you just looked straight at it and pulled the trigger. But her skill with knives was less impressive. In hand-to-hand combat, her slight size worked against her.

"Claire, you will never take down a man if you try to behave like one. You need to use your size to your advantage. They will think a skinny little thing like you will be a walkover. You have to prove them wrong."

Over and over she practised, until her instructor was finally fairly happy with her, although he still advised her to shoot rather than get into a situation where she had to fight up close and personal.

The one area of training in which she failed dismally was killing for food. She couldn't bring herself to kill a rabbit. While her colleagues thought nothing of it, she still couldn't bear the smell or sight of blood. Some agent she was going to make.

"You okay there, Frenchie? You're muttering away to yourself."

Adèle wanted to tell the lad to get lost, but she couldn't. He was one of the few who hadn't laughed at her fears. He assumed her problem was killing the animal, not the sight of blood, so he had been doing it for her when the instructor's back was turned.

"I was just thinking of my brother. He would have disowned me if he knew I was being such a fool."

"Where's your brother? Is he over there fighting?"

Adèle hesitated. They had been warned not to divulge any personal information, but surely it couldn't hurt to tell the truth. But thankfully the moment passed as her instructor called her over.

"Claire, Major wants to see you. Pronto."

Despite the nervous looks of some of her colleagues, Adèle wasn't afraid. She knew she had aced all her classes.

She knocked on the door, entering without being asked.

He didn't look up but left her standing in front of the desk for a few seconds. The silence grew uncomfortable. She coughed, discreetly, to remind him of her presence but she seemed to be invisible. Deciding enough was enough, she sat down.

"Stand to attention."

Adèle jumped up at the sharp command, glaring at him as she did so.

"And therein lies your problem, Mademoiselle Bélanger. Yes, I know your real name and your background. You do not behave like the agent Claire, but like the pampered, spoiled brat you are."

"Sir!"

"You come top of your class. That is to be commended if you showed an inch of behaving like you are part of a team.

This is not a one-man or -woman show. If, and it is a big if, we drop you in France as an agent, you will be part of a team."

Adèle dug her nails into the palms of her hands. This was so unfair. She had worked hard. She was better than the rest of the people out there.

"Yes, you have come top of your class and yes, you are the fastest person in many events. You, being French, have the native tongue, a sharp mind and an aptitude for training. You have the makings of a magnificent agent, yet I am going to recommend your training cease with immediate effect."

Adèle swayed, shocked by what he said. "But, sir—"

"Don't interrupt. You show no regard for your superiors. You also show no fear. Both are dangerous. Frankly, they could be fatal not just to yourself but to your team."

She waited for him to continue but with him staring at her, she thought he might be waiting for her to say something. She opened her mouth but then realised it might be a trap. She stayed silent.

"Well?"

"Sir?"

"What do you have to say?"

"I thought we weren't supposed to show fear. It's not like the torture is real. Is it?"

He lit a cigarette and stared out the window, his back to her.

"I don't know what you expect of me. I can't pretend to be afraid."

"You should be. Do you think the Gestapo will believe you are innocent if you stand in front of them looking like you are ready for everything they throw at you? If you stare them in the eye just as you do everyone here, with that look of disdain, they will arrest you immediately."

"Sir!"

He turned to look at her. "You don't hide your contempt for the British people. You make disparaging remarks. I know you have had a difficult time in France, but it hasn't been a picnic for people over here. Especially those in the cities facing bombs every night, not to mention the reality of their brothers, fathers, husbands, and sons being killed every day. Or taken prisoner. *We* may not be under the Nazi jackboot – yes, those were the exact words you used – but that is not to say we are immune."

Chastened, Adèle looked at the floor. She had to fix this, and fast.

"I apologise for any offence I gave."

He thumped the desk, making her jump. "That's it, right there. That attitude. You believe you are better than the rest of us. How do you know what your colleagues have already lived through? Do you think you are the only one to lose a brother? Or a mother or father, or maybe even your whole family. You judge those around you and find them lacking when you know nothing about them. The paths that brought them to this house, to this role. There are easier ways to make a difference to this war."

Tears pricked her eyes, but they weren't of anger but shame. He was right. In everything he said.

"Give me one good reason why I shouldn't send you to the cooler."

"Excuse me?" Adèle didn't know what that meant, although it didn't sound like something she wanted to know more about.

"It's a place in Scotland for failed agents who know too much about our operations here. In time, when the information they've learned is less relevant and thus lacks the potential to harm our agents, we release them back into normal life."

Adèle stared at him, horror making her speechless. She didn't want to go to Scotland or anywhere else, but home to France.

"Look, sir, I'm sorry. No, really, I am. I know I am a spoiled brat; my twin sister used to tell me all the time. Jean-Pierre thought so too. But I must go back. I must. Please let me try again. I will do better. Anything you ask me to do. I just have to go back to France."

He stared at her, but she didn't smile or flirt. She sensed that would be a waste of time.

"Sit down, Adèle."

She sat at the edge of the seat, holding her hands pressed tight on her knees to stop them shaking. Her stomach churned as he read the papers on his desk. The silence became too uncomfortable.

"I really want to play my part, sir."

"Of that, there is no doubt. You have the makings of a fantastic agent. God help me for admitting this, but possibly one of the best we ever had. But take a team approach. In the field, your men will depend on you. The locals will look to you for instruction on how to blow up a railway or secure landing fields. Your sex is already against you. Don't look so surprised; I've lived in France. I know how difficult it can be for a woman to take on what is traditionally viewed as a man's role. But I believe you can do it. So does Miss Atkins and, believe me, her recommendation carries a lot of weight. In ways, you remind me of her, but don't you go telling her that."

"I appreciate the comparison, but I know I have a lot to learn. Let me prove myself." She bit her lip, trying not to let her emotions spill over. "I need to do this. I have to do this."

He studied her intently for a few seconds. "All right, I'll give you another chance. But this is the last one. Don't mess it up."

She stood, her legs shaking. "Thank you, sir. You won't regret it."

"I think I probably will, but off you go."

She saluted and walked to the door, but before she reached the handle, he muttered, "Jean-Pierre would be proud of you."

She stood, her back towards him, not able to look at him. She couldn't speak, couldn't think.

"He saved my life and that of my pilot. They shot us down over Paris. He got us out. Confident young man, he showed no fear either – must be something in the blood. Go on."

She opened the door and marched out, her nerves in pieces. Only when the door was closed behind her did she let the tears fall.

SIXTY-ONE

The days dragged by as Adèle continued her training. Feeling like she was constantly being watched, she made a genuine effort to get involved in team activities. She walked over to the window, holding back the curtains to look outside at the stretch of never-ending green grass. And the rain. It never stopped. She missed home so much.

"Darn it, anyway." Gabrielle's voice came from behind her. "I'm never going to get the hang of this stupid language."

Adèle turned and ducked just in time to avoid Gabrielle's shoe.

"Sorry, Claire. I just get so frustrated. Major Hunter says I speak French like a tongue-tied debutante."

"That's ridiculous."

Gabrielle's eyes widened. "You really think so?"

"Debutantes don't kill people by throwing their shoes."

Gabrielle glared at her before bursting into a fit of giggles. Adèle laughed too. She picked up the shoe her roommate had thrown and put it down beside Gabrielle's bed. She walked over to the other side of the large, freezing-cold room, to her own bed and sat down. "Stop thinking so hard. Make it more natural."

"That's easy for you; you sleep, eat, and dream in French. Actually – do you?"

"What?"

"Dream in French?"

Adèle threw her pillow at Gabrielle. Before long, there were feathers everywhere as they released some of the tension of the last few weeks. When they were done, sitting on the floor, spitting at the feathers, Gabrielle asked, "Could you help me? I mean it, Claire. I really want to get to France. They ... oh, I know we aren't supposed to share but I have to tell someone. They took my whole family. There's nobody left. Just me. I want to kick them where it hurts."

"Then it is martial arts you should learn, not French." Adèle's joke fell a little flat. She wasn't sure how to react, not being used to girls taking her into their confidence. At the look of hurt in Gabrielle's eyes, she tried again. "I'm sorry, that was crass. I can't imagine how you feel. They killed my brother and that is bad enough."

"Was he a soldier?"

"No, he worked in a museum."

"Ah, a bomb? Like my family."

Adèle didn't correct Gabrielle's assumptions. There was little point in telling a would-be agent that the Germans had shot her younger brother.

"So, come on, talk to me in French. Say something. Anything."

Gabrielle stared at her.

Adèle picked up a feather. "Speak or be tickled to death."

Gabrielle giggled, but when Adèle made a move, she shot out of the way, speaking French.

"Major Hunter is wrong; you don't speak like a debutante."

Gabrielle looked hopeful.

"A German governess, maybe." Adèle shrugged before bending as Gabrielle threw another object in her direction.

"Come on, French. We will have you speaking like a native in
no time."

* * *

Besides helping Gabrielle, Adèle tutored some of the other
agents, not only in French, but in the ways of the French.

"Tommy, you don't have butter and jam on your bread. It is
one or the other. Maël, leave the bread on the table. It doesn't
belong on the plate. Milk goes in last, not first. We don't drink
tea, at least most people don't. Amy, we spread out the courses
for dinner; we do not pile our plates high thinking we will never
see another meal again."

In time, the other agents came to her individually, asking
questions about this or that. It surprised her to find while they
might have excellent language skills, many didn't understand
the customs in France. She did her best to explain, knowing
they would give themselves away if they didn't learn. To her
surprise, it was fun, and the time passed faster.

"Want us to teach you how to skin a rabbit?" Maël asked.

Adèle's stomach churned. "No, but thank you. I will have
the men under my command do that for me. I don't intend
breaking my nails."

The men laughed just as she intended. She looked up to
catch Major Hunter staring at her. She held his gaze and after a
few seconds, he seemed to smile, but it was gone before she
could be sure. He was called away before she could ask if she
was making progress.

SIXTY-TWO

Early one afternoon when they were eating lunch, Major Hunter appeared. They all stood to attention.

"As you were. Claire, my office, please."

She went to stand.

"No, finish your meal."

"Thank you, sir. I've finished." Her stomach churned. All thoughts of food went out the window. Her colleagues' eyes followed her through the door, no doubt wondering why he'd singled her out. He strode to his office, their footsteps the only sound echoing around the large hall. At the entrance to his office, he stood back to let her enter first. She risked a look at his face, but his closed expression didn't give her any clues. Her mind flitted over the previous weeks; she hadn't done anything to give him cause for concern. She fought the panic rising in her chest; he wasn't going to dismiss her, was he?

He closed the door behind him but didn't take a seat at his desk. He reached into his pocket, removing a pack of cigarettes. He offered her one, but she declined. He lit his and took a deep drag before saying, "You've made some good progress since our last meeting."

"Thank you, sir." Adèle wished her knees would quit shaking. She didn't want him to think she was afraid, although she was terrified. Was he going to send her to Scotland, to the place for failed agents? Had she not done enough?

He held her gaze for seconds, the silence growing uncomfortable. Just as she was about to break it, he picked up a piece of paper from his desk and glanced at it. But he wasn't reading it – was he nervous?

"Seems they need you urgently over there. Grab your stuff. Someone from head office will be here shortly to collect you. Be quick – this is an emergency situation."

Stunned, she stared at him. It took a moment for her mind to catch up. She saluted. "Yes, sir."

Major Hunter looked at her, his expression stormy, his eyes filled with a mixture of disgust and sadness. "Be careful. Some git brought down the entire network. Don't trust anyone, not even your own mother." He threw his cigarette down, grinding it into the ashtray.

"You've done yourself proud. Now, I would be happy to be part of your team. Ever need backup, send for me."

Adèle hesitated, unsure of how to respond. Major Hunter held out his hand. She shook it. "Thank you, Major Hunter."

This was it. She was going home. She opened the door, letting it slam shut behind her. She ran up the stairs before realising everyone was staring. Slowing down to a walk, she packed her bag and was soon ready and waiting for her lift. Gabrielle came running.

"Claire, don't tell me you weren't going to say goodbye."

Adèle hugged the other girl. "Major Hunter said it was an emergency. I hoped you would find me. This is it."

"I shall miss you." Gabrielle stepped back and held out her hand. "Bonne chance."

Adèle grinned. "Gabrielle! You spoke like a native. Take no chances over there. Maybe we will meet again after the war."

A smile hovered on Gabrielle's lips. "I hope you learn how to skin rabbits; wouldn't want you to die from starvation."

Adèle couldn't respond. Her throat was closing because of a growing lump. She wished her lift would hurry up.

"Au revoir, Claire."

Gabrielle was gone before she could reply. Wheels crunched on the gravel drive.

The female driver wore a FANY uniform, just like Adèle.

"Name's Betty," she said. "Don't stand there with your mouth open. Hop in. The brass won't wait for us." The driver grinned at her before turning the car around and heading for the rendezvous point.

Adèle stared at the house until it disappeared into the distance. *Au revoir, mes amis.*

Betty drove to a small farmhouse situated close to an airfield, judging by the sound of the planes. "Go on inside and get changed; the boss will be here, later."

Adèle went upstairs to change out of her uniform into a set of French clothes. She fingered the cotton underwear, wishing she had brought her silks with her when she left. The dress wasn't much better, like something a peasant would wear.

A knock on the door admitted Miss Atkins. She took in Adèle's expression and smiled.

"Not what you are used to. Still, you look the part. Can't be rushing around the French countryside dressed as if you belong in Maxim's."

The reminder of her old life made her cringe. She laced up the shoes, wanting her blushes to cool before she faced Miss Atkins.

"You've done well. Rocky start, but you came through in the end."

"I will not cause problems."

"Don't be defensive, mon amie. It is natural to want to avenge your brother, but you know better than most, you are going into a male-dominated world. Gain the trust of the men you will be leading. Men expect us women to stand behind a cooker or have babies."

Adèle laughed. Anyone who expected her to cook was in for a shock.

"You have the makings of a wonderful agent, so long as you curb your inclination to be impulsive."

Adèle stayed quiet. She knew now she had underestimated this woman when they'd first met. Miss Atkins cared for all her agents.

"And this is for you."

Adèle recognised the cyanide capsule. "I don't need that."

"Yes, you do."

"I am Catholic, Miss Atkins, despite what the Germans say. What you are suggesting is a sin."

"And killing a man isn't? This isn't Sunday school, sweetheart. If the Germans get you, you will want this. Take it. Please."

Adèle took the pill and tucked it into her pocket, despite resolving never to use it. Her mind wandered as Miss Atkins reiterated her previous warnings about Adèle seeking personal vengeance for Jean-Pierre's death. Adèle stared at the full moon. This was it. Finally, the flight could leave, and she would soon be in France. She glanced at the woman beside her. Miss Atkins looked grim. Adèle wondered how many times Miss Atkins would have to go through this same routine before the war was over.

Adèle got out of the car, closely followed by Miss Atkins.

"Bonne chance, Claire."

Miss Atkins embraced her and Adèle hugged her back. How things had changed from their first meeting, all those weeks ago.

"Merci, au revoir."

Adèle held her head up and tried not to run over to the plane.

I'm going home.

SIXTY-THREE

RIVESALTES

Chloé's descriptions hadn't come close to the horror waiting for Sophie. She put a hand up to her nose as they came closer to the double rows of barbed wire encircled by a sea of mud, not a blade of grass visible. There were barely any trees, just rows of barracks one after the other.

Chloé pointed out some old women who walked with the aid of sticks. "They are trying to reach the latrines but the sea of mud on the already swampy ground makes it too difficult. Even if they had enough to eat and proper medication, it would be hard for them to survive here."

"Who are they? Why are they here?"

"They are Jews, some German, some from the Alsace region, others are refugees, and some are French. It's mainly women and children left now. The men, those who could work, were transferred out to forced labour units. Some of them are in France while others have been sent to Germany. They weren't given a chance to say goodbye to their families. Look – there is Mary."

Sophie saw the woman Chloé pointed out. She was

surrounded by the camp inmates, and they were all holding out their hands, begging her for something.

"Mary works with the Quakers and other organisations to bring relief. She was in Spain helping the refugees from that war and escaped when it became too dangerous for the people helping. She works at different camps, setting up hospitals, schools and whatever else she can do in the way of improving things. She's a real way about her, she makes people do what she wants, but not by shouting. She gives the impression she expects the person she is speaking to to do something and they do. She's going to be thrilled to have a real doctor to help her."

"I'm not qualified yet; I didn't get a chance to finish."

Chloé grinned at her. "No need for honesty now. As far as everyone is concerned, you're a doctor. That way the camp orderlies may pay a little more attention to you. You won't be dismissed as another busybody woman who should be at home having children."

Her new friend's words reminded her of her father. How was he dealing with the reality of his son's death – or did he even think about it?

Up close, she saw the woman wasn't as old as she looked from the distance. In her early thirties, her face was lined with exhaustion but her eyes were bright and intelligent, and she gave a large smile of welcome.

"Mary, this is Sophie Bélanger, a doctor from the American Hospital in Paris."

"Thank you for coming to help us, Sophie. As you can see, your help is badly needed."

"How can they let people live like this?"

"Live?" Mary lowered her voice, the Irish lilt reminding Sophie of the nun who'd spirited away Captain M. "That's not the intention. No, I'm afraid the people held here are being slowly put to death. Their rations, when they show up, are pitiable but the conditions are a hazard. Disease spreads like wildfire, not helped by the mosquitos, the muck, and God knows what else. We lost sixty babies in the last two months alone."

Sophie couldn't find the words. She stood staring at the spectacle in front of her, her mind going back to the Vél d'Hiv. She thought she'd seen the worst back then, but that was a luxury compared to what these people were enduring.

"Come, let's show you around and introduce you to the people in charge. Be firm with them; you are here in an official capacity. Use your education, your beauty, and your feminine wiles. Anything and everything so that we can save these poor mites."

Sophie nodded, too choked up to respond. She followed the woman, looking at the ground as she picked her steps before finally giving up. They walked into one of the barracks where a school seemed to be in progress. The children stopped and stared at them, the fear palpable until some recognised Mary and came running to greet her.

"Forgive me, Rachelle, for interrupting your class."

"No apology necessary, Mary." The teacher's expression was one of adoration. Mary seemed oblivious.

"Rachelle, this is Sophie. She's a doctor, here to help."

Rachelle grasped Sophie's hand. "Thank you. There are too many of us who are sick. We try to keep the place clean but as you can see, we fail dismally."

Sophie smiled. "Your children are very well-behaved." She meant the compliment.

"It is easy to control children too hungry and tired to move." Rachelle's voice didn't break, her wearied tone telling Sophie more than her words had. She'd given up hope.

Sophie looked around her at the children's faces, at the exhausted women who worked so tirelessly to try and help them, and she knew she was in the right place. She had lost so much, but she had not lost hope. All her training had prepared her for this moment. She was here, she was ready to work to give these children a fighting chance, and nothing was going to stop her.

A LETTER FROM THE AUTHOR

Dear reader, thank you for reading my book and I hope you are looking forward to reading the rest of the twins' story in the next book, *Light Rises*. If you'd like to be the first to find out about new releases, please sign to my newsletter!

www.stormpublishing.co/rachel-wesson

If you enjoyed this book and could spare a few moments to leave a review that would be hugely appreciated. Even a short review can make all the difference in encouraging a reader to discover my books for the first time. Thank you so much!

People often ask me how I come up with my stories. I love to read and often when reading non-fiction, my imagination starts firing. The character of Sophie is based on the stories of the incredibly brave staff who worked in the American Hospital in Paris during the war. Many of the incidents described in this book are true – the staff did resist the German occupation, and many helped Jews and Allied pilots to escape. Dr Sumner Jackson, his family and many of his staff paid a high price for their bravery.

I've long been fascinated by the story of what was effectively the first resistance cell in Paris, the group Jean-Pierre was a member of. René Sénéchal, nicknamed *Le Gosse*, was the model I used for Jean-Pierre. I wanted to write about how the decisions and actions of one person would influence those of his family. As we saw in the book, some family members supported him while others believed him to be a traitor. Just like in real life.

Adèle is also modelled on many real-life people who for various reasons decided the war had nothing to do with them, all they needed to do was to live. But then as the actions of the enemy grew more abhorrent many realized they couldn't stand on the sidelines any longer.

I'm often asked why I concentrate on the women in the war. I write about female heroes of the Second World War to honour their memory and ensure that their contributions are not forgotten. In sharing their stories, I hope to inspire a sense of gratitude, admiration, and respect for these remarkable women, whose lives were forever changed by the war. Although the twins are fictional characters, Mary Elmes and Sister Marie-Lawrence were real individuals, two of my own countrywomen, and their actions make me proud to be Irish.

Once again, thank you for your interest in my work, and I appreciate your support in helping me share these important stories with the world. If you have any questions or comments, please feel free to reach out to me.

Rachel x

www.rachelwesson.com

HISTORICAL NOTE

Where possible, I have used the correct date and times of historical events. I have taken some liberties.

Dr Michael Murphy is modelled on Dr Sumner Jackson – Dr Jackson, an American who worked at the American hospital – was in the résistance and gave his life for France. His wife and son were also involved.

René Sénéchal, nicknamed *Le Gosse*, was the model I used for Jean-Pierre. While René was a Resistant and a hero and died for France, he didn't have twin sisters. All the elements of Jean-Pierre's family are made up from my imagination.

Jacques Bonsergent has the dubious honour of being the first civilian executed by the Germans after a wedding in 1940. I used him as inspiration for Léo Favreau.

Captain Ernst Roskothen, the presiding judge at the museum trial, was arrested at the end of the war. But numerous letters including one from Agnès Humbert, one of the women he sentenced to five years' imprisonment in Germany, asked he be given clemency. She and the others all commented on his civility, his fairness, and his only doing the job he had to do. It worked and he was released. He voluntarily returned to France in 1949 to give evidence in the trial of Albert Gaveau. Gaveau, the son of a German woman, was in the employment of the Gestapo for years and nobody knows how many members of resistance circuits he gave up to the Germans. Roskothen's evidence and that of the surviving members of the resistance circuit convicted Gaveau of treason. Unlike the people he had denounced, he was not shot but sentenced to life imprisonment.

Sister Marie-Laurence is a real figure, an Irish nun living in France, who was one of the many heroes in the resistance. Mary Elmes stayed living in France after the war.

ACKNOWLEDGMENTS

To all my readers, especially those in my Facebook readers group. You don't know how much your lovely comments about my books inspire my writing. Thank you.

To my husband for helping run our home and look after our children. I don't miss those school runs.

To my children for having patience while Mam works on her next book.

Made in the USA
Columbia, SC
08 December 2023

28041026R00271